Praise for Erica James

'Erica James' sensitive story . . . is as sparklingly fresh as dew on the village's surrounding meadows . . . thoroughly enjoyable and fully deserving of a place in the crowded market of women's fiction' *Sunday Express*

'This book draws you into the lives of these characters, and often makes you want to scream at them to try and make them see reason. Funny, sad and frustrating, but an excellent, compulsive read' *Woman's Realm*

'There is humour and warmth in this engaging story of love's triumphs and disappointments, with two well-realised and intriguing subplots' *Woman & Home*

'Joanna Trollope fans, dismayed by the high gloom factor and complete absence of Agas in her latest books, will turn with relief to James' . . . delightful novel about English village life . . . a blend of emotion and wry social observation'
Daily Mail

'Scandal, fury, accusations and revenge are all included in Erica James' compelling novel . . . this story of village life in Cheshire is told with wit and humour' *Stirling Observer*

'An entertaining read with some wickedly well-painted cameo characters. It's a perfect read if you're in the mood for romance' *Prima*

'An engaging and friendly novel . . . very readable'
Woman's Own

'A bubbling, delightful comedy which is laced with a bittersweet tang . . . a good story, always well observed, and full of wit' *Publishing News*

'James is a seasoned champion of the genre . . . *Promises, Promises* has an extraordinary deftness of touch, coupled with some searing insights into both how relationships fail, and can work' *Daily Mirror*

With an insatiable appetite for other people's business, Erica James will readily strike up conversation with strangers in the hope of unearthing a useful gem for her writing. She finds it the best way to write authentic characters for her novels, although her two grown-up sons claim they will never recover from a childhood spent in a perpetual state of embarrassment at their mother's compulsion.

Erica is the author of sixteen bestselling novels, including *Gardens of Delight*, which won the Romantic Novel of the Year Award, and her recent *Sunday Times* top ten bestseller, *The Queen of New Beginnings*. She now divides her time between Cheshire and Lake Como in Italy, where she strikes up conversation with unsuspecting Italians. Visit her website at www.ericajames.co.uk

By Erica James

Precious Time

ERICA JAMES

An Orion paperback

First published in Great Britain in 2001
by Orion
This paperback edition published in 2002
by Orion Books Ltd,
Orion House, 5 Upper St Martin's Lane,
London WC2H 9EA

An Hachette UK company

Reissued 2011

A CIP catalogue record for this book
is available from the British Library.

Typeset by Deltatype Limited, Birkenhead, Merseyside

Printed and bound in Great Britain by Clays Ltd, St Ives plc

The Orion Publishing Group's policy is to use papers
that are natural, renewable and recyclable products and
made from wood grown in sustainable forests. The logging
and manufacturing processes are expected to conform to
the environmental regulations of the country of origin.

www.orionbooks.co.uk

To Edward and Samuel,
whose time with me is
ultra precious

Acknowledgements

Heartfelt thanks to all my new and old friends at Orion, in and out of the office.

I shan't single anyone out for preferential treatment (not even my wonderful dancing partners from Bournemouth) because you're all special. But just to make his day, this is for Andrew Taylor: 'Thank you, Mr Taylor, for all your help. I wish I could say it's been a pleasure!'

Take good care of time, how you spend it
For nothing is more precious than time.
In one little moment, short as it is,
Heaven may be won or lost.

From *The Cloud of Unknowing*,
fourteenth-century mystical prose work

Chapter One

Clara Costello's friends were all of one opinion: that she was mad. Away with the fairies, crazy, doolally, Harpic, not the full shilling, and two bricks short of a load was just a random sample of what they had to say about her. And just for the record, Harpic was her favourite: it was their cute way of saying she was clean round the bend.

They had reached this diagnosis six weeks ago, at the end of January, when she had announced she was giving up her job – her well-paid and secure job, as was repeatedly pointed out to her – to take to the road in a second-hand camper-van with her four-year-old son.

Louise, her closest friend and biggest critic, had been disappointed that her gallivanting was to be restricted to the shores of Britain. 'Well, if you must indulge yourself with an early mid-life crisis, you might at least have come up with something a little more adventurous,' she had said. 'Backpacking round south-east Asia in search of spiritual enlightenment would sound so much more interesting.'

'That's because you and David are such dreadful snobs and want nothing but the most exotic postcards adorning your kitchen noticeboard,' Clara had responded good-humouredly.

'And what about Ned? You've only just got him into St Chad's. You'll lose his place, and even I know the waiting-list for that school gets longer the older your child becomes.'

'I don't care. He's only just turned four and he'll learn more doing this than he would stuck in a boring classroom every day. This will be fun for him, something he'll always remember. And, anyway, school will be waiting for him in the autumn. If I don't do it now, I'll never do it. This chance will never come round again.'

The car in front braked sharply and Clara did likewise. The carrier-bag of good-luck cards and presents she had been given during her farewell lunch slid forward on the passenger seat and dropped to the floor. She left them where they were, her attention caught by the sticker on the rear window of the rusting Fiat Panda in front of her. 'No Fear', it read. Did that mean 'No fear' as in 'Not likely', or 'No fear' as in 'Hey, look at me, I'm a free-falling daredevil who's not scared of anyone or anything'? Either way, Clara fancied a sticker like that. Her friends were always saying how fearless she was. 'You're too intrepid for your own good,' David had said, more than once.

'Not true,' she had argued. 'I always reason everything out before I dive in head first.'

But what neither her friends nor her parents knew was that they were all partly to blame for this rush of blood to the head, as Louise had so charmingly referred to Clara's shift of perspective.

It had started in the new year, when Clara's parents had embarked on their trip of a lifetime to Australia, where they would be spending an open-ended amount of time with her brother Michael, his wife and their newborn baby. Kissing them goodbye at the airport, Clara had felt the sting of being left behind.

It wasn't jealousy, more a case of acknowledging that it was too easy to stand still, too easy to let the glorious opportunities of life slip by without catching hold of them. For as long as she could remember her parents had talked about travelling the world, but it was only now, since her father had retired, that they felt they could justify such an extravagant trip, as if it was his reward for all the years he had put in at the insurance company he had worked for. But what if, after all that patient anticipation, one of them had fallen ill at the last minute

2

or, worse still and heaven forbid, died? What would have been the point in all that waiting? Why, oh why, did we spend so much time putting life on hold?

Pondering this in the busy airport, she had suddenly realised Ned was crying. His tearstained face was pressed against the smeared glass of the window as he tried in vain to see his grandparents for one last time – they had promised to wave to him from their plane on the tarmac. She bent down and held him tightly, wondering how she would ever fill the vast gap in his world created by Nanna and Granda's departure.

The following evening she had gone for dinner at Louise and David's. It was their usual fivesome: David and Louise, Guy and Moira, and herself. At around midnight, the time when Guy was most likely to start philosophising, once he'd progressed from wine to liqueurs, he had asked, 'If you only had a year left to live, what would you do?'

'In your case I'd donate the time to Help the Aged,' David had laughed. 'You'd fit in nicely now you're losing your hair.'

'And, knowing you, you'd waste your year.'

Helping herself to a grape, Louise had said, 'I'd stop dieting. I'd let myself become as fat as a pig and die happy.' She sighed and, with her teeth, peeled a tiny length of skin off the grape. She was going through another of her weigh-myself-and-hate-myself phases.

'I'd buy the house I'd always wanted,' Moira said, 'my dream home, and to hell with the expense.'

'So what's wrong with the one we've just bought?' Guy frowned. 'I thought it *was* your dream house.'

'It doesn't have a conservatory and the garden's too small.'

'It's got five bedrooms and very nearly an acre of paddock. What more do you want?'

'I just said what I wanted, a conservatory and—'

'Well, I know what I'd do,' David interrupted. 'I'd give up work and travel.'

'No, you wouldn't,' smiled Louise. 'You'd be bored to death within a week. 'You can't even go on a fortnight's holiday without reporting in. Besides, seeing too much of each other might send us over the edge.'

It was daft, drink-loaded, late-into-the-night talk, no one giving a sensible answer, no one giving the question the thought it deserved. They were a group of thirty-somethings, with no children (apart from Clara) and no real responsibility to anyone other than themselves. But driving home later, Clara did give it some serious thought, and after she had paid the babysitter and watched her drive away, she had gone upstairs to check on Ned. Kneeling by his bed she had experienced the fierce tenderness of love that she always felt for him in moments like this. As she stroked his smooth, rounded cheek, she knew exactly what she would do if her days were numbered. She would spend her time with Ned.

As a single mother and working long hours as a production manager for an international pharmaceutical company, she was all too aware of how little time she had with her son. It was hard to admit, but somewhere along the line she had got her priorities wrong and had ended up squeezing Ned into her busy schedule when and how she could, giving him the tired, worn-out bits of herself rather than the best.

How had she allowed herself to become the kind of person she would once have despised? The kind of person who, at the age of thirty-four, couldn't stay awake long enough to watch the ten o'clock news through to the weather, who perpetually worked late because there was yet another problem on the packing line. The kind of person who justified it all by saying there was a mortgage to pay, nursery-school fees to find, and a voracious pension fund to feed.

The reality was that, like her friends, she had confused success with happiness. And having built that happiness on the shifting sands of material success, she was feeling the strain of sustaining it. Financial security was a severe

4

taskmaster, and she knew that only a monumental change of heart would alter her outlook. It had happened to her when she least expected it.

With her parents away, taking care of Ned had become even more of a juggling act. They had looked after Ned for her most days. They were wonderful with him and adored him, and were as much a part of his life as she was. They would pick him up from nursery, drive him to the park where he could play on the swings and ride his bike, then take him home to give him his tea and generally spoil him. But since they had gone to Sydney, to make the acquaintance of their new grandson, Clara had had to persuade Ned that he had to go to a new nursery school where he could stay in the after-school activity club until she came to collect him.

On his first morning his dark eyes had pleaded with her not to leave him, his tiny hand squeezing hers, sending her silent messages that this wasn't what he wanted. It wasn't what she wanted either, but she didn't have any choice. She helped him wriggle out of his stiff new blazer and hung it with his satchel and plimsoll bag on his hook, which was level with her waist. She stooped to kiss him goodbye and saw to her horror that, beneath his shiny fringe, his eyes were filling. 'It'll be okay, Ned,' she said, her throat so clenched she could hardly get the words out. 'You'll have so much fun that the day will whiz by and before you know where you are I'll be here to take you home.'

He swallowed. 'I want to go home. I want Nanna and Granda.'

'Oh, Ned,' she whispered, 'I wish they were here too.' Then, all business-like, she tilted up his chin and straightened the knot of his red and grey tie, although it was already perfectly straight.

Two bigger boys cruised by, and gave Ned a contemptuous once-over. One said, 'What's that in your hand?'

He smiled his best engaging smile, the one that his grandmother said was a gift from the angels, and proudly

5

showed them what he was holding. It was a small plastic mermaid that had belonged to Clara when she was little and had gone everywhere with her. Now it went everywhere with Ned: it was his talisman and he was never without it. 'It's old,' he said brightly, 'nearly as old as my mummy.'

The boys drew in close for a better look. 'It's a doll,' one sneered. 'Dolls are for girls.' Sniggering, they sauntered away.

'Shall I look after Mermy today for you?' Clara asked, wanting to scoop Ned up and get him out of this place and away from bigger-boy superiority.

He shook his head, and pushed Mermy back into his pocket. With her heart fit to break she watched him square his shoulders ready to brave the day ahead.

That day, she had worried about Ned constantly. She didn't care a jot about the production of the latest infertility drug, nor about the rumours that, once again, Phoenix Pharmaceuticals USA were thinking of selling their UK division in Epsom, Surrey, to a French company. From their offices on the floor above her, Guy and David had e-mailed her with what was allegedly going on. Both suggested that she brush up on her French: 'Zut alors! Avec les Frenchies, nous will be out of le pan et dans le feu,' Guy had messaged, which had probably stretched his linguistic repertoire to its limit.

She left as early as she could and drove like the wind, dreading to find Ned in a crumpled heap of misery.

What she found was a tired-looking little boy sitting cross-legged on the floor with a group of glassy-eyed children watching a cartoon on a large-screen television. She was approached by one of his teachers who said she wanted a *little word*.

'He's been all right, hasn't he?'

'Oh, he's an absolute delight,' the woman said. 'He's fitted in just fine. But – and I know it's only his first day with us – goodness, what a disorganised little boy he is. A head full of clutter. And he never stops talking. But don't worry, I'm sure that between us we'll soon have him licked into shape.' There was laughter in her voice and Clara could see that she wasn't speaking unkindly. Even so, she could have slapped her face. For heaven's sake, he was four years old. What did she expect? A personal organiser tucked into his briefcase? Looking around her and seeing the orderly rows of blazers, satchels and plimsoll bags hanging from their hooks Clara felt angry. This was the future for Ned. At the age of four he was already on a conveyor-belt of uniformity. His next stop would be an office where he could hang his jacket and the rest of his life.

It was while she was driving home, with Ned almost asleep, his head tipped to one side, his hands wrapped around Mermy, that Clara made her decision. It was now or never. She had until September to give Ned what he deserved. She would use the precious time available and give him her undivided attention and, hopefully, a little adventure into the bargain.

Chapter Two

More than two hundred and fifty miles away, in Deacons-bridge, a small market town in the Peak District where luscious hills of tranquil beauty gave way to peaty moors of savage wildness, a man sat brooding restlessly on an uncomfortable orange plastic chair. His name was Gabriel Liberty, and at the age of seventy-nine he believed he had earned the right not to be kept waiting.

Half an hour he had been stuck here, confined in this airtight room, exposed to any number of germs. He stretched out his stiff legs and knocked over a tower of building bricks, which an ugly, snivelling brat had just spent the last five minutes constructing.

'Watch it, can't you?' the child's mother said. She put down her magazine, shuffled a handbag and a small baby on her lap, and bent to the brat who was now producing an annoyingly loud wail.

'It serves him right for being in my way,' Gabriel said. 'And while you're down there, wipe his nose. It's disgusting.'

A shrill ring sounded, followed by an even shriller voice announcing that the doctor was ready for patient number sixteen.

Gabriel hauled himself out of his chair. 'And about time too,' he muttered.

'I think you'll find I'm number sixteen,' said a hesitant voice from across the room.

Gabriel glared at a pasty-faced man in a flat cap, daring him to mount any kind of a real challenge.

'Oh, let him go,' said the mother of two, 'give us all some peace.'

8

Without bothering to knock, Gabriel entered Dr Cunningham's surgery. 'Humph, not seen you before,' he said, sitting down in front of the fake teak desk with a computer on one end and a shiny brass statue of a dancing woman with too many hands at the other. Sandwiched between the two was a spry little Indian man in his shirtsleeves. His name was Dr Singh, if the engraved plaque in front of him was to be believed. 'What happened to Dr Cunningham?' asked Gabriel.

'He died.'

'Mm . . . that doesn't surprise me. He never did strike me as a good advertisement for his profession. Always looked overworked and underfed. Clearly wasn't practising what he preached. What got him, then? Every doctor's weakness, the booze and fags?'

'No. A car crash in Portugal while he was on holiday with his family. Did you not read about it in the local paper?'

'I've no time for local rags. Nothing but a load of old cods about jumble sales and potting-shed break-ins. The Portuguese are the worst drivers on earth, aren't they? Mind you, your lot aren't much better. I was in Delhi once, never seen anything like it. Just passing through, are you?'

Dr Singh gave him a thin smile. 'No, I'm here for the duration. How about you?'

'All depends.'

'On anything in particular?'

'Yes. On how soon I can get out of here. I'll either die of boredom being cooped up in this surgery a moment longer, or I'll catch something fatal.'

'Well, let's see if I can oblige you and send you on your speedy way.' Dr Singh turned and stared into the computer screen. 'I see it's some months since you last paid us a visit, Mr Shawcross. How's that lazy bowel of yours?'

Gabriel bristled at the man's effrontery. 'I'll have you know my bowel is in perfect working order, nothing remotely lazy about it. And the name's Liberty. Gabriel Liberty. You could at least get that right.'

Dr Singh frowned and tapped away at his keyboard. 'I thought Mr Shawcross was next on my list.'

'Oh, him – he wasn't fast enough. Probably that lazy bowel of his holding him back.'

Gabriel snorted at his own joke, but Dr Singh attacked his keyboard once more. 'Ah, here we are. Gabriel Liberty of Mermaid House, Hollow Edge Moor, Deaconsbridge. Is that you? Have I got *that* right?'

'It'll do right enough.'

Another glance at the screen gave Dr Singh his next question. 'So how are you getting on with your diet? Still keeping an eye on your cholesterol?'

'A weather eye at all times,' Gabriel answered. He almost licked his lips at the thought of the steak and kidney pudding with chips that he would be tucking into as soon as he got out of here.

Another glance at the screen. 'And your arthritis?'

Gabriel waved his distorted large-knuckled hands. 'I'm giving them a rest, decided to ease up on the fiddly work of brain surgery. Truth is, I can't find the brains. Not round here anyway.'

Dr Singh rested his elbows on the desk. 'So what can I help you with?'

'I was wondering when you'd get to the point. It's this . . .'

Lunch wasn't proving as enjoyable as Gabriel had hoped it would be. For a start his usual table was occupied by a couple of day-trippers, and then there had been no steak and kidney pudding on the menu; he'd had to make do with egg and sausage instead. He didn't like change. And he didn't like having to make do. Besides, egg and sausage he could do at home. Nothing to it. But steak and kidney pudding was another matter.

He was sitting in the Mermaid café overlooking the square where Friday's market was in full flow – local people were going about their business while tourists, brought out by the warm spring weather, were getting in their way. He sprinkled extra salt on to his chips, folded the newspaper that the café supplied and prepared himself for a satisfying assault on the crossword. To his annoyance someone had beaten him to it. He pushed it aside. The day was not going well.

As pathetic as it was, coming into Deaconsbridge had become the high spot of his week. It was the only day that had any structure to it. He came here every Friday to browse in the antiquarian bookshop, to pick up the odd item of food – kippers for his supper that evening – and to go to the bank and the post office. And, of course, to have his lunch cooked for him.

He munched a mouthful of sausage slowly and wondered at the tedium of his life. It wasn't an easy confession for him to make, but he was bored. Other than his younger son, Jonah, who did the bulk of his shopping for him, he rarely saw anyone during the week. And Jonah only ever made a fleeting visit. As for Caspar and Damson, well, if it hadn't been for Val's funeral, he might not have seen them at all these last couple of years.

It was strange, but since the death of his second wife eighteen months ago, he had thought more and more of Anastasia, his first wife. The memory of her had grown sharper as Val's faded. Anastasia had been the mother of his children and had died thirty-four years ago.

He had been away on business in Nigeria when it happened and had missed her death by twelve hours. In those days communication wasn't what it is today, and he had arrived home to be told that he was the widowed father of three children – Anastasia had died giving birth to Jonah. Help was brought in to take care of the children, but nothing was ever the same again. As the years passed, it was clear that the children, in particular the twins, Caspar and Damson, who were growing wilder by the day, needed a mother. So he married Val. It was a union of convenience on both sides: he had needed someone to organise the house and his family so that he could devote himself to the running of Liberty Engineering, and Val had wanted the security a husband could offer. They never deluded themselves that the arrangement was perfect, but he liked to think that it had worked well for the most part.

His plate had been cleared away some time ago and he was ready for his dessert now. He banged his spoon sharply on the table and caught the eye of a waitress. Fellow diners looked his way and he returned their stares disdainfully. Someone muttered how rude he was, but the waitress came over with his bowl of apple pie and custard, just as she always did when he summoned her with his spoon.

'Everything all right?' she said.

She asked this every time she served him. He supposed it was her equivalent to 'Have a nice day' and went with the ridiculous outfit she and the other waitresses wore – silly red baseball caps with short red overalls, which made them look as though they belonged in a theme park.

'No,' he said, 'everything is far from all right. I'm at the wrong table, there was no steak and kidney on the menu and what's more,' he thrust the paper at her, 'someone has completed my crossword.'

'We'll have to see if we can do better next Friday,' she said breezily. 'Tea or coffee?'

'You know I always have tea.'

He spent the rest of the afternoon doing his errands before awarding himself an hour of browsing in the bookshop.

Eventually he drove back to Mermaid House in a foul mood. He had had to abort his first attempt because he had forgotten to call in at the chemist's. With Dr Singh's words echoing in his ears he had turned the Land Rover round and gone back into town. The man was probably overreacting but he had said it was imperative that he started the course of antibiotics as soon as possible. He had also said that Gabriel would have to come into the surgery again in a couple of days to have the dressing changed.

A lot of fuss and bother about nothing.

Even so, it wouldn't hurt to take the quack at his word, seeing as the pain in his arm had been getting worse. It had been so bad the last two nights he hadn't been able to sleep.

'That's a very nasty burn, Mr Liberty,' the doctor had said, when Gabriel had rolled up his sleeve. 'It's also infected. When and how did you do it?'

'Some time last week. I . . . I was careless with the kettle.'

'And you didn't think to get it seen to?'

'I thought it would heal on its own.'

'Do you live alone, Mr Liberty?'

'What's that got to do with the price of eggs?'

Once again the doctor's eyes had scanned his computer screen. 'Your wife died not so long ago, didn't she?'

'She might have. What else have you got stored on there about me?'

'You'd be surprised. Now, push your sleeve right back as far as it will go and let me have a good gander.'

'You know, for a foreigner your English isn't bad.'

'And for a man with a burn the size of a chapati, you're lucky you're not in hospital. Any family to keep an eye on you?'

'Mind your own business.'

The approach to Mermaid House was almost a mile long and the bumpy track made for hard going; it was a toss-up whose suspension would give out first, the ancient Land Rover's or Gabriel's. Cursing as each bump jolted his arm, he knew he would rather die than be forced to move. What was a little discomfort when he had perfection on his doorstep?

Perched high on Hollow Edge Moor, and about a thousand feet above sea level, his home was surrounded by unrivalled scenery. The best in England, for his money.

From the front of the house, and beyond the expanse of moorland, Deaconsbridge nestled in the shallow plateau of the valley with its old mill and factory chimneys just visible, but turn to the right, to the south, and you had the swell of the dales of the White Peak. Walk round to the side of the house, and on a clear day, the windswept hulk of Kinder Scout dominated the skyline.

When he let himself in, Gabriel saw that Jonah had been and gone. There were three carrier-bags of shopping on the table with a note saying he had put away the perishable items in the fridge and freezer.

Damn the boy!

It had become Jonah's habit to call when he knew his father was out.

Chapter Three

The nature of Archie Merryman's work meant that he saw more than his fair share of bereavement. A house-clearance job usually meant that he was tidying up the loose ends of someone's life and death, and it never failed to touch him. Stripping a property of its furniture and possessions, hearing the echoing footsteps on floors where once there had been carpets, always made him feel that he had personally removed the heart from the house. No longer was it a home: it was an empty shell. It was only the thought of the next family moving in that kept him from becoming maudlin. He liked to visualise them taking up residence, children crashing down the stairs, doors banging, chairs scraping, cutlery rattling, the radio playing.

He was glad that after twenty-five years in the business he hadn't become hardened to it, and not just because it gave him a good reputation and the edge on the other second-hand dealers in the area, but because it proved to him that he was still the same old Archie. 'You always were a soft beggar,' his mother used to say to him, 'soft as cottongrass, that's what you are.'

He climbed into his van, smiled goodbye to the two women whose father's house he had just cleared. What wouldn't he give to hear a sentence as coherent as that from his mother these days?

He reversed the van slowly, mindful of the load in the back. None of it was particularly valuable – the best stuff had been taken away for auction – but to mistreat it seemed disrespectful to those who had once owned it. Some of it would end up at the tip – even he couldn't sell perished bath mats and crumbling cork tiles – but he would shift most of it.

It had been a big job and had taken him longer than he had expected. He preferred smaller houses, not because he was lazy but because he didn't like to get too involved. If you spent too long clearing a house, you ended up thinking like the family, unable to be objective. He had done it yesterday. 'Are you sure you wouldn't like to hang on to this?' he had asked the two sisters. From the expression in their eyes he had known he'd said the wrong thing. They had probably already put themselves through countless emotional hoops deciding what to keep and what to part with, and here was this outsider making it worse for them.

He trundled the van slowly down the hill, away from the stone-built farmhouse and its For Sale board. In his rear-view mirror he could see the two women still standing where he had left them. They were crying. It didn't surprise him – he had seen it all before. While there had been business to conduct they had held themselves together, but now that they were alone, they could go back to mourning the death of their father.

It was warm in the van and he lowered the window. Immediately he felt his spirits drag themselves up from his boots. At last it felt like spring was really here. He loved March: in lush green fields criss-crossed with a network of drystone walls, sheep grazed while skinny newborn lambs hopped and skipped on bandy legs. In the distance he could make out a kestrel hovering above something on the ground that had caught its eye. He sighed expansively. Despite all the sadness the world wasn't a bad place, and until someone came up with anything better, he'd stick with it a while longer.

He drove on and wondered what he would find at home that evening. Since his mother had moved in with them after her stroke, things between him and Stella had gone from bad to worse. 'Over my dead body' had been her exact words when he had suggested it, and he hadn't been surprised by her hostility: Stella and his mother had never hit it off – but he had hoped she would come round to the idea. Thankfully she had, and Bessie had moved in last month.

When Archie had invited his mother to come and stay with them, as he had euphemistically put it to her, she had agreed quite readily – to his relief: he knew how independent she was. 'We'll treat it as a holiday,' he had said, 'but without the sunburn.' He suspected that she knew she would never go back to her house in Derby. Meanwhile, her neighbours were keeping an eye on it so that she could return when she was able. The fact that a second stroke was likely to follow the first, and that it would probably be more debilitating, was not mentioned.

She had had the stroke just before Christmas, not a massive one but bad enough to knock the stuffing out of her. The tough, uncompromising woman he had always known became fragile and unsure. The stroke had robbed her of nearly all the strength in her right arm and hand, and her right leg had also taken a beating, which made walking slow and difficult. Making herself understood had been a problem too. Her speech was a lot clearer now, and that was down to weeks of diligent speech therapy, although at times it was still a puzzle to know what she was saying. If she was tired or anxious the words came out slurred or just plain jumbled – 'hum-dryer' for tumble-dryer, 'rare hush' for hairbrush. He had tried to turn understanding her into a game, calming her frustration with light-hearted humour, but Stella didn't have the patience for this and recently had shown signs of losing her temper. He didn't blame her – Bessie wasn't her mother after all.

The strain of being caught between a rock and a hard place – wanting to keep the peace with his wife and do the right thing by his mother – was taking its toll. Initially things had gone smoothly, but then the niggles had turned into rows and recently he and Stella had both said things that should never have been voiced. Until then their skirmishes had been conducted in low voices. 'She's my mother,' he had whispered one night in the kitchen, as Stella slammed cupboards and drawers. 'She's not well. What do you expect me to do with her?' It was a dangerous question, given that he knew exactly what Stella wanted him to do with her. But he would never do that. He saw too often the hurt and sense of betrayal as families, as well meaning as they were, shepherded their elderly relatives out of the houses they knew and loved and into nursing homes. Sometimes they went willingly, looked forward to giving up the reins of running a house in exchange for having everything done for them. But more often than not they were sad and confused, not quite understanding that they would never see home again.

No. He would not do that to Bessie Merryman.

What saddened him most was that his mother apologised frequently for having become a burden and there was nothing he could do to convince her that she wasn't. The woman who had brought him up single-handedly, and taught him always to see the best in others, would never be a burden to him.

His shop, Second Best, was situated on the corner of Millstone Row and Lower Haye in Deaconsbridge. It was a double-fronted Victorian building of stone that originally had been honey-gold but which was now blackened with age. Positioned just off the market square, it had the bonus of convenient parking to the side where, with Samson's help, Archie unloaded the van. Samson – his real name was Shane – was the extra brawn Archie relied upon for those larger items of furniture he couldn't manage on his own. At six feet two, Archie wasn't a small man, but Samson dwarfed him. His conversational skills were restricted to a nod and a grunt, but he was a godsend with a wardrobe on his back and a horsehair mattress between his teeth.

On the occasions when Samson was on a house-clearance job with Archie or they were delivering furniture to a customer, Comrade Norm – so-called because his parents had christened him Norman Lenin Jones – kept a part-time eye on the shop. There were days when they could have done with another pair of hands, but business wasn't consistently good. It could stretch to two and a half salaries, but any more and the financial knicker elastic would snap.

He said good night to Samson, checked that all was locked and secure, and set off for home, a ten-minute walk across town. The low evening sun brought a soft glow of light to the square, and now that everything was shut, apart from the Mermaid café, which stayed open until seven o'clock, a pleasing calm had descended. The market traders had gone, leaving behind a vacant cobbled square splattered with squashed fruit and veg and discarded hot-dog wrappers. Over by the war memorial, a blue and white carrier-bag was swept along by the breeze until it came to rest at the foot of a litter-bin. It was only a few yards out of his way so Archie strolled over and popped it in. Straightening up, he waved to Joe Shelmerdine, who was just locking his bookshop.

Further along the street was the Deaconsbridge Arms, and although it had been done up by the brewery to draw in tourists, it was still where the old die-hard drinkers gathered to sup their beer and indulge in local gossip. Archie rarely showed his face in there. He wasn't a drinker: he had seen alcohol turn his father into a vicious bully and had grown up with a horror of it doing the same to him. He had come home too many times from school to find his father drunk and ready to take out his anger on the first person to hand. From a young age Archie had known that it was better for him to take the beating than his mother.

He carried on briskly – it was the nearest he got to working out like Samson did – but slowed when he got to Cross Street: it was one of the steepest roads in the town and it always took him by surprise, squeezed the air out of his chest and turned his relatively healthy fifty-five-year-old body into that of a wheezing ninety-year-old. He paused to catch his breath, leaning against the painted handrail on which generations of small children had swung upside-down like rows of multicoloured fruit bats.

He and Stella had wanted children, but sadly it wasn't to be, and as the years passed they had resigned themselves to being one of those childless couples who never quite fit in. They had moved to Deaconsbridge not long after they had married and had lived in a rented flat until they had enough money to put down a deposit on a three-storey end-of-terrace house in Cross Street. They had been here ever since. They could have moved, and Stella had been keener than him to do so, but somehow they had never got round to it.

When he reached home he let himself in at the back door and was surprised by how quiet it was. Usually the radio or the television was on, sometimes both competing to be heard.

A sixth sense told him something was wrong – the same sixth sense that had dried his mouth and made his hair stand on end just before Christmas when he had found his mother's home dark and silent. She had been lying on the floor by the side of her bed, her face twisted, her nightdress exposing more of her than was fair. When she saw him her eyes had filled with tears. She had been there since morning, unable to move, unable to call for help.

He moved fast now, calling her name as he took the stairs two at a time. He burst into what had been the spare room, but which was now her room.

She wasn't there.

Into the bathroom next.

Nothing.

He was just about to go into his and Stella's room when he heard her voice. He bent over the balustrade and saw his mother looking up at him from the bottom of the stairs.

'Ser-late,' she said, pointing to her watch.

He put his heart back where it belonged and joined her in the hall. 'Only a little late tonight,' he said, adrenaline still pumping through him. 'I had a busy day. Where were you? Didn't you hear me calling?'

She took his arm for support and led him slowly towards the front room. Once again the hairs on the back of his neck warned him of an impending shock.

On the mantelpiece, between a pair of decorative china plates, was an envelope with his name on it. He knew without opening it what it would say.

Stella had left him.

Chapter Four

It was Sunday morning and Ned and Clara were being treated to a brunch-party send-off. While Moira helped Ned to the last of the chipolatas and crispy bacon, Clara watched the goings-on outside where Guy and David were putting the finishing touches to Winnie, the three-year-old camper-van that was soon to be Ned and Clara's new home.

Parting with her lovely Mazda MX5 yesterday morning had been a wrench for Clara, and even Ned had looked sad when they had watched the smart two-seater sports car being driven away by its new owner – it had always been a source of pride to Ned that he was the only child he knew who got to sit in the front of his mother's car. He had brightened, though, when the camper-van arrived.

It was second-hand, but in excellent condition, and unlike a brand new car it seemed to have a highly developed personality. There was a cosy feel to it that suggested happy times ahead.

When Clara had first seen it, the salesman had explained that its previous owners were a nice couple who had only parted with it because they were upgrading to something bigger. 'I had no idea camper-vans could be so well kitted out,' she had said, as they stepped inside and she felt the soft fitted carpet beneath her shoes.

'This is actually what we call a motorhome, and quite a modest one at that. You should see what we have at the top end of the market. The Winnebago, now that's what we call deluxe.' He pointed through one of the side windows to a massive bus-like vehicle that looked as if it might accommodate at least two touring rock bands.

'Heavens! How many does that sleep?' she asked.

'Eight. One of the beds is queen-size. There's even a washing-machine and tumble-dryer on board.'

Then, feeling disloyal to the modest camper-van they were supposed to be viewing, she said, 'Well, how about you show me what this baby has to offer?'

While Ned carried out his own inspection – opening doors, trying the driver's seat complete with armrests – the salesman had filled her in on the superior coachbuilt workmanship, the elegant interior, the spacious dinette, the two-burner combination cooker, the tilt-tolerant fridge and the swivel cab seats. Ned had already discovered those – one minute he was facing the front, the next the back. With growing enthusiasm the young man showed her rattle-free lockers and cabinets. There were recessed halogen reading-lights, upholstered bench-seats, two surprisingly large wardrobes, a drop-down contoured hand-basin in the ingenious bathroom that contained a flushable toilet as well as a shower. He left the sleeping arrangements till last, showing her, with a magician's flourish, the double bed over the cab, complete with little ladder, and the two single beds in the dinette area that could also convert to a comfortable double.

'Did the previous owners have a name for it?' she asked, when at last he drew breath.

He gave her an odd look. 'Not that I know of. I could check the registration document if you want – it's in the office.'

'No, that's okay.' She sensed he was humouring her, probably thinking that after everything he had just gone through, she was just another time-waster. 'May I have a test drive, please?' she said, keen to re-inflate him. 'I'd like to see how it handles.'

He was immediately back into his stride. 'Certainly. Have you driven one before? It will feel quite different from what you've been used to.' He cast an eye in the direction of her sports car.

'I'm sure I'll get the hang of it.'

'Is it ours now?' asked Ned, climbing down the ladder from the bed above the cab while the salesman went to fetch the keys.

'Would you like it to be ours?'

He slipped into the driver's seat, grabbed the steering-wheel and *brrmm*ed noisily, trying to reach the pedals.

'I'll take that as a yes.' She smiled.

It was while they were driving home, after she had written a cheque for the deposit, that the camper-van had been christened. Clara had been thinking of the ridiculous eight-berth monstrosity and had said scornfully, to no one in particular, 'Winnebago. What kind of a name is that?'

'Winnie, Winnie, Bago,' chanted Ned. 'Is that what we're calling our camper-van?' he asked, looking up from the pile of glossy brochures he'd gathered from the salesman's office.

'We could shorten it to Winnie,' she said. 'What do you think?'

He considered her suggestion earnestly, then smiled. 'Poo,' he said.

'Oh dear, can you hang on until we get home?'

A grin extended across his face. 'Not that. Winnie-the-*Pooh*.'

Apart from filling Winnie with provisions, clothes, books, toys, games, cassettes, a basic tool kit, and anything else they might need for the next five months, they had also had to pack up other possessions. During their absence, a young professional couple would be renting their house and were moving in on Monday. Initially Clara hadn't wanted to let it, but common sense had dictated that she might as well have the money coming in to pay off the mortgage. Then her savings wouldn't receive such a large dent. It also meant that she would be committed to what she had started. With no

24

house to come back to until the end of August, she would have to make a go of the trip.

Her friends had been concerned about money. 'I just don't understand how you'll manage,' Moira said.

'I've got a PEP that's just dying to be let loose,' she had said. 'I know that would only get you through a long weekend, Moira, but our needs will be quite modest while we're away. And if the worst comes to the worst we could resort to busking.'

'I wouldn't put it past you.'

'Oh, and since when did I become such a rebel?'

'You've always been a rebel, Clarabelle,' Guy had said. 'You've never been fully in step with the rest of us.'

Though Clara knew that there was an element of truth in what he had said, she was hurt to hear it voiced so openly. She and Ned had not yet travelled a mile, but already a gap was opening between her and the gang. 'You mean I'm different from you lot because I'm not married and I don't trade in my house every other year for something bigger and better?'

'Now, don't get nasty with Guy,' Moira had said. 'It's not his fault he still hasn't forgiven you for spilling the beans about Margaret Thatcher not being the Tooth Fairy.'

Suddenly everyone had an opinion about her.

David said, 'You know jolly well that you're the resourceful one of us. For goodness' sake, you're the only one sitting round this table who knows what to do with a power drill. When was the last time you had to have a "little man" in? Eh?'

'Nothing ever fazes you, Clara,' Louise put in. 'While we've become childishly self-indulgent as we've grown older, you've turned into a sensible adult.'

'That sounds worryingly like a criticism to me,' Clara said defensively.

They ignored her and carried on, warming to their theme. 'You're a natural facilitator,' Guy said. 'A doer who has to do things her way.'

'Are you saying I'm bossy?'

'Well, you do like to be in charge, don't you?'

'Not always!'

'Face it, Clara,' David said. 'You put us all to shame. Just look at what you've achieved single-handedly. You've carved out a great career for yourself, you have—'

'A great career I'm wilfully throwing away,' she chipped in, wanting to redress the balance of this cringe-making conversation.

He had waved her interruption aside. 'And you have a fantastic son, who even you would admit is your crowning glory.'

'Enough!' she had cried.

Clara was still watching the antics of her friends outside when Louise came and joined her at the window. 'Just look at them! Anyone would think you were getting married.'

Decorated with party streamers and shaving foam, Winnie indeed looked like the archetypal honeymoon getaway vehicle.

'You know, it's not too late to change your mind about this hare-brained caper,' Louise said.

Without turning her head, Clara said, 'And why would I want to do that?'

'Oh, you know, now that it's the day you're finally setting off, it might be dawning on you – the extent of your madness and the terrible mistake you're making. Only you're too proud to admit you might have been a little hasty.'

Now Clara did turn and look at her friend. 'And you're too proud to admit that you're envious of what I'm doing.'

'Me? Jealous of being cooped up in a box on wheels for five months with a chemical loo? You must be joking!'

'Come on, Louise. Admit it! Aren't you just a teensy-weensy bit envious that I'm escaping, taking time out so that I can enjoy each day as it comes?'

'No, I'm not. I'm more concerned with living in the real

world, not this frothy concoction you've invented for yourself.'

'It feels real enough to me.'

'Mm . . . let's see how it feels in a week's time when you're bored of your own company and Ned says he's homesick.'

Clara looked across Louise and David's sitting room to where Ned was on the sofa with Moira. A momentary pang of uncertainty made her wonder if she wasn't being entirely honest with herself. Who did she think would benefit most from this trip? Herself or Ned?

Both of them, she told herself firmly. She needed a break from work and to be with Ned. 'Boredom and homesickness won't be an issue,' she said. 'What we'll experience will be just as real and valid as anything that's going on round here.'

'But it will only be as real as a holiday, which, when it comes to an end, will bring you back to where you started.'

'Maybe it won't. Maybe I'll find my personal Utopia out on the road and never come home.'

'And you can take this as a first official warning. If you stop washing your hair, pierce yourself just once and turn into a New Age hippie, I'll publicly disown you.'

Clara smiled. 'Is that a promise?'

'Oh, come here, and give me a hug. I'm going to miss you. You will write, won't you? I'll need the occasional phone call, too, to keep me going.'

Clara hugged her back. 'I'll miss you too. And of course I'll keep in touch. You don't think I'd pass up the opportunity to brag about what a wonderful time I'm having, do you? Rubbing your snooty nose in my happiness will give me the greatest pleasure.'

They drew apart. 'And don't you dare quote me,' Louise said, 'but, yes, part of me is jealous of what you're doing. Who wouldn't be?'

Clara embraced her again. 'And that happy thought will be with me every time I clean out the Chemi-loo!'

A bang on the window made them both jump. Guy and David's open-mouthed faces were pressed against the glass; it wasn't a pretty sight.

'And there's another happy memory for you to take with you,' laughed Louise. 'A matching pair of gargoyles!'

At last they were ready to go.

'Come on, you intrepid explorers,' David said, lifting Ned down from his shoulders, 'that's enough of the goodbyes. It's time you were on your way.'

'Glad to know you're eager for us to be gone,' said Clara. She settled Ned into the front passenger seat.

'That's because the sooner you go, the sooner you'll be back, sweetie-pie.'

'I wouldn't count on it.'

'You're all talk, Clarabelle. A hundred quid says you'll be crawling back to us within the month and applying for your old job.'

She held out her hand to Guy. 'Two hundred says I won't.'

He grasped it firmly. 'Done!'

Clara hugged everyone all over again and received their unhelpful words of advice with good grace. No, she wouldn't talk to strangers. No, she wouldn't hold the traffic up too much. And yes, she would remember to respect the countryside.

Louise moved in to have the last word. 'And don't do anything stupid while you're away.'

'Such as?'

'Such as taking any unnecessary risks. We want you to come back in one piece. Okay?'

'This may come as a shock to you, Louise, but that's something I'm keen to do myself.'

An hour into the journey and with Walton-on-Whinge – as she and the gang referred to Walton-on-Wineham where they all lived – well behind her, Ned had fallen asleep: the combination of excitement and anticipation had caught up with him. She turned off his story tape, and now that she was used to driving Winnie and had more or less mastered the vagaries of the gear-lever – roadworks and stop-start traffic on the M25 had seen to that – she relaxed a little and thought how wonderfully free she felt chugging along in the inside lane of the M40 with High Wycombe soon to be ticked off on her mental route-planner. She loved the idea of being able to stop at a moment's notice, park up wherever and feel instantly at home. It was this that had appealed to her when the idea had first occurred to her to take Ned travelling. A camper-van would provide a home-from-home environment that would give them a comforting sense of self-sufficiency. And certainly, right now, with Ned at her side, she felt as if she had everything she would ever want in the world.

A car overtook her and the driver gave her a wide smile. She wondered why. But then she remembered what Guy and David had done to the van – most of the streamers had blown away, but the balloons were still tied to the wing mirrors and door handles.

She switched on the radio. A song came on that she recognised – it was Nanci Griffith singing 'Waiting for Love' – and it tugged painfully at her heart. She had first heard it when she was living in America, and it would be for ever synonymous with that period in her life.

She had only recently arrived there, single and carefree, looking forward to the challenges of a year-long second-ment at Phoenix's headquarters in Wilmington. Determined to work hard and further her career, she had wanted to make the most of the opportunity.

But it hadn't been quite the career move she had thought it would be. She had returned home before the end of her secondment with a bruised heart and a pregnancy to explain to her friends and family.

Chapter Five

Gabriel was up earlier than usual. Last night when he had drawn the curtains the track had fallen down. Dust and bits of plasterwork had showered over him and something had got into his eye. He had tried bathing it with an old eye-bath he had found in the medicine cupboard, but it hadn't helped. Now, after a sleepless night, his eye hurt like hell and every time he blinked it felt as if the lid was coated with sandpaper.

Before going downstairs to make himself some breakfast he went into the bathroom and had another rummage in the cabinet, hunting through the shelves of old pill bottles and pots of gunk Val had sworn by. Right at the back, on the top shelf, he found what he was looking for: an ancient eye patch. The elastic had perished but he tied a knot in it, and it held firmly enough around his head. His hands were so annoyingly stiff and clumsy that it took him a few minutes to achieve this. He closed the cabinet door and took a long, hard look at himself in the dirty, black-spotted mirror.

He was presented with an unshaven, grey-haired old man wearing a black eye-patch.

He smoothed down his thick uncombed hair, which was sticking up all over his scalp, then he turned his head, and decided he looked no better sideways on. The long straight nose Anastasia had described as proud and regal had turned into something that didn't fit on his face any more; it looked too big, as though he had borrowed it from an older brother in the hope that he might grow into it. His cheeks had lost their firmness and sagged under the weight of so many lines. His mouth had withered into a rigid downward curve. Thick drooping earlobes hung at either side of his face and abundant bristly tufts sprouted from them. Dear God, when had he become such an ugly brute?

He walked the creaking length of the balustraded landing, avoiding the rucks in the threadbare runner, and paused, as he did every morning, to look down on the garden. The sun was still low in the eastern sky, but a pale light shone on the sloping lawn, planted sporadically with daffodils. It stretched down to a thick bank of rhododendrons that were yet to burst into flower, and beyond was Hollow Edge Woods, a copse where generations of foxes and badgers had lived. Way off in the distance, the swell of sheep-grazed hills rose up to the morning sky. He rested his hands on the stone sill and thought that Byron had got it right when he had compared Derbyshire with Greece and Switzerland, saying it was just as noble.

It had been love at first sight for Anastasia when she had seen Mermaid House. She had been an incurable romantic who acted on impulse and was inventively quirky, hence their children's bizarre names. But she had had her work cut out in convincing him to buy the house – he was so conventional and analytical. It cost much more than they could afford, and was miles from where Liberty Engineering's factory was situated, but eventually he had given in to her. He could still see her bright eyes flashing with delight as she whirled him round the room when he agreed to put in an offer.

It was only when they moved in that they appreciated the state of the place. It dated back to the mid-nineteenth century, and it was a wreck: dry rot, wet rot, any rot you cared to think of, Mermaid House had it in spades. Busy with work, he had left Anastasia to deal with it – it was her baby, after all. She threw herself into its restoration, determined to see the job thoroughly well done – and their bank balance just as thoroughly depleted. He had never regretted it, though. To see her happy was enough. And then Caspar and Damson had arrived. The upheaval in their lives was colossal, but Anastasia took the twins in her stride. She never complained of being tired, when night after night she sat in the nursery in the rocking-chair with one or other of the blighters on her shoulder. She never minded how little they slept, or how mischievous they were once they began to explore their surroundings, pulling themselves up on to their chubby legs and ransacking cupboards, drawers, shelves, constantly searching for something new to play with – and break. They were an inseparable two-man destruction derby: nothing was safe with them around. Gabriel had wanted to employ a nanny to help Anastasia, but she wouldn't hear of it, claiming that she loved the challenge of two such lively children.

It was five years before they took the plunge again and tried for another child. Then Jonah was born.

And Anastasia died.

By craning his neck to the left and pressing his head against the window, which was cloudy with dirt, Gabriel could just see the spire of the church in Deaconsbridge; it was where both of his wives were buried.

He tightened the belt of his dressing-gown and continued along the landing, passing closed doors to dusty rooms he hadn't been inside for months. He took the stairs slowly: his one-eyed view gave him a misleading impression of the floor – it wasn't as close as he thought it was. The staircase was yet another reminder of Anastasia: she used to refer to herself as Scarlett O'Hara as she swept down it in a graceful rush of laughter, her long hair tumbling around her shoulders.

The kitchen didn't catch the morning sun, and even in the height of summer it was the coldest room in the house. Val had had an Aga installed and had stoked it with coal morning, noon and night. It had been worse than a demanding baby: as she shovelled in fuel at one end, it deposited ashes at the other. She had soon tired of that and had had it converted to gas. Not long after her death it, too, had given up the ghost – something to do with a faulty thermostat that couldn't be replaced.

Since then Gabriel had bought himself a bog-standard electric cooker and one of those portable heaters on wheels with a large gas cylinder inside it. He switched it on now – he had to keep clicking the button until eventually a spark ignited the gas and a whoomph of flame shot across the blackened panels. It had been when he was doing this, the other week, that he had burned his arm. He had deliberately lied to Dr Singh about being careless with the kettle because he had thought that otherwise it might seem that he couldn't be trusted with a gas fire. Scalding oneself sounded less dangerous, somehow.

It was four days since he had been into Deaconsbridge and had his arm seen to. He hadn't been back to the surgery; he had decided there was no point. He had finished the short course of antibiotics several days earlier than he should have, working on the theory that the pills would take effect faster if he tripled the dosage on days one and two. What was more, he had changed the dressing himself, swapping the bandages and gauze for a clean handkerchief and securing it with a couple of safety-pins. By rights the doctor should be grateful for being let off the extra work. If more people were like Gabriel, the National Health Service wouldn't be in such a mess.

But now he had this wretched eye to deal with. He would give it a day or so, and if there was no improvement, he would go into Deaconsbridge – make his Friday visit on Thursday perhaps. He pressed the heel of his hand against the eye patch, resisting the urge to give it a damn good rub. It was so itchy and sore. To distract himself he set about making a pot of tea for his breakfast.

For such a large kitchen, there was little space to work in: every surface was crowded with crockery and paperwork that lay in untidy piles awaiting his attention. As did all those things that needed mending, but which he never got round to: an Anglepoise lamp that wouldn't stay in position; a battery charger he'd ordered from one of those junk catalogues and had dropped and broken; an iron that needed a new plug; a wobbly mug tree; a wooden bread bin that wouldn't open properly; and several shirts that were down to just a few buttons. But the mess was getting to him; there was something tidal in the stealthy manner in which it was creeping up on him. He would have to do something about it soon.

But not today.

Domesticity didn't suit him. He wasn't cut out for defrosting freezers or knowing how to get a crease-free wash out of the washing-machine. Val had taken care of all that. It had been her domain and he had willingly left her to it. He wasn't ashamed to admit that he was old school when it came to defining the boundaries of a husband and wife. The system had worked perfectly until the world had gone mad and everyone had become obsessed with equality and role reversal.

He switched on the wireless to listen to the *Today* programme, sweeping aside several days' worth of plates, cups, knives and forks, dirty pots and pans and a couple of empty pilchard tins, until at last he had cleared a space around the kettle and toaster. His breakfast made, he added a tot of twelve-year-old Glenlivet to his tea, just a drop to kick-start his day. Time was when a new day for him had been like cracking an egg – short, sharp, and he was off. Now he had to ease himself into it. He sat at the cluttered table and answered the wireless back, dishing out his objections and criticism with a fair hand: he disagreed on principle with everything the presenters or politicians said.

He was still sitting at the table when he heard a knock at the door. He checked his watch, as though it would tell him who was bothering him at such an unsociably early hour. But it was later than he had thought, almost ten o'clock. Even so, who could it be? Callers at Mermaid House were rarer than hens' teeth.

There was another knock, louder this time. Whoever it

was seemed determined to summon him to the door. He pushed his feet into his slippers and shuffled off reluctantly to deal with whoever had come to bother him. He slid the bolts back, top and bottom, turned the key and opened the door.

'What the hell do you want?' Gabriel growled, when he saw Dr Singh standing before him. 'And don't tell me you were just passing and thought you'd see if I was in.'

'No, Mr Liberty, I wouldn't dream of lying to you. I am here because you didn't keep your appointment with me. You didn't return to the surgery for me to check your arm.'

'Very considerate of you, I'm sure. But (a) I didn't make an appointment, and (b) you've wasted your time in coming here because my arm is better.'

'Perhaps you would be good enough to let me be the judge of that.'

Gabriel gave him a hard stare. 'Persistent, aren't you?'

'Professional is how I like to view myself. Now, then, are we to conduct surgery business on the doorstep, or am I permitted to come in?'

'Suit yourself.'

Gabriel showed him through to the kitchen and realised at once that this was a mistake. He could feel Dr Singh's dark eyes appraising the situation, and the mess seemed a hundred times worse. The bottle of Glenlivet on the table didn't give quite the right impression either, especially as he was still in his shabby old pyjamas. Damn! He should have taken him into the drawing room. In fact, any room but this. He pushed up the sleeve on his dressing-gown, deciding that the sooner the infuriating man had examined his arm, the sooner he would be gone. 'There,' he said, removing the makeshift bandage, 'just as I told you. Practically as good as new.'

Dr Singh gave the handkerchief a disapproving look, but nodded at the improvement in Gabriel's arm. 'You're right, it's healing nicely. But since I'm here I might just as well apply a proper dressing, and while I do that, you can tell me what you've done to your eye.'

'I got something in it last night,' Gabriel said airily. 'It's a bit sore, that's all. There's no need for you to have a gawp at that too.'

But Dr Singh insisted that he be allowed to do his job. 'And how did you come by this?' he asked, when Gabriel had removed the patch and the eye began to water at the sudden brightness.

'A curtain track fell on top of me, if you must know.'

After pulling a small-beamed torch on him, Doctor Singh said, 'I don't like the look of it. You need to see a specialist. It's inflamed and you might have damaged the retina.'

'Don't be absurd. I've just got dust in it, that's all. Can't you give me some drops or something?'

'The "something" is a trip to hospital, Mr Liberty. Do you really want to risk going blind in that eye?'

'God! You foreigners make me sick. You're all the same, you come over here, you get yourselves an education at our expense, then start telling us what to do. Well, you know what you can do with your trip to hospital, don't you?'

Dr Singh put away his torch and snapped shut his medical case. 'Mr Liberty, listen very carefully to what I am about to say. Either you do as I say or I shall inform Social Services that you are living in squalor and that you are incapable of looking after yourself. And, trust me, they will descend upon you faster than you can say Enoch Powell and you will rue the day you ever ignored my advice. So, *old chap*, what's it to be?'

Gabriel's jaw dropped. 'You wouldn't dare.'

'Care to put me to the test?'

'Couldn't we just try the eye drops first?'

'No. Now, if you would be so good as to get dressed, I will drive you to the hospital. I was going there anyway.'

'What? Right now?'

'No time like the present.'

*

36

'I don't approve of blackmail,' Gabriel said, as he folded himself into the doctor's Honda hatchback. His knees were almost tucked under his chin, the top of his head jammed against the roof. Typical of the bloody Japanese to build cars for midgets then inflict them on the rest of the world.

'It wasn't blackmail,' Dr Singh said, 'it was a straight-forward deal. We negotiated quite openly. There was nothing underhand about it. But tell me, why don't you have any help around your mausoleum of a house?'

'Who said I didn't?'

'Your standards must be low if you let a cleaner off so lightly.'

'If it's any of your business, I got rid of the last woman after I caught her stealing from me. I didn't object to her helping herself to the odd bit of loose change lying about the place, but I drew the line at her sneaking out of the house with my best single malt whisky stuffed up her knickers.'

'How long ago was that?'

'Nearly a year.'

'And no other help since then?'

'What is this? Twenty questions and then you file your report to Social Services?'

They juddered over the cattle grid at the end of the track where two stone pillars marked the entrance to Mermaid House, then joined the main road. 'Tell me about your family. Do they live nearby?'

Gabriel shifted the seat-belt that was cutting into his neck. 'Are you asking me why they don't act the part of doting children and pop in every other day to see how the old man's doing?'

'I might be.'

A slight pause hung between them before Gabriel said, 'We have a perfectly balanced relationship: they can't stand me and I can't stand them.'

Dr Singh slowed down for a sheep that was noncha-lantly crossing the road. 'Those are harsh words,' he said.

He turned to face Gabriel, looked at him gravely. 'Do you not feel the heavy weight of them? Do you not wish it could be otherwise?'

Seconds passed.

'The sheep's gone now,' Gabriel muttered. 'You can drive on.'

Chapter Six

With no class before lunch, Jonah decided to bunk off school. He pulled on his jacket and took the stairs two at a time. At the bottom, pressed against the lockers in a slobbering, face-washing clinch, he found Tim Allerton wrapped around Shazzie Butler. They hadn't heard him coming, so he stood perfectly still, just long enough to induce in them the right level of embarrassment when they noticed him. He gave a discreet little tap on the locker beside them. 'A-hem.'

They sprang apart, which wasn't easy, given the tangle of arms and legs.

Assuming a deadpan expression, he said, 'On the basis that by now you've fully explored each other's dental work, perhaps you would be so good as to find your way to whatever lesson you should be attending. You know how I value your input as regards helping the school to sprint up the league tables.'

He strode off, leaving them to wipe themselves down.

Outside in the car park, he opened the rusting door of his J-reg Ford Escort, wondering, as he always did, why he bothered to lock it. Half the kids he taught at Deaconsbridge High – or Dick High, as its inmates affectionately referred to it – would have it open without the aid of a key in seconds flat.

He turned right out of the school gates and took the Lower Moor Road towards the centre of town, passing a dismal housing estate and an even uglier industrial complex. Back in the early 1970s, liberal town-planners had been assiduously fair with their unimaginative architectural handouts and had given Deaconsbridge High the same ugly status as its immediate neighbours. At roughly the same time as decimalisation had made its mark on the country, the evils of cheap flat-roofed urbanisation had hit Deaconsbridge. Since then, and in the last decade when restoration had become the watchword, money had been lavished on the small town centre so that it might compete with rival tourist attractions like Castleton and Buxton, but the outlying areas had received no such philanthropic gestures. Occasionally there were calls for a bypass, since the hordes of lucrative trippers had been successfully drawn to the town, but the seasonal density of traffic didn't yet warrant such outlandish expenditure.

And it was just as well that the traffic was so light, as Jonah was in a hurry. In the centre of the town, he joined the one-way system, drove along the war memorial end of the market square, then up towards Hollow Edge Moor. He was going to see his father, and had planned it this way deliberately. With only an hour and a half available to him, he would be able to say what he needed to say then get out. Direct and to the point, that's what he had to be. Above all else he must not flinch at his father's response, which would, of course, be of the ballistic variety. Many times he had witnessed, and been on the receiving end of, one of his father's furious dressing-downs, and on this occasion he was preparing himself to be stripped to the bone.

In his mind he had every line of the conversation already figured out, with every vindictive word his father would throw at him.

For starters he would be accused of being devious and too big for his boots, not to say conniving. Next he would be told he was the messenger of his cowardly brother, and that he was weak and too stupid to make a proper life for himself. It wouldn't be the same if that old line wasn't given an airing. Jonah was quite used to the torrent of scorn that was regularly poured on his teaching career.

'It's only those who can't get a proper job who teach,' his father had said, when Jonah had graduated from university and announced that he was applying for a year's teacher training course.

He didn't discuss it further with Gabriel, and certainly he didn't look to him for financial support. He paid his own way through college by working shifts in a meat-processing factory and as a consequence hadn't been able to look a meat and potato pie in the eye since.

That had been thirteen years ago, and still Gabriel hadn't forgiven Jonah for settling for such a 'second-rate' career.

Jonah always felt a chill run through him when he came home to Mermaid House. A knot of anxiety formed in the pit of his stomach, with the desire to make his visit as short as possible. He tried to kid himself that it was the bleakness of the house and its remote situation that made him feel like this, but he knew it wasn't. It was the memories.

Mermaid House was of an unusual, almost whimsical design, with a tower, four wings and a central cobbled courtyard. It was built of locally quarried stone that had turned depressingly dark and dreary with the passing of time. Now, as Jonah drove through the wide stone archway, the rumble of his car engine was amplified: it bounced off the walls and came back at him louder than it normally did. It confirmed what he had suspected earlier that morning when he had driven to work, that his exhaust was blowing.

He parked next to his father's mud-splattered Land Rover in front of what had always been known, rather ostentatiously, as the banqueting hall: it boasted original timbers, trusses and a massive fireplace.

Getting out of his car, he noticed that the tax disc on the Land Rover had expired and that the tread on one of the tyres looked borderline legal.

He crossed the courtyard and found the back door unlocked. He knocked cursorily, let himself in and nearly took a flyer over a pair of old boots lying on the floor. He pushed them to one side, called to his father, and walked through to the rest of the house. He passed the laundry room, noting the piles of unwashed clothes, bedding and towels in front of the washing-machine, and kept going, past the gun room, until he came to the kitchen.

These days, the mess seldom shocked him; it shocked him more that he had grown used to the conditions in which Gabriel was prepared to live. There was the unappetising smell of gone-off fish and he located the source of this as an empty tin of pilchards in tomato sauce on the draining-board. He went to throw it in the swing-bin but found that it was full to the brim. It was indicative of the scale of the problems at Mermaid House. No job was ever in isolation. There was always a knock-on effect. To change a light-bulb, you had to find the stepladder, and to find the stepladder you had to find the key to the cellar, and the key was anywhere but where it should be on the row of hooks in the kitchen.

It hadn't always been like this. When Val had been in her prime she had run the house with military precision, determined, against the odds, to instil in the three children a sense of shared duty. 'It's a large house, so I would be grateful if you could all pull your weight,' she had told them. On the first day of their holidays, when they were home from school, she would line them up and go through the running order. 'Damson, I'd like you to do the dusting and polishing in the dining room, and Caspar, you can clear out the ashes from the grate in the drawing room and bring in some fresh kindling. Jonah, I've put the silver on the kitchen table for you to clean.'

'Why does he always get the easy jobs?' Damson had pouted mutinously.

'Because he's the youngest. He's not as big and strong as the pair of you.'

Just as rebellious as his sister, Caspar would argue frequently that their father was rich enough to have a host of servants to do the work. But Val would have none of it. 'We no longer live in an age of servants, young man. We have Mrs Harper to help us, but she is not a servant.'

Ignoring whatever scornful comment Caspar would make, she would clap her hands and send them on their way. And always there would be the same music played at full volume while they did their chores. Even now, Jonah could never hear a piece of Gilbert and Sullivan without wanting to reach for the silver polish.

The meticulous order that Val so prized was lost when she suffered the first of a series of minor heart-attacks. As she slowly slipped away from them, she took with her the smooth running of the household. Mrs Harper, who was well past retirement age, handed in her notice and a succession of local cleaners proved unsatisfactory: the sheer size of Mermaid House overwhelmed them: ten bedrooms and three bathrooms was more than they wanted to take on.

It was more than any sane person would want to take on, thought Jonah, as he stood in the middle of the chaos. Suddenly he had the urge to hire the largest skip he could get hold of and throw everything into it. How tempting it was to clear the decks and start again. He would give his stubborn, sore-headed father the clean slate he needed. But he knew that that would never happen. Only a nuclear bomb would clear these particular decks.

But it was a bomb of sorts that he had come here to drop.

He called to Gabriel again, and helped himself to an apple from the bowl of fruit he bought religiously every week for his father, and which Gabriel rarely touched, then wandered out of the hall. He checked the drawing room, the dining room, and finally the library, where the curtains were drawn to protect the shelves of books from being damaged by sunlight. But there was no sign of his father. He stood at the bottom of the stairs and shouted, his voice echoing in the musty emptiness of the high-ceilinged house. There was no answer.

The irony was not lost on Jonah. Every week he did his father's shopping for him, and tried to time his appearance at Mermaid House for when he knew his father

43

would be in Deaconsbridge so that he could avoid speaking to him. Now he wanted to talk to him and he couldn't.

Where was he?

Perhaps he had gone for a walk. Well, if he had, there was no point in looking for him. Jonah didn't have time to mount a search party. He would have to come back another day.

To his shame, he felt relieved as he retraced his steps the length of the house, knowing that, for now, he wouldn't have to go through with what Caspar had asked him to do.

He was about to use his own key to lock the back door – Gabriel really shouldn't leave the house unlocked – when he thought better of it. His father might have forgotten to take a key with him.

Outside in the pleasantly warm sun and taking another bite of the apple, Jonah looked at his watch and decided he had time to see to the balding tyre on the Land Rover. But when he checked the spare, he found that it was in an even worse condition.

Sometimes there was just no helping Gabriel Liberty.

Chapter Seven

It was four days since Stella had left him, and while Archie wasn't entirely surprised by her departure, he had been taken aback by the way she had gone about it. It was the coward's way out and he had never thought of Stella in that light.

The note had been blunt and to the point. It seemed that the affair he had thought was over had picked up again and Stella had decided, at last, where her future lay. And it was not with Archie, the man to whom she had been married for twenty-six years and who had failed to give her the children she had always wanted.

Indicating right, he pulled off the main road and turned sharply into the hospital car park. He felt angry. It was always Stella who was supposed to feel the loss of not having children. What about him? Why hadn't his feelings been taken into account? After all, it was he who had to live with the knowledge that he wasn't man enough to become a father, he who had taken the jibes when Stella's disappointment turned to bitterness. He had wanted children, too, but no one had thought he was bothered by his and Stella's incompleteness as a couple and no one had thought to ask.

Next to him, now that they were parked, his mother was struggling with her seat-belt. 'Here, love,' he said. 'Let me.' He pressed the red button and released the strap.

She straightened her hat and smiled at him. 'Ready now,' she said.

'Ready.' He smiled back.

She had dressed specially for the occasion – a trip to the speech therapist was a big day out for her. Archie had been roped in as chief style guru. 'Pink or glue?' she had asked, holding out two dresses as he sat on the edge of her bed eating his cornflakes.

'Definitely the pink,' he had said, trying to sound decisive. A hint of dithering on his part and they'd never get out of the house this side of sunset.

It seemed to work, and she held the dress against her in front of the long mirror. Then, lowering it, she said, 'Or maybe the . . . the . . . the . . .' She squeezed her eyes shut, pursed her lips, and at the back of her mind, where some prankster was rewriting the English language for her, she located the word. She snapped her eyes open and said, proudly, 'Or the cheese?'

He proceeded carefully. If he gave the wrong answer, the limited supply of good words available to her this morning would shrivel to nothing. He gave the matter serious consideration before he tapped the air with his spoon. 'No, I still think the pink would be best. Very Liz Taylor, when she was at her best. Shall I help you?'

He helped her now to take her seat in the hospital waiting room, and could feel the heavy tiredness in her body: the short walk from the car park had sapped most of her strength. But it did nothing to dampen her desire to enjoy her big day out. She smiled at the woman opposite, who also looked as if she was dressed in her best party frock – she had overdone the makeup, though, and the red lipstick clashed with the frilly purple neckline. The man sitting next to her, presumably her husband, looked dog-tired, and Archie wondered what unearthly time the pair of them had got up to get ready for their appointment.

But the woman didn't respond to the warmth of his mother's smile. Disappointed, Bessie turned to Archie and, in a voice that should have been a whisper but missed the mark by several decibels, she said, 'Cobbly cow.'

He tried not to laugh, and was still trying to contain himself when it was Bessie's turn to see the young girl who was patiently teaching her to speak again. Though with a phrase as beautiful as 'cobbly cow' – so much better than 'snobby cow' – he wondered whether it wouldn't be more fun to teach the rest of the world to speak as Bessie did now. He left them to their phonetics and flashcards and went in search of a polystyrene-flavoured cup of tea that would scald the top layer of skin clean off his tongue.

The vending-machine was situated in a bright, airy space where pieces of artwork from the local comprehensive were displayed on the stark white walls. There was an atrium-style roof to this modern extension – opened by a local soap star last year – and it felt more akin to a fancy hotel than a hospital. Not that Archie had had any first-hand experience of fancy hotels: the nearest he had got to one was when he and Stella were celebrating their twenty-fourth wedding anniversary. He had planned it as a surprise. He let her think he had forgotten about it, then on the day, while she was getting ready for work, he had presented her with tickets for the train to London and a show.

But it hadn't turned out the way he had hoped it would. She was moody and distant with him, and found fault with almost everything: the train took too long, the hotel was too small, the food too expensive and the show too loud. During the journey home he had wondered if everything would have been to her liking had she been with someone else. He kept the thought to himself, but he soon knew the answer. He found letters and a couple of photographs. He hadn't gone snooping, they had been left casually in a drawer, not even covered up; it was as if she had wanted him to find out. If she had been hoping for a confrontation, he must have disappointed her: he simply carried on as though everything was normal, convincing himself that if he ignored it she would get it out of her system and things would soon be okay again. Plenty of marriages had glitches; it was all about riding the storm. After a while he thought he had done the right thing. She stopped inventing reasons to be out of an evening, there were no sudden trips to see her sister, and the phone no longer rang with no one on the other end when he answered it. But she wasn't happy. If anything, she was worse – tearful, or irrationally angry. He almost felt sorry for her, imagining that her lover had decided to call a halt to the affair. Perhaps he, too, was married and hadn't wanted to jeopardise what he already had.

Stupidly, Archie spent more time than was healthy putting together a background for this unknown man. Was he younger than Archie? Better-looking? Funnier? More intelligent? Rich?

With the benefit of hindsight, he had been nothing but a coward. Instead of wasting time dwelling on her lover, he should have been talking to Stella, making an effort to understand where he had gone wrong.

But he had left it too late. All the talking in the world wouldn't make things right now. She was gone, no doubt to this perfect man who understood her. Who didn't . . . who didn't have an ageing mother to care for.

He swallowed the last of his tea and suddenly felt weary.

How would he manage Second Best and look after Bessie on his own? She wasn't so bad at the moment, but he could see that in the future she would need a constant eye on her. He crumpled the empty cup, dropped it into the nearest bin, and cursed himself for having taken advantage of Stella in the way that he had. In relying on her to be at home during the afternoons – she only worked mornings – he had felt that he was doing the right thing by his mother. It served him right that Stella had left him. He had given her a gold-plated final straw.

With ten more minutes before Bessie would be finished, he went for a stroll. He was just passing a couple of pretty nurses who were chatting about a hen party they'd been to last night when he caught sight of a face he recognised. It was that nice Indian doctor from the surgery in town, the one who was always so good with his mother. He was friendly without being overly familiar, which Bessie liked.

48

She always used to say that if you had to undress for a doctor, the least he could do was look the other way, and Dr Singh was wonderfully courteous and proper with her.

Archie went over to say hello. 'Touting for business, Dr Singh?'

'Ah, Mr Merryman, how good to see you. Are you here with your mother?'

'Yes. She's with the speech therapist. It's slow going.'

'Patience, Mr Merryman, she'll get there in the end. Remember what I told you, there's life after a stroke so long as everyone involved pitches in. You just have to keep the faith.'

'I know. Some days she's quite clear, but others I can't make head nor tail of what she's saying. So what brings you here?'

'An errand of mercy. And here he comes right now.'

A tall, spectacularly grizzled man came towards them. A white dressing covered one of his eyes but not the scowl that darkened the rest of his face. 'Bloody hours I've been stuck here, and it's all your fault, you interfering little man!'

Not missing a step, Dr Singh was the epitome of politeness: 'Do you know Mr Liberty, Mr Merryman?'

'Er . . . no.' Archie held out his hand. 'Pleased to meet you, Mr Liberty,' he said affably. But when the other man made no attempt to shake it, he said, 'Well, then, I ought to be getting back. Bessie will be wondering where I am.' He turned to go.

Behind him, he heard, 'A bloody waste of time. Nothing that eye drops wouldn't have sorted. Just as I told you!'

'So aren't you the lucky one, Mr Liberty!'

After calling in at the shop and checking that Samson had everything under control, Archie took Bessie for a cream tea at the Mermaid café. A treat to round off the day for her.

'We should do this more often,' he said, when Shirley

had served them with her customary good humour. She was a good sort, was Shirley; nothing seemed to bring her down, not even the break-up of her marriage several years ago. He passed his mother a cup of tea then set to work on the scones. He cut one in half, spread a dollop of strawberry jam on it then topped it off with a layer of cream, but when he gave it to her, his heart fell. From her pained expression he could see that he had assumed too much. He had treated her as an incapable invalid and robbed her of her dignity. 'I'm sorry,' he murmured, appalled at his lack of thought. 'Would you rather do it yourself?'

She shook her head. 'I'm well,' she said softly. 'Not ill, Archie.'

'Of course you are,' he agreed. 'You're absolutely fine. Now, tell me what the speech therapist said to you. Did she give you any gossip about that cobbly cow with too much lipstick?'

She brought her eyebrows together as she always had when she rebuked him as a child. 'Serious,' she said, pointing a finger at him. 'No fish pies. Tell me the truth about Stella.'

'What about?'

'Why?'

He knew what she was asking, but he didn't want to go down that route. Not yet.

When he had read the letter Stella had left him, he had shoved it into his pocket and gone out to the kitchen to make a start on their supper. Minutes later Bessie had appeared in the doorway and gone along with his need to pretend that nothing out of the ordinary had happened. Helping her into bed that night he had made up a story that seemed to satisfy her.

But now, four days on, she wanted to know what was going on.

'Why?' she repeated.

'Stella's left me, love,' he said. 'She's not coming back. I lied when I said she'd gone to her sister in Nottingham for a few days.'

For once Archie was glad that his mother's speech was so limited. They sat in a long, awkward silence, their eyes cast down as they concentrated on their scones. Then he heard her say, 'Is it me? Left you because of *me*?'

He looked up and saw that his mother's eyes had filled with tears. One of her hands had started to tremble and crumbs were scattered around her plate. His heart went out to her. 'No, love. She didn't leave because of you. It was me. I should have been a better husband.'

He had to turn away. He knew exactly what she was thinking: that she had become a burden to him, and that she had wrecked his marriage. She was wrong.

Chapter Eight

When the phone rang Jonah was standing on the top rung of the stepladder. He knew straight away who it was. Caspar was the only person he knew who could make the telephone ring with menace, and could be relied upon to do it at the worst possible moment.

He put the brush between his teeth, picked up the pot of paint, and made his descent. By the time he had found the phone under the dust-sheet by the side of his bed, and had switched off the Haydn piano sonata, he could easily picture his brother's tight-lipped face at the other end of the line. Just for the sheer hell of it he let it ring three more times before he put the receiver to his ear.

'Liberty Escort Agency, how may I help you?'

'Yeah, very funny, Jonah. Now, if you could act like the adult you're supposed to be and quit fooling around like one of those idiots you teach, perhaps you'd tell me how you got on. What did the old man say?'

'Absolutely nothing.'

'I find that hard to believe.'

'Not a word.'

There was a pause.

'Oh, I know what happened, you didn't see him, did you? You lost your bottle just as I thought you would. You always were a coward.' Caspar's voice was hard.

'You could always talk to him yourself,' Jonah said mildly. 'It *is* your idea.'

'Look, we've been through this before. These days, you're the only one who can get anything sensible out of him. He'll listen to you.'

Exasperated, Jonah pushed a hand through his hair.

52

Too late he realised there had been a smear of Windsor Blue emulsion on his palm. He turned to look at himself in the mirror above the chest of drawers and saw that his wavy dark hair – the bane of his life as a boy – now had a blue streak running through it. Better than yellow, he thought, with a rueful smile.

'Jonah? Are you still there?'

'Sadly, yes. And I don't know why you think I'm any different from you and Damson.'

A loud snort told Jonah that if he didn't divert his brother, he would be subjected to the familiar lecture on what it was to be the hard-done-by Caspar Nobody-loves-me Liberty. 'Actually, I did go and see him this morning, but he wasn't there.'

'So what was wrong with trying again when you'd finished work?'

'This might come as a surprise to you, but when I'm not carrying out your dirty work, I do have a life of my own.'

'But you fetch and carry so well, brother dear. Who else can I rely on in this splintered family of ours?'

'It's not a family you need, Caspar,' Jonah said, 'it's a battalion of henchmen. Now, if there's nothing else, I'm in the middle of decorating, so I'd appreciate it if you would let me get on.'

'Good God, why do you insist on living like a peasant? Get a genuine peasant in to do it for you.'

'Caspar, was there anything else?'

'Yes. Speak to Dad as soon as you can. Every day you botch this up, is another day of . . . well, never mind that, just do it.'

Back on the stepladder, Jonah resumed painting his bedroom ceiling. If ever a child had been born to upset the sibling apple cart, it had been him: Caspar and Damson had never let him forget that his birth had precipitated their mother's death. As children they had been cunning and wilful, had taken pleasure in setting him up as the fall-guy and enjoying the spectacle of him being punished. If anything went missing, you could bet your bottom dollar it would be found in his bedroom, hidden at the bottom of the wardrobe. If anything got broken, you could guarantee that he would be positioned right by the smashed window-pane or the shattered vase.

Their devious schemes worked every time. They would pretend they had decided to let him be a part of their coterie and, like the fool he was, so desperate to be accepted, he would go along with whatever dare or initiation ceremony they felt inclined to put him through. He fell for it time and time again, hook, line and sinker. He was the perfect stooge, trailing behind in their contemptuous wake, needing their approval, wanting to be just like them: the mysterious, all-powerful twins who were at the centre of their own universe where, stupidly, he also wanted to be.

That was before he became scared of them.

Once, when they had said he could join in with their latest game, they had put a blindfold around his head and shoved him into cold water. He was only six and they said all he had to do was swim to the other side of the river. It had rained constantly for the last week and the river was higher than usual; as the force of the water rushed pell-mell down the hillside, the strengthening swell had swept him away. He could still remember their laughter as they ran along the bank beside him, and it wasn't until he banged his head on a rock and began to scream that they hauled him out. They shook him hard, pulled his hair and slapped his face to make sure he didn't pass out, then marched him back up to the house. 'We found him down by the river,' Caspar told Val, 'causing trouble again. It was lucky for him we happened to be passing, otherwise he might have died.'

Caspar was the most convincing liar Jonah had ever come across, then or since.

By the age of nine he had wised up and kept his distance from his brother and sister, shutting himself away in his room. But whenever they got the opportunity they played their games with him. They would sneak into his room late at night when he was asleep and steal whatever was precious to him – stamps, comics, books, pocket money. Gradually, though, he learned to outwit or second-guess them. He discovered that he was smarter than they were, and by the age of eleven he was spending more time in their father's library than anywhere else. He discovered that trying to gain Gabriel's approval and respect was infinitely more worthwhile than being accepted by Caspar and Damson.

Until then his father had been little more than an occasional visitor in his life, forever away on business, immersed in his own affairs, an autocratic figure. But when Jonah showed an interest in the books Gabriel had collected over the years, the two almost connected.

Jealousy caused the twins to step up their bullying campaign but they soon found themselves in more trouble than they could have imagined. Late one night Gabriel discovered them in his library, defacing two of his most highly prized first editions. Their plan had backfired. They were grounded for a month, their allowance was stopped, their combined birthday party cancelled, and they were put to work by Val to clean out the attic. It was then that Val began to question the previous crimes Jonah was supposed to have committed.

They never discussed any of these things as a family, that would have been far too open and communicative, much better to sweep it under the mat and pretend it never happened.

On one occasion, aged thirteen, Jonah had behaved completely out of character. It only happened once, but it was such a shocking act of violence that, even now, the memory made him flinch. He had been away at school, and the bully of his year had picked on him once too often: he had stolen a fountain pen Val had given Jonah for Christmas. Incensed, Jonah flung himself at the boy, pushed him to the floor and beat him mercilessly. With no teacher in the classroom, everyone else had left their desks and grouped around to watch the mild-mannered swot bashing the living daylights out of the boy who, in Jonah's mind, had become Caspar and Damson rolled into one. But while he was hailed by his peers as a hero, the headmaster was less inclined to praise him: Jonah was caned and made to write a five-page essay, answering the question 'Which offers man the greater chance of survival: pacifism or violence?' Ironically, his essay was so good that he was awarded a prize for it at the end of term.

If Jonah had a less than generous opinion of his brother and sister, the regard they held each other in could not have been higher. In Caspar's view Damson could do no wrong, but as far as Jonah could see she had spent most of her adult life switching from one good cause to another with intermittent bouts of selfabsorption. Of the three, she was the only one to have married. She was also the only one to have divorced twice, and lucratively so. She was currently going through what she called her 'centred space' phase and was living, in peace and harmony, in a commune in Northumberland, which she had described as a self-help therapy centre in a hand-crafted Christmas card to Jonah last year.

This latest search for her inner self was just another in a long line of explorations from which she would doubtless emerge to plunge back into the hedonistic lifestyle she enjoyed: men, partying, shopping, and whatever else made her think she was happy.

Jonah didn't think she had ever been truly happy.

On the stroke of midnight, Jonah called it a day. It was handy living next door to a church: there was no danger of losing track of the time when the bells rang out every hour and slipped in a quick chime on the half-hour too.

He had moved into Church Cottage last August when he had come back to the area as head of history at Deaconsbridge High. Before then he had been living over yonder border – as die-hard Deaconites called it – in neighbouring Cheshire. He had been ready for a change and had followed his instinct when he had seen the post advertised. It had seemed the right thing to do, given that his father was now on his own with little sign of Caspar or Damson offering any help around the house.

And it was the house that was at the bottom of Caspar's insistence that Jonah speak to Gabriel. Caspar could dress it up any way he liked, but Jonah knew his brother too well. Caspar didn't give a damn about their father's welfare: all he was concerned about was getting his hands on the capital that would be released if Mermaid House was sold. Jonah had no idea what Caspar did with the money he earned – he owned one of the most prestigious car dealerships in south Manchester and had to be ripping people off for a decent amount – but however much it was, it clearly wasn't enough. Jonah had dared to query this the other day when Caspar had hinted that money from the sale would come in handy. He had been told in no uncertain terms to keep his nose out of things he didn't understand. 'Money is hardly your area of expertise, Jonah, so butt out! Just convince the old fool that he needs to move into something smaller and we'll all be better off.'

Much of what Caspar had said was true. Jonah wasn't a financial pundit and their father had reached an age when he might be better off living in a property a tenth of the size of Mermaid House. He had been thinking the same thing ever since Val had died, but had never found the right time, or the courage, to broach it with Gabriel, not when he knew how insincere and grasping it might sound to their father. It was annoying, though, that Caspar's thoughts had coincided with his, albeit for different reasons.

What his brother didn't know was that Jonah intended – if his father would listen to him – to make it clear that if Mermaid House was to be sold, Gabriel should not siphon off a penny of what it brought to his children to avoid inheritance tax, which, naturally, was the main thrust of Caspar's argument for selling up now.

Caspar would capitalise on a third-world disaster if he

thought he could get away with it. And there were many things Caspar had got away with over the years. Just as he had stolen from Jonah as a child, he had continued through adulthood to help himself to anything else to which he took a fancy. So far Jonah had lost two girlfriends and a fiancée to his brother.

Admittedly the loss of the girlfriends had taken place during his teens, but Emily had been another matter altogether and he wasn't sure that he could ever forgive Caspar for what he had done.

Downstairs in the kitchen, while he washed the paintbrush under the tap and squirted a dose of Fairy Liquid on to the bristles, Jonah wondered if a family as bitterly divided as his could ever be reconciled.

Chapter Nine

With Ned's help, and with the aid of a simple device that turned the white plastic barrel into a mini garden roller, Clara was pushing their fresh supply of water across the dewy grass of the Happy Dell campsite towards Winnie. It was one of the many things about camper-vanning that Clara enjoyed: the multitude of unexpectedly clever gadgets that made life a little easier.

This was their fourth day on the road, and already Clara and Ned considered themselves old hands at it. They were perfectly at one with the intricacies of their cassette toilet, could turn a dinette seat into a double bed with the speed and professionalism of a Formula One pit stop, could knock up mouth-watering meals on the two-burner stove at the flick of a hand and, perhaps more importantly, they could do it all without once feeling as though they were living on top of each other. It was extraordinary how quickly they had adapted to living life in miniature. It reminded Clara of when she'd been a little girl and had played constantly with the doll's house her father had made for her. She had been fascinated with the scaled-down world he had created, and it was the same for her now with Winnie. Everything was so incredibly well designed, and appealed to her logical way of thinking and her need for order. As a child she had been ridiculously organised: her mud-pies were always neatly prepared, her bedroom was tidier than any other room in the house, her schoolwork immaculately presented – and always handed in on time – her social life thought out with every consideration given to when, how, where and with whom. And woe betide anyone who interfered with this carefully ordered infrastructure. At the age of ten, she had spent hours drawing cut-away sections of houses, each room in minute detail, and people joked that one day she would become an architect, or maybe an interior designer. When she expanded her repertoire to sketch the roads the houses occupied, then mapped out whole villages and communities of harmonious synchrony, they suggested town planning. Her brother accused her of being a control freak.

But if Winnie appealed to Clara's desire for pigeon-holed regularity, it was a joy to see how Ned, too, loved their new home, especially his bed over the cab. He would lie up there with Mermy and his battalion of cuddly toys, pretending to read to them from his favourite storybooks, and Clara was relieved that, so far, he had shown no sign of missing anything he had left behind. But, as Louise would have been quick to point out, it was early days yet.

Much as Ned loved the bed to which he had to climb up, there was a disadvantage in the arrangement, which had come to light on their first night. At three in the morning he had woken needing the toilet. It was the kerfuffle of him sitting up, bumping his head and letting out a cry that had woken Clara. It took her a few seconds to gather her wits, switch on the reading light and climb up to him. Parting the curtains, she had helped him down and carried him to the loo. He was so drowsy that she had had him tucked in again and fast asleep before she was back in her own bed.

But he had always been a good sleeper, even as a baby. At two days old he had slipped straight into a comfort-able, convenient routine of feeds and napping that had rendered her parents nostalgically envious. 'Why weren't you and Michael like this as babies?' her mother had said, bending over the Moses basket and itching to smother her first grandchild with love as he slept on, his tiny hands balled into fists the size of walnuts, his lips quivering like butterfly wings. 'You both had me up at all hours, never gave me a minute's peace. Ooh, look, he's opened his eyes. Do you think I could . . . ?'

Clara and her father had exchanged a smile. 'Go on, Mum, while I make us a cup of tea; he's all yours.'

'And you can stop right there, young lady,' her father had said. '*I* will make the tea. And if I catch you moving just one inch from that chair, there'll be trouble.'

'Better do as he says, Clara, you know what a tyrant he can be.'

For years it had been a family joke that her father was a tyrant: the truth was, he was the biggest softie going. And he had been particularly kind and loving with his grandson. Once Ned was walking and talking, her father had come into his own, reading to him, teaching him to do simple jigsaws and taking him to the park. 'Come on, my little pumpernickel,' he would say, helping Ned into his hat and coat, then strapping him into the pushchair. 'Time for some man-to-man business down at the park. Let's go and feed the ducks.'

Clara knew that Ned's lack of a father tapped into her parents' old-fashioned instinct for a nuclear family, but she was happy to let her own father fill the void created by the man who could never be in Ned's life. He did it so well, never overstepping the mark, just quietly providing that indefinable extra for which Clara would always be grateful.

In the last few days she had noticed a change in Ned: he was fast becoming what her mother would describe as 'quite the little man'. He was forever insisting that he help her with everything he could. He particularly liked doing the washing-up. He would stand at the small sink on the step that was supposed to be used for getting in and out of the camper-van, up to his elbows in sudsy water. The job took a lot longer than if she did it herself, but it was such a pleasure to see him so involved that she didn't have the heart, or inclination, to stop him. And what did it matter how long anything took to do? They were in no hurry now.

Since leaving home on Sunday they had slowly made their way north. Their first night had been spent at a campsite in Stratford-upon-Avon, where the following day they had immersed themselves in all things Shakespearean and, more to Ned's liking, had visited a museum devoted to teddy bears. They had seen the original Sooty, and Clara had reminisced about her first pantomime, when she had sat in the front row and been soaked by Sooty and Sweep with water pistols.

From Stratford they had moved on to the West Midlands, taking in Cadbury World and the Museum of Science and Industry in Birmingham. Ned had been as pleased as punch when their guide picked him out from the crowd to press the button to start the steam engine. He was happier still when they left an hour later with a model of it, and he had spent the evening back at Winnie explaining enthusiastically to Clara how it worked.

Until now, they had decided together where to go each day while curled up in bed and flicking through touring books and maps. But their next port of call was to be a surprise for Ned, which Clara hoped he would enjoy.

When they had packed everything neatly away, and had paid the man in the campsite office, they were ready to go.

'Chocks ahoy,' said Ned, as he did each morning when they set off.

She smiled. She had given up telling him it was 'chocks away'. 'Chocks ahoy' sounded just fine to her. The people on the next pitch waved goodbye. They were an interesting couple in their mid-fifties who called themselves 'full-timers'. They lived all year round in their camper-van, which they had personalised by painting Ron's name on the driver's door and Eileen's on the passenger's. Over a glass of wine late last night, when Ned was asleep, they had given Clara their list of the top ten campsites in Britain. They were out of the way, not always listed in the touring guides: it was to one of these that Clara was heading today. Ron and Eileen had also shared with her how they had become 'full-timers': after giving up secure jobs, they had spent the last two years fruit picking in the summer and early autumn, then hooking up with fellow full-timers and travelling south to Spain and Tunisia for the winter.

Now, as she tooted Winnie's horn at them, Clara wondered what Louise and the rest of her friends would make of Ron and Eileen.

With the map spread open on his lap, his elbows resting on the armrests at either side of him, and his finger planted firmly on the streak of blue that was the motorway they were following, Ned looked every inch the seasoned navigator. That the map was upside down was neither here nor there. By Clara's reckoning they had about thirty miles of motorway driving left before they would strike out cross-country.

'Shall we stop at the next service station to stretch our legs?' she asked. Ron and Eileen had said that if there were free facilities to be had it was their duty to take full advantage of them rather than waste their own resources.

Ned looked up from the map. 'When Nanna says that, Granda says his legs don't need stretching. He says he's tall enough already.'

Clara smiled. 'It's called a euphemism.'

He tried the word out for himself. '*Eu-fer-miz-um*. What does that mean?'

'Well, it's when we use a word or phrase to disguise what we're really saying, to make it sound more polite. I was really asking you if you wanted to stop and go to the toilet.'

He thought about this. 'Like when Nanna asks me if I want to spend a penny?'

'Exactly.'

'*Eu-fer-miz-um*,' he said again.

Ned's vocabulary was quite advanced for his age, and Clara put this down to his having spent more time with adults than children. Neither her parents nor her friends had ever talked down to him: they had always treated him as a mini-adult and he had responded accordingly, absorbing information at a phenomenal rate. With so much adult company around him, she had dreaded him turning into a precocious brat, but thankfully there seemed little likelihood of that.

After they had euphemistically stretched their legs and spent their pennies, they joined the motorway once more, and, with the map the right way round, Ned looked at it hard and asked where they were going.

She gave him a sideways smile. 'You're not catching me out that easily. I told you, it's a surprise. Wait and see.'

'But will I like it? Surprises aren't always nice.'

'I'll make you a promise. If you don't like it we'll move on somewhere else.'

An hour later, and with the M6 behind them, Clara took the B5470 out of Macclesfield and found herself driving through rolling hills of lush green farmland criss-crossed with a threadwork of drystone walls. It came as such a surprise that she slowed down to take a better look. It was beautiful, just as Ron and Eileen had said it would be. 'If we could get the work up there, that's where we'd spend our summers,' Ron had said. 'Believe me, you'll love it. It's terrific walking country.'

But it wasn't hill walking that had drawn Clara to this part of the Peak District, it was what, according to the guide books, had also drawn Victorian day-trippers from the neighbouring industrial towns and villages: the chance to see a mermaid. Not a live one, but an underground cavern that claimed to have a rock formation that looked just like the real thing and granted wishes for those prepared to dip their fingers into the clear still water of its pool. Given Ned's love of Mermy – who was currently in his hand – and his desire to meet a real one, this was probably as near as she could get to fulfilling a dream for him.

They drove on, the road becoming steeper, the houses fewer and the scenery even more stunning as it stretched before them beneath a picture-postcard blue sky with puffy white clouds. Suddenly, making her jump, Ned pointed Mermy at the window to his left and cried, 'Mummy, look at all the sheep on the green mountains.'

'Those are what people round here call hills, Ned.'

'Even that big one over there?'

Clara smiled. 'A mere Brussels sprout. Perhaps later on our trip we'll go up to Scotland and see some real mountains.'

'I like it here. Is this my surprise?'

'Not quite. Now, I'm going to have to concentrate on the road. I'm looking for a sign that says Deaconsbridge. Shout if you see anything with a big D on it.'

The road climbed higher and higher, until eventually they reached the summit of a hill. Dropping into a lower gear, Clara took the descent steadily, with extra care on the tight bends.

Their first sighting of Deaconsbridge revealed a small town nestling in the shallow dip of a valley. From a distance it looked a soft shade of industrial grey with rows of terraced houses tucked into the slope of the hillsides, their uniformity broken by a scattering of old mills and stately chimneys. A church with an elegant spire stood self-consciously to one side of the town, surrounded by a cemetery, whose gravestones seemed to flow out into the expanse of moorland behind. As final resting places went, Clara thought it was pretty spectacular.

With a queue of cars itching to overtake them, they trundled ever nearer, and just as the road began to level, narrow and guide them to the centre of the town and its one-way system, Ned bounced in his seat and let out a loud, excited cry. 'Look, a mermaid! And there's another. Over there! Mummy, there's lots of them!'

Once Clara had squeezed Winnie into the pay-and-display car park – no mean feat, given how busy the small town was and the lack of space available – she could see that Ned was right: Deaconsbridge was awash with mermaids. Almost every shop front in the market square where they were parked had a sign depicting a mermaid, and each one was different. They ranged from shy lovelies coyly submerged in water, showing just a modest hint of scaly tail, to pert blonde bathing belles posing on rocks, and buxom Page Three beauties flaunting themselves shamelessly. But the sign Clara liked best was the one above the antiquarian bookshop, which portrayed a sylph-like creature reclining in an armchair reading – the spectacles were a nice touch, she thought.

Across the square, and opposite where they were parked, a sign showed a rosy-cheeked mermaid wearing an apron and holding a large wooden spoon. It was a convivial and inviting sight. 'Welcome to Deaconsbridge, Ned,' Clara said. 'Ready for some lunch?'

Chapter Ten

The Mermaid café was busy and at first glance Clara thought they would have to try somewhere else. But in the furthest corner, and beneath a large mirror flanked by two prettily stencilled mermaids on the wall, she could see a waitress clearing a table that had just been vacated by a couple of intimidating-looking leather-clad bikers now queuing at the counter to pay their bill. One smiled at Ned, who stared at his pony-tail, earrings and the shiny studs on his fringed jacket, then smiled back, revealing two rows of perfect milk teeth.

The waitress continued to add dirty plates to a tray already stacked high with an assortment of crockery and metal teapots, and for a few moments Clara and Ned were forced to stand with the two bikers. The one who had smiled at Ned did so again, this time adding a wink. Then he turned to Clara. 'He's a cute-looking kid,' he said. 'A dead ringer for his mum, or his older sister, perhaps? If you want a worthwhile tip,' he went on, 'we can recommend the chef's special. You can't go wrong with it.'

'Insider knowledge,' said his friend, tapping his long straight nose. He reached into a small basket of lollipops for younger diners and gave one to Ned. 'Here, have this on us.'

Ned's face lit up. 'Thank you,' he said.

'You'd better keep it for when you've had your lunch, though. We don't want any trouble from your big sister.'

Clara was about to add her thanks to Ned's when the waitress came over. 'Sorry to keep you waiting, dear,' she said, 'but these leather joy-boys make so much mess.' She gave the two bikers a broad grin.

The one who had spoken first to Clara gave the waitress's red cap a light flick. 'Mum, I've told you before, keep the wisecracks for when we're at home. Do you want me to take that tray through to the back for you?'

'No, Robbie, I want you to pay your bill and sling your hook. You're cluttering the place up. Now, are you or are you not going to make a start on the spare room for me this evening? I've got the wallpaper and paste for you.'

'Wouldn't miss it for the world.'

Thanking the two young men for the lollipop, Clara shepherded Ned towards their table, and quickly, before anyone else nipped in ahead of them to claim it.

'Those men were nice,' said Ned, settling himself into his chair and placing his unexpected gift on the checked plastic tablecloth. He propped Mermy against a bowl of sugar.

'They were, weren't they?' she replied, letting him get away, just this once, with pilfering a sugar cube. She could see that he was now wondering how to slip it into his mouth without her noticing so she bent down to her bag on the floor. She thought about the two young men, one of whom had treated her to some friendly flattery. He must have been at least ten years her junior. Big sister indeed!

Catching sight of herself in the mirror above Ned's head, she supposed the new haircut made her look younger. She had gone for a radical change in Stratford, deciding that her shoulder-length hair would be a pain to take care of while they were away. In the salon, everyone had agreed that the new style took years off her, that her dark hair now framed her small oval face perfectly and accentuated her brown eyes.

She turned away from the mirror and, with the two bikers – who admittedly had not been her type – still on her mind, asked herself when had been the last time a man had paid her an unexpected compliment?

She couldn't remember and wondered when she had become so unaware of or immune to male charm.

Since Ned had been born, she had had little time, inclination, or opportunity to seek out a boyfriend, although there had been one or two skirmishes, in particular a disagreeable incident on an industrial-relations course eighteen months ago. Then a pushy type with groping hands and gin-soaked breath had tried his luck with her in the bar one night. She had blown him clean away: 'What makes you think an intelligent woman like me would be interested in a prat like you? Now, push off before I throw my drink in your face.'

It wasn't that she didn't feel comfortable with men, far from it, she usually preferred their company to that of a crowd of women, but she knew that to embark upon a series of going-nowhere relationships would do her no good. Also, she didn't want to confuse Ned by bringing home a succession of men. And, perhaps more import-antly, she had a very real fear of accidentally getting pregnant again.

Not that she had ever regretted having Ned. She loved him just as much as if she had planned his conception down to the last detail.

Through the café window she watched the pair of swaggering lads in their leathers cross the road to the car park where two powerful-looking motorbikes were wait-ing for them, their well-polished chromework glinting in the afternoon sun. She watched them strap on their helmets, then heard the throaty roar of the engines, and though she had never before had any desire to sit astride anything more dangerous than a tricycle, she thought she could detect a change in her view now. Goodness, less than a week on the road and she was considering a wind-in-the-hair experience!

She plucked the menu from its wooden holder, and saw that the chef's special they had recommended was not a body-building tough-boy three-pounder burger but a vegetarian lasagne.

'What are you smiling at, Mummy?'

She raised her eyes from the menu. 'Myself, Ned. Now, what would you like to eat?'

They feasted on sausages, beans and chips, followed by the best Bakewell tart Clara had ever tasted. When she commented on this to their waitress – biker-Robbie's mother – she was told, 'I'll tell my sister that, she'll be well pleased. It's an old family recipe.'

'Is this a family business, then?'

'No. It's just a coincidence that we work together. Are you here for the day, or staying longer? The weather's supposed to be breaking by the weekend, so you'd best do your walking sooner rather than later.'

'Is that what everyone does round here – walk?'

'That, and go down the cavern to see the mermaid. To be honest, there's not a lot else to do.'

Ned leaned forward in his seat. 'A mermaid? Is it real?'

The waitress's eyes flickered over Mermy on the table. She sucked in her breath. 'Well, now, it's as real as you want it to be, I suppose. But if you've come to see it, you're too early. It doesn't open for another week. The tourist season round here hasn't got into full swing yet. You could always go across to Castleton or down to Buxton. Between them they've got more caverns than they know what do to with.'

'Do they have mermaids?'

'No, my fine little fella, it's only us that can boast something as special as that.'

They left the café unsure what to do next. If the Mermaid Cavern wasn't open for another week, should they move on somewhere else and come back, or stay put and use Deaconsbridge as a base for visiting the surrounding area?

Keeping her options open, Clara decided they would inspect the campsite Ron and Eileen had raved about and take it from there. She put this to Ned as she unlocked Winnie and stood back to let out the fuggy warmth that had built up inside the van while they had been having lunch. But now that Ned had heard about the Mermaid Cavern, he clearly didn't want to move on. 'If we don't like the campsite,' he said anxiously, climbing into his seat, 'we could find another, couldn't we?'

'If that's what you'd like to do, then yes.'

She started the engine, reached for the map, then regretted not having thought to ask their friendly waitress for directions to the Hollow Edge View campsite. It wasn't mentioned in the *Touring Parks* magazine she had used so far on the trip, but Eileen had said it was somewhere off the Hollow Edge Moor road. The road, or what Clara thought was the right road, was marked on the map and, with hope rather than solid conviction, she manoeuvred Winnie out of the market-square car park and went in search of a pitch for the night.

Nearly an hour had passed before she gave up. 'This is ridiculous,' she said, exasperated, when they found themselves, yet again, on irritatingly familiar ground. 'We've been up and down this road so many times we're on first-name terms with all the sheep. I'm sure they're laughing at us behind our backs.'

'Sheep don't laugh,' Ned said seriously. 'They go *baa*.'

'And I'll go *baa*-ing mad if I don't find this wretched campsite. I could also do with going to the loo. I'll just drive down this handy little track and park up.'

Ignoring the 'Private – No Entry' sign turned out to have been a mistake. The handy little track was longer and narrower than Clara had expected, and with drystone walls almost touching Winnie's sides there was no space to turn round. She had no choice but to keep going until it either branched off into another road, or offered her the opportunity to do a ten-point turn – reversing was not a viable proposition: it was the only trick of driving a camper-van that she hadn't yet mastered.

However, as mistakes went, it presented them with some of the best views they had seen so far and confirmed what Clara had read in the guide book last night, that Deaconsbridge, sandwiched as it was between the Dark

Peak of Derbyshire and its southern White Peak counterpart, was home to an interesting combination of the two. Way off in the distance, and after checking the map, she could see the bleak windswept moor of Kinder Scout to the north. Referring to the map again, she could see that if she carried on along this road they would eventually come to a belt of trees and a dwelling called Mermaid House. It looked as though the road widened sufficiently by the trees to allow her to turn and drive back to join the main road once more.

Her guesswork proved right, and in the shelter of the trees, she brought Winnie to a halt. 'Time to stretch my legs,' she said, smiling at Ned as she climbed out of her seat to go through to the toilet.

When she came out, Ned said, 'Can we go for a paddle? I can see a bridge over a stream and there might be some fish we could catch for our tea.'

'They'll have to be very lazy fish, the type we can catch with our bare hands.'

He slipped out from his seat. 'It's easy. I saw it on the television. This man had a stick and he watched until the fish came right up to him and then he—'

'Yes, I get your drift,' she interrupted, not wanting the gory details. 'Couldn't we just shake hands with them and invite them in for a fish supper?'

He rolled his eyes. 'Fish don't have hands, Mummy.'

'You sure about that? What about octopuses? I thought they had eight hands.'

'Now you're being silly. Everyone knows they're called testicles.'

She laughed. 'Tentacles, Ned. Come on, my little genius, let's see if there's a nice bit of smoked salmon just waiting to make our acquaintance. But it will have to be quick. I really do want to find that campsite before the light goes.'

Taking a rolled-up towel with them they approached the bridge and the length of river Ned had spied. It twisted along the lower edge of the screen of trees, tumbled down the slope under the bridge and, gaining speed, gushed on further down the hillside.

'It'll be cold in there,' Clara said, looking doubtfully at the clear shallow water as it rushed over the stones. 'Wouldn't you rather play Pooh sticks?'

Beside her Ned was already sitting on the grassy bank and tugging at his laces. 'We could play that after. Help me, please, Mummy. This one's in a knot.'

She untied the lace for him and rebuked herself for sounding so old and boring. Where was the spirit of adventure that had brought her here in the first place?

Despite the warmth of the spring sunshine, the water was icy cold, just as Clara had predicted; it made them both gasp and squeal as they dipped in their toes. They rolled up their jeans, and bravely went in deeper. Clara held Ned's hand as they waded out, and now that she couldn't feel her toes, she joined in the game of looking for their supper. 'Do you think there are sharks here, Ned?'

'Ssh!' he whispered. 'I can see something.' He let go of her, bent down to the water, cupped his hands, and made a sudden scooping movement. 'I've caught something!' he cried. He peered through the gaps between his fingers.

Amazed, she lowered her head to see what he had.

He shrieked with delight and splashed her face. 'Fooled you!'

'Why, you little monkey! For that, you can have a taste of your own medicine.'

The water fight was noisy and spectacular, and left them both drenched. Shivering, but still laughing, they slipped on their shoes and went back to Winnie to change into some dry clothes. They were soon warm again, and just as Clara was about to make them a drink – tea for her and blackcurrant juice for Ned – they heard an engine. Ned, who was sitting in the driver's seat, stuck his head out of the window.

'It's a car,' he said. 'A green one. It's got two men in it and it's stopped behind us. They're getting out.'

Clara decided it was time to investigate. After all, she had ignored that 'Private – No Entry' sign. Maybe the owner had come to move them along. She stepped outside and didn't like what she saw. Two lads of about the same age as the bikers came towards her. One had a baseball bat and was smacking it against one of his palms. They both looked her over. She swallowed, every instinct in her screaming that these two meant trouble. She moved back a pace to shield Ned who was still leaning out of the window. 'Get down,' she whispered, turning her head to the side, 'and don't say a word.' They came in close and, one on either side of her, they pushed her hard against the driver's door: they smelt of sour beer and stale cigarette smoke.

'Please,' she said, conscious of Ned behind her and their gaze flickering from her to him, 'just take what you want and leave us alone.' Outwardly she was doing her best to appear calm, but inwardly she was frantic.

They both laughed, and a coarse, fleshy hand stroked her throat. For a split second she considered bringing her knee up into the youth's groin, but as the hand began to exert more pressure on her windpipe, squeezing it painfully, she heard another man's voice say, 'Take your hands off that woman and get the hell out of here.'

The grip loosened. Twisting her head, Clara saw an elderly man dressed in a flat cap and a waxed jacket coming towards them. A patch covered one of his eyes and raised to the other was a double-barrelled shotgun. Her legs began to wobble and she hoped to God that the old man knew what he was doing with it.

The gun still held high, he drew nearer. 'And do it before I lose my patience and blast both your heads off!' The voice that had started with a low warning rumble, had now pitched itself forward into a snarl of intent. 'Go on, get out of here!'

Chapter Eleven

The hand dropped from Clara's throat. 'Take it easy, Granddad, don't go giving yourself a heart-attack.'

'Less of the lip, you scum. You're on my land and I want you off it. Pronto! Do you understand that, or do I have to spell it out into simple words that louts like you can understand?'

The two lads started backing away. 'Bloody cocky with your words, aren't you, you stupid old git?'

Tightening his finger on the trigger and lowering the shotgun until it was aimed directly at the youth's crotch, the man growled, 'So tell me, just how cocky do *you* feel? Get out of here.'

They fled to their car and, with the gun still trained on them, they turned it round and shot off down the track, leaving a dusty cloud hanging in the air.

Clara realised she had been holding her breath and let it out now, in a long sigh of relief. Her legs were still shaking and the sky spun. She leaned against the van, steeled herself, then opened the door and reached in for Ned. His face was as white as she felt hers must be. He trembled in her arms and she hugged him to her.

She turned to face the formidable man who had come to their rescue. 'I'm so grateful to you,' she said. 'If you hadn't turned up . . .' She swallowed, then tried again. 'Well, I'm not sure how I would have got out of that. Thank you very much.'

To her surprise, the man made no attempt to offer any further reassurance. He simply stared at her, bristling with disapproval. Then with a loud crack, he broke the gun and shoved the butt under his arm. 'You can save the fawning pleasantries,' he growled. 'I'm not interested. Maybe in future you'll think twice about trespassing on private property, especially somewhere as remote as this. Damn stupid of you to put yourself and the child in danger. Women! Bloody fools, the lot of you!' He turned his back and started to walk away.

Clara was outraged. 'Why, you miserable old bugger!' she burst out angrily. 'Come back here and apologise this instant.'

He slowed his step and twisted his head round. 'What did you call me?'

'You heard. And if I wasn't holding a terrified child I'd call you a lot worse.'

'If that child is terrified, then you have only yourself to blame.'

'Oh, because I'm a woman on my own I'm not allowed to take my son paddling. Is that what you're saying?'

'Paddling?' he echoed. 'Paddling in *my* water? I ought to bloody charge you for that.'

'Do that, you old skinflint, and I'll report you to the police for behaving in a threatening manner with a dangerous firearm. It's crazy old fools like you with guns who get innocent people killed!' Her voice was filled with rage.

'I'll wager that wasn't what you were thinking a few moments ago. I bet you'd never been so pleased to see a crazy old fool with a gun.'

'If I'd known it would be you, I'd sooner have taken my chances single-handed.'

'The hell you would have!' he guffawed.

They stared at each other. In the silence that followed, Ned lifted his head from Clara's shoulder. 'I need a wee,' he murmured, and started to sob. Then Clara felt a wet warmth run down her front.

The grumpy old man lowered his one eye to the puddle forming on the ground at her feet. 'Poor little beggar,' he said gruffly. 'Get him changed and I'll make you some tea.'

Near to tears herself, but determined to hang on to her self-respect, she said, 'I can manage, thank you. I wouldn't want to take up any more of your valuable—'

He silenced her with a fierce one-eyed stare. 'Don't look a gift horse in the mouth, young lady, until you're sure you can really do without it.'

Winnie seemed terribly cramped with the three of them inside it: their guest, as he fumbled around making a pot of tea, was too tall and bulky for such a confined space. By the time Clara had calmed Ned and changed their clothes, and they were sitting at the little table with their tea, she thought she should introduce herself. An apology seemed appropriate too.

'My name's Clara Costello, and I'm sorry for some of the things I said out there. This is my son, Ned.'

He took off his cap and laid it on the table. 'Well, Miss Costello, the name's Liberty, Mr Liberty, and I never apologise for anything I say.'

In spite of herself, she smiled. 'You know, that doesn't surprise me. Do you often go for an afternoon stroll with a gun?'

'When I feel like shooting something, yes.'

'Well, much as I disagree with the ownership of guns, I'm glad you felt the need to shoot something today.'

'Don't be so bloody patronising. Drink your tea and be quiet. That goes for you too, young man.'

'But it's got sugar in,' Ned said, taking a sip from his mug and screwing up his face that had now resumed its usual healthy glow.

The man gave a snort of derision. 'Hell's bells and buckets of blood! Don't tell me your mother's one of those new-fandangled creatures who doesn't believe in sugar.'

'I'm allowed sugar on cornflakes,' Ned said proudly. 'And grapefruit,' he added.

'Very generous of her, I'm sure.'

'What's wrong with your eye?'

'And what's wrong with your manners, Mr Nosy Parker?'

Unabashed, Ned carried on, 'You look like a pirate.'

This seemed to amuse their guest. 'A black-bearded, buccaneering, lash-him-to-the-mainmast-m'hearty type of pirate, I hope, not some white-frilled, swashbuckling nancy-boy.'

The distinction was lost on Ned. 'If you chopped a hand off, you could be Captain Hook.'

The man looked down at the badly swollen fingers that were wrapped around his mug of tea. 'I'll bear that in mind.'

'Come on, Ned,' Clara said gently, 'drink your tea and leave our guest alone.'

'Do I have to? It's horrible. It's too sweet. Can't I have some blackcurrant juice? Please.'

Sliding out from the seat she was sharing with Ned, Clara went over to the fridge, poured a cup of blackcurrant juice, and reached into a locker for a packet of biscuits. She had no desire to prolong their rescuer's stay with them, but she felt she owed him a Jaffa Cake at the very least.

He was a funny old stick, shabbily dressed in a motheaten green pullover with frayed cuffs and the elbows worn through. The points of his shirt collar were also worn and his brown corduroy trousers were scruffy and dirty. His shoes were unpolished and the stitching had been redone recently, but in the wrong colour. She sat opposite him and offered the packet of biscuits. His distorted fingers poked clumsily at the plastic wrapping as he helped himself and she wondered just how good a shot he would have been if he had fired that wretched gun. Thinking of it now, she gave it a censorious glance. It was resting against the wardrobe at the far end of the van, along with its owner's smelly old waxed jacket.

'Stop worrying,' he said, seeing her face. 'It's safe enough. I've taken the cartridges out. They're in my coat pocket.'

She made no comment, but thinking that she could take advantage of his local knowledge, she said, 'We're trying to find a campsite for the night. Perhaps you know where it is.' She got to her feet to fetch the map.

'I doubt that very much,' he said, when she returned. 'Camping's hardly my scene.'

'Heavens, are you always this helpful?'

He swallowed the last of his tea. 'You've got me on a good day.'

'Lucky old us.' She put the map down on the table between them and pointed to where Ron and Eileen had said the campsite was. 'It's called Hollow Edge View. I was told it was—'

'It's gone,' he interrupted. 'The owners beggared off down south last winter. Bankrupted themselves. Not an ounce of business sense. Softies from London who thought it would be an easy option playing Old Macdonald Had a Farm. I knew they'd never make a go of it. I told them so too.'

'Wow, and to think they didn't stick around to enjoy more of your warm neighbourliness. What were they thinking of?'

He looked up sharply, nostrils flaring. 'Nothing wrong in speaking one's mind.'

'Depends on the state of the mind. Can you recommend anywhere else for us to stay?'

'No.'

'Well, then, and since we've clearly exhausted you of your charm, you can leave us to sort ourselves out. I wish I could say it was a pleasure meeting you. Close the door after you, won't you, *Mr* Liberty?'

Gabriel was smiling to himself as he trudged home across the fields in the late-afternoon sunshine. He hadn't enjoyed himself so much in a long while. It wasn't often he came up against somebody brave enough to cross words with him, but that spiky, sharp-tongued young woman had made more of a go of it than anyone else ever had. Dr Singh had tried it on, although he was too conscious of his professional status to take a real verbal swing. But that Costello girl hadn't cared a jot for what his response would be. And fair play to her. Though he still maintained that she was a damned fool to go wandering about the countryside on her own with a young child. Asking for trouble in this day and age. One never knew who or what was around the corner.

Back at Mermaid House he let himself in and went through to the gun room. It was only then, as he stood in front of the locked glass-fronted cabinet, that he realised he didn't have the gun with him.

Damn and blast! He had left it behind with that girl and her son. A shiver of unease crept over him as he recalled the cartridges he had put into his coat pocket, which he had also stupidly left behind. He hoped to God that just as that little boy had been indoctrinated with the evils of sugar, he had been instilled with the belief that guns were a no-go area for children.

He was about to retrace his steps across the fields, to see if the camper-van was still there, when the telephone rang.

To his surprise he heard Jonah's voice at the other end of the line. Now what was this about? When was the last time any of his children had phoned him?

It was Ned who spotted it. 'Look, Mummy, Mr Liberty's forgotten his coat and gun.' He reached out to the twin barrels and Clara shouted, 'Don't touch!'

Ned jumped. 'I was only looking,' he said, hurt.

'I'm sorry,' she said, 'but those things can kill, and it's better that you never get within touching distance of something as dangerous.'

'What shall we do with it?' he asked, anxiously.

'We could either wait and see if Mr Liberty comes back for it, or we could go and find him.' She turned and looked at the map that was still laid out on the table. 'My guess is,' she mused, 'and since he claimed to own this land, that our friend Mr Grumpy-Pants Liberty lives here.'

Ned climbed on to the seat to see what she was pointing at. 'Where? Show me.'

She indicated with her finger.

'If we go back the way we came, join the main road, then turn right, just here, it's likely we'll find ourselves once again in the company of the rudest man on earth. What do you think? Is it worth the trouble?'

He stood up on the bench seat so that he was eye to eye with her. 'I thought he was funny.'

'I didn't. He was rude to us.'

Ned looked thoughtful. 'He stopped those horrible men from hurting you. And he made us tea because I was frightened.' He lowered his gaze beneath his long lashes. 'I'm . . . I'm sorry I wet myself.'

At the poignant reminder of what the old devil had done for them, Clara put her arms around her precious son. 'I nearly wet myself too,' she admitted. 'It was scary. And you're right,' she added decisively, 'it's time I learned to be more tolerant of other people's shortcomings.'

After Clara had put the gun inside a wardrobe, they washed up their cups, stored them away and set a course for Mermaid House.

As to be expected, there was no helpful sign at the end of the track that Clara was convinced would lead them to where Mr Liberty lived. She turned off the main road, juddered over a cattle grid, and pressed on. She soon realised that she had to slow to a steady crawl. They rattled along for almost half a mile before they set eyes on the most extraordinary sight. Clara whistled. 'Now that's what I call a house.'

Ned was impressed too. 'It's a castle, Mummy!'

There weren't any battlements, but there was a tower built into one of the corners of the house and it didn't take much imagination to picture a cursing Mr Liberty standing at the window, shotgun in hand, ready to defend his home from the onslaught of double-glazing salesmen.

They came to an archway that led to a central courtyard. Clara parked alongside a battered old Land Rover, pulled on the handbrake and turned off the engine. Close up, the house was gloomier than it had appeared from a distance. The sun was low in the sky now, and the cobbled courtyard was in shadow. The stonework was almost black in places and looked to be in need of a good restorative clean. One wall was almost covered in ivy, which helped to soften the grim effect of so much discoloured stone, but otherwise the house was as saturnine and forbidding as its owner.

But how different it must have been when it was originally built, Clara thought, as she hooked Mr Liberty's coat over her shoulder and picked up the gun. She and Ned walked towards what she hoped was a regularly used door – a deduction based on the pile of rubbish bags grouped around a collection of dustbins. A nose-wrinkling pong of rotting detritus floated out to them. 'Home, not-so-Sweet Home,' she muttered, under her breath, as she stood on the doorstep looking for a bell. Not finding one, she rapped loudly with her knuckles.

'No doubt he's preparing the hot oil and flaming arrows,' she said to Ned.

'Shall I call him?' he said, pushing open the letterbox.

'That's probably not a good idea,' Clara said.

But it was too late. Ned was already peering through the gap. 'Ooh,' he exclaimed, 'it's really untidy. There's things everywhere. Oh, I can see Mr Liberty. Hello, Mr Liberty, it's us, you forgot your gun and we've brought it for you.'

'No need to make such a song and dance about it, young man.'

Bending down, Clara could see that Ned was nose to nose with the formidable one-eyed owner of the house.

'We've brought your coat too,' Ned carried on, as though it was the most reasonable thing in the world to be holding a conversation through a letterbox. 'Your house is nice. It's just like a castle. Can I come in and see it, please? I'll be very good. I'll take my shoes off like I have to at Nanna and Granda's so I won't spoil your carpets. And I promise I won't run about and knock things over.'

It was time to intervene. 'It's okay, Mr Liberty,' Clara said. 'We're not here to bother you. I'll put your gun and coat here on the step and leave you in peace. Thanks for your help earlier this afternoon. Ned and I really appreciated what you did.' Taking her son's hand, she lowered her voice. 'Come on, Ned, we mustn't make a nuisance of ourselves. Besides, it's getting late and we have to find a campsite.' She turned to go.

The door opened suddenly. 'You're too early.'

'Too early for what?' asked Clara.

'There's only one campsite in this area and it doesn't open for another two weeks.'

She sighed. 'Oh, that's brilliant. Just what I needed to hear. Why didn't you tell me that before?'

'Oh, so it's my fault you didn't do sufficient background research before you came here, is it? How typical of a woman to blame her inadequacies on the nearest man to hand.'

She sighed again. But now it was edged with a spark of annoyance. 'Mr Liberty, do you realise just how rude you are? Because if not, let me tell you here and now that I have seldom come across a more cantankerous and mean-spirited man.'

He smiled. Well, she thought it was a smile. It was more a case of his lips stretching into what she assumed was an unaccustomed position, resulting in the baring of two rows of large, uneven teeth.

'And I have seldom come across a woman with as much ungracious impudence as you, Miss Costello,' he snarled, 'so I know that if I were to suggest you use one of my fields for the night, it would be a pointless gesture. You would only throw it back in my face.'

Astonished, Clara hesitated. It was getting late, the light had almost gone and she was tired. Embarking on a lengthy search for somewhere to hitch up for the night didn't appeal. Also, the incident that afternoon had left her more rattled than she cared to admit. Just thinking about it again caused her heart to beat faster. It seemed eminently sensible to be within shouting distance of help. Even if it came in the person of this misogynist old-timer with a serious attitude problem.

'Perhaps we could come to some other arrangement,' she said, choosing her words with care. 'Rather than spoil one of your fields by driving across it, how about we stay right where we are in the courtyard?'

He considered this. 'Just the one night?' he reiterated.

'Just the one night,' she confirmed. 'In fact, we'll be gone first thing in the morning. It will be as though we'd never been here.'

He switched his gaze to Ned. 'And you, young man, you promise you'll behave? I don't want any trouble from you. No crying. No running about the place. And definitely no shouting through my letterbox. I like things nice and quiet round here. If I hear so much as a snore out of you tonight, there'll be trouble. Got that?'

Ned gave a solemn nod. And then one of his most engaging smiles. 'Would you like to have tea with us, Mr Liberty? We're having pancakes. Oh, Mummy, please say Mr Liberty can have tea with us.'

Clara pushed her hands into the pockets of her jeans. Oh, well done, Ned, she thought. A cosy evening with Mr Misery. Perfect. 'You're more than welcome, Mr Liberty,' she lied, 'but it will be very simple. Nothing fancy, I'm afraid.'

Mr Liberty's enthusiasm for the idea seemed as great as her own. He said, and dismissively so, 'Pancakes? I can't stand them. I've got a nice bit of rump steak and a glass of claret I'm looking forward to.' He turned back towards the house, but before he disappeared, he tossed them one last piece of invective. 'And remember, no noise or trouble.'

Chapter Twelve

Gabriel went to bed early that night. He often did. Sleep was a welcome antidote to boredom. And, thank God, it was something he was still good at. The rest of his body might be betraying him – his hands, his bladder, his heart and the occasional limb given over to an attack of tremors – but sleep was a nut he could still crack.

He stepped over the mess of plaster and curtains that he hadn't done anything about since he'd pulled the track off the wall two nights ago, and got into bed. The sheets felt cold and damp. He didn't turn out the light straight away, but sat for a while to contemplate his day, a habit of Anastasia's that had rubbed off on him. 'Every day is a challenge,' she would say, 'but the real challenge is reflecting on the bad aspects of that day and learning from them.' It was another of her idealistic foibles that had contrasted with his more pragmatic approach to life: anything he didn't like about his day he wrote off. 'I haven't got the time to dwell on what's past,' he had said once.

Smiling her knowing smile, Anastasia had stretched out beside him in bed and stroked his cheek. 'Gabriel Liberty, I promise you that one day, when you're old and grey, you will find you have more time on your hands than you know what to do with and then you'll understand.'

'We're never going to be old,' he had responded fiercely. 'I would rather be dead than ancient and decrepit.'

He hadn't been much older than the age his children were now when he had said this, but as he shifted his pillows against the mahogany bed-head, Gabriel could remember uttering those words as though it were yesterday. Anastasia had shushed him with a finger against his lips. 'Yesterday, today, tomorrow, young or old, what does any of it matter so long as we're together and making the most of what we have?' Then she had kissed him. One of those long, lingering kisses that had promised him the world. With his eyes shut he could still feel the warmth of her moist mouth against his.

He snapped his eyes open. This was absurd. What did he think he was doing? He reached for the book by the side of the bed – a heavy tome of political memoirs guaranteed to see off such sentimental nonsense. But it remained closed as his train of thought was distracted again. Not by the distant past, but by the events of today. He wondered how his guests were getting on.

Thinking of the pancakes they must have enjoyed, he thought of his own supper – a lukewarm tin of Heinz tomato soup. He had lied about the rump steak and claret just as he frequently lied to Jonah about what he ate. Often he didn't eat what Jonah fetched from the shops for him. The fresh fruit, the vegetables, the chicken breasts – it was too much trouble. Cooking for one was bad enough, but eating alone was worse.

So why hadn't he accepted the invitation to join that well-mannered little boy and his mother for supper? Especially as their appearance down by the river had provided him with the highlight of an otherwise tedious day.

Since Val's illness, and her death, he had got out of the habit of being sociable, not that he had ever been gregarious. Val had been the driving force when it came to showing one's face at local functions; he had gone along with it to keep the peace. He had preferred to devote himself to work. But even that had palled as the years went on. And then came the day when, finally, he had had to resign himself to the truth that none of his children was interested in taking over the business he had inherited from his own father. It had been a bitter day indeed when he sold up and retired. He had never forgiven Caspar and Jonah for letting him down – in his heart, Damson had never really been in the running. They could not have found a more hurtful way to snub him. Everything he had worked for and hoped to pass on to them, they had, by their actions, despised and rejected. A solid engineering company with a name that was known and respected around the world wasn't good enough for them, was it? Oh, dear me, no.

And what had they chosen to do instead?

Not much.

After dropping out of university, Caspar, whose colossal self-regard far exceeded his willingness to get his hands dirty with real work, had thrown himself into a series of get-rich-quick scams that had all turned into financial disasters. During the eighties he had fancied himself one of Thatcher's boys, but his entrepreneurial skills were never going to sustain that ideal. He was an idle beggar who thought the world owed him a favour. His worst commercial disaster had been selling time-shares in Spain. When the bottom dropped out of the *hacienda* market the banks foreclosed, investors lost their money and one of Caspar's partners was sent to prison for fraud. But what else would you expect from the Costa del Crime?

No two ways about it, Caspar was a dreadful businessman and an even worse judge of character. Now he peddled overpriced cars for a living.

As for Jonah, the brightest of the bunch, he was wasting what talents he had been given by teaching in a third-rate school and earning buttons.

It went without saying, of course, that Damson had never held down a proper job. She had been too preoccupied with enjoying herself.

So Gabriel had entered the twilight zone of retirement. It hadn't suited him, isolated from the only world he had been interested in – industrial engineering: pipes, gaskets and valves – he had soon realised he had few friends. The people he had mixed with had been business associates in the steel-producing heartlands of Sheffield, and other than his love of books, he had nothing else to occupy him. Without meaning to, he had allowed the days to run through his fingers like sand. Anastasia would never have let him do this: for her, every day had counted. Val had tried to persuade him that they should explore the world together, but because he had travelled so extensively on business, he had ignored the brochures she left lying about the house and withdrew to his library.

Then she had died, and it was easier to retreat further still: to batten down the hatches and let the world go hang.

He knew the house was a mess and that he should do something about it. But where to start? It had got so out of hand that the task now seemed insurmountable.

He knew, too, that at times he was offhand and acerbic, but he didn't have the patience to be polite. He had always been direct and to the point – that was how one survived in business. Fannying around with false pleasantries would have got him nowhere. If a spade was a shovel, what the dickens was wrong in declaring it so? When had mealy-mouthed insincerity become the alternative to good old-fashioned honesty?

That was what he had liked about the Costello woman. She had said exactly what she thought. She had had the guts to call him a miserable old bugger. Good for her. That was what he approved of and could respect. He hated it when his children took whatever he dished out to them. It made him want to shake them and shout, 'Why can't you be more like me? Where's your bloody backbone?'

She was smart too. He could tell that by her waspish, quick-witted manner. Take the way she had sized up the situation down in the courtyard. He had offered her the use of a field, but she had wanted somewhere better and hadn't been afraid to ask for it. She was a determined woman who was used to ploughing her own furrow. Though he doubted that she would have been able to talk her way out of that ugly situation with those two nasty pieces of work. Lucky for her that he frequently went down to the copse; lucky, too, that he had been seized with the urge to take a few pot-shots at the crows. He had hated those birds ever since, as a boy, he had seen one pluck out the eyes of a newborn lamb. Armed with his gun he had been intent on an afternoon's sport when he spotted the camper-van parked on his land. He had quickened his pace, preparing to give the trespasser a piece of his mind, when the car had appeared. It had been satisfying to see the expression on the two yobbos' faces change as they'd looked down the business end of a double-barrelled shotgun. And even better seeing them run off. Rotten cowards, picking on a young mother and her child.

Perhaps he had gone too far when he'd shouted at her, but anger had fuelled his words. Anger that this was the kind of world in which he lived, where young women and children weren't safe to set foot in the countryside for fear of being robbed or subjected to God knew what else. He thought of that poor mite wetting himself and wished now that he'd scared those bully-boys even more.

He hated the idea that the disease-ridden scum of the big towns and cities was now infiltrating what had always been a place of sanctuary to him. Anastasia had loved to walk alone in the hills, and so had the children. Jonah in particular had relished the solitude of the moors, disappearing for hours at a time.

He had offered Miss Costello and her son the field because he had been genuinely concerned about their welfare. What if she was too tired to find a decent campsite and had dropped anchor in any old place and attracted further trouble? He might be considered in some quarters to be a bad-tempered old devil, but he was not the kind of man who would let a young woman go without somewhere safe to stay.

Smiling to himself, he thought of all the names he had been called that day.

A miserable old bugger.
An old skinflint.
A crazy old fool.
A cantankerous and mean-spirited man.
Not bad for starters.

He switched off the light and wondered what he might be in for tomorrow morning. Then he remembered that his feisty little guest had said they would be gone by first thing in the morning – 'It will be as though we'd never been here.'

He turned the light back on, reached for his clock and set the alarm for six thirty. Just in case he overslept. It would be a shame to miss out on a parting shot.

Chapter Thirteen

That night, unable to sleep, Archie stared at the ceiling above his bed. The curtains at the window were thin and unlined, and from the street-lamp outside, a glow of orange light shone through the cheap fabric. It was sufficient, though, for his eyes to follow the cracks in the plasterwork as if he was tracing a route on a map. That's me, he thought tiredly, I'm looking for the way out. Or, at least, some kind of direction.

He turned on to his side, hoping sleep would come if he lay in a different position. It didn't. Now he could hear a gang of youngsters coming back from the pub: they were kicking a tin can between them and their carefree banter jarred on his troubled thoughts.

He had received a letter from Stella's solicitor. The grey paper with the overly pedantic language had told him what he already knew, that more than two decades of marriage was to be reduced to *Mrs S. Merryman versus Mr A. F. Merryman*. The tone of the letter suggested that the matter could be brought to a swift conclusion as Mrs Merryman was happy to leave her husband's business concerns out of the negotiations, but the house was another matter. As Mr Merryman no doubt understood, Mrs Merryman had been a party to the original purchase of the property as well as a regular contributor to the mortgage payments, so she was entitled to her share of the matrimonial home.

Archie had no argument with that. It was all true. And as much as he wanted to avoid the upheaval of selling the house, he knew he had no choice: he had no other means to pay off Stella.

Still restless, he rolled over on to his left side and tried to relax. But his mind was racing through the years he and Stella had shared. The good times, and the bad times.

It mattered to him that the past was kept intact, just as it mattered to him that, for now, there were still traces of Stella's presence in the house, painful as they were. Like the brush she had left on the dressing-table with hairs caught among the bristles; the clothes she hadn't taken with her; the magazine on the kitchen worktop, still open at a page showing some film star with the new love of his life.

Ten minutes later, as sleep continued to elude him, he let out a sigh of defeat.

Insomnia was a new phenomenon to him, and other than getting out of bed and making himself a brew, he didn't know what to do. He slipped on his towelling dressing-gown and went downstairs quietly, not wanting to disturb his mother. She had taken to waking during the night and thinking it was time to get up. She had done it last night: at three o'clock, he had heard a noise coming from the kitchen, and had shot downstairs ready to confront whoever had broken in. What he found was Bessie setting out the breakfast things: plates and bowls, packets of cereal and slices of bread ready to go under the grill. His appearance in the kitchen had startled her so much that she hadn't been able to get a coherent word out. It had taken him some time to convince her that it was still the middle of the night. As he led her back to her room, she had launched into a long, heartfelt and impassioned speech, not one word of which could he understand. He had sat on the edge of her bed, coaxing the words of lucidity from her, soothing her frustration, until gradually he had realised that she felt guilty Stella had left him and was trying to help by seeing to things around the house. 'But, Mum,' he had said, 'I can manage perfectly well. I don't want you to worry about anything like that.' He had wanted to add that Stella had never

92

made the breakfast anyway, that it had always been his job.

He had spent an hour reassuring his mother that he could cope, before he got back to his own bed. But by five o'clock she was up again, running herself a bath.

When it came to Bessie having a bath, the golden rule was that somebody had to be on hand to help her . . . just in case.

Just in case she slipped.

Just in case she fell asleep.

Just in case she scalded herself.

But if Archie's golden rule was that her bath time had to be supervised, her own golden rule was that he was not allowed in the bathroom while she was in a state of undress. With the door ajar, he could sit outside on the landing, keeping up a steady flow of conversation about the shop, Samson, Comrade Norm, and the customers that came in to haggle over a stainless-steel egg-cup.

Now, in the harsh glare of the overhead strip-light, he stood in the kitchen, listening to the kettle coming to the boil. The speech therapist at the hospital had said that Bessie was improving, and he hung on to this glimmer of hope, wanting to believe that his mother would make a good, if not full, recovery.

He poured boiling water into the badly stained teapot, thinking how unfair it was that Bessie should now be cheated of enjoying life. She had worked hard down the years, had accepted and overcome every challenge thrown at her. Most had been a direct result of Archie's father having walked out on her when she was pregnant, leaving her to cope with the daily grind of making ends meet while struggling to bring up a child on her own. If he had stayed away for ever, it would have been better all round, but he took advantage of Bessie's generous nature and returned to sponge off her when the mood took him. It was always a relief when he grew bored of regular meals and her willingness to forgive, and left them alone.

Archie sat at the kitchen table to drink his tea, and tried

to remember what Dr Singh had said about there being swings and roundabouts to face. He'd heard a snippet on the radio, too. Something about keeping the stroke patient as active as possible, not just physically, but mentally. Apparently the precariously balanced mental capacities had to be exercised and shored up. Boredom was to be avoided at all costs. Loneliness too.

It occurred to him that maybe he could get Bessie into the shop for a few hours a day. She might like that. As kind as the neighbours had been, Bessie hadn't made a lot of effort to get to know them and, anyway, it wasn't easy for her to talk to strangers now. Her speech embarrassed her, and she knew that it embarrassed them.

No, the solution was to get her involved in the shop. Give her little tasks to do, such as polishing some of the small pieces of furniture. And those horse brasses from the house-clearance job he'd done the other day would come up a treat with a bit of tender loving care. As would the box of commemorative plates, which were covered in dust and grime. If he planned it carefully, there would be any number of little jobs he could find for her to do. But he would have to be subtle about it: his mother was no fool. He would have to make out that she was doing him a big favour, that he needed her help. There again, one look at Samson's huge clumsy hands would tell her that the big guy wasn't made for cleaning delicate china.

He swallowed the last of his tea, rinsed the mug under the tap, put it ready for his breakfast in the morning, and went back upstairs to bed. As he pulled the duvet over him, life didn't seem so bad after all.

He had always believed that for every problem there was a solution. It was just a matter of reasoning it through.

Drifting off to sleep, he felt better than he had in days. Maybe things would start to pick up now.

Chapter Fourteen

Clara woke to the sound of rain pattering on the roof of the camper-van. Stretching beneath the duvet, she opened her eyes and looked at her watch. It was eight o'clock. Goodness, as late as that. Still, there was no hurry, and as Ned was sleeping soundly, she could savour a rare lie-in. She closed her eyes, listened to the rain, and hoped it wouldn't develop into a full-blown downpour. Sadly, it seemed that the waitress's prediction at the café yesterday had been less than accurate: the rain had come early. They had been lucky so far on their trip: this was their first wet day. 'Captain's Log, Star Date 29 March,' she thought, with a smile, 'Day Five – rain.'

She should be keeping a diary. In years to come, when she was slogging away on the treadmill, it would make interesting reading. It would be nice for Ned, too. A keepsake to prove that they had been brave enough to flout convention.

Well, it wasn't too late to start. She would buy a book in Deaconsbridge and encourage Ned to play his part too. He could write his own entries, draw a few pictures, and maybe stick in postcards of where they had stayed. Another oversight. Postcards. She was supposed to be keeping her friends and parents up to date with their travels, but somehow she just hadn't got round to it. Nor had she phoned Louise. But that had been a conscious effort on her part to distance herself from home: to get the most out of this trip, she had wanted to separate herself from what she had left behind.

So, buying some postcards was another job for today, she thought, her orderly mind now putting together a list of things she had to do. They needed a supermarket, and a launderette would be useful. She didn't mind hand-washing a few pairs of pants and socks, but larger items were a drag. After yesterday, and their several changes of clothes, she could do with throwing everything into a machine, while she and Ned had a nose round the shops in the market square. Maybe they could have another meal at the Mermaid café and decide what they were going to do next. If it looked like the rain was going to settle in for the day, they could perhaps drive across to Castleton and visit the underground caverns, some of which, according to the guide books, were open all year.

She stretched again, and sighed contentedly. How pleasant it was to know that one's only concern for the day was to find a washing-machine and something to eat, with a little amusement thrown in. It was a far cry from worrying about meeting the latest production-line quotas. She didn't miss any of it – except, perhaps, the silly e-mails from the boys – Guy and David – and their antics. Guy had lifted the tension on many a head-banging-against-the-wall day. He would burst through her door like a member of the SAS, rolling across the floor and jumping up to declare that he had her covered – usually with a staple gun. The first time he had done it she had nearly fallen off her chair in alarm. It was also the first time she had met him. 'Hi,' he'd said, slipping the staple gun into the waistband of his suit trousers. 'I've been sent to introduce myself, seeing as you're new to the depart-ment. How're you getting on, Miss Clarabelle Costello?'

'Fine until you burst in and tried to staple me to the spot. Could you try knocking in future? You never know what I might be doing in here. And my name's Clara, not a ding-dong to be heard.' He never did knock, but she soon got used to his entrance – and the pet name.

She smiled at the memory. It was the camaraderie she missed, not the job. Already she was discovering that, away from home, her sense of perspective was undergoing further change. Though she and Ned had had holidays before, this one was different. There was no rush to their days. They did not have to cram everything into a week.

Even yesterday's horrible incident hadn't dampened her enthusiasm. She wasn't nervous by nature, but last night she had been grateful to Mr Liberty for allowing them to stay here – for her own peace of mind and Ned's. But she need not have worried about him: Ned had tucked into his supper with relish and gone to bed happily. The campsites they had stayed at previously had never been free of noise – of caravan doors clicking shut, toilets flushing, radios and televisions playing. Here, in the courtyard at Mermaid House, it had been the quietest night she had known. Other than a faint rustling of leaves on trees and the occasional distant animal noise, it had been as silent as the grave.

Which probably accounted for the good night's sleep she'd had. Overcome with a general sense of well-being, she thought that perhaps when she and Ned went into Deaconsbridge that morning they would buy a small present for Mr Liberty to thank him. She also wanted to try to make amends for being so rude to him – fear and tiredness must have got the better of her. She wondered if he was a one-off, or whether there were more like him inside Mermaid House. A whole family of eccentric Libertys slowly driving each other round the bend. If so, it was straight out of *Cold Comfort Farm*.

Putting aside its cranky, eccentric owner, the house was a veritable piece of whimsy. She had never seen anything like it before. She hoped there would be a chance, if she made peace with Mr Liberty, to have a look round. Maybe she could get Ned to ask him. It would sound less intrusive coming from a four-year-old boy.

Thinking of Ned, Clara rolled onto her side and looked towards his sleeping compartment. There was still no sign of movement from behind the curtain. He must have been shattered last night to sleep so long. It's all the fresh air, she thought. That would meet with her mother's approval. As babies, she and Michael had been put outside in their prams in all weathers. 'Toughened you up nicely,' said her mother, who had tried to do the same with Ned. 'Just airing him,' she claimed, when Clara arrived to collect him after work and found him on the patio with a strong wind buffeting the pram.

'Airing him or freeze-drying him, Mum?'

Though she had made her views clear on how she wanted her son treated, Clara knew that while her back was turned her mother did as she pleased, but so long as Ned thrived Clara couldn't complain. Anyway, she was glad to have parents prepared to help out. Without them, she wouldn't have coped nearly so well.

When she had discovered she was pregnant there had been no dilemma over whether or not to keep the baby. She had loved her unborn child's father, so it had seemed natural to want his baby. Telling her parents that she was pregnant had been one of the hardest things she had ever done. She knew she had let them down.

'Is there really no chance of the father taking on his responsibility?' her mother had asked, stricken.

'No, Mum. He's already married.'

That had been the second shock they'd had to cope with: that their sensible, well-brought-up daughter had been stupid enough to have an affair with a married man. Initially they had wanted to blame the despicable rotter for tricking her into a relationship with him when he should have known better, but she told them, 'I knew all along that he was married. At the time, though, he was separated from his wife.'

They had seized on this glimmer of hope.

'Is he divorced now?' her father asked.

'No. He and his wife are reconciled.'

Her father had picked up on the one aspect of the tale she had tried to gloss over. 'Did you tell him you were pregnant?' he asked.

'No.'

'But, darling, why not? He's the father, he should know,' her mother remonstrated.

'You only think that because you want to believe he'll wave a magic wand over my pregnancy and make it nice and respectable.'

'That's a little hard on us,' her father said.

'But it's true, isn't it? Imagine this year's Christmas cards: "Oh, and by the way, Clara's expecting our first grandchild but we don't know who the father is."'

'You haven't told us his name,' her mother said, pushing this uncomfortable home truth to one side.

'There's no need to. You won't ever meet him.'

In the end, and once the shock had worn off, her parents made it clear that they would be standing right by her. 'It's your life,' they told her, 'and we'll do all we can to help.' Their love and solidarity was just what she needed. It still brought a lump to her throat when she thought of their support and devotion.

By the time Ned was due, they were ready to fend off the merest hint of criticism from anyone and drove her to the hospital when she went into labour. She had never seen her father drive as fast as he had that night, crashing through red lights, the horn blaring. In the back of the car, next to Clara, her mother was breathing so hard it was difficult to know which of them was about to give birth. Louise met them at the hospital. She had been co-opted into being Clara's birthing partner, much to the rest of the gang's relief. 'You know I'm your biggest fan, Clarabelle,' Guy had said, 'but to see you flat on your back and screaming like a banshee would dispel the beautiful illusion I have of you.'

In the early hours of the morning, Ned made his appearance. He was the most amazing, tiny, wide-eyed, dark-haired bundle of wonder Clara could have imagined. She couldn't take her eyes off him. As she gazed into his little face she felt as if she had always known him. 'So there you are,' she almost said. 'I was wondering where you'd got to.' Even Louise, the world's biggest child-hater, had been moved to tears when he had wrapped his tiny

99

fingers around her thumb – though she claimed later that hunger and exhaustion had overwhelmed her.

Clara's parents had been equally moved by their grandson. Her father had hidden his wet cheeks behind a brand new Pentax – specially bought for the occasion – saying that somebody had to capture the moment, but her mother had sniffed and gulped quite openly, holding Ned in her arms and posing proudly for the camera.

At visiting-time later that day the gang were in her ward, presenting her with flowers and champagne, chocolates, and a huge teddy bear.

'It'll scare the poor mite witless,' Moira had said, taking a cautious but curious peek at Ned, who was asleep in Clara's arms. 'Was it as bad as Louise told us it was?'

Louise held up her hands. 'Sorry, Clara, but yes, I'm guilty of giving the sordid details. Frankly, from where I was standing, it was bloody awful. You've done me an enormous favour in putting me off for life.'

Four years on, Louise said that the moment she ever felt her hormones creeping up on her, she only had to think of that night in hospital with Clara and they shrank back into line without another word.

Though none of her friends had ever wanted children, they loved Ned, and went out of their way to spoil him. He might not be in possession of a full deck of parents, but in all other respects, he was a lucky boy: devoted grandparents and a set of the most doting aunts and uncles a child could wish for.

Clara slipped out of bed and filled the kettle. As she set it on the gas ring, she made a mental note to top up the water barrel before leaving. It held enough for two days of showers, cooking and washing-up, but she hated the idea of running out, so she kept a sharp eye on it. And while she was about it, she'd check their gas supply.

After wiping away the condensation that had formed on the window above the cooker, she opened one of the large vents in Winnie's roof, just enough to freshen the air but not to let the rain in, by which time the kettle had boiled and the van had acquired what she called a comforting happy-camper smell of burning gas. She made a pot of tea, then, surprised that the whistling of the kettle hadn't woken Ned, she stepped on to the first rung of the ladder and poked her head through the curtains.

Her heart leaped into her mouth.

Ned's bed was empty.

Chapter Fifteen

It was every parent's worst nightmare. Cold, debilitating fear consumed her, then sick panic took hold. She leaned across Ned's rumpled bed and flung back the duvet as though he might be there after all. She threw aside his pillow, too, and rummaged through his collection of cuddly toys.

Next she stumbled down from the ladder and checked the rest of the van, spurring herself on with the faint hope that in the night, and without disturbing her, Ned might have used the toilet and fallen asleep in there. No sign of him.

She stood for a moment to gather her thoughts. Had someone sneaked into the van while she slept and abducted him? She recalled a harrowing case several years ago of a young girl who had been taken from a tent and murdered.

No. Ned must simply have gone for a walk. In the rain?

Without bothering to change out of the oversized T-shirt she had slept in, she pulled on a pair of jeans and pushed her feet into her trainers. She opened the door and stepped outside. The rain was coming down heavier now and splashed against her face as she scanned the court-yard. If she had thought Mermaid House gloomy yester-day, it was even more so in the pouring rain. Beneath a pewter sky, the walls seemed darker than ever and water was cascading from a broken section of guttering. She made a dash for the door and, not caring that she had promised Mr Liberty they wouldn't cause any noise or trouble, she banged on it loudly. If she was going to find

Ned, she needed his help. He would have some idea where a curious child might wander on his land.

Impatiently, she crashed her knuckles against the frosted-glass panel of the door again. 'Come on, come on,' she cried frantically. Then, just as Ned had done yesterday, she bent down, pushed open the letterbox and peered inside. 'Mr Liberty,' she called, 'I'm sorry to disturb you, but I need your help. Please answer the door.'

Still no response.

Desperation set in, and with no shelter from the rain, she was now thoroughly wet and cold. Fear was making her nauseous, and conjuring up yet more disturbing images, of Ned lost in this unknown landscape, wandering across the fields and finding his way down to the river where they had paddled yesterday. The water hadn't been deep there, but what if he had discovered a more dangerous section where . . . where a small boy could drown?

She hammered wildly on the door. At last, and almost in tears, she heard the familiar, but welcome sound of Mr Liberty cursing. 'Hell's teeth, what's all the rumpus?' he growled, throwing open the door and staring at her fiercely.

'It's Ned.' She gulped. 'He's missing and I don't know where to start looking for him. Will you help me? Please. I thought you might know—' From behind him a head appeared, followed swiftly by the rest of Ned in his slippers, pyjamas and stripy dressing-gown whose belt was trailing on the ground. Clara went weak with relief. He was safe. She pushed past Mr Liberty, knelt on the stone-flagged floor and hugged Ned. But hot on the heels of relief came irrational anger and, to her shame, it was all she could do to stop herself shaking him. 'You know you're not supposed to leave the camper-van on your own,' she said, as calmly as she could. 'I was so worried. I thought something terrible had happened to you.'

'Please don't be cross with me, Mummy,' he said, tremulously. 'Mr Liberty said it would be all right.'

If Clara had felt like shaking Ned, she now felt like punching Mr Liberty's good eye right out of its socket. She got to her feet. 'Let me get this straight. This was all *your* idea?'

He cleared his throat. 'Saw the little lad peering out of his window and thought he might appreciate some company. Which he did. Isn't that right, young man?'

His cavalier attitude pushed Clara's anger to its zenith. 'What gives you the right to think you can encourage my son to break a rule? What did you think you were doing?'

'Mummy—'

'Ned, please, I'm talking.'

'But, Mummy, Mr Liberty showed me a secret door and the tower. He said there used to be a ghost up there. He told me that—'

'Ahem, possibly not the time, young man,' Mr Liberty murmured. 'Maybe we both ought to be apologising to your mother. She's looking a mite bothered to me.'

Clara flashed him a look of pure fury. 'Bothered? I was out of my mind with worry. I thought—' She stopped. She didn't want to relive the horror of thinking Ned might have been kidnapped by some perverted beast, that he might be lying dead somewhere, that she might never see him again and never feel his little body crushed against hers. That she might never stroke his soft cheek and silky smooth hair. Her anger subsided, and the heart-thumping pain of relief returned. 'I thought you didn't go in for making apologies.'

He looked uncomfortable. 'On this occasion I'm prepared to make an exception.'

'So what are you waiting for?'

'Miss Costello, I meant you and your boy no harm, and I'm very sorry that I caused you a moment's concern.'

'I'm sorry too, Mummy.' Ned's hand crept into hers. 'Don't be cross,' he added, shooting down any remaining vestiges of anger with one of his heart-melting smiles.

Suddenly she couldn't speak, but Mr Liberty filled in the silence. 'Well, if we're through with the sentiment, can you decide what you want to do next?' Contrition dispensed with, he went on, 'You can either stand here for the rest of the day letting in the rain and freezing to death or you can warm yourself by the fire in the kitchen while I make you some tea. A task I've proved myself more than capable of doing once before.'

Clara decided to accept, and she and Ned followed as Mr Liberty led the way. She was appalled at what she saw. Mess and clutter lay everywhere, piles of junk as far as the eye could see. The house smelt too. She had imagined a comforting old-fashioned kitchen with a massive fireplace where once upon a time a whole pig would have been roasted on a spit with a lowly scullery-maid to turn the handle. This dingy, bone-chilling room, with its grimy walls and flaking paintwork – especially above the cooker, which was covered in a thick film of grease – was not what she had envisaged. Nor was the gas-fired contraption with which Mr Liberty was now fiddling. She wondered why on earth he used such a device when behind it stood an Aga the size of a small car.

'It's the very devil to get going sometimes,' Mr Liberty complained, as he clicked away at a button on the side of the heater in an effort to ignite the flame. At last it caught and he straightened up triumphantly. 'There! That showed it who's boss.' She could see from his face that the coaxing of the heater into life was a daily battle of wills.

'Don't stand on ceremony,' he commanded. 'Sit your-self down.' He scraped one of the heavy chairs away from the long table and put it a few feet short of the heater. She crossed the room reluctantly, her shoes sticking to the scummy floor with each step, and sat in front of the meagre source of warmth. Mr Liberty threw a tea-towel at Ned. 'Don't stand there idly, young man,' he said. 'Help your mother to dry her hair. We don't want her catching her death, do we?'

'You wouldn't be spoiling me with your best Irish linen, would you?' she said, taking the grubby cloth from Ned.

He harrumphed loudly, turned away from her and set about the business of making tea.

A dubious brown crust on the tea-towel made her wonder if a mug of tea was such a good idea. Lord knows what she might catch. She tried to lose the tea-towel discreetly by folding it to slip it under some conveniently placed object, but Ned took it from her and tried helpfully to dab at her hair. She ducked out of his reach. 'No, Ned,' she whispered. 'It's dirty.'

'Shall I ask Mr Liberty for a clean one?' he whispered back. He might as well have placed a megaphone to his lips and relayed the message for the whole of the Peak District to hear.

Mr Liberty was rinsing mugs under the tap, and whipped round. 'Complaining again, Miss Costello? And there was me on the verge of offering you something to eat.'

The very idea made Clara want to gag. But, to her horror, Ned said, 'Breakfast would be nice.' He smiled at Mr Liberty. 'What have you got to eat? I'm very hungry.'

Clara stepped in fast. 'Why don't I cook us all a fry-up in the van?' She'd do anything to avoid being laid low with gastro-enteritis – even cook for this vinegary old man. 'We've got plenty of eggs and bacon.'

He looked at her shrewdly. 'Are you implying that my house isn't good enough for you? That it's not clean?'

'I'm not implying anything of the kind,' she said, rising from the chair to escape the gas heater and its noxious fumes. 'I'm telling you straight. The house, what I've seen of it, is a health hazard.'

He flared his nostrils. 'For one so young, you have quite a nerve, Miss Costello. Are you always so direct with people you hardly know?'

She gave him a conciliatory smile. 'Like you said earlier, sometimes there are occasions when one is forced into a position of making an exception. Which means I'm being unusually restrained with you. You should think yourself lucky.'

He gave a short bark of a laugh. 'Ned, m'boy, you have an extraordinary mother, did you know that? And just to prove that I don't harbour any ill feelings, I'm going to take up her offer of a cooked breakfast. That should teach her a lesson for shooting her impertinent mouth off, shouldn't it?'

Inside the camper-van, Gabriel tucked hungrily into his plate of bacon and eggs, relishing every mouthful. He couldn't remember the last time he had eaten a cooked breakfast.

'Would you like some ketchup, Mr Liberty?' asked Ned, from across the narrow table, a piece of streaky bacon dangling from his fork.

'Ketchup's for *caffs*,' Gabriel replied tersely. 'It's the opium of the common folk.'

'What's opium?'

'He doesn't need to know,' his mother chipped in, 'and don't speak with your mouth full.'

'Are you referring to me or your son?'

'To both of you.'

'Why don't I need to know?'

'Yes, Miss Costello, come along now, don't be shy. Surely you have an answer for your naturally inquisitive son. You seem to have an answer for just about everything else.' To his delight, a slightly raised eyebrow indicated that he had scored a point.

'It's a drug made from poppies, Ned,' she said, 'and it's highly addictive. It melts your brain. And before you ask what addictive means, it means that you want it all the time.'

'Like chocolate?'

'Yes. But you want it even more than chocolate.'

'But how does it melt your brain? And if I ate too much chocolate, would my brain melt? Would it pour out through my ears, going gloopy-gloopy-gloop if I shook my head?' He gave them a demonstration, his eyes swivelling.

Gabriel was reminded of Caspar and Damson as small children. They had always been on at him, question after tiresome question. There had never seemed enough answers in the world for them. Jonah had been the opposite, hardly opening his mouth. If he wanted to know something he found it out for himself. 'Jonah's an intelligent boy, Gabriel,' Val often said. 'You should do more to encourage him. Try to show how proud you are of him.' But Jonah had thrown away his potential.

Sighing inwardly and feeling his good humour drain out of him, Gabriel stabbed a piece of toast into the yolk of his second egg. He could remember the stinging blow Jonah had dealt him when he had announced his intention to become a teacher. They had been in the library, the setting sun turning the room amber, shafts of light catching the motes of dust in the warm air, music coming from some other part of the house. 'Please, Dad,' he had said, his hands stuffed into his trouser pockets, 'don't make this any harder for me than it already is. Just hear me out and respect my decision. That's all I ask.'

'And all I've ever asked of you is your respect, loyalty and duty, as my father expected them of me.'

'And maybe your father was wrong to expect so much of you. Perhaps if he had treated you differently, you might have treated *us* differently.'

Incensed at the doubled-edged criticism levelled at both himself and his father – a man he had both feared and idolised – Gabriel had done the unthinkable: he had lashed out and struck Jonah, knocking him clean off his feet. In shock he had watched his younger son pick himself up from the floor, then touch the bloodied corner of his mouth. But something more than anger was raging inside Gabriel, something far worse that made his fists itch to strike Jonah again. He never knew whether Jonah had done it deliberately, but his gaze, as he dusted himself down, moved from Gabriel's face to the portrait of Anastasia above the fireplace. It was as if he was saying, 'And what would she say of your behaviour?' But in a quiet, and wholly restrained voice, he had said, 'Why can't you trust me to cock up my own life, Dad? Why try to do it for me?'

Not another word passed between them. Not for the rest of that evening, that week or the months that followed. When Jonah walked out on him that night, Gabriel didn't set eyes on him again for a year. He had never thought of his younger son as stubborn – that was more Caspar and Damson's style – but his absence from Mermaid House during those twelve months proved beyond measure that he was as stubborn as Gabriel himself. He could almost respect his son for that.

The sound of an engine jolted Gabriel out of his thoughts. 'Shall I go and see who it is?' asked Ned, already slipping down from his seat and opening the top half of the camper-van door so that he could peer out. 'It's a car,' he announced, standing on tiptoe. 'There's someone to see you, Mr Liberty.'

'Top marks, young man,' said Gabriel, using his hand to wipe a peephole through the steamed-up window and recognising, with annoyance, the mobile Japanese torture chamber that had pulled into the courtyard. Didn't the wretched man have the sick and the dying to attend to?

'Shall I invite him in, Mummy?'

'No, Ned, I'm sure Mr Liberty would rather entertain his guest in the comfort of his own home.'

Gabriel put a last piece of sausage into his mouth and rose stiffly to his feet. He had a nasty feeling that he knew why Dr Singh had called today, and if he was ever going to get the irritating quack off his case, he was going to have to engage his brain in some nimble thinking.

Dr Singh was already knocking on the back door by the time Gabriel made it across the courtyard in the rain. 'You know what your trouble is,' he said to the doctor, 'you've got too much time on your hands. I suppose you want to come in?'

'Good morning to you, Mr Liberty. Yes, entry to your

fine house so that we can both get out of this terrible rain would be in both our interests, I suspect.'

'And I suspect you of foul play,' Gabriel said when they were standing in the kitchen, and Dr Singh had removed his wet coat and was requesting a look at his arm. 'You're keeping a close watch on me and I don't like it.'

'Mm . . . that's good. It's improving nicely. Eye next. Foul play? In what way?'

'You're biding your time before you start insisting that I do something about getting help around my house. You'll pull another of your blackmail stunts on me if I don't do as you say.'

'Tsk, tsk, Mr Liberty. I can't think what you're referring to. Mm . . . yes, your eye looks much better. But you do need help and I'm determined to make you see that. It's a big house you have here. And you're not—'

'And I'm not getting any younger,' Gabriel finished for him. 'Blah-di-blah-di-blah. You're just dying to get Social Services on to me, aren't you? You'd like nothing better than to have me rehoused in a tiny box with a warden banging on the door every ten minutes to check I haven't gassed myself through boredom. Why don't you just have done with it and measure me up for a coffin?'

'A tempting suggestion, and certainly something to consider. As risky as it is, may I wash my hands?' He pulled out a small hand towel from his medical bag, along with a tiny bar of wrapped soap.

'Oh, please, be my guest.'

'Talking of which, would I be correct in thinking you have one?' The doctor looked through the window, out across the courtyard. 'A member of your family, perhaps? Or are you about to take to the road and broaden your horizons?'

'My horizons are plenty broad enough, thank you. If you must know . . .' But his words petered out. 'Family,' he repeated, 'why did you say that?'

'A shot in the dark.'

Family, echoed Gabriel privately. Now there was an

idea. But would it work? Surely it had to be worth a try?

'Actually, your stab in the dark is spot on. My daughter's come to stay with me.'

Dr Singh turned off the tap with the tip of a forefinger, picked the small white towel from his shoulder, and dried his hands. 'You've had a change of heart, then?'

Gabriel looked at him blankly. 'What do you mean?'

'The last time we spoke you gave the impression that your family meant little to you. Has a reconciliation taken place?'

'Ah . . . something like that, yes.'

Dr Singh smiled. 'That is wonderful news. So, will you be allowing your daughter to play a more active role in your life from now on?'

'Oh, do me the honour of getting to the point. What you're really asking is, am I going to let her help me clean up my act?'

'You put it so well, Mr Liberty.'

'And if that were to happen, would you leave me alone? Would you stop turning up here with spurious excuses to check on my welfare with blackmail on your mind?'

'I might.'

'Well, you stay right there while I go and fetch my daughter for you to meet. You'll soon see that I'm now in thoroughly good hands.'

Crossing the courtyard, Gabriel had no idea if Miss Costello would play ball with him, but as he had just reasoned with himself, it had to be worth a try. All he had to do was inveigle her into telling a white lie or two and everyone would be happy.

Or, more precisely, *he* would be happy.

Chapter Sixteen

As she stacked the dirty plates to be washed, with Ned at her side on his little step ready to help, Clara listened to Mr Liberty's extraordinary proposal. Amused, she let him grind on until at last he came to a halt and his words were left hanging awkwardly in the confined space between them. Waiting for her response, he shuffled his big feet from side to side like a naughty schoolboy up before the headmaster. 'Now let me get this straight,' she said, 'you want *me* to pretend to be your daughter?'

He shuffled again. 'I thought I'd just made that abundantly clear.'

'Would it be too much of an imposition to ask why?'

'I might have known you'd make matters difficult. Why can't you just accept what I've asked you to do?'

'Because it's not in my nature. I like to be presented with all the salient facts before I make up my mind about anything. If I'm going to play along with your curious game of subterfuge, I think I ought to be allowed to know the whys, the hows, and the whats. So divvy up the information or leave Ned and me to get on. We have a busy day ahead of us.'

'God *damn* it! You're the most infuriating woman I have had the misfortune to meet, Miss Costello.'

'With all due respect, Mr Liberty, it strikes me that you need my help more than I need your impertinence, so if you're through with the name-calling, perhaps—'

'All right, all right. I need you to pretend to be my daughter so that annoying quack will leave me alone. I need to prove to him that I have a loving member of my family clasped to my bosom who is eager to keep a watchful eye over me.'

'And if you can't prove that is the case?'

'I'll probably have Social Services snooping round here faster than you can say meals on bloody wheels. And they won't leave it there. You've seen the state of the house – their next move will be to have me rehoused, claiming I'm incapable of taking care of myself.'

'You don't think you're overreacting just a touch? They couldn't do that unless you allowed them to.'

'If it was your freedom in the balance, would you want to risk it?'

She considered what he had said. Okay, maybe he was being paranoid, and perhaps he might be better off in a more wholesome environment with a regular supply of meals, but who was to say, other than the man himself, whether he would *feel* better off living that way? If he wanted to spend the rest of his life, until he died from bubonic plague, surrounded by his own mess, wasn't that his right? She didn't know anything about taking care of the elderly and what powers Social Services had, but she knew enough to understand that a matter of principle was at stake. Clearly Mr Liberty felt that this Dr Singh, who was currently waiting to meet his patient's loving, caring daughter inside Mermaid House, wasn't going to leave him alone until he had been convinced that his patient was to be looked after. If a couple of fibs was all it would take to make everyone happy, why not tell them?

'Okay,' she said, 'I'll do it. And given that your doctor has been kept waiting long enough, we ought to get this over and done with immediately. We don't have time to concoct anything elaborate so we'll have to keep our story simple. Agreed?'

He nodded. 'If he asks, I thought you could tell him you were coming to stay indefinitely.'

'And Ned? What do we say about him?'

Mr Liberty hesitated. 'I hadn't thought of him. I suppose he'll have to be my grandson.'

At this last remark, and with his hands cupping an enormous bubble, Ned turned from the sink. He beamed and gave the bubble a long, steady blow. It moved slowly from his hands, drifted up towards Mr Liberty and came to rest on his shoulder. Where it burst.

'Let's hope that's not what's going to happen to our story when we meet your Dr Singh,' Clara remarked.

Dr Singh was absorbed in a three-month-old *Daily Telegraph* that was lying on top of a box of old shoes and jam-jars when Gabriel and his newly acquired family entered the kitchen. He raised his head when he heard their footsteps.

In a loud, jovial voice, Gabriel said, 'Dr Singh, I'd like you to meet my daughter, Damson, and my grandson, Ned.'

'I'm very pleased to meet you,' the doctor said, coming forward to shake hands. 'But, Mr Liberty, you didn't tell me you were fortunate enough to be a grandfather. And such a fine-looking boy. So like his mother. The resemblance is uncanny.'

'You're not my priest, I don't have to confess everything to you.'

Dr Singh shared a conspiratorial smile with Miss Costello. 'Your father is a very unusual man. His sense of humour is not to everyone's taste, I think.'

'Oh, he's always been a quirky old devil, but that's his charm. Affectionately curmudgeonly, is what we say about him. Isn't that right, *Dad*?'

She's enjoying every moment of this, thought Gabriel, with a half-smile. But then, truth to tell, so was he. It was particularly satisfying knowing that he was getting one over on this interfering quack. 'If you say so, *dear*.'

'He tells me that you're coming to stay with him,' Dr Singh said.

'Yes, that's right. I thought I'd take him in hand, you know, tidy the place up a bit, maybe even encourage him to find himself a housekeeper.'

Dr Singh smiled again. 'I wish you luck in those tasks.' He cast his eyes meaningfully around the kitchen.

'Oh, I think I'm more than up to the task of whipping my rascal of a father into shape. No worries on that score.'

'Well, if you've both finished discussing me as though I were a dimwit,' Gabriel said tersely, 'perhaps you'd be kind enough to show the doctor to the door, *Damson*. There's a whole world of terminally ill people out there who must be desperate for a good dying scene in the arms of their local GP.'

'Yes, *Dad*, of course.'

Thinking how easily they'd got away with it, Gabriel watched the doctor being led out of the kitchen. He heard the back door open and was on the verge of a congratulatory pat on the back when the doctor re-appeared. Gabriel froze. Damn! Had the wretched man merely been playing along with them?

'Dear, oh dear,' the doctor said, 'you would think I'd know better by now.' He came towards Gabriel and reached for his medical bag, which he'd left on a chair beside the table. 'I've been told so many times that I would lose my head if it were not joined to the rest of me.' He laughed brightly.

Gabriel forced himself to join in. 'Got everything now?' he asked.

'I do hope so. I certainly don't want to have to make another trip out here today. Your drive is murder on my little car's suspension.'

'You'd better keep away, then.'

Despite the rain, Miss Costello walked the doctor to his car. Through the window, Gabriel could see that they were deep in conversation. No need to ask who or what they were discussing. Doubtless the good doctor was pumping the prodigal daughter about her pathetic old father.

'Well?' he said, when she came back into the kitchen.

'Well what?' she asked, shaking the droplets of rain from her hair.

'Did we get away with it?'

'For the time being, yes.'

'Uh?'

'You've earned yourself a reprieve until next week. He said he's going to try and pop in on Monday to make sure your eye has recovered.'

'This is victimisation,' Gabriel roared. 'I won't stand for it. It's outrageous!'

'A lot of people would give their back teeth for such a caring doctor.'

'Well, I'm not one of them! I'll – I'll pretend I'm not in. Or, better still, I'll go to the surgery. That'll show the stupid little man.' Then, in a less acerbic tone, 'Why can't people understand that I just want to be left alone? Is that really too much to ask?' He slumped into a chair at the table.

With her hands resting on Ned's shoulders, Clara observed him from across the room. The poor man made a desolate picture. And for the first time since meeting him, she saw not a growling, teeth-baring tyrant but an elderly man who wanted to preserve his dignity. It was just that he was going about it in the wrong way.

The modern world didn't work by the old rules of dictatorship. Nowadays it was run on different lines, by compromise, tact, guile, and subtle manipulation. She should know: she had used them well enough during her time with Phoenix. She had lost count of the number of management training courses she had been on where she had been told that there is no such thing as a problem: problems are challenges, and challenges are to be shared.

But how could this old man ever adapt? How could he ever wise up to the great universal truth that it was all about give and take?

Chapter Seventeen

There was nothing else she could say so Clara took Ned's hand and turned to leave. 'Why is Mr Liberty so sad?' Ned asked, his voice too loud and too clear.

'I'm not sad,' rumbled Mr Liberty, his head still in his hands. 'I've never been sad in my life.'

Pulling his hand out of Clara's grasp, Ned went back to the table, stood next to the old man and peered at him. 'Why are you hiding behind your hands?' he asked. 'Are you playing a game? Granda does that with me. He sits very still, makes gaps in his fingers, then suddenly goes, *boo*! It makes me jump every time. Shall I show you?' Before either Clara or Mr Liberty could stop him, Ned let out an almighty BOO! Mr Liberty jumped, but Clara could see that he was trying to pretend he hadn't. 'Do you want to play that game with me?' asked Ned. 'It might cheer you up.'

'Ned, I don't think Mr Liberty wants to play anything right now. He's not in the mood. And, anyway, we've got to keep our part of the bargain.'

At this, Mr Liberty raised his head. 'Bargain?'

'You generously gave us a place to stop for the night on the understanding we wouldn't cause you any trouble and that we would be gone first thing.' She looked at her watch. 'First thing was several hours ago, but by lunch-time we should be out of your way.'

Mr Liberty seemed to pull himself together. 'Of course. Well, I mustn't keep you. An agreement is an agreement. Where are you going? Have you sorted out a campsite?'

'Not yet, but I thought we'd go into Deaconsbridge and stock up on supplies. I also need to find a launderette.'

'You've as much chance of finding one of those round here as tripping over a crock of gold.' He was sounding much more his indomitable self. 'We used to have one, but it was turned into a fancy art gallery selling tacky paintings to dumb tourists who wouldn't know art if it jumped up and bit them on the nose.'

Clara smiled. 'We'll make it our first port of call, then.' Once more she turned to go, then hesitated. 'Would you like us to fetch you anything? It wouldn't be any trouble.'

He regarded her uncertainly. 'You're coming back in this direction?'

'Not specifically, but I don't mind making the trip. You're not that far out of the town, are you?'

'That's good of you,' he said gruffly. He took a ballpoint pen from Ned, who was making an irritating noise by repeatedly clicking the top of it with his thumb. 'But there's nothing I need.'

She looked at him thoughtfully. 'You're not used to kindness, are you?'

He squared his shoulders and straightened his back. 'At my age, kindness and charity become indistinguishable.'

'So you'd be much happier if you believed my offer was born out of a desire to interfere, rather than accept it as a genuine offer to help?'

He didn't say anything, but removed from Ned's hands a magnifying-glass he had unearthed from an overflowing shoebox of junk on the table. He had been using it to inspect Mermy at close quarters.

'Look,' she said, trying to be conciliatory, 'I'm sorry things didn't pan out better with your tenacious doctor, but the only way you're going to get him off your back is to meet him half-way. Clean the place up and prove to him you can fend for yourself. Can't you enlist your real daughter's help?'

Mr Liberty brought the magnifying-glass down on the table with a sharp bang. 'Damson doesn't show her face here unless she has to.' His voice was hard, scornful.

'Damson's an unusual name. I meant to ask you about it earlier.'

'Sounds more like a cat's name, doesn't it? Which is quite appropriate. Damson can be as sleek and cunning as any feline creature I've ever known. Scratchy too, when she wants to be.'

'Was the name your idea?'

He shook his head. 'The credit goes to my first wife. She had a fondness for the eccentric.'

Clara realised that this was the first time he had referred to his family. 'Do you have any other children?' she asked.

'A pair of sons who are both two shades of stupid. Caspar is a conman with as much head for business as a watermelon. He's a chippy brat who, like Icarus, hasn't yet learned the hazards of flying too close to the sun. My other son, Jonah, is a weak-willed idealist.'

'And what terrible crime did he commit to gain such familial approval?'

'*That*, Miss Costello, is none of your business. And while we're on the subject, why have you started asking me so many questions? I thought you said you were going.'

'I was simply wondering why you don't ask for their help. And you've given me the answer. You've scared them off, haven't you? But, like you said, it's none of my business so I'll say goodbye. It's been an education meeting you.' She held out her hand.

He stared at it hard, rose to his feet, and took it in his large distorted paw. Then he withdrew it, looking as if he was about to say something important. 'Tell me, Miss Costello,' he said slowly, 'you strike me as a woman who enjoys a challenge. Am I right?'

'It has been said of me, yes.'

'And you told me over breakfast that you don't have any real plans, that you and your son are just drifting from one place to another. Is that so?'

'Absolutely nothing wrong with your memory. Your point being?'

'I'd like to make you an offer. Help rid me of that interfering quack by pretending to be my daughter for a while longer.'

'Are we talking more lies? And perhaps you'd elaborate on what *a while longer* actually means. Another day? Another two days?' She watched him swallow and sensed that he was hoping for more than that from her.

'It depends on how long you think it would take to sort out this mess.' He indicated the kitchen.

Clara was stunned. He couldn't be serious. 'Whoa there, I'm not sure I like where this is going. What on earth makes you think I would be remotely interested in dealing with this little lot? Ned and I are on holiday. Cleaning up after somebody else doesn't feature on our itinerary.'

'But you do owe me a favour.'

'Since when?'

'Since I rescued you from those goons when you were trespassing on my land.'

The breathtaking cheek of the man! 'Oh, nice try,' she said derisively. 'You think you can toss that one in and hold my conscience to ransom. Well, think again, buddy, because you've got me all wrong. Anyway, I've already carried out one favour for you by lying to Dr Singh about being your daughter.'

'If I can't appeal to your good nature, then maybe your purse will be a better option.'

'Sorry, still not interested. Try flaunting your money at the *Yellow Pages*.'

'I'd sooner flaunt it at a person I know and trust.'

'How can you be so sure I won't fleece you?'

'I pride myself on being a good judge of character.'

'The flattery, even from you, won't work. Get hold of a firm of contract cleaners with a good reputation.'

'I don't want strangers in my house. Please, won't you

even consider my offer? I'm willing to pay you whatever it takes.'

She held her ground. 'Look, you might be used to bullying people into doing what you want them to do, but you can't do the same with me. And, for your information, I'm not for sale.'

'Come, come, everything is for sale, surely you know that. And just think of the challenge.'

'The answer is still a resounding no.'

It was the most monstrously ludicrous idea Clara had ever heard, and as she and Ned packed up Winnie, she didn't know whether to feel flattered by Mr Liberty's proposal, that he clearly approved of her, or downright insulted that he had thought she might want to waste her holiday cleaning up his mess.

'Completely off his trolley,' she muttered under her breath, as she moved about Winnie, putting packets and jars into their respective cubby-holes and slamming the locker doors. 'Just who does he think he is?'

It was a power thing, she suspected. Old Laughing Boy needed someone he could treat as a skivvy. That was what this was about. Well, not this girl. She was nobody's skivvy. No sirree. And how dare he think she could be bought off? She hadn't given up a well-paid job to become a cleaner for that miserable old goat!

Gabriel watched the camper-van trundle slowly along the drive until it was out of sight. He turned from the rain-lashed stone mullion window in the tower, angry and disappointed: angry because he had been reduced to the humiliating level of begging somebody to help him and disappointed because he knew he was going to miss having that Costello woman and her son around. They hadn't been with him long, but there had been something about them he had liked, something about their company that had appealed to him.

The woman's forthrightness had been a refreshing

change from the patronising sycophancy with which he was frequently treated, and the boy had been as bright as a button, not missing anything that was going on around him. He had forgotten how honest children could be. How they could put their finger on a raw spot and prod it mercilessly. Sad, was how the youngster had described him. Well, yes, in that moment he had felt sad. Weary too. Worn out. Shrivelled up. A husk of his former self. Old, and ready to throw in the towel.

He knew he was bucking against the system, which held all the trump cards. It was only a matter of time before Dr Singh and his kind would have their pernicious way with him. It was his greatest fear that the time would come when he would be carted off to live the remainder of his life among a crowd of insufferable strangers whose only excitement would be a change of incontinence pad after a game of bingo. It was, he knew, a fear that was bordering on the pathological, and not one based on personal experience of these places. But he had read enough horror stories in the papers to know that dreadful things went on in retirement homes. Last year, before the television had broken, he had watched an appalling series of programmes about a bunch of poor old dears and ageing Jack the Lads living out their lives to the tune of 'It's a Long Way to Tipperary' and 'The Hokey-Cokey'. Sometimes he had nightmares about this from which he woke in a sweat, heart pounding, terrified that he would end his days with sickeningly motherly women calling him 'dear' and offering to take him to the lavatory. Dear God, he'd rather take one of his shotguns to his head.

That was why he had resorted to pleading with the Costello woman. He had seen in her someone capable and strong, someone he could trust to help him sort out Mermaid House. He knew it had to be done, and if somebody could just get the job started for him, he felt confident he would see it through.

Nothing had been done since well before Val's death, and all of her things were still lying about the place –

clothes, jewellery, perfume, books, stuff he didn't need, but felt he couldn't discard. It seemed sacrilegious to dismantle her life like that.

It had been the same when Anastasia had died. It had been years before he had emptied her wardrobes and dressing-table. But then it had been different: he hadn't wanted to part with Anastasia's belongings. Having them around had kept her alive somehow. For a long time after her death, and before going to bed at night, he would open a cupboard and run his hands through her dresses, holding the smooth fabrics against his face, breathing in her sweet, sensual fragrance. One night, when he had thought the children were asleep, Damson had crept up on him and asked what he was doing. She had stood in the doorway, her head tilted to one side, looking at him as though he were quite mad. 'You should throw everything away,' she had said matter-of-factly, 'or burn it. Caspar and I could make a bonfire for you.'

He could scarcely believe what he was hearing: seven years old and she was offering to burn the few tangible keepsakes they had of her mother. The cruelty of her words had horrified him. 'Why are you being so disgustingly insensitive, Damson?' he had asked.

She hadn't answered, just stared at him until he closed the wardrobe door.

He had told the twins that no amount of tears would bring their mother back, and he could not recall seeing either Caspar or Damson cry for her. Not even at the funeral, when they had stood beside him beneath the hot summer sun, perfectly composed, their dry-eyed gaze on their mother's coffin as they held hands, united by something that had excluded him.

He crossed the dusty wooden floor to the narrow staircase that led back to a short, unlit passageway, then on to the library, where a secret door opened to the right of the fireplace. It was this that he had shown Ned that morning. The little lad's eyes had grown as large as hubcaps when Gabriel had shown him the hidden handle that made the lower half of the bookcase swing open. 'Where does it go?' Ned had asked, peering cautiously into the darkness.

'It goes up to the tower you can see from the front of the house.'

'Will you take me to see it, please? I'll be very good.'

'If you promise to take care where you put your feet,' Gabriel had told him, as he dipped his head and led the way. 'It's as black as pitch, so stay close to me.'

'Are there any spiders?'

'Lots.'

'Big ones?'

'Enormous, and wearing hobnail boots and carrying sawn-off shotguns. So mind you don't look them in the eye or they'll have you for breakfast.'

He had enjoyed seeing the look on the lad's face as he tried to figure out how much to believe, and it had made him spin even more yarns of mysterious intrigue, of ghosts who lived in the tower, shook their chains and slammed doors at dead of night. All nonsense, of course, but it was what children lapped up.

When he had looked through the kitchen window first thing that morning and had seen Ned's face staring back at him from the camper-van, he had acted on a rare impulse and gone outside to see if the boy wanted to go round the house. He knew now that it had been a mistake to encourage him to go against his mother's rule – that he wasn't to leave the van without her permission – but it had seemed harmless at the time. She had been sound asleep and it had seemed better to let her enjoy a lie-in while her son had a bit of fun.

Which he had. He'd been thrilled by the secret passage-way and had loved the tower, asking politely to be held up high so that he could look out at the view.

It had been ages since Gabriel had been to the tower and it had looked worse than he had remembered it. The last time he'd ventured up there had been to let out a bird that had got in through a broken window – droppings were still stuck to the floor and walls.

As children, Caspar and Damson had regularly holed up in the tower. Jonah had never been allowed in. Even when Val had intervened, they had refused him entry. 'He's a stupid baby,' they had yelled through the door, 'and we're not having him in here with us. He'll spoil what we're doing.'

Back in the library, and shutting the secret door behind him, Gabriel sighed. So many memories contained in one house. Some good. Some not so good. And some plain awful.

Perhaps if he could get rid of some of the rubbish from the house he might cleanse it of the memories he would rather forget. Selective memory via a damn good spring-clean, that's what he needed.

When he'd been widowed for the second time he had imagined he would more than cope with all this domestic malarkey. Nothing to it, he had thought, so long as he could boil himself an egg and remember to fill the washing-machine once a week. But he hadn't bargained on things going wrong, or fiddly, time-consuming jobs piling up until they had the better of him.

He cursed under his breath that the Costello woman hadn't accepted his offer. Now she and her son were gone.

Well, good riddance! Coming here and cadging off him for free!

Pah!

Chapter Eighteen

Clara had hoped to prove Mr Liberty wrong, but so far her search had revealed that Deaconsbridge was a launderette-free zone, just as he had said. It hadn't been a complete waste of time, though: she now had the lie of the land and knew that there was a modest supermarket a short distance from the market square where they could stock up on supplies.

'Ho hum,' she said to Ned, as they circled the market square one last time, the rain coming down harder still and the long wiper blades swishing across the windscreen, 'I guess this is one of those rare occasions when I'll have to admit defeat. Perhaps the next campsite we stay at will have a machine we can use. Shall we get the shopping done now?'

'Then can we go to the Mermaid café for lunch?'

'Good thinking, and while we're there, we'll make our plans. We'll look at the map and see if we can find a campsite we like the sound of. Oh, and something else we need to do before we leave. We must buy a large notebook and some postcards.'

Taking the next left, Clara told Ned about her idea that they should keep a diary. He liked the sound of this. 'Ooh, can we buy some new crayons, please?'

She smiled. What was it with children and crayons? It didn't matter how many packets you bought them, they could never have enough new ones. From the moment Ned had been old enough to grasp a crayon between his fingers, he had turned into a stationery fiend. At home, he was forever setting out his stash of felt-tip pens, rubbers, paper-clips and pads of paper. Her mother claimed that

Clara had been the same as a child, except her collection had boasted several hundred pencil-sharpeners. Apparently she had always been striving for the ultimate sharp point. 'I think the budget will stretch to that,' she said.

'I'm going to draw Mr Liberty and his castle.'

'Steady on, Ned, this is a diary we're writing, not a horror story.'

'And next I'll draw the secret passageway and the tower he showed me,' Ned said enthusiastically. 'He told me it was full of spiders, but I didn't see any. He also said they wore boots and had guns, but I knew he was joking. Spiders aren't big enough to carry guns, are they, Mummy?'

'They might need to, living with a man like Mr Liberty. Right, here we are. And thank the Lord, it's free parking if we're only here for an hour. Life just gets better and better, Ned.'

The supermarket was a small independent one that Clara had never heard of. Built of local stone and tinted glass, it was conspicuous among the old buildings that surrounded it.

They dashed through the rain from the van to the front of the store, grabbed a trolley and made a start. But with Ned at the helm it was only a matter of time before they crashed into someone or something. He gave the job his entire concentration, and their first target was a freezer offering two packs of chicken Kiev for the price of one and placed inconveniently in the middle of an aisle. Next they scored a direct hit on a large wire basket of Walker's crisps. And finally, coming into the home straight, through wines and spirits, they rammed a trolley being pushed by a long-faced man in an expensive suit. Miraculously they arrived at the checkout relatively unscathed and with everything they'd gone in for, except the notebook and crayons.

There were only two checkouts in use, so they joined the one with the smallest queue. To Clara's embarrassment, the long-faced man pulled in behind them. She noticed that his trolley contained a dozen bottles of champagne that was on special offer. For a Champagne Charlie, he looked wildly out of place. 'Come on,' he muttered irritably after a few minutes. He tapped an expensively shod foot impatiently. 'What's the hold-up?'

The question was directed at nobody in particular, and Clara had no intention of answering it. Instead, she finished loading their shopping on to the conveyor belt, and looked at the woman in front of her. She was in her mid- to late seventies, Clara reckoned, and was wearing the type of felt hat Clara's grandmother used to wear. She looked upset and was glancing from the checkout girl to the purse in her trembling hands. She said something that Clara didn't catch. In response an over-plucked eyebrow hitched itself skyward. 'You what?'

Whatever the older woman had said, it wasn't getting her anywhere, and the girl – a sullen piece of work dressed in a pink and white overall – drummed her sparkly false nails on the till and rolled her eyes at Clara as if to say, 'Got a right one here.'

'Will you please get a move on?' the suit demanded from behind Clara. 'Unlike most people round here in Hicksville, I don't have all day to waste.'

Queue rage, thought Clara, with disgust. She left Ned scaling the side of their trolley and went to see if she could help. 'What's the problem?' she asked the checkout girl.

'Search me. The daft old bat's not making any sense.'

Clara turned to the older woman. 'Can I help?'

A pale anxious face, brimming with confusion and distress, looked at Clara. Trembling hands showed her the snap-fastened purse: it was empty. Oh, Lord, thought Clara, now what?

'Oh, for heaven's sake, this is ridiculous. Will some-body *do* something?'

Clara turned and smiled sweetly at the suit. 'For a start, you could try piping down, mate. No, better still, take your bargain-price bubbly and go and join the other queue.'

He stared at her furiously. 'And *you* should try keeping your brat under control. He's stepped on my foot three times since I've been standing here.'

She did the adult thing, poked her tongue out at him, then turned back to the woman and her empty purse. 'How much is it?' she asked the girl on the till.

'How much is what?'

'This customer's *bill*,' she said, slowly and with sarcastic emphasis. 'Please, do stop me if I'm going too fast for you.'

'It's three pounds seventeen.' The girl pouted.

'Goodness, a king's ransom.' Digging into her bag, Clara offered her credit card. 'Right, stick it on this and put my shopping through as fast as your helpful little fingers can manage it. *Okay?*'

'Stuck-up bitch,' the girl muttered, as Clara turned to explain the situation to the woman. She was looking even more confused and distressed.

'There's no need to worry,' Clara said. 'It's been taken care of. I've paid it for you.' But her words seemed to add to the poor woman's anxiety and she started speaking so fast that Clara couldn't understand what she was saying. 'Here,' she said slowly. 'This is your bag of shopping. Will you be all right now?'

But the head shook again, and a hand squeezed Clara's arm. After an agonising pause, she said, 'You ... with me.'

'You want me to come with you?'

A smile of relief and a nod confirmed that she had understood correctly.

'But where to?'

Another chaotic burst of words brought forth no further illumination.

'Do you want me to take you home?'

Clara didn't understand the answer, but after she had bagged up her shopping, paid for it, and insisted that she, not Ned, push the trolley, the three left the store. It was slow going as their newly acquired friend had something wrong with one of her legs and took each step, with the aid of a stick, as if she was picking her way through a minefield. They had run out of time in the car park, so Clara explained to the woman that they would have to drive to wherever it was that she lived. Getting directions was going to prove interesting, though. Then she had the idea of asking the woman to write down her address.

But when she gave the woman a piece of paper and a pen, it became evident that her hands lacked the dexterity to hold anything firmly. Nevertheless, after she had made a huge effort, Clara read the word 'stroke'. Ah, so that was it. She asked the woman where she wanted to go. It took a long time, but 'Second Best' and 'Son' appeared.

Following the woman's hand signals, they drove back into the market square, past the bookshop and the Deaconsbridge Arms, then took a side road called Millstone Row and there, on the corner, they saw a double-fronted shop called Second Best. There was just room to park in front of it, and through the windows Clara could see an Aladdin's cave of bric-à-brac and second-hand furniture. Seeing that her passenger was struggling to release her seat-belt, Clara did it for her, then called through to Ned, 'Okay, you can get out now.'

They entered the shop, their arrival heralded by a tinkling bell. It was jam-packed with corner cupboards, wardrobes and three-piece suites. There were coffee tables, bookcases, lamp-stands, mirrors, ornaments, and any number of chairs – dining chairs, kitchen chairs, garden chairs, even a rocking chair, which drew Ned like a magnet – and bar stools. Despite the quantity of furniture and knick-knacks crammed into the confined space, there was a surprising degree of order to the shop and Vivaldi's Four Seasons was playing on a radio.

'I'll be right with you,' a man's voice told them. 'I'm just on my knees with Des O'Connor and Val Doonican, and how many blokes do you know who would admit to that?'

Before she had set eyes on the voice's owner, Clara had

decided she would like him: he sounded so cheerful, a real blast of fresh air.

The old woman took a few painfully slow steps through the shop and disappeared behind an old gas cooker.

'Hello, Mum, you back already with Samson? He found you all right, then? What's wrong?'

This was progress, thought Clara. They'd found the son. After a torrent of jumbled words, he appeared with his mother. In his arms he carried a cardboard box of old LPs.

Clara explained who she was and what had happened in the supermarket. At the man's side, his mother kept muttering something that sounded like 'Bunny. Blow bunny,' and twice showed him her empty purse. Then she started to cry. Her son placed the box of records on the floor and put his arm around her. 'Hey, it's okay, Mum, it doesn't matter. You took the wrong purse, that was all. It could have happened to anyone. Now, why don't you sit down, and I'll make you a cup of tea?'

Helping her out of her coat, he hung it on a convenient coat-stand and settled her into a chocolate-brown leatherette sofa. Clara was struck by his kindness and patience and that he didn't seem at all embarrassed that his mother was crying in front of a stranger. He was well over six feet tall and struck Clara as very much the gentle giant. She put him somewhere in his mid-fifties. He was overweight, but his bulk seemed to emphasise his naturally warm-hearted manner.

'Would you excuse me for a minute?' he said to Clara, when the worst of the tears were over. 'I'll just go and put the kettle on for a brew.' In his absence, Clara joined his mother on the sofa. The woman reached out to Clara's arm, squeezed it as she had in the supermarket, and eventually produced, 'Bes-sie. Name . . . Bessie.'

'I'm pleased to meet you, Bessie. We forgot to introduce ourselves earlier, didn't we, what with all those rude people at the checkout? My name's Clara, and in the rocking chair is my son, Ned.'

The anxious expression gave way to a smile. 'Juggly poy. Juggly pies.'

'Juggly poy?' Clara repeated, hoping for enlightenment.

'She's saying he's a lovely boy, and has lovely eyes.'

The son was back. He set a mug of tea on a small reproduction sherry table beside his mother, even rustled up a coaster from somewhere.

'I'm Archie Merryman, by the way,' he said, holding out a large, strong hand to Clara, 'and I'm extremely grateful to you. My mother had a stroke not so long ago and the words don't always come out as they should.'

'So I understand. I had what I thought was a brilliant idea of getting her to write things down, only I didn't realise it would be so difficult for her.'

'The stroke did its worst down your right side, Mum, didn't it?' he said, turning to his mother to include her in the conversation.

In the silence that followed, Clara realised that the music had stopped, as had the creaking of the rocking chair. She looked to see where Ned was, and located him on the other side of the shop where he was inspecting a commode. 'What's this for, Mummy?' he asked, his voice echoing slightly.

'I'll tell you later.' She glanced back at the owner of the shop, who was smiling. 'Children,' she said, with a shrug, 'questions, questions, questions. And at the least appropriate moment.'

'Eshooks berryou,' Bessie said.

Clara looked to Archie for help.

He interpreted, without a second's hesitation: 'She said he looks like you.'

'Yes, poor lad, there's no disputing his pedigree. You don't mind him poking around, do you?'

'Of course not. It's good to see someone enjoying themselves. He's a grand little chap. Are you here visiting Deaconsbridge?'

'Is it that obvious we're interlopers? I thought we were blending in rather nicely.'

He laughed. 'I've been here more than twenty years, and I still stick out like a sore thumb. But where are my manners? I should have offered you a drink. What can I get you?'

'That's kind, but no thanks. I've promised the chip off the old block lunch in the Mermaid café.' Ned had moved from the commode to a coffee table where he'd found a *Star Wars* jigsaw. 'No, don't tip it out, Ned,' she called, seeing him ready to settle in for the afternoon – there were enough things here to keep even the most hyperactive child amused. She stood up to go. 'Goodbye, Bessie, it was lovely meeting you. You take care now, won't you?' Then to Archie Merryman, she said, 'I know it's a cheek, but would it be all right if I left our van outside your shop while we have something to eat? We won't be very long.'

'Sure. It's the least I can do for you, sweetheart. Enjoy your lunch.'

The bell tinkled merrily behind them as they left, and while they waited for the traffic to pass so that they could cross the road to go back to the market square, Clara thought how nice Archie Merryman was. 'A juggly man,' she said to herself, with a smile.

'It's beginning to feel like home, this place,' Clara said to Ned, when they were sitting at the table they had used yesterday and had been served by the same waitress, whose name was Shirley.

'Why couldn't that lady speak properly?' Ned asked, while they waited for their food.

She told him that Bessie Merryman had had a stroke, and tried to explain what that was without frightening Ned. 'It can happen when you're young, but usually when you get older.'

He thought about this, tracing a finger along the squares on the checked tablecloth. 'Will it happen to Nanna and Granda?' he said, when his finger reached the salt cellar and knocked it over.

'I hope not, but we never know what's round the corner for any of us. It's what life is all about.'

'Why was she crying?'

'Well, in the supermarket people weren't treating her very kindly. The man in the smart suit probably doesn't think about anyone but himself, and the young girl on the till was probably worrying about what she ought to wear that night to go out. To them, poor Bessie was a nuisance who they couldn't be bothered to understand or help. She knew that, and it was horribly embarrassing for her and made her very upset.'

'I didn't like that man.'

'Was that why you kept stepping on his foot?'

He looked at her coyly from beneath his long lashes.

'I thought so, you little rascal.'

The café was even busier today and it was a while before the waitress brought them their meal. She explained that it was always like this when the weather turned wet. 'It brings the walkers down from the hills and moors in search of something warm to stick their ribs together,' she said. 'It'll be crazy like this for some days.'

'I thought you said the weather was breaking at the weekend. What went wrong with the forecast?'

She wiped her hands on her red overall. 'I was only out by a couple of days. And any road, we have our own climate round here. We're a law unto ourselves.'

'It means that, like any true Deaconite, she makes it up as she goes along.'

The three turned to see who had spoken.

'Ah, and what would you know about the weather, Archie Merryman? Are those flowers for me by any chance?'

He gave her a wink. 'Another bunch, another time, Shirley. Mind if I join you for a couple of seconds? I won't keep you,' he said to Clara.

'No, no, of course not. Please, sit down. What's wrong?'

'Nothing. It's just that I forgot to pay you back for my

mother's shopping. And . . . and I also wanted to give you these, to say thank you for what you did.' He handed the flowers across the table.

Clara was touched. 'I don't know what to say except thank you. They're lovely.' She breathed in the heady scent of the purple freesias. 'Mm . . . wonderful. But there was no need for you to go to all this trouble.'

'I'll have to disagree with you on that point. And this is for you, Ned.' From a carrier-bag that Clara hadn't noticed until now, he pulled out the *Star Wars* jigsaw Ned had been looking at in the shop.

'Ooh, thank you,' he said, putting down his knife and fork with a clatter and kneeling up on his chair for a better look.

'This is very generous of you,' Clara said, 'but really—'

'No buts, sweetheart. Definitely no buts.' From his shirt pocket he retrieved a roll of money. 'Now, then, how much was my mother's shopping?'

'Glory be, do you always carry that amount of money round with you?'

'In my trade, cash is the best currency.'

'Well, you can put it back in your pocket. I don't need reimbursing.'

He frowned. 'That arrangement really doesn't suit me. I'm used to paying my whack.'

'It was hardly anything. I was just pleased I was there to help.'

He turned to Ned who, while tracing the outline of Luke Skywalker on the lid of the jigsaw box with a finger, was working on a long strand of spaghetti. His cheeks were sucked in hard and his lips were pasted with Bolognese sauce. 'Ned, you have a peach of a mother. You take good care of her, won't you?'

Clara laughed. 'Please, stop it, you're embarrassing him. To say nothing of what you're doing to me.'

'In that case, I'd better go.' He stood up abruptly.

Disappointed to see him leave so soon, she said, 'Have you left your mother on her own in the shop?'

'No, Samson's with her now. He got held up in traffic and didn't make it in time to fetch Mum from the supermarket as we'd arranged. I'm trying to give her as much independence as possible, but it's not easy. Anyway, enough of the moaning from me. Are you leaving Deaconsbridge today or will we be lucky enough to see you around town for a few days yet?'

'If I can find a suitable campsite nearby, there's every chance you might see us again. Our plans are fairly flexible.'

'We're going to see the Mermaid Cavern,' Ned piped up. 'And I've got a mermaid of my own. She lives in my pocket. Do you want to see her?'

'A mermaid in your pocket? Now, this I have to see.' He watched as Ned dug around inside his pockets. 'You know the cavern's not open yet, don't you?' he said to Clara.

'Yes, Shirley gave us the bad news yesterday.'

'Mummy,' Ned said, his voice wavering and his face crumpling, 'I can't find Mermy.' His lower lip wobbled. He got down from his chair, came round to Clara and buried his tomatoey face in her lap. 'I've lost Mermy,' he wailed.

Chapter Nineteen

Ned was inconsolable. He had only ever mislaid Mermy once before, during an overnight stay with Nanna and Granda when Clara was away on business. He was so distraught that his grandparents had ransacked the house, combed every square inch of the garden and turned the car inside out. When, in desperation, they emptied the kitchen bin they had found Mermy hiding inside a crushed tea-bag box. Nobody knew how she had got there, but her reappearance had instantly dried Ned's tears.

Clara knew now that if she was going to calm her son, she would have to convince him that, no matter what it took, she would find Mermy.

With most of the occupants of the crowded café looking sympathetically in their direction, Clara lifted Ned on to her lap. She took a paper napkin from the holder on the table and wiped his eyes. 'It's okay, Ned,' she soothed, 'we'll find her. Don't worry. She probably slipped out of your pocket in the supermarket.'

'Or she might be back at my shop,' Archie said, bending down so that he was eye to eye with Ned.

But Ned was far from consoled. 'Someone might have taken her,' he whimpered, his breath catching in shaky gulps. He buried his face in Clara's shoulder.

Shirley came over. 'You been upsetting the little boy with your ugly mug, Archie?' she asked.

Clara explained what had happened.

'Oh, dearie me,' Shirley said. 'Nothing for it but to retrace your steps. Where've you been today?'

Ned peeled himself away from Clara's shoulder. 'Mummy, I think I know where she is.'

'You do?'

He sniffed loudly. 'I left her at Mr Liberty's house.'

Clara didn't know whether to be relieved or disappointed. A return visit to Mermaid House and its splenetic owner – just how much fun could a girl cope with? 'Are you sure?'

Another messy sniff and a nod. 'I was playing with her at the table when you were talking to Mr Liberty.'

Clara vaguely remembered Ned inspecting Mermy with a magnifying-glass. 'And you haven't seen her since?' she clarified. 'Not in Winnie, perhaps?'

'I don't think so.'

'Well, that looks like it's settled,' Archie said. 'Where does this Mr Liberty live, by the way? Will you have far to go?'

'He lives in a castle,' Ned said, wiping his eyes with the backs of his hands. 'He has a tower and I've been up it. *And* he has a secret passageway.'

'This wouldn't be Mr Liberty of Mermaid House, Hollow Edge Moor, would it?' asked Shirley.

'You know him?' Clara said.

'Probably safe to say that most folk know of him,' Shirley answered. 'He comes in here every Friday lunchtime. None of the others,' she tilted her head in the direction of the kitchen, 'will serve him. I'm the only one thick-skinned enough. The man never has a civil thing to say for himself. If I was being polite I'd say he was a poor old fool who was losing his marbles. But if I was being honest, I'd say he was a disagreeable old crosspatch who ought to learn some manners.'

'You don't think he's just a lonely old man who's a touch eccentric?' Clara wondered why she felt the need to defend him.

'Try serving him in here when you're rushed off your feet and he's banging his spoon on the table to grab your attention.'

'She's a sweet, tolerant little thing, isn't she?' Archie said, when Shirley had moved on to clear another table.

'So what's your opinion of Mr Liberty?'

'If he's the same chap I ran into at the hospital the other day, I'd say he's a man of elusive charm and has a way to go in the tact and diplomacy stakes. What will you do? Go up to Hollow Edge Moor now and see if the little lad's toy is there, or would you like a hand checking out places closer to home first?'

Touched again by his thoughtfulness, Clara said, 'Ned seems pretty sure that he's left Mermy at Mermaid House, so we'll start our search there. If we draw a blank,' she added, lowering her voice, not wanting to dash Ned's hopes, 'we'll come back and have a look at the supermarket. Thanks for the offer of help, though.'

'I'll give the shop a good going-over as well, just in case. If I find it, I'll put it somewhere safe for you. Anyway, I'd better be getting back. Take care now. And thank you again for what you did for Bessie.'

It had stopped raining by the time they left the café and crossed the market square to where they had left Winnie. Through the window of Second Best, Clara could see Archie talking to an enormous young man with a pair of weight-lifter's shoulders. As she started the engine, they both turned. In response to Archie's wave, she waved back and pipped the horn.

'Right,' she said to Ned, 'fingers crossed that Mermy is where you think she is.' And fingers crossed, she thought, joining the flow of traffic, that Mr Liberty hasn't done something unspeakable to her. And there you go again, she told herself. She was badmouthing a man she scarcely knew. Perhaps she ought to stop and ask herself why he was such a misery? What had happened to him to make him so unlovable? Why had he lost his respect for and pleasure in the world around him? And why was he deliberately isolating himself from it and those who should have given him the most reward: his children?

Having experienced nothing but love and support from her own close-knit family, and been lucky enough to have such wonderful friends, Clara couldn't imagine what it would feel like to be so alone. As for cutting herself off from Ned, she might just as well consider lopping off a limb.

Before she conceived Ned, she had never been one of those naturally maternal women who go all gooey at the merest glimpse of a Mothercare catalogue. Not once had she been conscious of her biological clock ticking away its indubitable message that time waits for no woman who wants to start a family. Perhaps it was because she had always thought that she would get married before she had a child. And with her not being married, or in any hurry to be so, she had not felt the lack of a baby in her life.

But then she had met Todd and she began to think that marriage might be something she could entertain, maybe even children. Being in love had made her think and act quite differently. She had thrown caution to the wind and tripped headlong into a passionate affair with a man recently separated from his wife. If she had been at home, her friends and family would have told her she was mad to get involved with a man on the rebound. But she was not and she gave no thought to the consequences.

Todd Mason Angel was his name and he was as attractive as his name sounded. He was seven years older than her and had a smile that lit up his face and softened the lines around his mouth. He was from Wichita, Kansas, and had worked for Phoenix at their head-quarters in Wilmington since graduating from Harvard. He was ambitious and dedicated to his career, but he wasn't ruthless and hard-nosed as his position within the company might have implied. He was honest and up-front, and never hid the facts from her about his marriage, which had recently broken down, or the emotional tie he still felt to the woman he had been married to for nearly ten years, and who was the mother of the two daughters he adored. Clara had insisted they kept their affair secret at work because she didn't want anyone to accuse her of getting on by sleeping with someone so senior. He had gone along with this, but she had always felt that it was less out of respect to her than because he hoped that one day he would be reconciled with his wife. To put it bluntly, she had known all along that she was playing with fire and that she would have no one to blame but herself should he end their relationship.

Ironically, the day of reconciliation came twenty-four hours after Clara discovered that she was pregnant. She and Todd had arranged to go away for a long weekend, during which she planned to tell him her news.

On the day they were due to set off, he had come into her office an hour before lunch, closed the door behind him, and told her that Gayle had phoned him to say that she wanted to give their marriage another try. Though he had tried his best to let Clara down gently, and to conceal his happiness, the thud with which her heart had hit the floor had rocked her world and she had known she could never tell him she was pregnant. She had smiled bravely and said she wished him well, that if there was a chance of his marriage being put back together, he had to take it: he owed it to himself and his children.

'I'll never forget what we had, Clara,' he had said, rising from his chair, already wanting to get on with rebuilding his marriage. He added, 'I've only ever loved two women, and you're one of them. I just hope you don't feel that I've used you, because I haven't. I'm really not that kind of a man.'

With an airy wave of her hand, she had said, 'Go on, get out of here. You've a family to get back to.'

'No hard feelings, then?'

'You know us Brits, stiff upper lip right to the finishing line.'

He had leaned over her desk and kissed her forehead. 'I'm sorry, Clara. I wish we didn't have to end it like this.'

Another shrug. 'Hey, it was always going to have to end. We both knew that. And I'm really pleased about you and Gayle. Now, let me get on with some work.' She had wanted him gone from her office. A moment longer, and her resolve would have been shattered. Much better to stay in control and nurse a shattered heart that no one could see.

Some might say that she had behaved heroically, but she saw it differently. Such was her love for Todd that she knew she had to sacrifice her own happiness for his by letting him go.

She had spent the rest of that day going through the motions at work, until eventually she gave up and went home early, claiming she was feeling sick. It was true. She did feel nauseous. For the next two months, her morning sickness was so bad the weight fell off her. A month later she returned home.

Louise was the first person she told and, predictably, she was horrified. But no amount of questioning would make Clara reveal who the father was. She tried lying to preserve Todd's anonymity, but made a poor job of it. Louise said, 'Don't give me any of that "it was just a casual fling" business. I know better than anyone that you're not into one-night stands, Clara Costello. This man must have meant something to you, or why would you want to keep his child?' But Clara held firm. It was the one area in her friendship with Louise, and the rest of the gang, that remained a closed subject. Much as she loved Louise, Clara knew that she was a blabbermouth and would be sure to tell David, who would tell Guy, and before long, the whole of Phoenix Pharmaceuticals would know that Todd Mason Angel, the company's newly appointed finance director, was the father of Clara Costello's baby.

And every time Clara's mother said that Ned had a smile straight from the angels, she had no idea how close to the truth she was. Todd's could warm the coldest heart and Ned had inherited it.

Now, as she drove over the cattle grid to Mermaid House, Clara hoped that Ned's face would soon be its normal smiling self when he was reunited with his pride and joy.

Whether Mr Liberty would be smiling when he saw them again, was another matter altogether.

When Gabriel looked out of the kitchen window as he washed his hands at the sink and saw the camper-van drive through the archway, his face broke into a wide, sardonic smile. So she was back, was she? The insolent little shrew had a price, after all. Well, now they were in for some fun.

He dried his hands on the back of his trousers and went to meet them. 'Looks as if you can't keep away from me, Miss Costello,' he said, as she climbed down from the driver's seat. 'But I knew you'd reconsider, that it would come down to a simple act of bartering. So, what figure have you in mind?'

But his words went unanswered. Ned came barrelling up to him: 'Mr Liberty, have you got my mermaid? Is she in the kitchen where I left her on the table?'

And then he understood why they were back: not to help him but to help themselves.

'You'd better go and take a look,' he said to the boy. 'You know the way. But be careful not to touch or disturb anything of mine,' he called after Ned as the little boy shot inside the house.

Embarrassed at his mistake, and staring down at the cracked leather of his shoes, he said, 'It seems I've just made a colossal fool of myself, haven't I?' His voice was mute with despondency and his shoulders sagged.

Clara felt a pang of sadness for him. How hard he made life for himself, she thought. And what a contrast he was to Archie Merryman, who would go out of his way to help anyone. 'Perhaps only a mild fool of yourself,' she said softly. 'But tell me, just as a matter of interest, when was the last time you bought anybody flowers?'

He raised his one-eyed gaze. 'I beg your pardon?'

'It's a simple enough question. But what I'm really getting at is, when was the last time you made a spontaneous gesture of kindness to another person and felt good about it? Because if you did it more often, I'm sure you wouldn't be in the position you are now – bullying a stranger into helping you. If you were nicer, people would be queuing up with offers of help.'

'Are you saying that if I was nicer you would want to help me?'

'I was talking generally, about you being nice to your fellow man.'

'I'm not interested in talking generally. And as for my fellow man—'

'Don't split hairs.'

'Why not? You are.'

'Look, Mr Liberty, stop being so quarrelsome. Be more gracious and see where it gets you. For instance, instead of blackmailing me this morning by saying I owed you a favour, you should have just asked me politely if I would help you. As it was, you got my back up. I suspect that's what you do to people all the time, isn't it?'

'A man should be allowed to be himself,' he said stubbornly, drawing in his breath and pulling himself up to his full height.

'I couldn't agree more with you, but some common courtesy wouldn't go amiss.'

The sound of Ned's voice made them both turn. 'Mummy,' he cried, 'I've found Mermy. She was on the table just where I left her.' He came running towards them, and threw himself against Clara, who scooped him up and hugged him. You see, she wanted to say to Mr Liberty, it doesn't take much to be happy, does it? Then a more dangerous thought occurred to her. What effort, what *real* effort on her part, would it take to make Mr Liberty happy? Why had it been so simple earlier today to help Archie Merryman's mother in her hour of need but so difficult now to help this pugnacious old man? Okay, his demands were on a different scale, and he might not seem such a worthy cause, but who was she to judge? Here she was lecturing him on how to be more gracious, so why wasn't she leading by example?

Because she was on holiday! His problems were not hers.

But it would still be a holiday, she argued with herself. And Ned would enjoy himself just as much here as somewhere new. Besides, if she agreed to help him for a week, how big a hole in their schedule would that make? On the up-side, it would be a week of earning some money as well as landing themselves free lodging, and by then the Mermaid Cavern would be open. She thought of what Ron and Eileen had told her about their lifestyle, which they so enjoyed, about taking each day as it came, of rising to the myriad challenges that crossed their path and of always being the richer for having experienced them.

But it was a decision that couldn't be made in isolation. Still holding Ned, whose legs were wrapped tightly around her hips, she whispered in his ear, 'How do you feel about staying on here for a short while?'

'Will we still go to see the mermaid in the cave?' His lips tickled her ear.

'Of course.'

He nodded and smiled.

She lowered him to the ground. 'Mr Liberty, I'll do you a deal. I'll give you one week of my precious time, and in return you have to agree to certain conditions, the principal one being that you must promise me you will try to be less disagreeable, so that when Ned and I have gone, you will be enough of a human being to attract further offers of assistance. How does that sound?'

'Sounds to me as though it's a deal heavily weighted in your favour. What are the other conditions?'

She smiled archly. 'We'll sort those out as we go along. For now, though, I need to hook the van up to an electricity supply. For which, I'd like it made clear, you will not be charging me. I also need water.'

'Anything else?'

'Yes. I want an up-to-date copy of the *Yellow Pages*.'

'I'm not having any contract cleaners in. I told you that. You do the job, or no one does it.'

'It's a skip I'm after. My guess is you have a lifetime's rubbish lying about this place and ditching it will be the only way forward. Well, don't just stand there, let's be about our business.'

'I'm not going to regret this, am I?'

'Let's hope that neither of us does.'

Chapter Twenty

It was raining again as Jonah drove home from school, the light already fading. Other than a stack of essays to mark on the rise of the Nazi Party in the 1920s, he was looking forward to a quiet, uneventful evening. Supper and the pleasure of listening to the latest recording of Mahler's Symphony No. 5 was all he had in mind.

Despite the dreary weather, he was in a relaxed and happy mood. The day had been constructive and rewarding. With the exception of a couple of students, he was pleased with his GCSE students and had high hopes for them when they sat their exams next term. If he could keep them motivated, crank them up another gear, and make them believe that education was power, he reckoned he could get the best history results Dick High had had in years. Already a large number of his students were saying that they wanted to take the subject on into the sixth form and it was particularly gratifying to know that within his short time as head of the department, he had turned it round so dramatically. His predecessor had long since lost the plot: he'd grown tired of battling against cuts, damning league tables and hostile Ofsted recommendations. Worse than this, he had lost the will to cope with disaffected pupils who, once they knew they had the upper hand, could grind a vulnerable teacher into the ground faster than a pile-driver. Last autumn a group in year eleven had tried it on with Jonah during his first week. They had sat in the back row with their feet on the desks, their ties no more than a stubby two inches long. Passing round copies of *Loaded* and *FHM* they had pretended to ignore him as they shared with the rest of the class the details of the previous night's excitement on the estate where they lived. Modern world history had as much relevance to them as the FTSE index to their future giro cheques, or so they thought.

'Warfare,' Jonah had announced, slipping off his jacket and putting it on the back of his chair. 'Anyone up for it?'

Their attention caught, just for a second, he wrote on the white board 'No Man's Land', 'War of Attrition' and 'Going Over the Top'. He then asked for a volunteer, specifically from the back row, to come and draw a rough map of the estate he and his mates lived on.

'Don't be shy, ladies and gentlemen,' he said, his eyes resting on one lad in particular. His name was Jase O'Dowd and Jonah had heard nothing but bad reports of him since he had arrived at Dick High. Like a lot of the boys in the class, he wore his hair intimidatingly short, but with the most extraordinary gelled-up quiff at the front. He gazed insolently at Jonah, tucked a half-smoked cigarette behind his ear, and said, 'I thought this was a bleeding history lesson. Maps is for geography.'

The others urged him on. 'Go on, Jase,' they chorused. 'Show Sir where we live.'

'Yeah, and don't forget to make it look pretty. We don't wanna be shamed with Sir thinking we're not as lah-di-dah as him.'

Whistles and chants accompanied Jase as he lumbered to the front of the class. He snatched the marker pen out of Jonah's hand, and drew two large rectangles facing each other separated by a thin strip. With stabs and slashes of the pen on the whiteboard, he marked off little boxes within the two rectangles.

'For that extra-artistic touch, can you put arrows where you and your friends live, please?' Jonah asked. Just as he knew they would be, they were all congregated in the one rectangle. 'And who lives here?'

To the side of the other rectangle, Jase drew a skull and cross-bones and wrote underneath it, the Tossers.

'Okay, so tell me what this space between the two rectangles is.'

'It's a friggin' road, Sir – what d'yer think it was? *Durr!*'

'So, would I be right in thinking that when you're in the mood to give someone a good kicking, you have to cross it?'

Jase smirked. 'Yeah, got it in one. You're not as stupid as you look, Sir, are you?'

'Well, Jase, you'll be delighted to know that the tactics you use to exert your reign of terror on your neighbours are based on the same rules employed by the generals who devised trench warfare on the Western Front in 1915.' Taking the pen from him, Jonah drew a German flag over one rectangle and a Union Jack over the other, then an arrow from the words No Man's Land to the road Jase had drawn. 'Now, one more job for you, Jase. While I draw a slightly more detailed map of Belgium and northern France, can you rig up the TV and video for me, please?'

A loud cheer went up. 'What're we watching, Sir? *Hot Mammas Spank My—*'

'I'm afraid not, you'll have to save that for your role-play sessions in Drama. For now you're going to watch *Blackadder Goes Forth.*'

By the end of the lesson, he knew he had achieved what he'd set out to do: he'd got their attention. It was all the start he needed. Six months on, and a class of low achievers who had long been dubbed in the staffroom as tomorrow's social misfits could now make a reasonable fist of an essay and display an above-average interest in a subject they had previously dismissed – just as *they* had been unfairly dismissed.

Skirting round the centre of town, he swung the car into Church Brow and took the steep, cobbled road slowly. A row of cars was parked on the right-hand side, and as he drew near to his cottage, at the top of the narrow road next to the church, the easy-going evening he had planned evaporated. Outside his front door, in a flashy electric-blue Maserati, was his brother, Caspar.

What was *he* doing here?

Jonah parked alongside the cottage, gathered up his old leather briefcase from the back seat of his dilapidated Ford Escort and approached the immaculate sports car, the latest in an ever-changing range. This one, even at trade, must have set his brother back a small fortune: the numberplate alone – *Caspar 1* – had probably cost him more than Jonah's heap of mobile rust when it had been showroom new.

The only thing that Jonah and his brother had in common was their love of classical music, although Caspar's penchant for the pretentiously esoteric works of some latterday composers was where their commonality divided. It was a piece of this shrill, discordant music that Jonah could hear now as he tapped on the driver's window to attract his brother's attention. Caspar's head was resting against the smooth cream leather of the headrest and his eyes were closed as his fingers conducted an imaginary orchestra lined up along the dashboard.

The electric window slid down. 'You're getting wet, brother dear,' Caspar said, above the excruciating ting, ping and scrape.

'Could be something to do with the inclement weather. Are you coming in, or are you happy to stay out here showing off your new car to my neighbours?'

Caspar gave him a look of disdain. 'You mean these little shacks are occupied by real people? Heavens, whatever next?'

Jonah let them in. He shed his leather jacket and hung it up in the understairs cupboard, then took his brother through to the kitchen. He knew Caspar hated his house, that he found the old weaver's cottage cramped and claustrophobic. Caspar lived alone in a stark loft apartment in Manchester that was a temple of clean lines and minimalism. To Jonah's knowledge, he never entertained there, never encouraged visitors. The only time Jonah had been allowed in had been when Caspar wanted to show it off. He had come away feeling that whatever his brother had paid to live in such superficial splendour, it wasn't money well spent.

He watched his brother prowl uneasily round the tiny, low-ceilinged kitchen, his cold grey eyes seeking out the least offensive spot on which to stand. He was dressed in an expensive dark blue suit with a crisp white shirt, a red silk tie and black lace-up shoes. His fine hair was a light-brown version of Michael Heseltine's, and showed signs of grey just above the ears. The contrast between the two brothers could not have been greater. Jonah wore baggy corduroy trousers, a loose-fitting shirt with the odd splash of paint on the shoulder, and a tie he'd owned for more years than he cared to recall. His dark brown hair was thick and wavy, the opposite of Caspar's smooth well-cut locks. The kids at school often teased Jonah that his tousled mop made him look like David Ginola on a bad-hair day.

'I see you haven't got round to doing anything about the state of this kitchen,' Caspar remarked, still prowling and trying to avoid hitting his head on the pans hanging from one of the beams. He came to a stop in front of a bookcase crammed with paperbacks and CDs. Giving the handpainted cupboards a dismissive glance, he added, 'It really is the last distasteful word in folksy charm. You should gut it and start again. Maybe extend it into something worthwhile.'

'Actually, Caspar, this *is* done. Are you stopping long enough to warrant me offering you a drink?'

'Depends what you've got.'

'You'll have to be a lot more honey-tongued if you want anything better than instant coffee.'

'What do I have to do for a decent glass of Chablis? Fawn all over you?'

'No, go out and buy one. I don't have anything here of the ilk that would agree with your sensitive nose and palate.'

Caspar gave him a pitying look. 'Ha, ha, as droll as ever, I see.'

'I like to keep my hand in. One never knows when one's older brother is going to come calling and wreck one's evening.'

'You had plans? You do surprise me. A night of unbridled passion with a colleague from the staffroom? A lissom games mistress fresh out of college? Oh, do tell.'

Jonah turned his back on Caspar and reached for a bottle of Merlot from the wine rack. 'An evening of marking essays on the rise of the Nazi Party is what I had in mind,' he said. 'Just think, if you'd been around at the time as one of Hitler's right-hand men, he might have made a go of it.' He poured two glasses of wine and passed one to Caspar.

Caspar sniffed his suspiciously, then made a great play of picking out a rogue piece of cork. 'Not bad,' he said, giving the wine a swirl. He took a sip. 'Better than that acidic, enamel-stripping Sauvignon you gave me last time I was here. Argentinian, wasn't it?'

'Chilean.'

'Whatever.'

Did he have any idea how ridiculous he was, thought Jonah, standing here in his expensive suit, pretentiously appraising a bottle of plonk that had cost three pounds from the local supermarket? How could anyone become such a monumental prat and assume such an affected air of moneyed arrogance? Sadly, affecting the right air had always been of paramount importance to his brother. Having the right credentials, knowing the right people, owning the right car, it was all part of Caspar's carefully projected image. For what it was worth, Jonah suspected that Caspar had become a victim of his own arrogance: he didn't have any real friends, only hangers-on.

'What are you doing here, Caspar?' he asked. 'The phone not good enough for you, these days?'

Caspar shifted position. He went and tried out a space by the old Rayburn that Jonah had bought second-hand

and patiently restored. 'I've been sampling the heady delights of Deaconsbridge,' he said, 'in particular, Mainwaring's, the estate agent. It's just as I thought. It's the perfect time to sell Mermaid House. I spoke to Mainwaring, and he's of the opinion that by the end of the summer the property boom will be over. It's now or wait another year, maybe longer, until things pick up again.'

'Anything wrong in doing that?'

Caspar narrowed his grey eyes. 'I told you, Jonah, we need to move on this sooner rather than later. If we let the old man stay put, the house will slide into a total decline. It's bad enough as it is, but another year and God knows what the place will be like.'

'And how do you know what state the house is in now? When was the last time you paid Dad a visit?'

Caspar banged his glass down on the table between them, his cool imperious manner giving way to temper. 'That is hardly the point! Why do you always have to be so damn picky? Can't you just accept that I'm right? *God!* You always were a bloody pain in the backside. I should have known better than to come here and expect a civilised conversation with you!'

Jonah leaned against the sink, casually crossed one ankle over the other, and considered his brother's outburst. He was used to seeing Caspar flip, but this struck him as different. Usually he could keep up the act of supercilious prig for at least two glasses of wine before he launched into an attack. What was the urgency about selling Mermaid House? Had he, yet again, got himself into a financial mess? He decided to push. 'Seeing as you're in the area,' he said blandly, 'why not go and see Dad this evening? If it's money you're short of, he might find it in his heart to bung you a few quid.' He knew his remarks would incense Caspar, but he didn't care. If it got his brother out of his house, so much the better.

Predictably, Caspar rose to the bait. 'Who the hell said anything about me being short of money? That's an accusation I find vaguely absurd coming from someone who knows nothing about business.'

'It was a logical assumption. You've been on at me to go and see Dad and—'

'Yes, and I'd like to know why you haven't.'

'I've been busy. If you must know, I've arranged to see him tomorrow.'

This seemed to mollify Caspar and he reached for his glass again. 'Oh. Right. Good. Well, it's about time too. But mind you be firm with him. Don't give in to his bullying.'

The amusing irony of this instruction stayed with Jonah, long after Caspar had left. The essays dealt with, his supper coming along nicely, and Mahler well into his stride, Jonah reflected on his brother's unwelcome visit.

He's desperate, he concluded, stirring the pan of mushroom risotto, then adding more stock. He must be, to have forced himself to drink cheap plonk in a house he hated with a man he despised. Caspar's need for money must be greater than it had ever been, which might mean that he was even more determined than usual to get what he wanted.

It was a grim prospect.

Caspar's scheming skulduggery over the years would make humorous reading if there wasn't always some poor soul who had lost out to his ruthlessness. Lying, cheating and trampling over other people's feelings to get what he wanted – it all came quite naturally to Caspar. It was a sport for him.

The most breathtaking example of this had occurred two and a half years ago when Jonah had unwisely, and against his better judgement, decided to introduce Emily to his family. He had been putting it off for nearly six months, but now that they were planning to marry, it seemed only right that Val and his father should meet his future wife. Val had been forever trying to bring them together as a family, and had insisted on a full Liberty turn-out with everyone spending the weekend at Mermaid House. Damson was in her most recent post-divorce state and Caspar came with his latest girlfriend, a model of half his age with a fake tan, whom he ignored for the entire weekend. He was much more interested in Emily.

It was just what Jonah had been terrified of. Until then he had deliberately kept Emily away from Caspar; he had even told her why. She hadn't taken him seriously, though, and had said he was being paranoid: 'It's you I love. Why would I be remotely interested in your brother?'

But that evening during dinner, he had seen Caspar working his charm on Emily, and that she was flattered by his attention. And why wouldn't she be? He was good-looking, and when he wanted to be, he was erudite and witty. He was the perfect dinner-party guest, regaling Emily with stories of Jonah growing up, telling her what a great kid brother he had been, what hilarious and companionable larks they had had together.

'You make your childhood sound so idyllic,' Emily had said, 'like something out of *Swallows and Amazons*.'

Looking across the table with his steely-eyed gaze on Jonah, Caspar had said, 'She's right, isn't she, Jonah? We did have a glorious childhood.'

To have told the truth would have seemed churlish and petty, so he had said, 'It had its moments.'

Caspar had laughed. 'Just listen to him.' Then, 'But what I don't understand, Jonah, is why the long face? Anyone would think this was a wake and not a celebration of your forthcoming nuptials with this heavenly creature. For heaven's sake, cheer up.'

While they were getting into bed that night, Emily had said, 'Your brother was right, you did look miserable during dinner. Are you sure you haven't exaggerated the stories you've told me about him?'

'Why would I do that?'

'Because you're jealous of him.'

'*Jealous?* You have to be joking!' He had tried to laugh

off her accusation, but she had pursued the subject doggedly.

'You kept looking at him as though you hated him, Jonah. I've never seen you like that before. It's very worrying. You're showing me a side to you that I didn't know existed.'

All he could say was, 'You've never seen me in the bosom of my family before.' He had tried to make love to her, to reassure himself that her feelings for him hadn't changed. But it hadn't worked. He had been too anxious, too convinced of his own failings. Defeated, he had slept with his back to her.

The next day, after breakfast, Caspar had suggested they treated themselves to some fresh air by going for a walk. Val said she wanted to go to church and their father said he had more important things to do. Damson said she needed to be alone so that she could meditate and realign her aura, and Caspar's girlfriend, who was getting the message that she was history, pouted and said she didn't have any suitable footwear. But Emily had reacted as though she had just been invited to fly to Paris for lunch. 'What a wonderful idea, Caspar. You must have been reading my mind. A walk is exactly what I need to blow away the cobwebs.'

'Cobwebs, Emily? Don't tell me my brother doesn't take you out enough and he's allowed you to collect cobwebs.'

It was no kind of joke, yet Emily seemed to find it hysterically funny, and Jonah knew that the only thing being blown away was his chance of marrying Emily.

Caspar and Emily strode on ahead, leaving Jonah to plod along with the sulky model, who was wearing a pair of Val's boots as well as a borrowed waxed jacket.

'Is Caspar always like this?' she said, pausing for the umpteenth time to catch her breath as they climbed the gentlest of slopes – she might have been racehorse thin, but she had as much stamina as a soggy Ryvita.

'Always like what?'

'So rude. And why don't you stop what he's doing with your girlfriend? Or are you so stupid you haven't noticed?'

Oh, he'd noticed all right, and if the skinny, lettuce-nibbling girl hadn't stopped every few hundred yards, Caspar and Emily wouldn't have got so far ahead. Way off in the distance, and in the shelter of a rocky outcrop, he could see Caspar standing behind Emily, an arm over her left shoulder as he supposedly pointed out the landmarks to her – Kinder Scout, Cracken Edge and Chinley. Then he saw the hand stroke her windblown hair. When Emily turned to face him, her face tilted upwards so that he could kiss her, Jonah knew it was over.

Leaving Caspar's girlfriend to sort herself out, he took off back to Mermaid House. He packed his things and left without telling Val or his father what he was doing.

Another man – a real man, as his father would have been quick to say – would have confronted Caspar and beaten the living daylights out of him. But apart from that one incident at school, Jonah had never resorted to violence and preferred to keep it that way.

That evening, Emily called to tell him what he already knew, that their engagement was off. Riding high on the euphoria created by Caspar's attention, she told Jonah she hadn't realised until now how dull he was. She told him that she was moving in with Caspar, that she had never known anyone so amazing. 'It was love at first sight,' she went on. 'I hope you can understand that. He's literally swept me off my feet.'

But in less than a month, she discovered what it felt like to be swept aside. As was to be expected, Caspar had lost interest in her. She wrote to Jonah, apologising for what had happened, saying that she had been a fool, that she didn't know what had come over her. She even asked if there was any chance of them getting back together.

He never replied to her letter. What was there to say?

He had warned her that Caspar liked nothing better than to play games with other people's emotions.

There was no point in him asking why Caspar had done it. His answer, as it had been the first time he had taken a girlfriend from Jonah, would have been, 'Because I can, Jonah.' When the dust had finally settled, all he said on the matter was, 'She clearly wasn't in love with you, Jonah. If she had been, I wouldn't have been a temptation for her. Think of the episode as my having done you a favour. You're better off without her. No need to thank me.'

Now, as he tipped his mushroom risotto on to his plate, and poured himself another glass of wine, Jonah wondered if anything, or anyone, could shame Caspar into behaving like a decent human being.

Chapter Twenty-One

Archie had been too tired to face cooking supper that evening, so he had picked up fish and chips on the way home from the shop. He unwrapped the two parcels and tipped the contents on to the plates he had warmed under the grill, then put them on the table where Bessie was doing her best to butter some slices of white bread. Her movements were heartbreakingly slow and clumsy, and all at once he was reminded of past Christmases, when Bessie would cook the largest turkey they could afford and invite any neighbours who were on their own to share it with them. One Christmas morning, she had sent Archie out on his bike to round up Miss Glenys Watson, a retired music teacher, who was so proud she would rather sit on her own listening to the radio than admit she couldn't afford to celebrate Christmas. Nor did she want it known that, other than her ageing cat, she didn't have anyone to spend it with. 'Please, Miss Watson,' he had said, after knocking on her door, 'Mum says she needs your help. She wants us all to sing carols after lunch and you're the only one she knows who can play the piano without her getting a headache. Will you come?'

Miss Watson must have known what his mother was up to, but she never let on. She had accepted the invitation graciously, pulled on her hat and scarf, her gloves and coat, locked the door and walked alongside him as he pushed his bike. They had almost reached home, when she said, 'Do you play the piano, Archie?'

'Oh, no, Miss Watson. I'm not at all musical.'

'Perhaps it's time someone taught you. I could give you lessons after school.'

He had said he would like that very much, but he didn't think his mother could afford it. 'But you mustn't tell her I said that,' he had confided.

She had smiled and said, 'I'm sure we can find a way round that little problem.'

At ten years old, he didn't understand that he had just become a bridge between his mother's warm-hearted generosity and an old lady's pride. All he knew was that it was Christmas morning and a whole day of seeing his mother happy lay ahead of him. She liked nothing better than having people around her, especially those she thought she was helping. 'The world is full of sad and lonely people,' she would say to Archie, 'so it's down to the rest of us to put a smile on their faces.' One of her favourite games was to sit on a bus and see how many people she could make smile during their journey. The bigger the challenge, the more she enjoyed herself. 'See that poor old soul just getting on, the one in the tatty gabardine and the rucked-up face to match,' she whispered to him one day. 'Two peppermint humbugs says I can have her lips twitching by the time she gets off.' And, of course, she had, and with so little effort. 'It doesn't take much to spread a little happiness,' she always claimed.

The first Christmas Miss Watson spent with them was also the year his father had turned up unexpectedly on Boxing Day. They had heard nothing from him for years, then out of the blue there he was, sprawled on the settee, throwing peanuts into the air and catching them in his mouth, expecting to be fed before he strolled down to the pub to pick up where he had left off with his drinking cronies. In bed that night, Archie had heard his mother telling his dad that, for the sake of their son, if he was back, it had to be for ever or not at all. Archie had held his breath. He didn't want his father around: he knew it would make his mother unhappy, that it would mean more drunken, violent rages. There would be no more amusing bus rides together, no more cosy evenings by the fire while his mother read to him. His heart had crashed to a stop when he heard his father say, ''Course I'm back for good, Bess. What can I do to convince you I'm a reformed character? I'm gonna take the first job that comes along and prove to you I'm as good as my word.'

That first job never did come along and he lay on the settee smoking and drinking beer while Bessie worked at the bakery. He even suggested, since he was around to see to the boy – he always called Archie 'the boy' – that she ought to work more shifts because the extra money would come in handy.

Archie had never been able to understand why his mother, when she could be so strong – she was known as the rock of the neighbourhood – was so weak when it came to dealing with a husband who treated her so badly. Perhaps her feelings for him overruled common sense and allowed her to compromise where otherwise she would have held firm.

And wasn't that what he had done with Stella? Even when he had known she was having an affair, he had held on to the hope that she would once again feel for him what he still felt for her.

When he had met Stella, she had bowled him over: she was tall, elegant and knew how to dress to make the most of her long legs. How proud he had been to catch such a stunner. She could have had anyone, but she had settled for plain old Archie Merryman. 'It's because you're going to take me away from all this,' she would laugh, when he asked her why she loved him. 'All this' had been the noisy, robust family in which she had grown up. Archie had thought her parents, brothers and sisters were full of fun and knew how to enjoy themselves, but she said they embarrassed her, that they didn't aspire to anything. There was so much Stella wanted out of life, and that was one of the reasons he had started up his own business. Nobody in her family had done that: the men had all been employed at the local steel works in Sheffield, while the women had cleaned and had babies.

'Archie?'

He looked up from his plate, realising that his mother had been trying to talk to him. 'Sorry, Mum, what did you say?'

'Sad?'

He shook his head. 'No, just tired. It's been a long day.'

She forked up a chip with her good hand. 'Sorry.'

'What for?'

Her words came out in a long jumble, but eventually he disentangled them. 'I told you earlier, there's nothing to apologise for. It was great that you felt strong enough to go shopping, and it was a simple mistake you made, taking the wrong purse with you. It was only because you got flustered that your speech went all to cock. Remember what the therapist said? It's when you get upset that the words get clogged up inside your head.'

And if those people at the supermarket had been more understanding, she wouldn't have got into such a pickle, he thought, and stood up to put the kettle on. Thank heavens that young woman and her little lad had been on hand to help. He didn't like to think what would have happened if they hadn't been there. It broke his heart to think how distressed Bessie must have been at not being able to explain what was wrong with her.

Water was gushing over the top of the kettle and he turned off the tap as his sadness turned to anger. His mother had been treated as if she was batty, until a stranger had come to her aid. Not so long ago, Bessie had been as strong and capable as any of them.

His mother was still eating her fish and chips when he sat down again with their mugs of tea. She never had been one to rush her food, but now she took twice as long. He wasn't bothered. He didn't have anything else to do that evening and was happy to sit with her. He reached for the local paper and flicked through to the classifieds to make sure his regular house-clearance advert had gone in. The 'What's On' section caught his eye. It was years since he had been to the cinema – Stella could never sit still long enough to watch a film – and he was seized with the urge to go. 'What do you think to seeing a film at the weekend?' he asked his mother.

Without needing to disentangle her response, he could see that she approved of the idea. In the old days, going to the flicks had always been something of a treat for her. Clark Gable, Rex Harrison, Audrey Hepburn and Omar Sharif had provided her with a much-needed touch of glamour and excitement.

He folded the newspaper and laid it flat on the table so that they could make their choice. Today's movie stars might not be as glamorous as they'd been in Bessie's day, but they might give her a chance to escape the unfairness of her life for a little while.

Chapter Twenty-Two

Their breakfast eaten and everything tidied away, Clara was keen to make a start on Mermaid House. Her only concern was keeping Ned occupied while she got down to work. Though he could amuse himself for quite long spells, she wasn't sure how soon it would be before he was bored. And, like any parent, she knew that boredom might lead him into danger or mischief.

The answer was to keep him busy, and having already glimpsed some of the ground-floor rooms, she felt there was enough relatively safe-looking junk lying about the place with which Ned could play for hours.

Mr Liberty had offered to give them a tour of the house last night, but Clara had declined. Instead she and Ned had driven back into Deaconsbridge and made a return visit to the supermarket where, with a sub from Mr Liberty's wallet, she had bought several carrier bags of cleaning products, rubber gloves, cloths, tins of polish, air-fresheners, and several rolls of bin-bags.

She never did anything by halves, and having made a deal with the old man she was determined to see it through. There had been no danger of her waking this morning and regretting her decision. That was not her style. She had always been the same, even as a child – so her mother had frequently told her. If she had wanted to come top in French she went all out to achieve it. Conversely, if she didn't want to do something, like finish a piece of embroidery for a needlework lesson, there was no making her do it.

Louise and the gang had always teased her that she saw life so clearly. 'Nothing ever muddies the water of your vision and thinking, does it?' Guy had said to her one day at work, after she had dealt with a dispute on the packing line between two women who claimed they couldn't work together. And she supposed he was right. She wished, though, that he hadn't made it sound like a criticism.

Much to her amusement, and Ned's delight, Mr Liberty had joined them for supper in the van last night. 'No steak and claret this evening?' she had asked, when he had accepted her offer of grilled lamb chops and easy-cook noodles. His gruff reply had got lost somewhere in his rattling throat and confirmed what she had suspected: that it was a while since he had cooked himself such a meal. If ever.

Over supper he had brought up the subject of how much she expected to be paid. 'I'm nobody's fool,' he said, pointing his knife at her. 'You're not going to con me.'

'And I'm no mug, either, so you'd better brace yourself. This won't be cheap. If you want the best – me – you're going to have to pay accordingly. I assume you have sufficient funds.'

'That's damned impertinent!'

'Just making sure we both know where we stand. For all I know, you might be a penniless old codger who's down to his last shirt button.'

'I resent the implications of that last remark. I'll have you know that I'm not an old codger and, what's more, I'd bet my last shirt button that I'm better off than you.'

'I'm glad to hear it. So why haven't you got around to throwing a wad of cash at some other idiot to do the job for you? Or are you just mean with your money?'

'I've never been mean with money, just prudent. If I was a Scrooge, do you think I'd be providing you with free electricity and water while you're here? And I didn't replace my last cleaner because I saw no reason to put up with another light-fingered woman helping herself to my belongings.'

'So what changed your thinking?'

'That blasted doctor started poking his nose in.' He went on to tell her how he had burnt his arm and reluctantly paid a visit to the surgery. 'I knew I was in trouble the moment that doctor started asking me how I was coping after my wife's death. Fine, I told him. But they don't want to believe that, do they? And then he turned up here and I'd got something in my eye and he blackmailed me into going to the hospital to have it checked.'

'Blackmailed you?'

'It was what happened, true as I'm sitting here. He threatened me with Social Services if I didn't get into the car with him there and then to go to the hospital.'

Clara had wanted to laugh at the doctor's audacity, but refrained, and again she felt sorry for Mr Liberty. He was clearly terrified that he was going to have his independence taken from him. It convinced her that she was doing the right thing in helping him and that her main objective was to make him see the sense in getting regular help once she had gone. If he didn't, he would be back to square one within weeks with the threat of Social Services still hanging over him. If indeed they were a real threat.

She had smiled at the thought of the days ahead when she would be giving Mr Liberty a taste of his own medicine – a generous dose of bullying.

Carrying the bags of cleaning things, Clara let Ned run on ahead to knock at the door. It was opened almost immediately, as if her employer had been waiting for her to arrive and clock on. 'Is your eye better now, Mr Liberty?' asked Ned. The patch had gone and without it he looked a little less fierce.

'It's as good as new,' he replied starchily, and stood back to let them in. 'Where will you start? The kitchen?'

'We'll start first with improving labour relations,' Clara said. '*You* will bid *us* a good morning, then *you* will offer to put the kettle on. And while *you* are making *us* some coffee, I will survey the wreckage and assess the extent of the damage.' She handed him one of the carrier bags.

'There's a jar of instant in there, along with a packet of biscuits which will add to your onerous duties as tea and coffee-maker.'

He grunted and led them through to the kitchen.

'Ever thought of buying a dishwasher?' she asked, when she saw once more the piles of dirty crockery still untouched on the draining-board.

'A waste of money just for one person.'

'There are some reasonably priced ones on the market, small machines designed for people on their own.'

'Reasonably priced,' he repeated. 'I don't need things to be *reasonably priced*. I told you, I have money.'

'Well, try spending it! Or are you hell bent on leaving it to the family of whom you've spoken so highly?'

He snorted, then reached for a pen and a used envelope. He handed them to Clara. 'Make a list of all the things you think I need.'

'I'll put "new heart" at the top of it, shall I?'

Her first job was to clear the decks by shifting most of the junk on to either the table or the floor so that she could get at the work surfaces to scrub them clean. Once she had done the sink, she tackled the washing-up, then moved on to the cupboards, which were chock full of things she doubted were ever used. At the back of one she found a two-year-old bag of self-raising flour crawling with weevils. Cringing, she threw it into a bin-bag, along with a dozen pots of out-of-date Shippam's paste, two opened jars of pickled cabbage, another of horseradish sauce that was a dubious shade of yellow, and a tin of rock-hard Oxo cubes. It wasn't difficult to work out what the poor man was eating on a daily basis: the stockpiled cans of pilchards and tomato soup were a dead give-away.

With Ned helping to empty the lower cupboards of old pans, buckled lids, steamers and fish kettles, the like and size of which Clara had never seen before, she called Mr Liberty. He appeared in the doorway and looked aghast at the mess. 'You've made it worse,' he said, as he surveyed the scene.

'Oh, bring on the gratitude, why don't you?' said Clara sharply. 'Now, listen, I need you to decide what you want to keep.'

He shrugged. 'You decide for me.'

She took him at his word, and deciding that it was highly unlikely that he would be cooking a whole salmon in the near future, or steaming enough vegetables to feed an army marching on its stomach, or making vats of jam and marmalade, she put together a modest collection of pans for his basic cooking needs and instructed Ned to take them over to the sink. He could mess around with soapy water under the guise of washing them.

'What will you do with the others?' asked Mr Liberty.

'Some are fit for the dustbin – which reminds me, that skip I ordered should be here around lunchtime – but the better ones could go to a charity shop. Do you have such a thing in Deaconsbridge?'

'There was one, but when the rents on all the shops in the market square went up, it closed.'

'It seems a shame to ditch them when they're in pretty good nick. Put the kettle on again and I'll have a think.'

With a bucket of hot water dosed liberally with disinfectant, she started to clean inside the cupboards. There was something satisfying about bringing order to chaos, and though she would never admit it to Mr Liberty, she was enjoying herself. By the end of the day she would have the pleasure of knowing that she had personally conquered this grubby wreck of a kitchen. She would have it shipshape and Bristol fashion, or her name wasn't Miss Clara Costello.

Calling herself by her full name made her think about the formal way in which she and Mr Liberty referred to each other. It amused her, and if she wasn't mistaken, it amused him.

Behind her, she could hear Ned talking to Mr Liberty as he spooned coffee into mugs. He was chattering nineteen to the dozen, just like he did at home with Granda, and she realised that as long as Ned had someone to talk to, he would not get bored.

When Mr Liberty handed her a mug of coffee, and she indicated for him to place it on the floor next to her, he said, 'You've been working like a Trojan ever since you got here, why don't you take a break?'

She wrung out the cloth into the bucket and doffed an imaginary cap. 'Gawd bless you, guv'nor, for taking pity on a humble scullery-maid. I'm touched.'

She was even more touched when he held out a hand and helped her to her feet. 'Bring your coffee with you, and I'll give you a guided tour,' he said gruffly.

She tugged off her rubber gloves and, Ned following with the biscuits, Mr Liberty led the way. He stood for a moment in the vast hall, as though getting his bearings – it was a large house, after all.

'Do we need a map?' she asked, good-humouredly.

He threw her a disparaging look. 'Suggesting I'm so far gone I don't know how to get round my own home?'

'Not at all. I was merely implying you live in an above-average-sized house. How many bedrooms are there?'

'Just the ten.'

'Just the ten,' she repeated. 'A bit cramped, then?'

'I know the way,' said Ned, and sped off down the gloomy length of the hall, whose panelled walls were decorated with an incongruous mixture of African masks, a barometer, a large, heavily worked brass plate that looked Indian, and a moth-eaten bear's head. Everything was covered with a peppering of dust, including the ornate gilt frame of a massive oil painting depicting a Highland stag.

'Where's he taking us?' she asked. 'And do you mind?'

'To the library, and it doesn't look as if I have much choice.'

When they caught up with Ned, he was swinging open a heavy door. 'Slow down, partner,' Clara told him. 'And you've had enough biscuits.'

She took the packet and handed it to Mr Liberty. For the first time she noticed his arthritic hands, how swollen and clenched they were. Slipping a thumbnail under the top biscuit, she raised it so that he could easily get at it. He caught her eye. 'Don't go putting yourself out on my account,' he muttered.

'Don't flatter yourself.'

The library felt cold and damp, but was comparatively tidy, in as much as it contained a few basic items of furniture: two leather armchairs either side of a stone fireplace, another two in the bay window either side of a large rent table, a footstool, and a lampstand with a dented shade and an unravelling gold fringe. Two of the walls were lined from floor to ceiling with books. But it was difficult to make out anything in any detail: the curtains were drawn, keeping out the light – and holding in the musty smell of age and soot. Clara guessed that the chimney needed sweeping. 'Do you always have the curtains like this?'

'Not always.' He went over to the window and gave the burgundy velvet drapes a hefty tug. 'But it stops the light destroying the books.'

So the man had a weak spot. Books above humans, by the looks of things.

She changed her mind when light flooded the room and she saw the painting above the fireplace. 'Who's that?' she asked.

Mr Liberty stood beside her. 'My first wife, Anastasia.'

Clara stared at the young woman, her confident gaze and the beguiling gentleness in her expression. The eyes were full of warmth and humour and were as dark as her thickly tousled hair, which was painted so luxuriantly and with such depth that Clara could almost feel the silky curls in her fingers. 'Is it a good likeness?' she asked softly.

He took a noisy swallow of his coffee. 'Yes.'

'She was very beautiful.'

'And I suppose you're wondering what she saw in someone like me?'

Before she could deny or refute this, Ned called, 'Mummy, come over here. This is where the secret passage is.'

She went to where he was standing. She stared at the rows of leatherbound books that he was pointing to. 'Are you sure?' she asked, playing along with him. 'All I can see is a load of old books.'

His eyes danced with excitement as he glanced at Mr Liberty. 'Shall I show her?' he asked, his hand already reaching to the shelf where, presumably, the handle was hidden.

Mr Liberty sucked in his breath, then let it out slowly with a doubtful shake of his head. 'I don't know, lad. Can she keep a secret? We don't want her blabbing all over the county, do we?'

Ned's face grew solemn. 'Mummy, you won't tell anyone, will you? Do you promise?'

'Hand on heart,' she said, as seriously as she could. 'I promise not to tell a living soul about Mr Liberty's back passage.'

Mr Liberty snorted. But the hint of a smile on his face didn't escape Clara.

Despite the misty rain, the views from the tower were spectacular. They would be even better if the windows were clean, thought Clara, wondering if there would be sufficient time in the coming week to add the tower to her agenda. But was there any point? Dr Singh was hardly going to rate his patient's ability to stand on his own two feet according to whether this extraordinary piece of whimsical architecture was spick and span. Stick to the essentials, she told herself.

'When was the house built?' she asked.

'In 1851. John Temple, a local quarry owner, had it built for him and his family. He called it Temple House, but when his son inherited it, and later discovered an underground cavern in the area with its dubious rock formation, the whole ridiculous mermaid saga was set in motion. As a consequence, and to plump up the son's ego, the house was renamed.'

'You sound like you don't approve.'

'I don't approve of scams.'

'What's a scam?' asked Ned.

Not wanting Ned's anticipation spoiled, Clara gave Mr Liberty a warning look. To her grateful surprise, he said, 'Nothing you need worry about, young man.'

'Any particular reason why the secret passageway was built?' asked Clara. 'The age of the house precludes priest-holes, and the geography's certainly wrong for smuggling.'

'No real reason as far as I'm aware, other than that John Temple wanted something none of his neighbours had. Now, if you've seen enough, shall we get on?'

He took them down the creaking narrow staircase, along the dark corridor and back into the library. From there he showed them the rest of the ground floor: the dining and drawing rooms that, like the library, both smelt of soot, the gun room, where Clara had no wish to linger, and the laundry room, which was a glory-hole with bells on. Piles of yellowing newspapers and boxes of empty whisky bottles littered the stone-flagged floor, with dirty clothes, towels and bed-linen. Mr Liberty kicked at the heap of washing. 'Machine's not working,' he muttered, embarrassed. He picked up a wooden clothes horse and set it against one of the damp-spotted walls.

'Do you know what's wrong with it?' She bent down to investigate.

'Haven't a clue. It's too modern and fancy for me. Jonah bought it last year and it's been nothing but a damned waste of money. It's supposed to dry as well as wash. All it does is bang about a lot.'

'I'll take a look at it later,' she said, 'though presumably it's still within its guarantee.'

He looked at her scornfully. 'You can mend a washing-machine?'

'Sure. So long as it's not the electronics, they're usually

straightforward enough. Sounds like the drum belt may have worked itself loose.'

'Mummy can mend all sorts of things,' Ned said, helping himself to an empty whisky bottle and unscrewing the lid. He pulled a face when he held it to his nose. 'Pooh!'

'Is that right?' Mr Liberty said, taking the bottle from him and replacing the lid.

'I don't like things to get the better of me,' she responded.

'Or people, I should imagine.'

'How astute of you. Now, then, shall I get back to work, or will you show us the rest of the house?'

The tour continued upstairs, and mercifully the mess didn't get any worse. As far as she could see, the damage was relatively superficial, but it was the scale that was so awesome. That, and the poignancy of some of the bedrooms.

'This was my second wife's room . . . It was where she died.' Mr Liberty unlocked the door and let them in. It was strange the way he said it, and prompted Clara to ask how many wives he had had.

'Just the two. And don't look at me as though I was careless with them.'

It was a long oblong room with a view over the garden and the moors beyond. 'Val loved to look across to Kinder Scout,' he said, moving to the window, 'which is why she chose this room. We never shared . . .' He cleared his throat. 'We didn't have that kind of relationship.'

Clara would have liked to pursue this tantalising confidence, but wisely held back. Instead, she said, 'What did she die of? Ned, don't touch!'

They both looked at Ned, who had settled himself on a stool in front of a dressing-table. Set out before him was a dusty array of scent atomisers, pots and tubes of cream, lipsticks, powder compacts, necklaces, and bottles of nail varnish. At his mother's words his hands, which had been hovering over a pair of reading glasses, dropped to his sides.

'It was heart trouble,' Mr Liberty said, joining Ned. He picked up the glasses and slipped them inside a tapestry case. 'I should have got rid of this lot, but I couldn't bring myself to do it. Makes me look like a sentimental old fool, doesn't it?'

Without answering him, she said, 'Would you like me to sort it out for you?'

'There's clothes too.' He indicated two large mahogany wardrobes and a matching pair of chests of drawers.

'Just let me know what you want to keep, and I'll bag it up for you . . . if that's what you'd like.'

Next he showed her the rooms that had belonged to his children. It was at this point, standing in what had been his daughter's room, that Clara realised it was what Mr Liberty didn't say, coupled with the emptiness of some of the rooms in this huge house, that revealed most about him. She realised, too, that she hadn't seen a single photograph of any of his children. Other than the portrait of the first Mrs Liberty, and the second wife's belongings, there was no record of anyone else having lived here. She thought of her parents' modest little semi-detached house and the rogues' gallery of pictures they had of her and Michael growing up, with treasured photographs of Ned and their latest grandchild. As a teenager she had been mortified at the number of photos around the house recording her transition from gummy baby to spotty adolescent. But by the time her graduation photo adorned the wall of the dining room, along with Michael's, she had come to terms with her parents' pride, and knew that when the time came she would probably do exactly the same.

Which she had. From his birth, Ned's likeness had been framed many times over. When she had been clearing the house ready for the young couple who would be renting it, she had spent hours removing them, wrapping them and storing them in a box to go in the attic. Ned had been captured in every conceivable pose: smiling, frowning, chewing, laughing, crawling, clapping, sitting, walking, even sleeping.

Caspar, Damson and Jonah's bedrooms were shabby and bare. Each contained an uncovered wooden-framed bed, a rug, a few pieces of functional furniture and a series of ghostly marks on the walls where once there had been shelves and pictures. It struck Clara that someone had gone to a lot of trouble to strip these rooms. It seemed such a callous act. Vindictive. Almost a threat.

But as Mr Liberty went on to show them the rest of the bedrooms, which were piled high with trunks and huge ugly pieces of furniture, with faded wallpaper coming away from the walls, she began to think it was no wonder he was so miserable. If she had to live in this mausoleum, she too would turn into a crabby old devil. Suddenly she felt angry with his children. How could they have left him to rot here? Okay, he clearly wasn't an easy man, but why hadn't they persisted and won him over? Because it was easier to turn their backs and forget him. They were a bunch of idle, pathetic cowards and they ought to be ashamed of themselves.

This thought was still with her when Mr Liberty showed her his bedroom. It was almost thirty feet long with a spectacular view over the garden and the moors beyond. She made a mental note to deal with the curtains, which were lying on the floor.

When he made a surprising offer to take Ned off her hands and play a game with him, she returned to the kitchen with renewed vigour and determination. She switched on the radio, moved the dial to Classic FM and pulled on her rubber gloves. Her plan now was to tackle at least one room a day, so that by the end of the week, a minimum of seven would have been scrubbed and polished, which would go some way to restoring the house to what it had been.

She turned her attention to the Aga and hoped it wasn't

a lost cause. If she could get that running smoothly, it would make all the difference to the dreary atmosphere in the kitchen.

Chapter Twenty-Three

Gabriel passed Ned the pack of playing cards and told him to shuffle them.

'I'm not very good at that,' Ned said, kneeling up on the chair and taking the pack uncertainly in his small hands.

'I'm sure you'll make a better job of it than I would.'

As he jumbled the grubby cards, Ned said, 'Why are your fingers so funny, Mr Liberty? They're all knobbly and crooked.'

'That's because I'm the crooked old man who lives in the crooked old house.'

'No, you're not. And your house isn't crooked at all. What are we going to play?'

'What can you play?'

'Um . . . Pairs. But we usually use picture cards. Nanna gave them to me for my birthday.'

'Well, let's try it with these. Have you finished messing them up yet?'

'I think so. Shall I spread them out for us?'

'Be my guest.'

Leaning across the dusty table, placing the cards face down, Ned said, 'That's what Granda always says to me.'

'Uh?'

'If I ask him if I can play outside, he says, "Be my guest."'

'I'm surprised Granda ever gets a word in edgeways with you around. Don't you ever stop talking?'

'Nanna and Granda are in Australia,' Ned carried on. 'Granda sometimes calls me his little pumpernickel. I have a baby cousin now. I've seen pictures of him on the

Internet. Do you think Nanna and Granda will see any kangaroos? Kangaroos are funny. They go *boing, boing, boing.*'

Just as Gabriel was despairing of ever keeping up with such a butterfly brain, the child got down from his seat and gave an impromptu demonstration of how he thought a kangaroo would bounce around the library of Mermaid House: ankles together, elbows tucked in and hands sticking out in front of him.

'And you'll go *boing* in a moment if you don't get back into your chair. I thought we were playing Pairs.'

Gabriel watched the boy climb up into the leather armchair and resume setting out the cards. At least he wasn't cheeky and constantly running about the place, smashing into the furniture. He had an enquiring nature, and Gabriel approved of that. His spitfire of a mother was doing a good job of bringing him up. Just as she was doing a good job of sorting out the kitchen. He was still surprised that she had changed her mind about helping him. Perhaps, after all, the money had swayed her.

But she didn't seem the sort to be strapped for cash. People like her – quick-witted, intelligent, well-spoken and confident – didn't usually struggle to make ends meet. They knew where they were going; they had a goal and went for it. They weren't drifters who sponged off others in the hope of handouts. Which brought him right back to where he had started: why the dickens was she mucking out his kitchen?

He hoped it hadn't been an act of charity. Charity was for those too weak to help themselves. That wasn't him. And it never would be.

He caught the sound of music coming from the kitchen – blast the woman, she'd gone and fiddled with his radio – and his gaze moved from the boy to Anastasia's portrait above the fireplace.

She was very beautiful, had been Miss Costello's words earlier, but they didn't cover half of what Anastasia had meant to him.

Her inner strength, humour, and dazzling candour had attracted him to her when they had first met at a mutual friend's wedding. Compared to his contemporaries he had left marriage relatively late. He claimed it was because he was so busy, but until Anastasia he had never met a woman with whom he had wanted to spend more than a night, let alone the rest of his life. She had changed that as soon as he had taken his seat beside her at the back of the church. During the excessively long sermon on the sanctity of marriage, delivered by a vicar who plainly liked nothing better than a captive audience, she had leaned into him and whispered, 'I know one is supposed to be awfully generous in these moments but, goodness, don't you just want to heckle the man down from the pulpit so that we can get on and enjoy ourselves at the reception, which, hopefully, will be a lot more jolly?'

He had smiled and agreed.

'I can't tell you how tempted I was a few moments ago to leap to my feet and say I had a just cause and impediment as to why the marriage shouldn't be taking place,' she had added, her wide-brimmed hat knocking his head as she leaned closer to him.

'What is it?' he had asked, amused.

'That I know they'll split up within the year. I can't think of a more unsuited couple.'

When they were outside the church, watching the ill-fated bride and groom pose for the photographer, she said, 'Do you think anyone would object if I removed my hat?'

He had wanted to say that if anyone did, he would personally knock them to the ground. He had watched her take it off, remove several pins and let an autumnal rustle of curly brown hair fall around her shoulders: it enhanced her long, slender neck and made her even more alluring. 'I don't think you should bother with hats. You look perfect without one,' he said.

She had given him a brilliant smile. Not one of those brittle, glued-on social smiles, but a flash of sunny brightness. 'Do you really think so?' she said. 'Between you and me, I paid a ridiculous amount of money for that one, and all to disguise my unfashionable hair. Every other woman here, including the bride, is dyed blonde like Grace Kelly. Had you noticed?'

Truth was, he hadn't noticed a single woman until he had sat next to her.

'I went all the way to London for that hat. It seems a shame to let it go to waste,' she said.

There was no vanity in her, just a mild touch of irony. It was something he soon came to love. She was at her best when she was being entirely herself.

'Have you seen Grace Kelly's latest film, *The Country Girl*?' she asked. 'For such a natural beauty, she was surprisingly good as a plain girl.'

'No. I don't go to the cinema. I don't have time.'

'What *do* you have time for?'

'Work mostly. Sorry if that sounds dull.'

'You need someone to change that for you.'

He stared at her to see if she was mocking him, but she wasn't. Her smile was genuine and he knew in his heart that there was no guile or cunning in her. He didn't know her name or where she lived, but suddenly he wanted to know everything about her. More importantly, he wanted to know that he would see her again. He said, 'What are you doing when this tortuous shindig is over?'

Confident brown eyes as dark as her hair had gazed at him, and he had momentarily lost his nerve. Why would this dazzling young beauty be remotely interested in a man whose friends described him as a confirmed, gone-to-seed bachelor?

'Having dinner with you, I hope,' was her answer.

A year later, in 1956, her prediction that their mutual friends' marriage would end in separation was proved right. They heard the news two days before their own wedding, and it prompted him to say, 'Do you know any just cause or impediment why our marriage should not go ahead?'

'None whatsoever. We are the best suited couple I know.'

She had been right. They had been the best of companions, the best of lovers. She was reassuringly self-sufficient, which suited him: being so busy with work and travelling as extensively as he did, he had needed to know that she wouldn't be lonely without him, or unable to cope with the running of such a large house on her own. Too often he had seen marriages collapse because one half of the couple relied too much upon the other. He and Anastasia relished being independent spirits, but the welcome he received when he came home after a long trip away never left him in any doubt that his wife loved him as passionately as he loved her.

Still staring at the portrait above the fireplace, he sensed that, in many ways, Miss Costello was from the same mould as Anastasia. She was a confident young woman who would glide through life on the strength of her own determination. She was just the kind of person to take everything in her stride and make the most of it. Anastasia had never made a drama out of anything that went wrong – not even when the tower had been struck by lightning while he had been in Canada. No doubt about it, they were two of a kind, and perhaps that was why he had felt compelled to seek Miss Costello's help. He had known instinctively that because she saw things so simply, she would be able to cut through the chaos of Mermaid House so that he could take control again.

But while he could appreciate her many strengths, he realised that he knew little about her. What did she do when she wasn't roaming the countryside in a camper-van with her young son? Where did she and the boy live? *How* did they live? Where was the boy's father? Was he her husband? And why had he himself made the assumption that she wasn't married? He tried to picture her left hand to see if he could recall a ring. He couldn't, but observation had never been his strong suit.

He knew he shouldn't do it, but with his curiosity fully

aroused, and with the means to satisfy it sitting opposite him, he saw no reason not to ask a few questions.

'Finished!' Ned said, sitting back in the large chair and admiring his handiwork. The circular table was now a patchwork of blue and green tartan. 'Shall I go first?'

'As Granda would say, be my guest.'

A short while later, when Ned's pile of successfully matched cards was greater than his own, Gabriel said, 'You're not bad at this. You sure you didn't look at the cards before you put them down?'

'No!' Ned's voice rang with indignation. 'I just have a better memory than you.'

'Depends what one uses one's memory for. I can remember things very clearly a long time ago—'

'But not where the Queen of Hearts is!' Gabriel turned over the wrong card and Ned claimed the pair. 'I'm beating you, aren't I?'

'Do you play this a lot at home with your mother?'

'I do now. But not when we were at home. Mummy was too busy then.'

'Oh? Busy with what?'

'Work. She had a very important job. She told lots of people what to do.'

Gabriel caught the past tense – *had* a very important job. Redundancy, eh? Well, there was a lot of it about.

'She gave up her job to be with me,' Ned said, with unashamed pride. He claimed another pair of cards. 'She said she wanted to give me an adventure I wouldn't forget.'

'And here you are playing cards with an old man who can't remember where the nine of clubs is . . . Aha, got it.'

'You're getting better, Mr Liberty. But I'm still winning.'

'So who looked after you when your mother was busy telling people what to do?'

'Nanna and Granda. And I went to nursery too. Nanna and Granda are in Australia.'

'You said. Do you miss them?'

He nodded. 'Yes. But not so much now.'

'Why's that?'

'Because I see Mummy all the time now.'

'And you prefer that, do you?'

'Ooh, yes. I wish it could be like this for ever and ever. I wish I never had to go to school.'

'But you'll have to go home some day, won't you?'

'I suppose so.'

'And your mother will have to go back to bossing people about. I can see she'd be good at that.'

'She's not bossy with me.'

'She isn't? You sure?'

'She loves me.'

When he heard the boy express himself so simply and honestly Gabriel was jolted by something he didn't understand. It was a faint stirring of an emotion that was buried deep. There was a squeal from across the table.

'Look! I've found the Jokers.'

'And what about your father?' Gabriel ventured, after he had watched Ned rapidly unearth another series of pairs. There was hardly anything left on the table now: the child's memory was extraordinary. 'You never speak of him.' As soon as the words were out, he regretted them. The boy, normally so bright and open, looked confused, as though he didn't understand the question or, perhaps, didn't know how to answer it. Gabriel suddenly felt horribly unworthy. Supposing his father was dead?

'There's lunch on offer if anyone's interested,' said a stiff voice.

It was the boy's mother and Gabriel reddened with shame. *Damn!* How long had she been standing there? And just how much had she heard?

His guilt was multiplied many times over when he stood in the kitchen and saw the transformation.

The surfaces were all cleared and scrubbed to a high sheen and the cupboard doors were so shiny that reflections bounced off them. The floor was no longer sticky underfoot, the windows looked as if the glass had been removed, and the cobwebs that had been hanging from the ceiling like last year's Christmas decorations were gone. There was no sign of grease or burnt-on stains on the cooker, the fridge door looked as if it had been given a coat of white gloss paint, the rubbish that had covered the table had vanished, and lunch had been set for three. There was a white embroidered tablecloth he didn't recognise, and in the centre of the plates of sandwiches and glasses of orange juice, there was a small vase containing some purple flowers. He could just about discern their delicate scent above the more powerful odour of cleaning fluids.

It was as if he had walked into someone else's kitchen. He wouldn't have thought that just a few hours could have wrought such a change. 'I don't know what to say,' he murmured. A lump was firmly wedged in his throat. The more he looked, the more he was staggered.

'"Thank you" would be a start.'

He could hear in her voice just how very cross she was with him.

'Ned, do you want to go to the loo before we eat?' she said, in a more kindly tone. 'It's down by the laundry room, where Mr Liberty keeps his empty bottles. Be sure to wash your hands. I've put a clean towel in there.'

Gabriel walked awkwardly over to the Aga, which had also been given a clean and a polish. He ran his hand over the smooth green enamel and caught a distorted view of a bulbous-nosed face in the shiny chrome of the hot-plate cover. 'Miss Costello, I'm truly amazed at what you've done. Thank you very much.'

She gave him a steely glance and turned off the radio, which she had moved from the top of the fridge to the window-sill. 'And if you want me to stick to our agreement I'll thank you not to interrogate my son. Got that?'

He hung his head. It was a long time since he had felt so ashamed. 'I'm sorry,' he mumbled.

'At least have the decency to look at me when you're apologising.'

'I'm sorry,' he repeated, more clearly this time and looking straight at her. 'Shouldn't have done that to the little lad. Not on at all. Not my business.'

'Good,' she said briskly. 'Should you feel the disreputable need to play the part of grand inquisitor, please just ask *me* what you want to know. Okay?'

'Agreed.' Contrite. Meek. These were strange feelings to him, but that was exactly what he felt. That and the need to put things right with another person, whom he'd clearly upset. But how?

What could he do to make her think better of him? And when was the last time he had ever been concerned with what anyone thought of him?

Chapter Twenty-Four

Still beside herself with barely controlled fury over Mr Liberty's scurrilous behaviour, Clara was putting the surge of energy to good use. After lunch, and after she had instructed him – rather curtly – to wash up the plates, cutlery and glasses, she took the grimy curtains she had earlier unhooked from the kitchen windows and took them outside into the courtyard. She wanted to get the worst of the dust and sticky cobwebs off before washing them. The fine misty rain had stopped, and as she shook the curtains her anger began to subside. 'Just let him try a stunt like that once more,' she muttered, 'and I'll be out of here faster than . . . well, faster than anything he's ever seen move!'

Marching through to the laundry room, she threw the curtains on to the floor. Then, with the contents of the toolbox she had fetched from Winnie, she started to take the washing-machine apart.

To her satisfaction, her diagnosis was correct. Fortunately nothing was damaged and in no time at all she had it in working order. Not only that, but she soon had two loads of washing pegged on a line she had rigged up in the courtyard. While a third load was sloshing around inside the machine, she went outside to catch her breath. The sun was making a valiant effort to shine now, and while she stood in the courtyard, watching the clothes and curtains billow in the light breeze, the skip arrived.

'Sorry I'm late,' the man said, when he had lowered it into position and she was signing the form confirming its delivery, 'but it's been one of them days.'

'Tell me about it,' she said, with feeling.

Ned and Mr Liberty came to investigate just as the man was driving away. 'You don't do anything by half, do you, Miss Costello?' Mr Liberty said, when he had surveyed the scene – a large yellow skip and a line of his freshly laundered clothes, including some items he would perhaps rather not have had on show quite so visibly.

'Not if I can help it,' she said. 'Aren't you going to thank me for mending your washing-machine?'

'I was just about to. But why aren't you using its dryer?'

'No need – not when we can dry your unmentionables for free. Looks to me as if you could do with investing in some new ones.'

He scowled in embarrassment.

Enjoying his discomfort, she said, 'Now then, as you're both here you can help me ditch some of the rubbish I've collected. First to go will be those boxes of bottles from the laundry room.'

Under her directions, they worked steadily for the next hour and a half, until Mr Liberty suggested he made some tea. 'Got to keep the workers happy,' he said, and sloped off.

The moment Jonah had driven through the school gates that morning and the exhaust had dropped off on to the tarmac, he knew that it was going to be one of those days.

Now it was three o'clock and he was accompanying Jase O'Dowd to the doctor's surgery in Deaconsbridge. He had been in the staff room, drinking a cup of coffee while standing over the temperamental photocopier and thinking about year eleven's parents' evening next week, when Larry Wilson, the design-technology teacher, poked his unwashed head of grey hair round the door and asked if anyone would mind taking O'Dowd to the vet's to be put down. 'The bloody idiot's tried to chisel off a finger,' he grumbled, when Jonah agreed to forgo his hour of free time. 'If I've told him once not to muck around in my lessons, I've told him till I'm blue in the face. Serve the time-wasting blighter right if he's done himself some serious harm.'

Jonah found Jase waiting outside the secretary's office, and while he looked his normal cocky self as he leaned against the wall, kicking it idly, his face was as white as the notices on the board behind him. He raised his temporarily bandaged hand at Jonah. 'I'm gonna sue,' he said. 'It's not safe making them chisels so friggin' sharp. I'm gonna get the best lawyer Legal Aid can give me.'

'A cracking idea, but first things first. Let's get you stitched up, shall we?'

Exhaustless, they roared unceremoniously through the school gates, through the town and into the surgery car park, where Jonah pulled on the handbrake, switched off the engine and said, 'I'm not doing much for your street cred, am I, Jase?'

'Could've been worse. Could've been old Ma Wilson bringing me here.'

'I was referring to my car, not the status and quality of one of my colleagues.'

'Yeah, but you agree with me all the same, don't you? He's a right poxy old woman.'

Jonah kept his expression unreadable. 'I couldn't possibly comment.'

They reported to the receptionist, then took a seat in the empty waiting room. Jonah said, 'By the way, Mr Wilson did contact your parents, didn't he?'

'Nah, I told him there was no point.'

Jonah sighed. 'Jase, school has to let them know. You know that as well as I do. We have to do things by the rule book or that hot-shot Legal Aid lawyer of yours will be down on us like a ton of bricks.'

His face set, Jase said, 'Leave it, Sir.' Then, 'How long do you think it will take for this to get better?'

Jonah looked at Jase's bandaged hand. 'Depending on how badly cut it is, a week or two. Why? Worried it might get in the way of your love life?' He knew from corridor and playground gossip that, since last Christmas,

Jase was devoting less time to fighting on the estate where he lived and more to Heidi Conners, an anxious girl who was painfully thin – Jonah thought she might be anorexic.

Jase's face coloured, all the way to his sharp-curled quiff. He got to his feet and went over to a table where there was a pile of pamphlets on family planning. 'Friggin' hell, Sir, you ain't 'alf got a filthy mind! I was thinking of my exams next term and whether or not I'd be able to write.'

Suitably put in his place, and mildly surprised, Jonah apologised. 'I expect it'll be fine by then.' He knew that Jase could now put together a history essay that covered enough salient points to get him a C grade, possibly even a B with a bit more attention to detail and the wind blowing in the right direction, but as to his other GCSE subjects, he wasn't so sure. Occasionally he heard mutterings in the staff room that Jase O'Dowd was nothing but a load of trouble and Jonah was annoyed that the youngster could be so easily written off.

'Sir?'

'Yes?'

'What d'yer think my chances are of getting a job when I leave in the summer?'

'Do you have something in mind?'

Jase gave him a withering look. 'I thought with the qualifications I'm likely to get I'd start off with something easy – investment banker, summat like that.'

Jonah ignored the sarcasm. 'You don't think you might want to stay on in the sixth form, then?'

'What? *Me?* Have you flipped or what?'

'Heidi's staying on, isn't she?'

Another flush rose to Jase's face. 'Yeah, well, it's okay for her, she's got brains.'

'And so have you, Jase. You're just a bit more selective about how you use yours. I think you should consider it.'

He came and sat down again. He chewed at a grubby thumbnail. 'No point in considering it. It's too late.'

'Says who?'

'Old Ma Wilson for one.'

Jonah mentally cursed Larry Wilson, remembering now that he was Jase's form teacher. What hope was there for this disillusioned sixteen-year-old boy if the person who was supposed to be offering support and guidance was consigning him to the burgeoning number of disenfranchised young people the length and breadth of the country?

A shrill bell announced that whoever would be attending to Jase was ready to see them. Looking at his watch and seeing that they had only been waiting a short while, Jonah was glad that Dick High's policy was to use the local surgery in Deaconsbridge rather than the hospital.

Expecting a nurse to stitch up Jase's finger, Jonah was surprised to be greeted by a slightly built man, who introduced himself as Dr Singh.

'I've heard of educational cutbacks,' the doctor said, unravelling the bandage from Jase's hand and focusing his attention on his patient, 'but removal of a pupil's finger is going a step too far in my opinion. Ah, there we are, and what an impressive attempt has been made to slice through this fine finger. And what a lot of blood you have to spare.'

It was at this point that Jase's eyes rolled back and he fainted.

Jonah caught the boy before he slid off the chair and helped the doctor resettle him. Then, at his instruction, he went over to the small sink in the corner of the room and filled a paper cup with cold water.

Conscious again, Jase took the cup from Jonah, but without meeting his eyes. Jonah knew that he was embarrassed by what had happened and would have liked to reassure him that nobody would hear of it from his lips, but the doctor was gesturing for him to get out of the way.

'Now, Mr O'Dowd, to avoid a repeat performance, I suggest you avert your eyes while I tidy you up.' While Jase studied a poster that advocated a healthy diet of fruit and vegetables, the doctor completed his task with speed and efficiency. His small-talk never once dried up as the needle dipped and rose, and a layer of gauze and a finger bandage were expertly applied. 'I see from your notes that you're up to date with your injections, which means you'll be spared the ignominy of a tetanus jab, so it's not all bad today, is it? Now, tell me, is school as awful as I remember it? Are your teachers, present company excluded, of course, as sadistic as they were in my day?'

Jase shrugged. 'Some of them are, but Mr Liberty's okay.'

Standing at the sink now and ripping off his surgical gloves, the doctor looked at Jonah. 'Either the young man is terrified of you, or you have a loyal and devoted fan.'

'He's terrified of me,' Jonah smiled. 'Terrified I'll do a better job of chopping off a finger next time.'

Coming back to his desk, the doctor paused. 'Forgive my inquisitiveness, but are you by any chance related to Mr Gabriel Liberty of Mermaid House?'

Surprised at the question, Jonah confirmed that Gabriel Liberty was his father.

The doctor sat down and rearranged his sleeves. 'Well, how extraordinary. And isn't life strange? Suddenly the world is full of Libertys. They are crawling out of the woodwork, so to speak.' He laughed at his own joke.

'I'm sorry, Dr Singh, I'm not with you.'

'Forgive me again, please. But in one week I meet first your father, then your sister, and now you.'

'You've met my sister?' It was news to Jonah that Damson was in Deaconsbridge. What had brought her here? Then he remembered Caspar. Of course, the two of them were planning a pincer move on their father.

'Oh, yes,' Dr Singh said. 'I met her yesterday, your nephew too. They're staying with your father, didn't you know?'

Jonah gaped. Nephew? Good grief, Damson had had a baby!

*

There was no point in going back to Dick High – school had finished twenty minutes ago. Jonah dropped off Jase at home, and headed back towards town and the supermarket, as he usually did at this time on a Friday afternoon. Next he went to Church Cottage where he left his own shopping, then drove on to Mermaid House, still unable to get his head round the idea that Damson was not only staying with their father but was a parent herself. He hadn't seen her since Val's funeral, but he couldn't imagine she had changed in the interim to the extent that she was now a doting mother.

The light was fading when Clara remembered to bring in the washing. It was dry enough to be ironed, so she folded it neatly into the pitiful excuse for a laundry basket, thinking that if she wasn't too tired, she might tackle it later that evening. She was just adding the last of Mr Liberty's threadbare underpants to the pile when she heard an almighty racket. The throaty rumble grew louder and nearer. Someone's car was in need of a new exhaust.

She went inside the house to find Mr Liberty, to warn him that he had a caller. It was probably Dr Singh again. And if it was, she needed to know if Mr Liberty wanted her to keep her head down, or to be a visible presence in the guise of helpful daughter.

Interrupting a rumbustious game of Snap in the library, she told Mr Liberty he had a visitor. Like her, he assumed it was Dr Singh. Instantly every inch of him was bristling, ready for battle. She followed a few steps behind him, but stayed out of sight when they reached the kitchen. Peeping round the doorframe, she saw that they had leaped to the wrong conclusion. Standing beside the table, and with several plastic bags at his feet, was a tall man in a leather jacket. His collar-length hair was thick and wavy and, as he stared round the kitchen in obvious amazement, his profile and stance reminded Clara of a Renaissance painting.

'Good God, Jonah, what are you doing here?'

He turned. 'It's Friday, Dad, the day I always go shopping for you, and the day we agreed I'd come and see you. What's been going on here? It looks fantastic. Has Damson done this?' He plonked the bags on the table, carefully avoiding the vase of flowers.

Mr Liberty looked incredulous. 'Damson?' He snorted. 'Damson be damned!'

Having sized up the situation, that this was the youngest of her employer's uncaring darlings made flesh, Clara decided to leave them to it. She turned to join Ned, who was still in the library, but a commanding voice bellowed, 'Oh no you don't, Miss Costello. You come right back here and take the credit for all your hard work.'

She stepped into the kitchen. 'I'm in no need of credit,' she said briskly, making her tone hostile. Irrationally she wanted this casual-looking Renaissance man to know that she disapproved of him. That she despised him for being too weak to take his father by the frayed scruff of his neck and whip him into shape.

'Miss Costello and I have what one might call an arrangement, Jonah,' Mr Liberty explained, a wry smile twisting his mouth. 'For an exorbitant sum of money, she is staying with me for the week to do my bidding.'

'What your father is trying to say, in his clumsy way,' Clara said sharply, 'is that I'm here to tidy up Mermaid House.' She gave them both an accusing look. 'And since you're clearly about to settle in for a family bonding session, Ned and I will be off.'

Mr Liberty guffawed loudly.

But his son continued to stare, confused. 'Could someone please explain exactly what's going on here?' he said. 'And where's Damson?'

'Hell's bells, what makes you think she's here?'

'I was told she was. Apparently I have a nephew, who I'm curious to meet.'

Clara exchanged glances with Mr Liberty. She said, 'Have you been talking to a certain Dr Singh?'

'Yes, this afternoon. I was at the surgery with a pupil and he told me—'

'That your sister was staying here,' interrupted Mr Liberty. He smiled triumphantly at Clara. 'Didn't I say we'd taken him in? Hah! We reeled in the poor stupid fool good and proper! What a team we make.'

But Clara wasn't so triumphant. 'Hang on a moment. Before you start ringing the bells of victory, hadn't you better check with your son that he didn't dispute the matter and blow your little scam out of the water?'

Liberty Junior held up his hands. 'Whatever scam it is that you've got going here, I'm not guilty of trying to spoil it.'

His father needed convincing. 'You sure about that?' His tone implied he might reach for a shotgun if the answer wasn't to his liking.

'I played my part beautifully, dumb schmuck, right to the end.'

'Now why doesn't that surprise me?' muttered Clara.

Even by her standards the remark sounded more caustic than she had intended, and Liberty Junior frowned at her. He started to unpack the bags of shopping, and said to his father, 'I'm sorry to run the risk of repeating myself and appearing doubly foolish, but would it be too much to ask you why you've gone to the trouble of duping Dr Singh into believing that you have a daughter staying with you?'

'I would have thought that was obvious.'

'Please, indulge me.'

A short while later, the shopping put away, a pot of tea made and explanations given, Jonah watched his father leave the kitchen to fetch Miss Costello's son. Standing in front of the Aga, and running his fingers over the shiny surfaces, he was overwhelmed by the shame this acerbic one-woman dream-team had made him feel. He wanted to thank her for what she had done, and for what she was prepared to go on doing for the rest of the week, but he was mortified that a stranger had walked into his father's life and achieved what no member of his own family could do. Or, more precisely, what none of them had even tried to do.

Behind him he could hear her opening a packet of biscuits he had brought. He turned and watched her tip the chocolate chip cookies on to a plate to form a perfect spiral. He wondered if things always turned out so well for her. 'This must seem strange to you,' he said. 'From the outside looking in, it must appear as though we, his children, don't care.' He hoped she wouldn't judge him too harshly.

She gazed at him severely. Astutely. Assessingly. 'You probably *don't* care. Not enough, anyway.'

'That's not fair,' he said, defensively.

She crumpled the empty packet into a tight ball and put it into the swing bin. 'Okay, then,' she said. 'I'll be generous and say you've simply got used to the chaos and squalor in which your father has been living and turned a blind eye to it.'

'Are you always so blunt?'

'Yes.'

'Then that's probably what my father likes about you. Few people ever gain his approval. And just because one is related to a person, it doesn't mean you understand each other. Or even get on.'

She surveyed him steadily, her eyes cool and measuring. Unnerved, he turned away.

As unlikely as it was, Jonah had never seen his father talk to a child before, and intrigued, he watched him with Miss Costello's young son, Ned. He was a sweet-faced boy, whose expression ran the gamut from solemn to bright as if at the flick of a switch. He was immensely confident, not at all shy, and seemed extraordinarily comfortable with Gabriel, whom Jonah would have expected to terrify the child senseless. He had a shiny cap of dark brown hair, the same colour as his mother's, intensely dark, alert eyes and an engaging smile. Jonah had no way of knowing if his mother had passed this on to him, too, because he had yet to see her smile. But from the disapproving glances she flung at him, Jonah was getting the message that she despised him for not doing more to help his father.

Though Jonah was more used to teenagers, he had to admit that, for four years old, Ned was remarkably well behaved, never once spilling his drink or dropping crumbs. The nearest he got to making a *faux pas* was when he had told his mother with his mouth full that Mr Liberty was going to teach him to play draughts tomorrow morning. 'He says I can be white and go first. He's shown me the board, it's very old.'

'Mr Liberty won't teach you anything if you spray everyone with biscuit crumbs, Ned,' his mother reprimanded him gently. 'Finish what's in your mouth, then talk to us.'

His lips tightly sealed now, he was chewing extra fast, his miniature eyebrows rising up and down. He swallowed hard and continued excitedly, 'But he says I might not be clever enough to play draughts because I'm so young. Do you think I'm clever enough to play, Mummy?' Suddenly he looked grave, his eyes wide.

'You're as clever as you need to be, Ned,' she said reassuringly. 'No more, no less.'

'Another of your inscrutable replies, Miss Costello. Bravo. Do you lie awake in bed at night practising them when you can't get to sleep?'

'Not at all, Mr Liberty. I'm naturally inscrutable. Moreover, I never have trouble sleeping. I put it down to having a guilt-free mind.'

As he got up to add more hot water to the teapot, Jonah felt strangely isolated. There was a level of light-hearted repartee going on between this woman and his father that seemed designed to exclude him. It was as if he had walked in on the middle of something – which, in a way, he had. Oddly, he felt as though he was playing gooseberry to their extraordinary double act of sparky lovebirds.

He stared out across the darkening courtyard to where the yellow skip stood and, beyond, to where Miss Costello's camper-van was parked. Lifting the kettle, he poured freshly boiled water into the pot and wondered what was really going on here. Who was this confident, efficient woman who could sit so at ease at his father's table playing verbal pit-pat with him? And why did their obvious rapport rankle so much with him? Why did it make him feel even more of a failure than he usually did at Mermaid House? It was the same every visit, as if the bricks and mortar contained a magnetic force that made him revert to the anxious boy he had once been.

Hearing his father laughing behind him – and not the usual scornful barked-out guffaw he was more used to but full-throated good cheer – an ugly thought occurred to him: he was jealous. Jealous that this stranger with her sharp, no-nonsense way of talking, who had probably never suffered a moment's doubt, could make his father happy and he could not.

Suddenly he felt a flash of searing pain. He hadn't been concentrating on what he was doing and had poured boiling water over his hand. Stifling a yelp of pain, he moved to the sink and shoved his fist under the cold tap.

'Here, let me see.' It was the efficient Miss Costello.

'It's nothing,' he said, but he allowed her to inspect his hand.

'Keep it under the tap while I go and fetch my first-aid kit,' she instructed.

While he watched her through the window as she hurried across the courtyard, his father joined him at the sink. 'You wouldn't be attention-seeking, would you, boy?'

And you wouldn't be making a fool of yourself over a pretty young girl, would you? Jonah wanted to retort.

Within minutes she was back and showing him a tube

of cream. Slightly out of breath, she said, 'It will sting at first, but then it will feel quite cool.'

'What is it?' he asked, turning off the tap and reaching for a clean handkerchief from his trouser pocket to dry his hand.

'A homeopathic remedy for burns. Works every time. Now remember, I said it would sting at first—'

'*Ouch!*' He pulled away his hand.

'You're worse than a baby. Honestly, men, you're all the same. Merest hint of pain and you go pathetically weak-kneed.'

'Whereas you brave women lap it up and ask for more.'

'No, we simply grin and bear it.'

He forced a grin and held out his hand again. 'Go on, then. I'll bear the agony just to prove to you that I'm no coward. I'm sure inflicting pain on a mere man will give you great pleasure.'

She smiled unexpectedly and for the first time he registered that there was more to her than the prim, judgemental woman he had thought her. 'Sorry to disappoint you,' she said, 'but I get my kicks in a much more satisfying way. There, that's it. And not one tear shed. Give yourself a pat on the back.'

'I would if I had any feeling left in my hand.'

'You have two hands, Mr Liberty Junior, or is the glass always half empty for you rather than half full?'

Before he could answer, she was screwing the top back on the tube of cream and had turned to his father. 'I think Ned and I have earned ourselves the rest of the day off. Eight o'clock suit you tomorrow morning? I want to finish sorting out the laundry room. Then I'll make a start on getting the dining room into apple-pie order.'

He grunted. 'Eight o'clock? Working part-time already, are you? Thought you were too good to be true.'

'And you're too full of sweetness. Come on, Ned. Time for some supper and our own more congenial company.'

Suppressing a yawn, Ned climbed down from his chair.

'Goodnight, Mr Liberty,' he said. 'You will teach me that game in the morning, won't you?'

'A promise is a promise, young man. Now be off with you before you fall asleep and I have to carry you across the courtyard to your bed.'

Both Jonah and his father saw them to the back door and watched them go. When a soft light glowed from the windows of the camper-van, giving it a warm, cosy look, Gabriel shut the door, led the way back into the kitchen and said, 'Right, then, what was it you wanted to talk to me about?'

Remembering why he was here, Jonah suddenly felt every inch the coward that only moments ago he had denied.

Chapter Twenty-Five

It didn't matter how many times Jonah replayed the scene at Mermaid House, or how often he tried to convince himself that he was overreacting, he knew that last night he had been judged by the snappish Miss Costello and, worse, that he had been found wanting.

It was Saturday morning, and he was lying in bed, trying to enjoy the slow, potentially relaxing start to the day. But it wasn't working. His enjoyment levels were at an all-time low. He laced his hands behind his head and stared up at the ceiling. His mood took a further nose-dive when he noticed that the indigo-blue paint he had applied earlier that week looked patchy in the bright sunlight shining through the uncurtained window.

No doubt that would never happen to Miss Costello. Anything she painted would be perfect.

Irritated that she had come into his thoughts again, and that he was forced to refer to her so formally – as though she were an old-fashioned school-marm – he reminded himself that what she didn't know, and could never understand, was that there were other dimensions to the truth about his family. A whole kaleidoscope of dimensions that no outsider could appreciate. But far from making him feel better, this added to his guilt. He was making excuses for himself.

He closed his eyes, then opened them again, hoping he had imagined the flaw in the paintwork. No, he hadn't. Haphazard criss-crosses were clearly visible. It was an infuriating mess. Why hadn't he noticed it before? And why hadn't he done something about his father instead of leaving him to turn to a stranger?

Frustrated with going round in this same futile circle, which kept dumping him where he had started, he launched himself out of bed. He went to the window and gazed down at the long stretch of garden at the back of the house, which he was in the process of taming. It ran parallel to the churchyard and fell away to merge with the landscape of gently rolling hills. At the bottom of the garden there was a tangle of brambles, which for years had got the better of a beautiful old rose that must once have reigned supreme. Against the wall of the brick-built shed there was a forsythia that had also taken more than its fair share of space, and that, too, needed his attention. He had always thought it was just the kind of space in which Val would have liked to potter. The garden at Mermaid House had never lent itself to a quiet afternoon's pottering. It was too big, much too wild and exposed for anything tender to flourish in it.

Normally the view from his bedroom window cheered him: the lush green pastureland had a pleasantly soothing effect. But this morning his mood was still clouded by the severity of Miss Costello's words and the reproachful way in which she had treated him. There had been something unnervingly proprietorial in her manner towards his father. He had wanted to explore this with Gabriel after she and her son had left them alone last night, but there had been no opportunity to steer the conversation in that direction, not without annoying his father. He had soon sensed that the proprietorial thing went both ways. Gabriel hadn't been prepared to divulge any information about her. Or maybe he hadn't anything to divulge. Certainly he didn't seem to know much about Miss Costello.

'What does it matter where she's from?' he had said, in response to Jonah's probing. 'She's on holiday with her son and doing some work for me. What more do I, or *you*, need to know about her?'

'But I still don't understand why you wanted to play a practical joke on Dr Singh.'

'And frankly, Jonah, I don't understand why you're suddenly paying me so much attention. Do I interfere in anything you do? No. I leave you to get on and cock up your own life, just as you told me to do when you walked out on me.'

Those words reminded Jonah too poignantly of the scene in the library when his father had struck him, so he had changed the subject and suggested that he cook them supper. But Gabriel had turned the offer down flat. 'I'm quite capable of getting my own supper. Why don't you stop wasting our time and get to the point as to why you've come here?'

Which he did, but only when his father was searching the cupboards for a bottle of whisky, banging doors and muttering, 'Where the hell did that infernal girl put it?'

'Dad, have you thought that maybe it might be a good time to think about selling Mermaid House?'

The last of the cupboard doors crashed shut and his father turned round, a bottle of single malt in hand. He banged it down on the table, spun off the top, poured himself a large measure and, without saying anything, raised it to his lips. He took a long gulp. 'And why would I want to do that?' he asked finally.

'Because you might be more comfortable in something smaller, easier to manage.'

Gabriel topped up his glass. 'How small were you thinking? Coffin size?'

'Don't be ridiculous, Dad.'

'That's rich! You don't think *you're* being ridiculous by coming here and suggesting I change my lifestyle to suit your conscience?'

'It's got nothing to do with my conscience.'

'No? Then perhaps it's more to do with lining your pockets. Caspar and Damson's bottomless pockets as well, no doubt. Have they bullied you into coming here tonight to convince the old duffer that it's in everybody's best interests for him to sell the house so they can get their hands on the loot?'

'Of course not!'

He gave a contemptuous snort. 'You never did have any talent for lying, Jonah. Unlike your brother. So what's the line he's taking? Death duties? Am I expected to sell my home and make a gift of the proceeds to my beloved children in the hope that I would live long enough for there to be no heavy tax penalties to pay? A happy-ever-after scenario for everyone . . . except me.'

'Whatever Caspar may or may not have in mind, you don't have to go along with it.'

He snorted again. 'What's this? Rebellion in the ranks?'

'Look, Dad, you might get some kind of vicarious thrill from pitching me against Caspar, but the truth is, I've come here tonight to suggest that it might be in *your* interest to think about moving to a house that would be more convenient for you to live in. No one else should come into the equation. What's more, what you chose to do with the proceeds of Mermaid House would be your affair. Personally, I'd rather you used them for your own pleasure and satisfaction, or gave them away to someone a whole lot more deserving than anyone with the name of Liberty.'

'A dog's home, perhaps? Or how about Miss Costello? She strikes me as being eminently deserving.'

In spite of himself, Jonah had looked up sharply at this. 'It's your money, you can do with it what you will. If you think Miss Costello would benefit from it, then give it to her.' Slipping his jacket on, he'd added, 'I've said all I came to say, so now I'll go before either of us says anything we'll regret. Goodnight.'

It wasn't until he was driving home that he knew he had omitted to say one important thing: that above all else, he cared about his father's welfare and happiness.

Downstairs in the kitchen, eating a piece of toast and scanning his mail, Jonah thought of how his father could never resist fanning the smouldering flames of a difficult conversation into a roaring argument. His comment that Miss Costello was an *eminently deserving case* had been a blatant attempt to keep their heated exchange going. Even so, he couldn't help wondering how Caspar would react if he thought there was a chance that the threat might be carried out.

The thought stayed with him for the rest of that day. So when the telephone rang later that afternoon and Caspar demanded to know the outcome of his visit to Mermaid House, he couldn't stop himself pursuing what could only be described as a wanton act of malicious stirring.

It was petty and foolish, but none the less he relayed the goings-on at Mermaid House to his brother, labouring the point that their father seemed very taken with the attractive woman who had appeared from nowhere to work for him.

To hear the taut shock in his brother's voice and visualise his fuming face was worth every second of the ear-bashing to which he was then subjected.

Chapter Twenty-Six

Caspar gave the matter no more than a minute's thought. He cancelled his plans for that evening – the opening of a new restaurant in Manchester – and phoned Damson. Not that he held out much hope of speaking to her.

Poor deluded Damson, so fully immersed in mystical mumbo-jumbo that she was away with the fairies at the bottom of some sacred garden, getting high on pungent candles and herbal tea-bags while extolling the merits of Celestial Sex.

It vexed him that he couldn't remember the last sensible conversation they had shared. She was constantly on about biorhythms and her karma. It was like being with her in an Edward Lear poem at times: the words came out fluently enough but he was damned if he could understand a word she was saying. As far as he was concerned, she was going from bad to worse. 'It's all New Age funk, Damson,' he'd said, 'shallow and meaningless. Dare one ask how much you're paying for the privilege of being brainwashed?'

'Darling Caspar, I know you only have my best interests at heart but, please, the reward of finding one's centred self is beyond measure. You should give it a try.'

Yes, he'd thought, when hell froze over. The idea that she could be taken in by such a massive con appalled him, though part of him admired the person who had set up the scam: as commercial ventures went, it had the potential to be a lucrative money-spinner.

Still waiting for some idiot in Northumberland to get off his or her backside and answer the phone, he crossed one leg over the other and stared around him. Of all the things he had ever possessed, his loft apartment was the one from which he derived the most pleasure. It was a conversion of an old brewery warehouse in close proximity to Manchester's gay village, and though a high percentage of his neighbours were gay, they had good taste, were tidy, and seldom gave him much trouble – so long as they kept their mattress-wrestling behind closed doors, he had no complaints. The local restaurants and wine bars weren't bad either, pandering to the strength of the local currency, the vibrantly pink pound.

Since the day he moved in, he had felt at home: the stark barrenness of the place appealed to his keen sense of the aesthetic. Not for him the wild confusion with which he had been surrounded while growing up at Mermaid House. He preferred everything stripped back to the purity of line and form. And that was exactly what he had achieved here: polished wooden floors, white-painted brickwork, large sheets of plate glass, stainless steel and slabs of granite gave him the austerity he craved. He had kept away from colour too, never straying into the garish palette of vulgar tones for which so many people opted. The only relief to this hard-edged simplicity was a large cream leather sofa and a specially commissioned circular bed on the mezzanine level.

But unless he could work a miracle in the next month or so, there was a danger that he would lose it. His car too. In his line of business he didn't need to own a car – a perk of the job was that he could have the use of more or less whatever he fancied – but such a transient arrangement didn't suit him. Outright ownership was what counted, and selling his Maserati would be a last resort. And he'd be damned before he did that. That was why his father had to see the sense in selling Mermaid House and freeing up its considerable capital. It was going to happen one day, no matter what. The old man couldn't stay there much longer, not at his age, so why not get it over and done with now and let his children have the benefit of the money that would come to them anyway?

It was spite that was stopping him from selling. It had been the same earlier that year when he had approached his father for a loan to get the bank off his back. 'Enough is enough!' Gabriel had roared. 'Not another penny, Caspar. So long as I'm breathing, you'll not scrounge another bean out of me.'

At last somebody in Northumberland answered the phone. 'Rosewood Manor Healing Centre,' announced a reedy voice, which sounded as though it needed a boot taking to it.

'This is an emergency,' lied Caspar, sitting upright and uncrossing his legs. 'I need to speak to Damson Liberty. Tell her it's her brother and that it's imperative she comes to the phone.'

'Damson who?'

'Damson Liberty – I mean Damson Ackerman,' he repeated impatiently. He never could keep up with the changes to her surname. Peevishly he added, 'Just how many Damsons do you have there?'

'Oh, you mean *Damson*. Hold the line and I'll see if she's available.'

'You do that. Now trot along quick as you can and find her for me. Meanwhile, I'll cope with the pain of your absence by slipping a rope around my neck and pulling it tight.'

Drumming his fingers on the smooth leather arm of the sofa, he listened to the woman's footsteps recede down what he imagined was a dark, draughty passageway, and in the minutes that passed, he went over what he was going to say to his sister. He had to attract her attention in the first nanosecond of their conversation. Let Damson run so much as an inch with the ball and he would never get a coherent word out of her. She would be off on one of her surreal planes of fantasy.

What he needed to get across to her was that they had to work together on their father, persuade him to sell Mermaid House now, while the property boom was still at its height. Leave it till next year and they would lose out. Despite what Jonah thought, every pound counted. For some annoyingly perverse reason, his brother seemed intent on missing the crucial point that they must cash in on a buoyant market. Just as he was woefully naïve about the appearance of this unknown woman at Mermaid House.

What the hell was their father up to? And just who was she? A gold-digging opportunist who had caught the whiff of money?

He brought the flat of his hand down on the arm of the sofa with a loud smack. As if he didn't have enough to worry about without his father getting involved with a travelling New Age hippie! He could picture her perfectly. An irresponsible single mother who was shaven-haired, pierced all over, and who clomped around in boots and khaki trousers that were three sizes too big for her. It was the thought of her getting her unwashed feet under the table at Mermaid House that was causing him to act without delay.

He wanted Damson to understand that unless they took immediate action they might find themselves out in the cold with a scheming new step-mother calling the shots. Gabriel Liberty wouldn't be the first or last old man to make a fool of himself over a much younger woman.

Footsteps in his ear told him Damson was about to pick up the receiver. He felt himself relax and realised how tense he had become. He knew that once he had his sister on board, it would be like old times, and they would be invincible.

But he was wrong. They weren't Damson's footsteps he had heard. They belonged to the woman with the reedy voice. 'Are you still there?' she asked.

'More's the pity, yes. Where's Damson?'

'I'm afraid she can't come to the phone just now. I've been told to tell you she's in the middle of a very important holistic—'

'But I need to speak to her!'

A timid silence seeped down the line, followed by the

sound of a loud gong. 'I'm terribly sorry,' the woman simpered, 'I'm going to have to go. I should ring back later if I were you.'

'And if I were you, I'd have a full-frontal lobotomy!' He slammed down the phone.

Now what?

He'd have to deal with the problem direct. Scooping up his keys from the glass bowl on the table by the front door, he locked his apartment, took the lift down to the garages on the ground floor and slipped behind the wheel of his Maserati. He nosed the car into the early evening traffic and tried to steady his temper by switching on the CD player, at the same time focusing his thoughts on the smoothness of the drive.

It worked.

By the time he had picked up the A6 and had driven through Disley, he could feel the knots easing in his neck and shoulders. He knew he shouldn't let things get the better of him, and knew, too, that as long as Damson was under the thumb of those hippies up in Northumberland, he could no longer rely on her. But old habits died hard: he still saw her as his rock. As children she had always been the more daring and cunning of the two of them. If ever he thought he was losing his nerve, it was always Damson who reassured him that nothing could go wrong.

But where was she now when he needed her support and reassurance?

Hanging around with a bunch of navel-gazing screwballs who had as much chance of finding their inner selves as he had of becoming the next Queen of England.

The tension was building again in his shoulders, and he tried not to think of how much he missed Damson. It was ages since he had last seen her – Val's funeral probably.

He pressed his foot down on the accelerator and sped on towards Mermaid House and the devious woman who had designs on his father.

She might have met his younger brother and concluded

that he was as much of a threat to her plans as a wet paper bag but she hadn't reckoned on coming face to face with Caspar Liberty.

Chapter Twenty-Seven

The day had gone well for Archie. The shop had been busy from the moment he had opened. A cold north-easterly wind had provided him with a steady flow of day-trippers coming in for a browse and a warm. There had also been a number of more serious customers, like the well-dressed couple who wanted to furnish a cottage in Castleton, which they were letting to the holiday trade. 'Naturally we don't want to fill it with anything new and expensive,' the wife had said, in a tight, haughty voice, 'not when cheap tat will do the job perfectly well. And what a lot you seem to have. I suppose it's all clean?'

Ignoring the implied slur, Archie smiled and got on with offloading as much furniture and knick-knacks as he could and arranging for its delivery on Monday morning.

Another couple had come in soon after them, a husband and wife in matching fleeces, whom he recognised from their monthly trawl of his shop. They were dealers from Buxton who made it their business to check out the bottom end of the market for the antiques of tomorrow. It always surprised him what they picked from his shelves. Last month it had been an ugly chrome ashtray – one of those silly things on a stand that always got knocked over. Today it had been a Bakelite clock. He couldn't see the attraction in Bakelite; in fact, he hated it. It reminded him of when he had been in his bedroom as a child, listening to his father shouting at his mother downstairs. To keep himself awake, just in case his mother needed his help, he would leave his bedside lamp switched on. But then it would overheat and give off a horrible fishy smell.

Alone in the shop now, he was locking up. Samson had

given Bessie a lift home earlier so that she could take her time to get ready for their big Saturday night out at the pictures. Just as he was slipping the last of the chains and bolts across the door, the telephone rang. Because Archie was thinking of his mother, he rushed through to the office and snatched up the receiver, fearing the worst.

'Is that Mr Merryman at Second Best?' asked a woman – an assured young woman.

'Yes, it is. What can I do for you?'

'You might not remember me, but my name is Clara Costello and my son and I—'

'Of course I remember you. How are you? Still enjoying the delights of Deaconsbridge?'

'Yes, but not quite in the way I thought I might. I know it's a bit late in the day but I've got a proposition for you. Have you got a moment?'

'I'm all ears.'

When he'd heard what she had to say, he laughed. 'Well, I think I could manage that. I'll put it in the diary for Monday afternoon, around three o'clock. That soon enough for you?'

'Yes, that'll be fine. Do you need directions?'

'No, thanks. I've a nose on me like a bloodhound.'

After he'd rung off, he reached for the diary to make a note of his appointment with Clara Costello at Mermaid House. It was only then that he remembered he'd be delivering an entire house's worth of 'cheap tat' for Mr and Mrs Hoity-Toity over in Castleton that morning. Oh, well, he and Samson would just have to make sure they got through the job in double-quick time.

Feeling surprisingly chipper, he left the shop to walk home. He crossed the square, waved at Shirley through the window of the Mermaid café, then made his way slowly up the steep hill of Cross Street. The early evening air was sharp and it sliced through his thin jacket. He paused to catch his breath in the usual spot, leaning against the rail. The coldness of the metal scorched his hand and he wondered if they were in for a late snap of winter. Just because they were on the verge of April, and had recently experienced a few welcome days of spring weather, it didn't mean they were out of the woods. He could recall many an April morning when he'd had to scrape ice off the windscreen. Then he remembered he had left his car at the shop. He had driven to work that morning because he had taken his mother in with him on the pretext of needing her help again. 'I'm knee-deep in stuff that needs cleaning,' he had told her the night before. 'I don't suppose you'd come in for another day and give me a hand with it, would you?'

By the time he had parked the Volvo outside his house, it was almost seven. He'd have to get his skates on now or they'd miss the opening minutes of the film. As he let himself into the house at the back, he called to his mother. It was the moment in the day he dreaded most, other than first thing in the morning when he knocked on Bessie's bedroom door. He told himself repeatedly not to keep imagining the worst, but the memory of finding Bessie on the floor of her own home last year was difficult to shake off.

Hearing voices, and thinking she was in the sitting room watching the television, he pushed open the door and found her rigged up in one of her best dresses – collar and buttons askew – listening attentively to an earnest young man who could be no more than seventeen. He was reading from a copy of the *Watch Tower* and next to him was an older woman pouring tea. All three looked up as he came into the room.

'Hello,' he said, cheerfully enough, but inwardly annoyed. 'What's going on here?'

'Archie,' his mother said, unaware of the tension that his presence had caused, 'this is Rickie and his hummer.'

'I think she means mother,' the woman said, lowering the teapot.

'And I think she may have lost track of the time,' Archie said firmly. 'We're due out shortly, so I think it would be better if we brought this cosy chat to an end.' He was livid now. How dare these people think they could take advantage of a defenceless woman and indoctrinate her with their religious beliefs?

'Another time perhaps?' the woman said smoothly, rising to her feet and pulling on her coat. She had probably been thrown out of more homes than Archie had had hot dinners.

When he had hustled them to the front door, he realised how uncharacteristically rude he was being. 'Look,' he said, 'I'm sorry, it's just that you could have been anyone – robbers, murderers, you name it. She's too sweet-natured for her own good. She thinks well of everyone.'

'A fault with which more people should be blessed,' the woman said, with a smile of such forgiveness that he felt twice as churlish.

Watching them close the wrought-iron gate behind them, Archie noticed that the boy's trousers were too short for his long thin legs and his conscience pricked again. He wished he could replay the scene and deal with it better. It's not your religion or beliefs I have a problem with, he wanted to call after them, it's the world we live in. A dog-eat-dog world that takes advantage of innocent children and old ladies.

Later, as he was driving to the cinema, he thought how heavy-handed he had been. He knew he had hurt his mother's feelings by behaving like a boorish, arrogant bully, taking it upon himself to censor her enjoyment, which was bad enough, but what pained him more, was that he had reminded himself of his father.

Determined not to let this thought put a dampener on the evening, and knowing that Bessie was still upset, he said, 'I'm sorry about turfing Rickie and his mother out, but in this day and age you really ought to be more careful who you let into the house.'

What she said next made him feel even worse. 'Lonely, Archie, on my bone.'

Cut to the quick, he drove on in silence. Then he thought of something that might cheer her up, and told her about the call he had had from Clara Costello. 'She's only gone and got herself working for that dreadful man I told you about at the hospital. You know, the one who was so rude to Dr Singh. I hope he doesn't take advantage of her.'

Chapter Twenty-Eight

'Mr Liberty, please don't think you can take advantage of
me. I'm really not that sort of a girl.'

Gabriel scowled. She was merciless in the way she kept
twisting his words. But two could play at that game. 'Miss
Costello, I may have lost some of my social skills of late,
and the use of plain English may have changed since I last
made anyone such an offer, but as far as I'm aware I
believe I only suggested I'd cook you supper. There's not
the slightest chance of me wanting to seduce you. As
disappointing as that might be to you.' Hah! Let's see you
bat that one back!

They were standing in the dining room, where she had
been hard at work all day. She was polishing a pair of
silver candlesticks he hadn't seen in a long while. He
couldn't even remember where they had come from. She
stopped what she was doing, folded the yellow duster in
half, then in half again and turned away to place the
candlesticks on the stone mantel above the fireplace.
Without looking at him, or giving him an answer, she
said, 'What are you hiding behind your back?'

He cleared his throat and mentally conceded the point
to her. She was good, very good. But now they'd got to
the tricky part. This was when he had to apologise. 'Ahem
. . . It's a peace-offering.'

She turned slowly and he held out a tightly wrapped
bunch of red tulips, their petals still closed. She didn't say
anything. Feeling a desperate compulsion to fill the
awkward silence with words, he heard himself rambling
out of embarrassment: 'You rather rudely asked me the
other day when was the last time I had bought anyone

flowers – well, I saw these when I was in Deaconsbridge this afternoon and they reminded me of you.'

She made no move to take the tulips from him, but lowered her gaze to them. He could see the curious doubt in her eyes. 'Reminded you of me, eh?' she said. 'Care to explain?'

He cleared his throat again. 'I've always thought of tulips as an efficient-looking flower. Upright and business-like. They give the impression of not wanting to waste their time frolicking about the flower-beds. In short, they strike me as purposeful. Like . . . like you.'

Her gaze met his. It was softer than it had been. 'Hush now, Mr Liberty, go easy on the schmooze or you'll have me blushing to the tips of my ears. But you mentioned they were an apology. For what exactly?'

'You wouldn't be trying to extract blood from a stone, would you?'

'But of course. That goes without saying. So, come on, let's hear it. And no mumbling. I like apologies to be loud and clear. Then I can be sure they're genuine.'

Corralling what was left of his shaky resolve, he pulled at his nose, scratched his chin, and tried to recall the exact words he had prepared for this moment while driving back from town. He pictured himself as a newsreader, lifting the words from an auto-cue, but trying to add some meaning to them. 'I just want to say that I've been left with a nasty taste in my mouth after that incident with your son. I had no business prying into your affairs and I wanted you to know just how sorry I am.' His mission completed, he clumsily thrust the flowers at her and turned to flee.

He was nearly at the door when she said, 'That was really quite good, Mr Liberty. Full marks for content but running off before taking a final bow loses you valuable points when it comes to artistic expression.'

He didn't risk looking at her, kept his face to the door. 'Please don't make fun of me. Not when I'm—'

'Trying to be nice?' she finished for him. 'Now, why

don't you come back here and let me thank you properly? That's if you have the nerve.'

It was a challenge he couldn't refuse. He'd never been short of nerve. Who did she think she was to accuse him of such a thing? But when he stood in front of her again and she raised herself on her toes and softly kissed his cheek, he wondered if he hadn't met his match. 'We'll make a decent human being of you yet, Mr Liberty.' She smiled.

Caught so thoroughly off guard, he couldn't stop himself from lifting a hand to his cheek and touching, with his fingertips, the spot where he could still feel the light pressure of where her lips had been. Then he discovered he hadn't shaved that day. Had he even washed? Burning with self-loathing, he edged away from her.

Still smiling at him, she said, 'I hope you're not going to withdraw your offer of supper.'

With a supreme effort of will, and managing to sound his normal self, he said, 'You should know well enough by now that I'm a man of my word. But don't expect anything other than plain fare. I've got some boil-in-the-bag cod in parsley sauce knocking about in the freezer. Jonah keeps buying it for me and I keep forgetting to eat it. Is that good enough for her ladyship and her son?'

'Quite good enough. Talking of Ned, where is he?'

Glad of the diversion, he led her out of the dining room and along the hall. 'I took the liberty – no pun intended – of buying him a little something while I was in Deaconsbridge.'

In the kitchen, Ned was kneeling on a chair, his head bent over the table. When they came in he looked up. 'Mummy, Mr Liberty bought me a scrapbook and some postcards. I've been drawing a picture of his house. Do you like it?'

Out of the corner of his eye, Gabriel watched the boy's mother anxiously. Had he overstepped the mark? Would she think he was interfering? But he had only done it because the boy had told him during their walk before lunch that she had forgotten to buy them for him. 'We're going to keep a diary of our holiday,' Ned had said, releasing himself from Gabriel's grasp and running on ahead like a giddy spring lamb.

'Don't go too far without me,' he had called after the lad, his voice catching on the wind. 'Your mother said you had to stay close to me. And if I have to go home and tell her I've lost you, she'll have my guts for garters.'

The boy had slowed down until Gabriel caught up with him. 'What are guts and garters?' he had asked.

Prodding at his small belly, he said, 'Guts are inside there, your squelchy innards. And garters are elastic bands that people used to wear years ago to hold up their socks.'

Considering this, the boy had unzipped his anorak and felt his stomach through his clothes. 'But how would Mummy get your guts out?'

'Depending how angry she was, and bearing in mind I'd just told her I'd lost you, she might take a large knife to me and cut my stomach open.' He drew a line from his own chest down to his trouser belt. 'Then she'd take a stick and coil my innards around it.'

'And then?'

'Well, she might hang them up on the washing-line and let them dry before cutting them into the required lengths for the garters.'

'Would she sew you up afterwards?'

'Probably with the biggest, rustiest and bluntest needle she could lay her hands on.'

They continued their walk, the child's small warm hand now locked in his. Gabriel was taking Ned to the copse, where he hoped to show him a badger's sett. As they took the downward slope of the field, their muddy shoes skidding on the wet grass, and a nippy wind hustling them from behind, Ned said, 'I don't believe you, Mr Liberty.'

'Hmm . . . what don't you believe?'

'About Mummy and your squelchy bits.'

'You think I'd tell you lies?'

'You were joking, weren't you? Are you frightened of my mummy?'

'Good Lord! Frightened of a slip of girl like your mother? Now it's you who's joking.'

But standing in the kitchen, as Gabriel awaited her verdict on his purchases, which had now been added to the bonanza of coloured pencils and glue that covered the table, he had to admit that part of him *was* scared of her – of stepping on her toes and offending her.

He watched her move in beside the lad. She stroked the top of his head absently and studied his drawing. 'Ned, it's brilliant. How clever of you to draw the tower so well.' She placed the tulips on the table and bent down to his level for a closer inspection. 'But, my goodness, who is that handsome man?'

The boy beamed. 'Mr Liberty.'

Curious, Gabriel drew near to see how he had been depicted. Expecting to see a scowling old man with wild hair, he saw instead an enormous matchstick man who dwarfed the tower of his house – which bore an uncanny resemblance to the leaning one in Pisa. His massive head was wearing a ridiculously large pair of ears, and stretched between them was a crescent-shaped smile. 'You've forgotten my nose,' he said.

The boy reached for a coloured pencil and gave the matchstick man a pastel pink swirl that obliterated one of his eyes.

'Perfect,' his mother praised him. 'And thank you, Mr Liberty. You couldn't have given Ned a better present. It was very kind and thoughtful of you.'

Twirling the pencil in his hand, then trying to balance it on his top lip, the boy said, 'Mr Liberty said he'd help me with some of the writing tomorrow.'

'But only if you're good,' Gabriel said, moving away from the table and crossing the kitchen to the freezer compartment above the fridge. When he had finished rummaging through the bags of frozen peas and sweetcorn, and had found the stockpiled cod in parsley sauce, he realised that Miss Costello was standing behind him. 'What's that smirk on your face for?' he asked.

'You wouldn't be going soft on me, would you?'

'Of course not. I'm feathering my own bed. By keeping the boy out of mischief I'm ensuring that you get more work done. I don't want you having an excuse for slacking.'

'And while I'm not slacking, I'll defrost that for you tomorrow . . . and in case you're wondering, I'm referring to the freezer, not your frosty exterior.'

To round things off, Clara decided that they would eat their supper in the room she had spent all day cleaning. It had proved a lot less trouble to sort out than the kitchen. The dining room had been left to its own devices and it was more a matter of treating neglect to a large dose of tender loving care.

She had started by throwing open the windows and letting in some much-needed fresh air, then vacuuming the parquet floor, the rugs and the curtains. Using a full-height ladder she had found in an outhouse, and putting the vacuum cleaner on to its lowest setting, so as not to shred the brittle fabric damaged by years of exposure to sunlight, she had carefully removed the thick blankets of dust. Balls of fluff the size of walnuts were rounded up from under the mahogany table, chair legs and the corners of the room, and thick-legged spiders found themselves given short shrift and an abrupt change of address.

Next she had dusted the faded wood panelling that went from floor to ceiling, and the framed antique maps of Derbyshire that hung on it. Then she cleared out the contents of the sideboard and the matching pair of glass-fronted cabinets that stood at either side of the fireplace. She immediately wished she hadn't. There was so much of it. Quite apart from the hundreds of crystal wine glasses, brandy balloons and whisky tumblers, all of which needed careful washing, there was a mind-blowing quantity of elegant but tarnished silverware: teapots, coffee-pots, cream jugs, coasters, sugar tongs, snuff boxes, candlesticks, candle snuffers and tea strainers. And every item had a brother or sister. It occurred to Clara, as she spread out the sheets of newspaper and set to with the silver polish, that everything in the house, except its owner, was multiplied by a factor of at least three. It had been the same in the kitchen yesterday: if she found one Kenwood mixer, she unearthed a whole family of them. It made her wonder who had collected such a hoard. Surely not Mr Liberty. His wives probably. Perhaps out of pure devilment he had considered leaving the mess for his children to deal with when he departed, just to teach them one last lesson.

Now, as Clara set the table for supper, with cutlery, mats, glasses, her lovely red tulips and a candelabrum at one end, she thought of the youngest member of the Liberty family she had met last night. He had seemed pleasant enough, which paradoxically had made her dislike him on principle. His slightly hesitant manner had irritated her, had made her want to say, 'How dare you live on the doorstep and do so little to help? Anyone can fetch the weekly shop. How about scrubbing the floor or cleaning the toilet?'

Mr Liberty seemed greatly amused by the splendour of the setting for their simple boil-in-the-bag supper. He had wanted to eat in the kitchen, but Clara had insisted on showing off her efforts, barring anyone entry until she had everything just right.

'Ta-daa!' she chorused, when at last she allowed him and Ned to come in.

She watched his face as he stood for a moment, taking in the scene, a large tray of steaming food in his hands. Even to her critical eyes the room looked and smelt magnificent. Darkness was pressing in from outside, so she had drawn the heavy brocade curtains and lit the room with candles, their flickering flames bouncing soft light off the furniture and panelled walls. There was a warm, burnished look of opulence to the room and copious amounts of fresh air and lavender polish had seen off the musty, depressing smell of neglect.

Ned's eyes were wide and luminous. 'It's like Christmas,' he said. 'Only bigger.'

Mr Liberty set down the tray on the table and made a low bow. 'Another day, another miracle for you, Miss Costello. I applaud you once again. A small point, though. Where did all the candles come from? I had no idea I had so many.'

'I found them on a shelf in the laundry room. Some of them are so old they're probably medieval church relics.'

'Well, just so long as we don't go up in flames. Will we be warm enough in here, do you think?' He cast his eyes over to the empty grate in the fireplace, where she had placed a pottery jug of daffodils picked from the garden.

'I wanted to light a fire but thought I wouldn't risk it. As well as antique candles you're probably the proud owner of a ton of antique soot. I'll get hold of a chimney sweep. But for now, I'm starving.'

Despite the blandness of the meal, it was their most convivial so far – the second bottle of Chablis they were roaring through might have had something to do with that. Ned, who was sitting on two cushions and a telephone directory to get him up to the right height, and who was surprisingly perky for one whose bedtime should have been more than an hour ago, was telling her Mr Liberty's gory tale of guts and garters when Clara heard a sound and interrupted. 'What was that?' She cocked her head towards the door.

'What was what?' asked Mr Liberty.

She allowed him to top up her glass. 'I must be spending too much time with you, I'm going mad and hearing things.'

He crashed his glass against hers. 'Here's to you. May you always speak your mind!'

'Just you try and stop me.'

'I suspect I'd need a Panzer tank to stop you doing something you'd put your mind to.'

They were both mid-laugh when Clara noticed the door open slowly at the far end of the room. She froze. Mr Liberty turned to see what she was looking at. A smartly dressed man had come in. Clara would have recognised him anywhere. It was the long-faced rude man from the supermarket with the trolley of bargain-priced champagne.

'Hello, Father,' he said, in a pompously creepy voice. 'Do hope I'm not interrupting anything.'

Chapter Twenty-Nine

'As a matter of fact you *are* interrupting. What is this? Suddenly everyone's treating my home as if it was Liberty Hall.'

Caspar forced a smile. 'Never underestimate those old jokes, Dad.' He stepped further into the candlelit room, his leather-soled shoes sounding loud in the sudden hush. 'Liberty Hall indeed.' His words were directed at his father, but he was more interested in Gabriel's dining companions, in particular the woman: the scheming Miss Costello. Though she was scruffily dressed in khaki trousers (he'd got that right!) and a loose-fitting T-shirt stained with something he didn't care to think about too deeply, and had the kind of childish, unattractive haircut he never approved of on a grown woman, she didn't match up to the pierced, tattooed New Age scrounger he'd pictured.

But appearances could be deceiving.

It was odd, though: the more he looked at her and the child, the more he felt he had come across them before. But where?

He could see that she was appraising him, and that his presence was not to her liking. Which confirmed his hunch: she was working a number on the old man but now knew that she had been confronted with a spanner in the works. Well, get ready, little lady, you're going to be out of here before you get your feet any further under the table.

'Caspar, are you going to stand there all night gawping at us?' his father barked. 'Or are you going to share with us what's brought you here? Or perhaps you were just passing through and thought you'd check up on your dear old pater. Make sure he hadn't snuffed it in his bed.'

'Passing through' was exactly the cover Caspar had decided to use and he slipped seamlessly into his prepared speech, pulling out a chair beside his father and imposing himself on the cosy scene of candles, flowers and best silver. 'As it happens, I *am* just passing through,' he said. 'I've been to see baby bro Jonah. I had no idea how concerned he is about you.'

Gabriel snorted. 'Hah! That'll be the day, when any of you worry about me.'

Caspar laughed expansively. 'Come on, Dad, there's no need to take that line. You know jolly well that we all care about you. But where are your manners? Aren't you going to introduce me to your dinner guests?' He leaned across the table, hand outstretched. 'Caspar Liberty, your humble servant and eldest custodian of my father's welfare. And you are?'

He had intended his words as a warning shot, but when his hand was ignored and Gabriel said, 'Is there any need to introduce you?' he felt the full force of one of his father's warning shots.

'Sorry, Dad, you've lost me. You know I'm no good at cryptic clues. That's much more your scene, what with all the crosswords you do. Any chance of a glass of that wine?'

'Cut it out, Caspar. I know exactly why you're here. And it won't do.' Gabriel slapped one of his knobbly hands on the table. The cutlery rattled and the small boy with staring dark eyes jumped and leaned in towards his mother.

'Steady on, Dad, you're frightening your guests. An unforgivable breach of etiquette in anyone's book. In some quarters poisoning one's guests is an acceptable mishap, but to scare them to death—'

'Caspar, while I'm familiar with the fact that you listen to nothing but the echo of your own voice, my guests are not so well informed, so will you do them a great kindness and shut up?'

'I think it's time we were going, Mr Liberty.'

The scheming minx was on her feet now and staring pointedly at him. But as she manhandled the child out of his seat and hooked his short legs around her waist, Caspar saw how small she was. Not the glowering Amazon she had appeared while seated. Quite insignificant, really.

'There's no need for you to leave, Miss Costello,' his father said. 'In fact, I would rather you stayed.' The voice was imperious, as Caspar remembered it from his childhood – *'You'll stay right where you are, young man. You'll leave this room on my say-so, and not before.'*

'No can do, Mr Liberty. Ned's tired and I need to get him to bed. Same time tomorrow morning?'

'As you wish, Miss Costello. Goodnight.'

What was all this? *'As you wish, Miss Costello'* and *'No can do, Mr Liberty'*? What kind of game did they think they were playing?

The door closed silently behind her, signalling that Caspar could get down to business. He pushed back his chair and turned to face his father. But Gabriel was ahead of him and gained the advantage by creaking to his feet. 'I hope you're satisfied, Caspar,' he glowered down at him, 'because for the first time in a long while I was enjoying myself, but as usual, you had to spoil everything. Nothing changes with you, does it?'

Caspar's jaw dropped. Good God, it was worse than he'd thought. The old fool had got it bad. He didn't know whether to laugh or jump out of his seat in horror. He played it cool, preferring to extract as much embarrassing detail from his father as possible. 'I'm not sure what you're getting at, Dad. What exactly did I interrupt here this evening?' He cast his eyes meaningfully over the remnants of the candlelit dinner.

Standing by the fireplace, one clenched fist jammed into his side, the other on the mantel, his father stared at him.

Then his withered features acquired a firmness that was both vital and tenaciously implacable. Inexplicably, he began to laugh. A nasty sneering laugh that started as a low rumble until it grew into a full-blown body-shaker before climaxing in a fit of wheezy coughing. Sweet Moses! Any more attacks like that and the man would kill himself! Caspar stood up. 'You all right, Dad?'

Gasping for breath, Gabriel swiped Caspar out of the way as if he were a fly. He moved back to the table and took a swig from his wine glass, then another. Just as he was confident that he had his breathing under control, he almost started to laugh again. The situation was hilarious.

Bloody hilarious!

Caspar, poor stupid, greedy Caspar, thought his father had finally lost his marbles and fallen for the charms of a pretty girl! Ha, ha, ha! Well, let the arrogant buffoon think what he wanted.

'Are you going to tell me what you were laughing at, Dad?'

Using all his guile, Gabriel kept his face poker straight and joined Caspar by the fireplace. He put a fatherly arm around his son's shoulder. 'Caspar, I know this may come as a shock to you. To be honest, it's been a seismic shock to me. The thing is, I'm fairly well smitten with the lovely Miss Costello. But you must have grasped that. You've seen what a beautiful woman she is. She's stunning, isn't she? Intelligent. Poised. And utterly charming. Quite a catch for an old thing like me.'

To his delight he felt his son stiffen and it was all he could do to stop himself grinning. He sighed the sigh of a man hopelessly in love and continued to turn the screw. 'And for some reason that is quite beyond my comprehension, she seems besotted with me. So, what I'm trying to say is, and I know she's much too young for an old duffer like me, but how do you feel about a new step-mother? Your approval matters to me, you know.'

Chapter Thirty

There was little to be gained from telling Caspar to calm down – Jonah had tried that already only to provoke a louder and more incoherent outburst – so he poured his brother a glass of wine.

Caspar took the glass and tossed back half of its contents in one gulp. To Jonah's relief, it brought him to a standstill, and he repeated, more calmly, what he had said on his arrival at Church Cottage. 'This proves beyond all doubt that the old man is definitely losing it.'

'You still haven't said—'

But Caspar was off again. 'I warned you something like this could happen. But would you listen to me? Oh, no, you had to carry on as you always do with your head buried in the sand. Maybe now you'll take more notice of what I say.'

'I might listen if you started talking sense,' Jonah replied, keeping his voice level. 'What's happened to cause such a rush of blood to your normally temperate head?'

'Oh, please, save the witty sarcasm for your brain-dead pupils. Haven't you heard a word I've said?'

'Every syllable, but I still haven't a clue as to what you're raving on about.'

Caspar's face hardened. 'Look, Jonah, our father is on the verge of marrying for the third time. Do you have any idea where that will leave us? Out in the cold, that's where.'

'Who is he thinking of marrying?'

'The gold-digging Miss Mop.'

'But that can't be right.' Jonah was stunned.

Caspar regarded him pityingly. 'Of course it's not! But

I'm pleased to see that I'm finally getting through to you. We've got to put a stop to this nonsense . . . Any more of this lighter fuel going?'

Jonah poured the remains of the bottle into Caspar's empty glass. Reaching for the corkscrew, he opened a second, wondering if the joke he had played on his brother had been trumped by a bigger one from their father. He simply could not equate the assured woman he had met yesterday with one who would be interested in marrying a man like Gabriel Liberty. Or was it possible that Caspar was right, that the efficient Miss Costello was nothing but a scheming gold-digger? He recalled how jealous he had felt in the kitchen at Mermaid House that she had an empathy with Gabriel that few other people had ever had, least of all the members of his family.

But despite this, he couldn't go along with Caspar's theory. There had been nothing in her manner to suggest that she was up to anything so devious as fooling an elderly man into marrying her for financial gain. But then why was she at Mermaid House?

He leaned against the Rayburn. 'Right, Caspar, tell me exactly what Dad said to you. Try to remember his exact words. Don't exaggerate.'

Caspar rolled his eyes. 'Stop treating me like a fool, Jonah. I may have flunked university, which Dad has never let me forget, but credit me with sufficient intelligence to read the signs. And it was you who alerted me to what was going on in the first place. If you hadn't told me on the phone last night—'

'Just tell me what he said.'

'My, how snappy you are these days. He asked me how I felt about having a new step-mother. And I think that even *you* can grasp the significance of that. He also said that he was smitten by the lovely Miss Costello and that she was equally besotted with him. *And* he put his arm round my shoulders.' He shuddered and took a long sip of his wine. 'I can't remember the last time he touched me.'

'Did he say anything else?'

'Plenty, most of which makes me cringe to think of it. Once he got started it was impossible to shut him up. He even asked me for my advice as to where they should honeymoon, and if I thought it might be worth his while to see the quack about some Viagra! He's certifiable if you ask me.' He put down his glass, tugged at the white cuffs of his shirt that poked out from his jacket sleeves, then straightened his cufflinks. 'Do you suppose that's a line we could pursue? Put a stop to the marriage by proving he's not in his right senses?'

Having listened to Caspar, Jonah was doubly suspicious that his brother had been duped. Never in a million years could he see their father seeking advice about Viagra. That put the tin lid on it as far as Jonah was concerned. The more he thought about it the more convinced he was that, just as their father had enjoyed pulling a fast one on Dr Singh with Miss Costello's help, so he had with Caspar. But why couldn't Caspar see that? 'Did the object of Dad's affections have anything to say on the matter?'

'No. This all happened after she'd left us alone. They were in the middle of a romantic candlelit dinner when I arrived.'

'And her son?'

'Oh, he was there too.'

'So, a romantic dinner *à trois*, then?'

Caspar looked at him hard. 'She could hardly have left him sitting on the doorstep with a bottle of pop and a bag of crisps.'

Side-stepping, Jonah said, 'I think our best policy is to stay quiet and see how things progress.'

'Oh, that's bloody typical of you, isn't it? Some tart is planning a move on our inheritance and you want to pretend nothing's going on. Don't you care that if Miss Costello becomes the third Mrs Liberty, we can kiss goodbye to Mermaid House?'

'You speak as though you have a right to it,' Jonah said.

Caspar's expression grew tight, and his nostrils flared just like their father's. 'That's because I do. A share of Mermaid House *is* my birthright. I hardly need point out to you that it's what our mother would have wanted for each of us.'

There was absolutely nothing Jonah could say to this last, dangerously weighted comment, so he kept quiet and waited for his brother to leave.

The next morning Jonah's curiosity had got the better of him, and after calling in at Kwik-Fit to have a new exhaust pipe fitted, he drove out on to Hollow Edge Moor.

Thick banks of clouds were being dragged across the sky and a blustery wind buffeted the car; rain was imminent. Only a few hardy walkers dressed in full-length cagoules with knapsacks were braving the elements up on the ridge, their distant figures leaning into the wind. Black-legged lambs sheltered with their mothers in the lee of a drystone wall, and the recent warm spring weather was now a distant memory. But the dismal nature of the day didn't bother Jonah: he found it invigorating.

As the brooding outline of Mermaid House came into view he felt a stab of doubt. What did he hope to achieve by seeing his father again? 'Two visits in one week, Jonah?' Gabriel would sneer. 'Suddenly I'm the most popular man in the Peak District.'

He supposed that, deep down, he hoped he was right that his father had played a prank on Caspar and might want to let him in on it.

'Sibling rivalry makes fools of us all,' he muttered, as he drove through the archway and parked alongside Miss Costello's camper-van, noting that the large yellow skip was still in residence.

He switched off the engine and felt nothing but contempt for himself. Why hadn't he just told Caspar last night that he thought their father was having a laugh at his expense?

Because they were all so used to fighting one another.

Out of his car, he looked across the courtyard to see the energetic figure of Miss Costello hurling a cardboard box into the skip. Only the other day he had wished he had the courage to clear the decks for his father and now an outsider was doing precisely that. The thought irritated him. He strolled over, uncomfortably aware that he was trying too hard to put on a casual air.

Seeing him, but not stopping what she was doing, she said, 'You've got your exhaust fixed then?'

'And Dad's got you hard at work even on a Sunday.'

She tipped another box into the skip and a gust of wind caught some sheets of newspaper. She pushed them down hard. Wiping her hands on the back of her close-fitting jeans, she said, 'Understand this, Master Liberty, it's me who sets the agenda. I decide the hours I work.'

'I don't doubt that for a minute. Here, let me help you.' He expected her to refuse his offer, but she didn't and between them they added a smelly rolled-up rug to the pile of rubbish. 'Caspar will be furious if he thinks you're chucking away the family heirlooms.' His tone was light, but she didn't say anything, merely reached for a black plastic sack and threw it on top of the rug. 'I believe you had the pleasure of meeting him last night,' he added.

'I'd had that pleasure already.'

'Really?'

'In the supermarket, in Deaconsbridge. I decided then and there that he was the rudest, most self-centred, arrogant man I'd ever set eyes on.'

Jonah tried not to smile. 'And did last night alter your opinion?'

She didn't answer him. Instead she said, 'If you're looking for your father, he's in the library.'

He was clearly being dismissed and, baffled, he wondered what he had done to deserve such frostiness. 'Miss Costello, you don't like me very much, do you?'

She paused, lifted her chin and looked him dead in the eye, her small face stern. 'Does that bother you?'

He took from her a dusty dried flower arrangement, which Val had put together a long time ago, and placed it carefully in the skip. He was used to brutal honesty from his family, but not from someone he hardly knew. He decided to fight back, force her to drop the annoying deadpan manner he was sure she had adopted for his benefit. 'If you're going to be my step-mother,' he said mildly, 'don't you think we ought to make more of an effort to get along?' He watched her closely for her response.

'Well, what can I say?' she said, her manner giving nothing away. 'I suppose you're right. How do you suggest we go about it, young Master Liberty?'

'First you can stop calling me Master Liberty. My name's Jonah. And second, you can be honest with me.'

'Oh, I don't know whether that's a good idea. Families are rarely honest with each other, are they? There's always something we like to keep from each other. By the way, who spilled the beans about your father and me getting hitched?'

'Dad told Caspar last night.'

The conversation wasn't going at all how Jonah had thought it would. Who was bluffing who? But he was determined to get a straight answer to a straight question. 'Miss Costello, please, will you level with me?'

She held up a hand. 'Don't be so formal. Call me Mother. Or would you prefer Mum?'

'Please,' he tried again, 'a straight answer for a straight question. Are you indulging my father by playing along with another of his self-satisfying games?'

'As I always tell Ned, you must believe what you want to believe.'

'In that case, I don't believe a word of what my father has told Caspar. Or that you're a gold-digger on the make as my brother thinks you are.'

She stuck out her chest and placed her hands on her hips provocatively. 'Is that because you don't fancy me in the role of step-mother?'

He knew she was teasing him, but her playful tone and the sight of her breasts showing through her thin T-shirt were an unexpected turn-on. 'I'm afraid that imagining you as my step-mother would take too much suspension of disbelief.' He lowered his gaze. He had no choice but to accept that he wouldn't get any further with her. Exasperated, he said, 'Where did you say my father was?'

'He's in the library with Ned.'

As Clara watched Jonah go inside, she almost felt sorry for him. What in the world was the incorrigible man up to now? He might have had the decency to warn her that not only was she his stand-in daughter but also his fiancée. How would they explain that to Dr Singh?

Chapter Thirty-One

On his way through the house to the library, Jonah noted the changes and improvements Miss Costello had single-handedly brought about. Whatever his feelings towards her – and he wasn't entirely sure what they were – he couldn't fail to be impressed by the effect she had had on Mermaid House. There was a lightness about it that he hadn't felt in years. No, more than that: it was as though, with each room she had touched, the house was being coaxed out of mourning, something which had been going on for as long as he could remember. He poked his head round the dining-room door, which was ajar. He saw and smelt yet more telltale signs of Miss Costello's refreshing handiwork – polished wood, flowers in the grate and on the table, sparkling glass and silverware on the shelves of the gleaming glass-fronted cabinets. The transformation was incredible.

Hearing a squeal of high-pitched laughter, he carried on towards the library, calling to his father so that he couldn't be accused of turning up unannounced. He pushed open the door and braced himself for another in a long line of difficult encounters. But he had miscalculated his father's mood.

'Jonah? Well, I can't say I'm surprised to see you, not when I'm suddenly flavour of the week, but your timing is perfect. Pull up a chair and help me. This cheeky whippersnapper has me on the run.'

The room hadn't yet received the Miss C treatment, and after shifting a dusty pile of *National Geographics* from a chair to the floor, Jonah joined them in the bay window where a game of draughts was in progress. The 'cheeky whippersnapper' smiled exuberantly at him. 'I've just taken another of Mr Liberty's pieces,' he said proudly. He waved the grubby ivory disc in front of Jonah. 'And look at all these other pieces I've got.'

'Enough of the boasting, young man. Now; ssh! I need peace and quiet while I think out my next move. What do you advise, Jonah?'

Jonah observed the board, the same board on which he had learned to play both chess and draughts – games his father had always played ruthlessly to win, no matter the age or ability of his opponent. On several occasions Val had told him to give Jonah a fighting chance. 'He's only a child. How will he ever improve if you don't encourage him?' Looking at the board now and its scene of one-sided carnage, Jonah could only conclude that either Ned was a child genius, or Val's advice had finally been heeded: Gabriel was down to just a few pieces. 'Strikes me that you're in real trouble, Dad,' he said. 'Any move open to you looks risky to me.'

'And since when have I ever been afraid of taking a risk?' Licking his mottled lips, Gabriel nudged one of his few remaining pieces forward. 'There now, you little rascal, pick the bones out of that!'

Lost in the depths of the leather chair opposite, and resting his chin on a knee drawn up close to his chest, the boy stared hard at the board, his bright eyes flicking from left to right. The only sound in the room was Gabriel's wheezing – was it louder than it had been? – and the steady ticking of the clock on the mantelpiece. Jonah willed Ned to see for himself that with one simple move he could win. A small hand hovered over the left of the board. Jonah felt disappointed; Ned had missed the obvious. He cleared his throat to attract Ned's attention and looked meaningfully at the other side of the board. A moment passed before Ned took the hint, but then his hand moved towards one of his kings, and with a burst of gleeful realisation he claimed the last of Gabriel's pieces.

He was gracious in his victory. He sat back in his chair and smiled. 'Mr Liberty, I think you've lost.'

Gabriel stared at the board and slowly smiled. 'Clearly I've been too good a teacher. Well done, young man.' He brought his hands together and gave him a short round of applause. Jonah noticed that each clap made his father wince.

Leaning forward in his chair and repositioning his triumphant army, Ned said, 'Can we play again?'

Gabriel groaned. 'Not now. Maybe after lunch. My poor old brain needs a rest. You run along and tell your mother what a smart lad you are while I have a chat with my son; I doubt I'll need my brain for that.'

Alone, and expecting his father's mood to change, Jonah started setting out the board ready for another game. He said, 'Do you remember teaching me to play?'

Gabriel pushed himself to his feet, setting off a crackle of dry joints. 'Like it was yesterday. And talking of yesterday, I imagine that's why you're here, isn't it? Come to get the news straight from the horse's mouth about my approaching marriage, I presume.'

The last of the draughtsmen lined up, Jonah said, 'Why are you doing this, Dad?'

'What? Marrying the delectable Miss Costello? Wouldn't you if you had the opportunity?'

Jonah had let one conversation slip out of his grasp and had no intention of this one going the same way. 'We're not talking about me, Dad,' he said firmly. 'We're discussing why you're pretending to Caspar that you're marrying the *delectable* Miss Costello, as you describe her.'

'Who said anything about pretending?'

'I did. It's another of your games, isn't it?'

'I'll say this for you, Jonah, you're verging on the astute.'

'So why taunt Caspar?'

'Because it was fun! You should have seen the feckless

238

little runt. I thought he was going to pass out on me with shock. I haven't enjoyed myself so much in years.'

'But is it right to do so at somebody else's expense?'

Gabriel waved aside the implied criticism. 'What do I care for Caspar's finer feelings? When did he or Damson ever care about mine, eh?'

'Am I not to be included in that condemnation?'

'Carry on with this interrogation and you might well find yourself top of the list!' His father turned abruptly and looked out of the window. 'Damn! It's started raining. I was hoping to take young Ned for a walk later on. Do you want to stay for lunch? Or have you something better to do?'

Jonah stood next to his father and stared through the dirty glass at the heavy downpour that was flattening the daffodils on the sloping lawn. He couldn't remember the last time his father had made an invitation so spontaneously. He didn't know how or why, but it felt as though a small bridge had just been crossed. Prepared to take whatever was on offer, he said, 'Lunch would be great. Thanks. Do you want me to see to it while you prepare yourself for another whipping at the hands of your protégé?'

Upstairs, in what had been Val Liberty's bedroom, Clara was sorting through the dead woman's belongings. She had wondered who had been responsible for the clutter in the house, and now felt sure she had found the culprit: the second Mrs Liberty had been an inveterate hoarder.

Judging from the drawers, cupboards, bedside cabinets and wardrobes, she had never thrown anything away. She had kept all sort of curious things: train tickets to Sheffield and Manchester, dental appointment cards, hairdresser's receipts, shopping lists, bent hairpins, ancient suspender belts, empty scent bottles, hairbrushes, crumbling bath cubes, packs of safety-pins and half-used tubes of hand-cream. There was a collection of hot-water bottles, so old and perished they had become glued together into the kind of rubbery collage the Tate Modern might exhibit. There were several boxes of Carmen heated rollers as well as one of those inflatable hood devices for drying your hair.

Mr Liberty had given her *carte blanche* to get rid of everything. 'None of it's of any use to me, so you might just as well ditch the lot,' he had said. This was after she had arrived for work first thing that morning and told him she wanted a change from scrubbing and polishing.

'Aha! Trying to get out of the heavy-duty work so you can take it easy with the light stuff, are you?'

'Keep the words of love and kindness for your family, Mr Liberty. Did you enjoy your late-night cigar-and-brandy session with your son?'

He had cracked the air with a bellow of laughter. 'Immensely. I'll tell you about it later when I bring you your elevenses. Ned, m'boy, you stay with me. Today's the day you learn to play draughts.'

Folding yet another thick woollen skirt and adding it to the bag of clothes she had already sorted – there were two piles, one destined for a charity shop and the other for the skip – Clara thought how funny it was that the three of them had slipped into such an unlikely but easy-going routine. Ned was perfectly at home with Mr Liberty, whom he probably regarded as a temporary grandfather. Which was fine by her, because, as far as she could see, they were all getting something out of the week. Mr Liberty was getting spring-cleaned, Ned was being entertained and taught to play draughts, and she was getting paid enough to convince herself that she hadn't been mad in taking on such an extraordinary assignment.

Last night, after reading Ned a bedtime story, she had written her first postcard home to Louise and the gang.

I can't believe it's only a week since Ned and I set off in Winnie. It feels like we've been away for ever.
Having the most unbelievable time. Not quite what I'd had in mind, but lots of fun all the same. We're doing

missionary work (I'll explain later), staying with a crazy man in the Peak District – so far north for you, Louise, you'd need a pocket phrase book! Ned is having the time of his life. He's four going on fourteen now. More news in the next card. Love to everyone, Clara.

P.S. Missing work? Get real!

She had deliberately omitted to mention that she had turned herself into a cleaner for a week, because she knew that Louise would despatch David to fetch her home.

With the rails of the first wardrobe empty now, she stood on a chair to clear out the stuff from the top shelf. She found a battered hatbox hidden beneath a pink candlewick bedspread. It was quite heavy, so she took off the lid and found that it contained a bundle of large notebooks.

She climbed down, sat on the bed, and pulled at the frayed satin ribbon that held them together. Picking one at random, she opened it, expecting to find nothing more interesting than a rambling extension of the cluttered woman she had so far glimpsed – a variety of recipes for prize-winning chutney, perhaps.

But she saw straight away that what she had in her hands was a diary.

She knew she shouldn't but she couldn't stop herself reading the erratic writing that covered the lined pages.

Sunday, 16 September

There are times when I hate this dreadful house! I know that sounds overly dramatic, but there it is, that's how I feel today.

I warned Gabriel something like this would happen, that Caspar wasn't above such an appalling act of treachery. But, as usual, the stubborn old fool refused to do anything about it. 'They're grown men, they should be able to deal with this themselves,' he said, when I told him this evening what had been going on.

'No man is ever fully grown,' I said, but he just gave me one of his baleful looks and went off to his wretched library.

The trouble started the moment Caspar and that dim girlfriend of his (whose name escapes me, I doubt we'll ever see her again, so it doesn't really matter) arrived to celebrate Jonah and Emily's engagement. During dinner I could see what Caspar was up to (I've seen him do it countless times before, so I could recognise the signs) and knew that no good would come of the weekend, and that it was my fault – it was me who had insisted on everyone being present. As soon as that silly girl Emily started giggling, I knew she had been taken in. Poor Jonah, he just sat there quietly seething, his head down, his mood darkening by the second. 'Do something!' I wanted to shout at him, but he didn't. He just let his brother walk all over him as he always has. He's frightened of him, I know. Frightened of Damson too. And Damson could see what Caspar was up to, and I think that maybe even she was a little shocked. But she made no attempt to stop him – she's the only one who can rein him in – and in doing nothing, she condoned his behaviour. Though to be fair, she's so caught up in herself she probably doesn't care. Half the time I can't understand what she's talking about. She hasn't got enough to do, of course. That's the real problem. If she had some real direction in her life, she wouldn't be like this. So airy-fairy.

By lunchtime today it was all over. Jonah left without saying a word. I watched him from the kitchen window as he drove out of the courtyard – I don't think I've ever seen anyone so angry and so unable to express themselves.

Minutes later, Caspar's girlfriend came hobbling into the house in my borrowed boots and, glory be, there's a creature who can express herself! Such language! (Calls herself a model too – not a model of decorum, that much is clear!) From what I could gather from her highly colourful language, she and Jonah had seen Caspar kissing Emily, in Jonah's favourite haunt by the rocks, where he likes to go and think. And while she waited for Caspar and Emily to reappear, she phoned for a taxi and packed her bag. When Caspar did deign to show his face, she slapped it hard for him and left. (Can't say I blame her!) Emily, the stupid girl, had the grace to look ashamed of what she had done, but Caspar was his normal arrogant self. 'Well,' he said, in that annoyingly cocky voice of his (I know it's wrong but my hand always itches to slap him when he puts that voice on!), 'there goes a girl with some spirit. I wish her next sparring partner all the luck in the world.' He then had the gall to say to me, 'Val, old love, it looks like lunch is off. Another time perhaps?'

And during all this commotion, where was Gabriel? Where he always is. Hiding in the library, of course. Why won't he deal with his family? Why does he always leave it to me? I'm tired of it, truly I am. I often wonder what would become of them all if I was no longer here.

A flurry of footsteps out on the landing had Clara shoving the books back into the hatbox, slapping the lid on it, and standing guiltily to attention. The door flew open and in came Ned. 'Mummy, guess what? I beat Mr Liberty at draughts.'

'Aren't you the clever one?' She went to him, knelt on the floor and hugged him.

Wriggling out of her grasp, and staring intently into her face, he said, 'It's a real grown-up game, Mummy, and I still won. I did, really I did. No help from anyone. Well, maybe a tiny bit from Mr Liberty's son.'

She kissed the tip of his nose, basking in the shining rays of his euphoria. 'Do you want to help me up here now? Or would that be too boring?'

He looked around the room, eyeing it for the fun factor. His gaze slid over the piles of clothes and he shook his head. 'I'll do my scrapbook downstairs with Mr Liberty.' He was already moving towards the door.

'Okay, then, but don't make a nuisance of yourself, will you?'

'I won't.'

'Oh, and while you're with Mr Liberty, remind him to bring me up some coffee. It's well past eleven.'

As soon as she was alone again, Clara slipped the lid off the hatbox and reached for another diary. Just a couple of pages, she told herself.

Friday, 2 December

Well, he's finally done it. I never thought he would, but he's sold up. And I know he feels terrible about it. He won't say anything, of course, but the whole thing has taken a far greater toll on him than he will ever admit to.

And why did he have to sell to a rival firm of engineers? A firm he's despised for as long as I can remember. A firm that will strip his business for its assets and throw the rest to the dogs. It's as if he's done it deliberately. As though out of spite he wants the whole thing to implode in on itself. He says he doesn't care what happens to it. 'I've washed my hands of it,' he said this afternoon, when he came home after his meeting with the lawyers and accountants and poured himself a large glass of his most expensive malt whisky. But I simply can't believe he meant it. 'What about all those men and women who have worked so loyally for you?' I asked him. 'Don't you care what will happen to them?' He grunted something I couldn't make out and told me I didn't understand. Maybe I don't. But what I do understand is that what Gabriel devoted his life to, and his father before him, has to mean something. I also understand how much it hurts him that none of his children wanted to step into his shoes – he so badly wanted at least one of them to do that. But I can see it from their point of view too: they have their own dreams to follow.

Why does he always have to take things so personally?

Again, the sound of footsteps – less hurried ones this time – had Clara furtively hiding the diary. She stuffed it back into the hatbox and pretended to be folding a matted Fair Isle sweater.

'Dad sent me up with your elevenses and an apology for being late.' It was Jonah with a mug and a plate of ginger nuts. He handed her the mug and put the plate on the dressing-table, clearing a space for it among the mess. 'How's it going?'

'Slowly.'

He looked about the room. 'I guess it's easier if you're detached from it. I know I'd struggle to be objective. I did try to do it for Dad, but it was probably too soon for him.' He settled his gaze on the sweater she had just folded. 'I remember Val knitting that. It was a Christmas present for Dad but it shrank and ended up fitting her better than him. She only ever wore it in the garden. Oh, and if it helps things between us, apparently the engagement's off.'

For a moment she thought he was referring to what she had just been reading in the diary – the engagement between him and Emily – but then she realised he couldn't possibly be talking about that. 'Sorry?'

He shrugged. 'It's okay, you don't have to carry on with the game any more. Dad's told me the truth. It was a wind-up for my brother's benefit last night.'

'Oh, so I don't even get the chance to be jilted at the altar. How disappointing. And to think I was so looking forward to being your wicked step-mother.'

Given the room they were in and its contents, Clara wished she hadn't said that. Her cheeks burned. How could she have been so insensitive?

He spoke before she could apologise. 'Not all stepmothers are wicked, you know.'

'I'm sorry.' Wanting to make good the damage, and intrigued by the entries in the diary, she said, 'What was your step-mother like?'

He hesitated fractionally, then said, 'To put up with us Libertys, Val was two parts saint and one part sergeant-major. On reflection I think we gave her a terrible time. I don't think she was always very happy.'

Though she couldn't comment on its accuracy, she was impressed by the incisiveness of his reply. 'How old were you when she married your father?' she asked.

He moved away from the bed, went over to the window. 'A little younger than Ned, and before you ask, no, I can't remember a time before that.'

'Not even your real mother?'

'Not likely, given that it was my birth that killed her.'

Once more Clara wished she could retract her words. 'Oh dear. I'm sorry. I keep putting my foot in it.'

'"Oh dear", indeed. It's quite the party-stopper, that line, isn't it?' He was moving again, this time towards the door. 'Don't forget your coffee. Lunch is in an hour, so you'd better not scoff too many ginger nuts or you'll upset Chef.'

'And we all know the consequences of annoying your father.'

'Sorry to disappoint you, but it's not my father's culinary delights you're being treated to. Lunch is on me.'

For the next hour, Clara worked doubly fast to make up for the time she had spent reading. But all the while she was sorting through Val Liberty's things she kept thinking what kind of a woman she must have been to take on such a family. What an enormous challenge she had accepted the day she had agreed to marry Mr Liberty – or Gabriel, as she now knew him as – a widower with three young children who between them must have tested her love and patience beyond endurance.

Clara had done many things in her life of which she had later thought better, but this one was perhaps the most unworthy. She knew she had no right to do it, but she was hooked. Having begun to see the Liberty family in a new light, she wanted to know more, understand them better.

She took the diaries from the hatbox and slipped them into a bag with the intention of reading them later. She would return them to Mermaid House tomorrow morning with no one else the wiser.

Where would be the harm in that? She was only borrowing them.

Chapter Thirty-Two

In bed that night, long after Ned had fallen asleep, Clara was reading the diaries. As she turned the pages in the soft beam of light, she was conscious that while she might refer to the diaries as 'borrowed', she was actually stealing the private thoughts of a woman who, if she were alive, would have every right to be furious at Clara's intrusion into her honest record of her own failings as well as the shortcomings of others. Clara knew from what she had read that Val had been a fair woman. She had tried hard to see a difficult situation from every angle. Yet there were times when Clara got annoyed with Val's 'understanding'. She longed to shout, 'Stop making excuses for them all!' The tricks that had been played on her by Caspar and his sister were breathtakingly diabolical, and as their father had turned a blind eye to what was going on, he was no better than his scheming brats.

The first diary began a month after Val, in her own words, had 'taken on the job of nanny and housekeeper at Mermaid House'. This bleak description of herself, so soon into her marriage, seemed to have been prompted by a case of good intentions on her part that had gone disastrously wrong.

I cannot believe what happened today! I'm still shaking with anger and indignation. The whole situation is so gruesomely destructive I have to get my thoughts and shock down on paper – hence this journal, something I haven't done in years, not since I was a child with TB and had to spend so much time in the sanatorium and thought I would die of loneliness. N.B. Clearly there is a connection here!! Will think about this in more detail when I have calmed down!

The trouble started last week, and I really could kick myself for not seeing how I was being manipulated – just like the heroine of *Rebecca* at the hands of Mrs Danvers – but in all truth, how was I to know? I suggested to Caspar and Damson that the three of us ought to get our heads together and do something about Jonah's birthday. 'How do you know it's his birthday?' Damson had asked, her closed face watching me slyly from behind her long curtain of hair. 'Why, is it a secret, darling?' I replied (and yes, I do try to call the children something endearing, even if I don't mean it half the time). She didn't say anything and I didn't think it strange that until that moment no one had mentioned the fact that Jonah's fourth birthday was just round the corner. I only found out about it by chance when I had been putting away some papers – just another example of the stuff that Gabriel is for-ever leaving about the house. Putting the letters and documents away in his desk I saw a card that must have come in the post that I hadn't seen. It was from the doctor's surgery in Deaconsbridge recommending that Jonah be brought in for his pre-school booster. It was then that I saw the date of his birth. The only thought that crossed my mind at that point was that it was lucky I had seen the card as otherwise, and knowing Gabriel and his lack of foresight when it came to anything to do with his children, the child's birthday would probably have been and gone without any of us realising.

Still sitting at the table with Caspar and Damson – Jonah was upstairs in bed – I asked them why neither of them had thought to tell me when their brother's birthday was. Damson shrugged and said, 'If you'd wanted to know, you only had to ask.' There was something in her voice that made me want to snap back at her. Cold and patronising, she was treating me no better than a charlady. Restraining myself, I said, 'Why don't we arrange a party for him? You'd like that, wouldn't you? Help me blow up the balloons and make the jellies.' I thought I was doing the right thing, involving them in something by treating them as equals, rather than tiresome children. (Goodness, how weary I am from trying to win them over! When all the time they begrudge me the very air I breathe!)

Eventually it was decided, between Caspar and Damson, that we would organise a surprise party the following Saturday for Jonah, and that it would coincide with the day their father was returning from his three-week trip to Helsinki. I should have smelt a rat when Caspar and Damson insisted I didn't mention what we were doing to Gabriel, but I was so caught up in my own pride and vanity that I was finally forging a link with the twins that I didn't see the warning signs. Oh, if only I had! The pair of them made the invitations – pieces of paper with a cake drawn on (rather crudely in my opinion, given their age), and I wrote out the envelopes with the addresses of Jonah's little friends from his nursery school. These were duly posted – or so I thought – by Caspar and Damson, who even today after all the commotion, swore blind they had walked to the end of the drive and handed them over to the postman, but I just know that if I were to tackle Mr Potts, he would confirm that no such thing occurred.

Meantime, I had forged ahead with the shopping and baking, and last night while the children slept, I worked like a mad thing in the Banqueting Hall, blowing up balloons, setting out the trestle tables, decorating them with colourful paper tablecloths, paper plates and cups. I put a tape-recorder on a table in front of the fireplace so that we could have games of musical chairs and pass the parcel, and before going to bed I iced the cake I'd made that morning, giving it the finishing touch of 'Happy Birthday Jonah' and placing four blue candles, one at each corner.

Then this morning, and on Caspar and Damson's instructions, I wished Jonah a happy birthday but kept quiet about the present we had for him – the twins had claimed that it wouldn't be fair to their father for Jonah to open it without him being there to share the moment. Again, I should have thought something was wrong when Jonah didn't pursue the matter. He just looked at the card I had given him, turned it over and ran his fingers over the embossed picture of a little boy flying along at top speed on a bicycle. So intent was his scrutiny, it was as though he had never seen anything like it before.

Why, oh why, didn't I put two and two together? Why didn't I question the fact that in the run-up to his birthday he never once referred to it? In my defence I shall have to put it down to my ignorance of children and their mores. Jonah's quietness is also a factor. I've never come across anyone with more natural reticence. Rarely does he speak unless spoken to directly, and even then his words are so reluctantly given one can hardly make them out. 'Speak up!' Gabriel yells at him. 'Stop muttering!' But that only makes it worse, as I often tell him. Jonah needs someone in his life with a gentler manner than his father has. Someone with the patience to tease out the words, to give him the confidence he so badly lacks. I can't imagine what kind of nannies these children have had in the past. The twins are practically out of control, little better than savages. In contrast, Jonah has the anxious look of somebody who's lost a shilling and found sixpence.

Just after breakfast, Gabriel phoned to say that his flight was going to be delayed, but he hoped to be home by three, which unbeknown to him, meant he would miss the first hour of the party. But I wasn't deterred. At least he would be there for when it came to blowing out the candles on the cake and singing Happy Birthday to Jonah. By now I was almost as excited as a small child myself, imagining the delight on Gabriel's face when he walked into the middle of his youngest son's party. But by half past three, my excitement left me. Not one child had shown up. Poor Jonah, there he was, standing in the Banqueting Hall wearing a party hat with a long feather poking out from the top that Damson had made him wear, tearful bewilderment all over his face.

'Looks like no one's going to turn up,' Caspar said, helping himself to a cocktail sausage and flicking the stick on to the floor.

Jonah went over to the tables, stared hard at the plates of crisps, sandwiches and jugs of juice. There was such a look on his face. I couldn't fathom it for the life of me. And then we heard the sound of a car. It was Gabriel. The twins rushed to meet him, but Jonah came and stood next to me. If I had known better, I would have realised he was frightened. The next thing to happen was that Gabriel came marching in, knocking a bunch of balloons out of the way that was hanging above the door. 'What the hell's going on here?' he roared. 'Whose idea was this?' Jonah stepped behind me – dear God, he was actually hiding from his own father! I could feel his small body shaking against my legs.

It breaks my heart to say what happened next, but Gabriel continued to shout, oblivious to the harm he was doing to Jonah, and probably has been doing these last four years. In the end I took hold of Jonah who looked as if he was going to be sick with fright and carried him across the courtyard and inside the main part of the house. Gabriel followed, the twins at either side of him, and told me I had had no right to do what I had. 'But why?' I demanded – I was close to tears myself now. And then it all came tumbling out. Jonah's birthday was never celebrated because that was the day his mother – Gabriel's first wife – had died. 'So – so why didn't anybody tell me?' I stammered, my stomach sinking right down to my toes, my head feeling light with shock. 'It's not something I care to mention,' Gabriel snapped back at me. 'And what about Jonah?' I pressed – the poor lad was still burying himself in my skirt. 'Doesn't he deserve better than this?' I got no answer, and after Gabriel had stormed off, the twins trailing in his wake, I was left to explain to Jonah that there had been a terrible mix-up. Oh, my saints! What an understatement! Just as Jonah must have thought he was at last having his very own birthday party, it was snatched away from him. And he never said a word. Just stood there holding back the tears, his chin up, his eyes blinking rapidly. I bent down and hugged him. 'Don't worry, darling, you'll have your party if it's the last thing I do.'

Silently cursing Caspar and Damson's deviousness – my goodness, how that sly pair took me for a fool and manipulated me for their own pleasure! – I knew that from then on I would have my work cut out bringing this family together.

There was a gap of several weeks before Val took up her pen again. It seemed she had won herself, and Jonah, a small but important victory. From the little she had read of the diaries, Clara decided that based on the randomness of the entries, and their heated, exasperated content, Val only wrote when she needed to get something off her chest. It made Clara wonder if the poor woman had had any friends to whom she could turn. And if she hadn't, how awful it must have been for her to be so isolated at Mermaid House where there was so much to contend with.

Never did I think I would have to assume the role of mediating diplomat to the extent I have. An agreement has been reached. Jonah is to be allowed to celebrate his birthday, but on the condition that it's done a week after the official date. According to Gabriel, this will give the memory of his first wife the degree of respect it deserves.

I know very little about the woman I have replaced, other than what her portrait in the library tells me – that she was beautiful and serene, with an edge of fun-loving determination beneath her gentle surface. To my shame, I am now desperate to listen to the snatches of gossip that come my way during my shopping trips into Deaconsbridge, as well as the snippets of information the cleaning lady lets slip. Until now I had forced myself not to dig too deeply into Gabriel's previous marriage, accepting his silence quite readily and acknowledging that the past was best left to deal with itself. But regrettably my shield of common sense has dropped and I'm eager for the smallest of details.

Also to my shame, I'm beginning to wonder if I didn't agree to this marriage a little too hastily. Would it have been so very bad to remain alone and unmarried? Hindsight tells me I should have got to know Gabriel better before I accepted his proposal, but I suppose we both saw the convenient opportunities each could offer the other. But how will I ever manage Caspar and Damson? Of course I understand that they're both hurting from losing their mother at so young and tender an age but, really, at some point in their lives they are going to have to knuckle down and move on. But there I go again, being too hard on them. I must remember that when all is said and done, they are only children.

Clara's eyelids were drooping, so she turned out the light reluctantly, but instead of falling asleep, her thoughts turned to Jonah and lunch that day, when they had been sitting at the table in the kitchen. She had watched him talking to his father as he served him a portion of tuna and pasta salad, and had realised that what she had previously condemned as his irritating casual manner was an act. The relaxed body language was there to cover his uneasiness: the reserve between father and son could not have been greater. And reflecting on his inability to do more than the weekly shop for his father, Clara wondered if this was the only way he felt able to help a man he was scared of. Admittedly, twenty-four hours ago she would have trounced him as a wimp for not standing up to his father, but now she was seeing things differently. She saw not a grown man but a small boy hiding behind the skirts of a woman he scarcely knew while his father ranted at his audacity in wanting to celebrate the day he was born.

And what of Gabriel Liberty? What heartbreak had he buried beneath that gruff exterior? What bitterness did he still harbour over his children's refusal to carry on the family business?

The next morning Clara woke early, made herself a cup of tea – careful not let the kettle whistle and disturb Ned – then slipped back into bed to carry on where she had left off last night. The diary had moved on to 1973.

Tuesday, 29 August.

Goodness! Gabriel left this morning on another of his big trips – it's Oslo this time, inspecting a pipeline he's supplied something or other for – and I feel like I'm living in a madhouse! Last week Caspar and Damson told the vicar I'd converted the household to Catholicism, which of course I haven't, I merely suggested that something a little more uplifting than the low-church service at St Edmund's would suit me better, to which Gabriel had snorted and called me a papist candle-worshipper . . . oh dear, I seem to be losing the thread here. What I was trying to say was that on top of that Caspar and Damson have now developed a morbid fascination with death and have been carrying out mock funerals with anything dead they've found on the hills and moors. Added to which, they now dress up like something out of a Gothic romance. I've no idea where or how they've got hold of the outfits, but they spend their days drifting about the house in black velvet cloaks. Damson spends her evenings winding her long hair up with bits of rag – a pillow case is missing from her bed I notice – so that in the morning she has what she thinks is an authentic hairstyle. Most suitable for 1973, I'm sure! She wears an old cotton nightdress under her cloak and seems to be modelling herself on Cathy in *Wuthering Heights*. Caspar, complete with riding boots and a floppy white shirt – drooping cuffs, limp collar – is a latterday Lord Byron. Oh, yes, he even has an absurd hat! Yesterday they spent all day out on the moors. When I asked them what they had been up to, they looked at me as though I had no right to ask such a question. With a vagueness that made me want to take a rolled-up newspaper to them, Caspar waved a book of poetry under my nose and said, 'If you must know, we were reading poetry.' While I applaud anyone for extending their knowledge, I can't help but think I'd prefer them to be more like other teenagers. Normal teenagers. What I wouldn't do to be worried about trivial matters like Damson defacing her bedroom walls with posters of pop stars and sighing from dawn till dusk with the ache of an unrequited crush on some boy or other, and Caspar pestering for a motorbike. I mean, that's what teenagers are about, aren't they? I wonder if it isn't just a little unhealthy the way Caspar and Damson cling to each other. I hardly dare bring myself to write this, but every time I look at them with their arms linked, their eyes fixed on each other, I come over with the most awful feeling. Surely I'm wrong? Oh, please let me be wrong. Please let their bizarre behaviour – this exclusive need to be apart from others, to scorn the rest of the world for its ignorance – be an adolescent phase. Nothing more worrying. Nothing untoward.

Saturday, 18 November.

Just as I thought life was beginning to settle down, the building bricks of normality, which I have been so carefully arranging, have come tumbling down on me yet again. For the fourth time in as many weeks, Jonah has run away from school. But at least now Gabriel will have to do something; he will have to get his stubborn head out of the sand and DO SOMETHING!

Knowing that Jonah has been so unhappy makes me feel negligent and useless. For some time now I had thought perhaps we had turned the corner with him. He was beginning to come out of his shell, talking more. Well, talking more to me – the moment his brother and sister showed their faces (or his father) he clammed up. Reports from school also confirmed that he was making good progress, claiming that he was 'participating' more actively. He had even joined in with a few clubs and was spending less time on his own. It had all sounded so encouraging, as if, at long last, he was through the worst of it. But then the phone call came from school to say that he had tried to run away, but we were not to worry. He had been found by a keen-eyed teacher who had come across him hitching a lift as she drove to school. 'All under control, Mrs Liberty,' the house-master said. 'Most of the little devils try it at some time or other.' His tone was oily and patronising, though he probably thought he was reassuring me.

The third time it happened I suggested to Gabriel that we ought to review the situation, which was a phrase Jonah's house-master had used on the phone when he called to say that Jonah had been found sleeping in a bus shelter: 'Perhaps, Mrs Liberty, it's time for us all to review the situation.' In response to this, Gabriel declared that Jonah was attention-seeking, that he just had to face facts – certain things in life were damned unpleasant but one simply had to square one's shoulders and accept one's lot. No further comment.

No further comment! Honestly, I could have hit him with a frying-pan!!

But instead of confronting Gabriel as I know I should have done, I phoned the house-master and demanded to know what they were doing to Jonah to cause him so much unhappiness. 'What kind of a school are you running, that you allow children in your care to sleep rough in bus shelters?'

'I understand your concern, Mrs Liberty, but let me assure you, we do the best we can. But if a pupil isn't prepared to co-operate, then frankly, it's an uphill struggle and there's not a lot we can do.'

Co-operate!

Uphill struggle!

Where was the love and support these children needed? And, yes, I noticed that not once in the conversation did the thoroughly irksome little man refer to Jonah as a child. He was nothing but a lump to be added to the sausage-meat that would be squeezed through the machine and pushed out the other side as a supposedly mature and responsible member of society.

'He's not happy,' I told Gabriel, when the fourth phone call came. This blatant truth was reinforced by the headmaster (we were obviously above the level of mere house-master now), when he summoned us to school to discuss the matter. Gabriel tried to wriggle out of the appointment, but I was having none of it. 'You will do this one small thing, Gabriel Liberty, or you will live to regret it.' It was the sternest I had ever been with him.

So there we were, in the bone-chilling inner sanctum of the headmaster's study, to discuss Jonah's fate. Gabriel was still of the opinion that Jonah needed to take the rough with the smooth, but I stuck my neck out (I knew I'd never forgive myself if I didn't) and said, 'I have seen and heard nothing here this afternoon to convince me that this is the right environment for a sensitive boy like Jonah.' Once Gabriel had got his furious throat-rattling under control, the headmaster said, 'I'm inclined to agree with you, Mrs Liberty. And let me tell you, rarely do I agree with parents on the issue of what they think is best for their offspring. Not enough objectivity in my opinion. But, in Jonah's case, I wholeheartedly agree that he would benefit from a different school.'

Yes, I thought, as we drove home with Jonah looking ashen-faced in the back of the car, you're washing your hands of a problem child who challenges the whole ethos of your horrible school.

Gabriel can't stomach the notion that he is the father of a problem child. 'There's no shame involved,' I told him, as he gripped the steering-wheel with steam practically coming out of his ears. His face was grim and he made no response, but I saw his eyes flicker to the rear-view mirror to look at his son in disgust.

Poor Jonah, eight years old and the weight and guilt of the world squarely on his young inadequate shoulders.

The sound of creaking from Ned's bed above the cab had Clara snapping the diary shut and sliding it under her mattress. She waited for him to make his way down the short ladder before slipping into bed with her to claim his all-important first hug of the day.

Just in time she remembered what day it was. When he appeared at her side, she said, 'Ooh, Ned, what's that on your nose?'

His hand flew to his face. 'What?' he said, alarmed.

'April Fool!' She laughed. Pulling him into bed with her, she planted a huge kiss on his cheek then blew the fruitiest of raspberries into his warm neck. As he squealed, giggled and wriggled, the strength of her love for him rose up within her and she held him tightly, vowing never to make him unhappy as Jonah Liberty had been. And God forbid that you should ever end up with a sadistic sibling like Caspar or Damson, she thought.

A better person might be prepared to make allowances for people like the Libertys because they had never truly come to terms with the death of Anastasia, who had been such a central figure in their lives, but Clara thought that nothing in the world would ever make her feel sympathetic towards Caspar and his freaky-sounding twin sister.

Still cuddling Ned, she despaired of Machiavellian men like Caspar. Vain men who revelled in their own perceived perfection. Not so much running on testosterone as functioning on super-strength narcissism. She had loathed him in the supermarket, and the second viewing on Saturday night had confirmed her initial reaction.

She hoped that he held the same opinion of her and that while she was still around he wouldn't be in any hurry to grace Mermaid House with his presence again.

Chapter Thirty-Three

Archie was relieved to be getting through the morning's workload faster than he'd thought they might. When they had turned up at the cottage in Castleton the woman who had done most of the gabbing in the shop on Saturday took one look at Samson and his battleship-sized body and said, 'You will be careful, won't you? We've only just had the decorators in.'

'We'll be like silk rubbing against velvet, love,' Archie had reassured her. The look she gave him said she didn't appreciate being called 'love'. No chance of a brew, then, he had thought, as he and Samson carried a three-seater sofa over the threshold, taking care not to scrape the twee Victorian-style wallpaper and mahogany-stained dado rail.

Now they had finished and went to settle up with Mrs Hoity-Toity. Like the good tradesmen they were, they humoured her by waiting in the hall while she wrote out the cheque in the kitchen, then beat a hasty retreat back to the shop, picking up sandwiches from the bakery in town for a late lunch.

Comrade Norm had been holding the fort, along with Bessie, who had been doing sterling work on some boxes of crockery. Dressed in an old nylon overall, which she used to wear when she was doing the housework, she seemed happy in the little kitchen with a stack of washed plates, cups and saucers on the draining-board. With slow, deliberate movements, she was drying the china carefully before arranging it on a set of cheap veneer shelves in the front of the shop. Archie pretended not to notice the broken sugar bowl in the bin, half hidden beneath an old newspaper.

Lunch dealt with, he took the van and drove home to check the post. These days, it never came before he left for work, but when he saw what was on the mat in the hall, he wished he hadn't bothered. It was another pompously worded letter from Stella's solicitor wanting to know which firm of solicitors he had instructed to take care of the divorce. It was ironic that today of all days – April Fool's Day – he should receive such a communication. It was the anniversary of the day on which he had proposed to Stella and it had been a long-standing joke between them that she had been a fool to accept.

'Running jump' and 'go stick it' were the words that were ready to leap from Archie's tongue after he had read through the letter. But he swallowed them, knowing that he should have taken on a solicitor by now. He hadn't consciously shied away from the task, it just hadn't figured too highly on his list of jobs to do. One way or another, he never had a minute to himself now. Still staring at the piece of stiff grey paper in his hand, he considered whether it was worth approaching Stella directly: that way they might save a lot of hassle and expense by cutting out the middlemen. But perhaps he was being naïve: in this greedy day and age, the winner took all. Except there could never be an outright winner in divorce. All there could ever be were two disappointed, wounded victims, who had to live with the sad knowledge that they had let each other down.

He sighed and went outside to the van. No time for such maudlin meanderings, he chided himself, not when a pretty young woman was waiting for him at Mermaid House.

It had rained for most of the weekend but today a weak sun was trying to find a crack in the thick blanket of grey cloud. It was still unseasonably cold and Archie was glad of the heater in the van.

Mermaid House was the most extraordinary place he

had seen in a long while. 'Well, I'll be blowed,' he said, when he first caught sight of it on the brow of a rise in the landscape. 'What a godforsaken place to live.' He carried on along the bone-shaking drive in awed amazement, the empty van rattling noisily as it splashed through muddy puddles. He pulled in beside Clara Costello's camper-van, and wondered how many times his modest end-of-terrace could fit into this vast old place. He got out and crossed the shiny wet cobbles of the courtyard but came to a stop when he drew level with the skip. He couldn't resist having a quick shufti – after all, one man's rubbish was another's livelihood. His surreptitious foray was brought to an abrupt end by a door being flung open and a none-too-friendly voice saying, 'Who the hell are you and what d'you think you're doing snooping through my belongings?'

Clara had warned Archie what to expect. 'Herr Liberty runs a boot-camp up here on the quiet,' she had told him on the phone, 'but take no notice of his commandant persona. He's a real sweetie when you get to know him.'

Archie stepped forward. 'Archie Merryman's the name. Miss Costello phoned me on Saturday about some odds and ends you wanted to get rid of.'

He was given a disdainful eyeball-frisking, followed by, 'Uh, so you're that rag-and-bone man she got in touch with, are you? I suppose you'd better come in. But be sure to wipe your feet.'

Archie did as instructed, then followed him to a large kitchen. He was allowed no further, though, and after he had been ordered to stay where he was, the cussed old man went over to an open doorway. 'Miss Costello,' he bellowed, 'your disreputable rag-and-bone man's here.'

A door opened and footsteps sounded.

'Mr Liberty, there is no need to shout. And how many times do I have to tell you, Mr Merryman runs a second-hand shop and he's the least disreputable man I know.' Her voice and footsteps grew louder until finally she came into the kitchen. She was dressed in dirty jeans, a grubby

T-shirt, and a cobweb decorated her dark hair; she looked younger than Archie had remembered her. The bright eyes and smile were the same, though. 'Hello, Archie,' she said. 'The Commandant treating you as rudely as I said he would?'

'Not so badly. How's that lad of yours? Did he find his mermaid?'

'Oh, yes. It was here just as he said it would be. How's your mother, everything okay with—'

'Great Scott! How much longer have I got to put up with this incessant tea-party chatter? I thought there was some business to be transacted.'

Clara winked at Archie and tutted. 'You leave the business to me, Mr Liberty. But talking of tea parties, bung the kettle on, would you? I'm sure Mr Merryman would appreciate a cup of your finest PG Tips.'

Mr Liberty's nostrils flared and Archie speculated as to who was the real commandant here. He fell in step beside Clara as she led him the length of the house, the rubber soles of her shoes squeaking on the polished wooden floor. 'I'm afraid none of it is of any great worth,' she said, 'but I've tried to organise everything into two piles: stuff you might be able to sell and stuff that's a little more dubious.'

She pushed open a heavy door and showed him into an enormous drawing room that had to be about thirty feet by twenty. Stella would have loved all this, Archie thought suddenly: the grandness of the room, the high ceiling, the massive stone fireplace and the beautiful mullion windows. For years she had been on at him to move. 'We need more space,' she would say, leafing through the local paper and admiring houses way out of their reach. He couldn't understand why she tormented herself looking at them. 'But why do we need more space?' he had argued back. 'There's only the two of us, and this is plenty.' In return, she had given him one of her standard you-don't-understand looks. Well, she'd been right on the button there. He didn't understand her need to stretch their finances just so that she could indulge in a bigger version of playing house. But this place might just about have satisfied her. It would have given her all the room she could have ever wanted. There was sufficient space here to swing a Tyrannosaurus Rex, never mind a cat.

The furniture wasn't up to much though, he reckoned. Most of it was shabby and not much better than the pieces he sold in his shop. The room was home to a hotchpotch of paraphernalia: an elephant's foot that had been turned into a stand for a tatty old Swiss-cheese plant, a bamboo table with a cracked glass top, a leather hand-tooled pouffe with a gaping hole and stuffing oozing out of it, a Chinese silk wall-hanging, a set of African drums, a lacquered chest, and a cabinet chock full of bits of jade, ivory and carved wooden animals. Souvenirs brought home by a man who had travelled, thought Archie, a little enviously.

He began to look at the room more critically, seeing the cracks in the high ceilings, and the gaping holes in the plasterwork above the moulded skirting-boards. Why, it was nothing but a demanding bugbear – and would cost a fortune to heat and keep clean. Other than Stella, who in their right mind would want to take this on?

He felt his mood turning bitter and he thought again of the solicitor's letter he had to deal with when he got home that evening. For the first time since she had left him he felt angry. Until now he had resigned himself to what had happened: he had failed his wife, so what else could he expect? But now he felt the unfairness of Stella's actions, the sting of the implied criticism and blame, the cruel, underhand way in which she had carried on her affair. Then there had been the continuous sniping at him for supposedly holding her back. 'I could have done so much better for myself if I hadn't married you,' she had told him once. She had apologised later for that, but once said, words can never be retracted. He had always thought of himself as a considerate man, who took people at face value, who didn't judge and condemn, because at the end of the day no one is perfect. And that was why he had never confronted Stella about her affair. He had wanted to give her space to resolve whatever she was going through. But now he saw how weak he had been, and that Stella had taken advantage of him and turned him into a fool.

An April Fool for sure.

Realising that Clara was waiting for him to speak, he shook himself out of his despondency. 'Sorry, what were you saying?'

'I was just saying that if any of these things are too awful to contemplate, you must ... Are you okay, Archie? You look a bit bothered.'

He forced himself to smile. 'I'm tired, that's all. Now, then, let's see about this little lot, shall we? Looks to me like you've got the whole bag of tricks here.' And with a supreme act of will, he focused his attention on the boxes on the floor. Without needing to sift too deeply through them he could see that the assorted junk was mostly saleable – pots, pans, ladles, a china toast rack in the shape of a loaf of bread, a rusting hand whisk, various discoloured and outdated kitchen gadgets, a bedside lamp and an old money-box. It was the usual household stuff he saw every day. What he couldn't get rid of he'd pass on to a fellow dealer up in New Mills whose customers weren't so choosy as his. He reached into his trouser pocket for his roll of money. 'No problem,' he said, 'I'll take the lot, save you the trouble of messing about with any of it. Is that it?'

She pulled a face. 'I'm afraid not. I've got a load more upstairs. Oh, and I should have said, the electrical items all work. I've tested them myself.'

He put his money away for now. 'I'll say this for you, you're doing a thorough job here.'

'A little too thorough at times.' Mr Liberty was lumbering in with two mugs in his hands. 'Having her around is akin to taking laxatives,' he said to Archie, handing him a mug of tea. 'She sweeps you clean, whether you like it or not.'

'Thank you for sharing that delightful analogy with us, Mr Liberty.' Clara smiled. She took her mug. 'Was there anything else?'

Judging from the twist to his mouth, the old boy had taken his dismissal with pleasure. Strange man, thought Archie. He sipped his tea. 'What on earth possessed you to take on this colossal task?' he asked Clara.

She laughed. 'A question I've been asking myself several times a day since I started.'

'And the answer?' he pressed.

'I'd like to say that it's down to pure altruism, but my friends would claim it's due to my perverse desire to take charge and organise everything around me.'

'Now that's just what I could do with.'

'Oh?'

Something in her tone made him want to unburden himself. The thought shocked him: until that moment he had never seen himself as a man who was burdened. He felt crushed. He looked at her enquiring expression and wondered if she would mind being used as a sounding board. Because that was what he needed. Someone objective in whom he could confide. He hadn't turned to his friends for advice. Male pride, he supposed. That, and he didn't want the whole of Deaconsbridge knowing his business. A small town was the devil for gossip. He also hated the idea of people feeling sorry for him, viewing him differently. He'd always been good old Archie, cheerful, dependable. He knew it was irrational, but he felt as if he would let everyone down by being anything else.

Go on, he urged himself, confide in her. She's an outsider. Who would she tell? Say something. Anything. Because if you stand there any longer looking like a prize idiot, she'll think the lights have gone out and you're a meter short of a shilling.

Staring at him over the top of her mug of tea, she said,

'It's none of my business, but is it something to do with your mother?'

Her gentle probing did away with the remnants of his resolve, and he acknowledged the dragging pain that had been with him since Stella had left. 'Yes and no,' he volunteered. 'Bessie is certainly one of my concerns, but . . . the thing is, my wife left me recently and I haven't a clue how to deal with it. I thought I was handling it, but now I'm not so sure.'

'How recently?'

'Just—' He swallowed and hung on grimly to his self-control. 'Just over a week ago.'

'Oh, Archie, I'm so sorry.' She reached out and touched his arm lightly. 'Come and sit down.' She led him across the room, avoiding the oozing pouffe and elephant's foot, to two high-backed armchairs in the bay of a window. 'It must be awful for you. Did you have any idea that this was going to happen?'

'I'd be lying if I said it came as a surprise. Things have been difficult for a while, and what with Bessie's stroke and her moving in with us, well . . . let's just say I haven't helped matters.'

'But it must have been a terrible blow.'

He ran a finger over the fraying fabric on the arm of his chair. 'I think it's only now that it's finally hitting home. I'm ashamed to say I feel angry at what she's done.'

'And what's wrong with that? Why shouldn't you?'

'Because . . .' He gave the chair a light thump: a cloud of dust rose into the air. 'Because I'm not like that. I never get angry.'

'*Never?* What an exceptional man you must be if that's true.'

'Not exceptional. Not by a long chalk.' In his mind's eye he saw his father losing his temper and lashing out at Bessie. Until Archie had been big enough to step in and end the nightmare for her.

'What does your solicitor advise?'

'I haven't got that far.' He told her about the letter that

had arrived that morning. 'You're probably thinking I've been stupidly slow and cowardly, aren't you?'

'Not at all. But you have to accept that the problem isn't going to go away on its own. Have you spoken to your wife since she left?'

'No.'

'Do you know where she is?'

'She's in Macclesfield with the man who—' He broke off. An agonising moment passed before he managed to pull himself together. 'Sorry, it's just hearing the words out loud makes it seem all the more real. I suppose that's what I've been doing this last week or so, keeping it to myself so that I don't have to face up to what I'm going to have to do.'

'And do you know what you *want* to do? What choices you need to make?'

He smiled ruefully. 'Oh, aye, I'm double-parked on what's to be done. I'll agree to the divorce, sell the house and move into something smaller and cheaper. I'll keep Second Best going and somehow look after Mum.'

'That takes care of today. What about tomorrow?'

In spite of his flagging spirits, he laughed, and felt better for it. 'That's just the kind of talk I need.' He drained his mug. 'Now, then, let's get back to work or your man Liberty will be after me.' They both rose to their feet. 'Thanks,' he said, 'thanks a million.'

'What for? I haven't helped you resolve anything. More's the pity.'

'No, sweetheart, but you've listened, and maybe that was all I needed.'

Chapter Thirty-Four

Before he had even opened his eyes Gabriel knew the day would not be a good one. It was Friday morning, and it was Ned and Miss Costello's final day at Mermaid House. He didn't know how it had happened, but somehow during the last week he had got so used to having them around he was going to miss them when they were gone.

A skew-eyed glance at the alarm clock on the bedside table told him it was a quarter past seven. He pushed back the bedclothes and, with a creak of springs, thumped his feet down on to the floor. He wriggled his buckled old toes, then launched himself stiffly upright. He went over to the window and gave a cautious tug at the curtains. They glided smoothly and soundlessly along the track and he imagined Miss Costello scolding him for not putting more faith in her ability to operate a drill and knowing which rawlplugs to use. She had even filled in the gaping holes left by the chunks of plaster that had fallen out. He stood at the window, breathing in the fresh outdoor smell of the curtains, which had been washed yesterday and left to dry in the blustery wind and sunshine. She had ironed them while they were still slightly damp and a comforting steamy warmth had filled the kitchen. While she had been doing that he had helped Ned with the latest page of his scrapbook – a drawing of a box on wheels (supposedly a camper-van) and three sloping lines of wonky writing. 'How do you spell diesel?' the boy had asked.

'D E I S E L,' Gabriel had answered.

'D I E,' Miss Costello had corrected him, from behind a cloud of steam.

'Should have been a school-teacher, your mother.' He winked at Ned.

'Jonah's a teacher, isn't he? Can you write "diesel" for me, please?' A scrap of paper was pushed across the table. 'He must be very clever to be a teacher. You have to know *everything*.'

'That's a matter for dispute.' He passed the piece of paper back. 'Any old fool can stand up in front of a class and tell them what to do. Even I could do it.'

There was a snigger from the direction of the ironing-board. 'Spelling lessons would be interesting.'

'I'll have you know that was a mere slip of the tongue.'

'How do you spell "engine"?'

'Here, let me write it down for you before your mother gets out her stick of chalk. Or, worse, her cane to beat me.'

'Six of the best and a detention would do you the world of good, Mr Liberty.'

'You'd have to catch me first.'

'A ten-minute head start suit you?'

'She's a cruel, heartless woman, your mother.'

The boy looked up from his wobbly writing. 'My mummy isn't cruel. She's nice. And she makes *you* laugh.'

'Pah! Who told you that? It's a shameless lie and one that I shall defend till the cows are blue in the face.'

'Ahem, don't you mean till the cows come home? Fine English teacher you'd be with your metaphors running away with themselves.'

'Yes, but which is more likely to happen? The cows wandering home, or their faces turning blue? I think I have you there, Miss Costello, the point is mine.'

Still standing at his bedroom window, Gabriel sighed heavily. Life was going to be dull without them around.

He washed, shaved and dressed in his pristine bathroom, put his dirty clothes tidily in the laundry basket, as instructed, and went downstairs. The kitchen was beautifully warm – another of Miss Costello's miracles. She had had the Aga serviced by a man who knew what he was talking about: turned out all that had been wrong with it was a faulty thermostat. The treacherous gas heater that had burnt his arm had been banished to the gun room. And talking of treachery, that interfering Dr Singh had been conspicuous by his absence. So much for turning up here on Monday as had been threatened. Not that Gabriel was complaining: as far as he was concerned, the less he saw of the annoying quack the better.

He put the kettle on and went to sit in one of the Windsor chairs placed in front of the Aga. This had been another of Miss Costello's reforms. By moving the table, she had created a space beside the Aga where he could comfortably warm his feet of a morning. The chairs had been brought down from one of the rooms upstairs and she had awarded him and Ned the job of polishing them while she tackled the unenviable task of cleaning the main bathroom.

On day one of her assignment to sort out Mermaid House, Miss Costello had taken him at his word and put together a shopping list of things she considered would make his life easier. Then, the day before yesterday, she had dragged him off to the shops with the intention of making him buy these so-called labour-saving products. 'You have remembered to bring your wallet, haven't you?' she said, as they drove to the other side of Deaconsbridge in her camper-van, to the retail development he had never before visited. The vast range of electrical appliances on sale in the store was bewildering. 'How long will this take?' he asked warily, looking at the shelves of brightly coloured kettles, irons and toasters, which all seemed to resemble toys.

He needn't have worried. She knew exactly what she was looking for and, much to his admiration, badgered the spotty young assistant into giving them a ten per cent discount, plus free delivery for that same evening.

He had watched in further admiration late that night after she had put Ned to bed and had got down on her hands and knees and plumbed in the dishwasher. 'Are you deliberately trying to make me feel completely useless?' he had said, passing her a spanner and wishing he was forty years younger.

'Not at all. You do too good a job of it yourself. Now, let's see if this baby's going to perform. I'll put it on a quick rinse cycle.' She wriggled out from under the work surface, stood up, and rocked the slimline dishwasher into place. She shut the door, turned the dial with a clickety-click and pressed the start button. Water rushed through the pipes and the machine whooshed and whirred. He looked at her doubtfully. 'Should it make that noise?'

'Absolutely. And trust me, it'll transform your life. You'll wonder how you ever managed without it. Shall we sort out the microwave next?'

'What do you do for an encore? Walk on water?'

'Give it time, Mr Liberty. Give it time.'

Eating his breakfast of toast and marmalade and resting the plate on his stomach as he sat by the Aga, Gabriel listened to the news on the radio – or, rather, listened to the news on his new all-in-one, all-singing-and-dancing radio-CD-cassette player. It was another of Miss Costello's fine-tunings. 'Treat yourself, Mr Liberty,' she had said. 'Or do I have to twist your arm up round your shoulder-blades?' The reception and sound quality were certainly better than he was used to from his old radio, but the news was still as tedious. And as from tomorrow, the highlight of his day would be answering back some jumped-up nobody who fancied himself a political smart-arse.

Clara and Ned were having their own breakfast, and as her son dipped his spoon in and out of his bowl of Coco-Pops while he looked at his scrapbook spread across the narrow table, Clara had the feeling that he wasn't looking forward to moving on. He hadn't said anything, but the way he was lingering over each page she knew that leaving Mermaid House was going to be a wrench for him.

But the same was true for her. What was the old song about having become accustomed to somebody or other's face? It was from a musical. Yes, *My Fair Lady*, one of her mother's favourite shows. And while she hadn't fallen in love with the cranky owner of Mermaid House, she had enjoyed seeing him mellow. She'd also enjoyed keeping up the game of formality between them. Despite the shift in their relationship that had taken place, she always made a point of calling him Mr Liberty to his face – and he still referred to her as Miss Costello – but in her mind he had become Gabriel; not exactly archangel material, but a man with a softer side to him than he was used to exposing.

It had been a week of hard slog, though: her aching back and sore hands were proof of that. But she would leave knowing that she had spent a week doing something positive and worthwhile. She wasn't so sure of how long the benefits of her work would last. If left to his own devices Gabriel would probably let things slide back to how they had been. But she couldn't do anything about that. Perhaps she could speak to Jonah before she left and impress upon him that his father needed a cleaner, or maybe a housekeeper.

But he knew that already. What would be the point?

In the back of her mind she heard Louise and the gang telling her to leave well alone: 'Stop trying to control what isn't your concern.'

Sound advice.

Mercifully Caspar had stayed away from Mermaid House, and she hadn't seen Jonah since Sunday. Apparently he had been away on a school history trip to northern France and Belgium. Having read some of Val's diaries she could only marvel that any of the Liberty children had survived their childhood. She had alternated between being furious with Gabriel for ignoring the needs of his family and feeling desperately sorry for him. Clearly the death of his first wife had left him a broken man with no one to turn to. At various times in the week she had been tempted to ask him more about his family and the past, but the moment had never seemed right. Either Ned was around, or he and Gabriel were off on one of their adventures.

During the last few days the weather had picked up again, and while she had been busy clearing out cupboards, polishing neglected furniture, arranging with Archie to pick up yet more junk, supervising the chimney sweep and the collection of the skip, Gabriel had taken Ned down to the river to play. Yesterday they had returned from one of their expeditions smelling of fresh air, their faces red from the wind, announcing that they were starving. 'Lucky I picked up some scones and crumpets from the baker this morning,' she had said, when they were kicking off their mud-caked boots and about to leave them in an untidy heap. One look from her and they were lining them up beneath their neatly hanging jackets.

But whatever Gabriel and his family had suffered in the past, it was really none of Clara's business and she had no right to pry. Just as he had had no right to interrogate Ned about his father. She winced. Where did that leave her with Val's diaries? Guiltily, she made a mental note to return them before she and Ned left.

Looking at Ned as he scraped up the last of his cereal, Clara knew that her priority that day was to keep him cheerful. She didn't want him to be upset about leaving and the only trick she had up her sleeve to soften the blow for him was that once she had finished her work here today, they would be free to visit the Mermaid Cavern.

At Gabriel's insistence they were to have lunch in town at the Mermaid café. 'It's one o'clock, and I declare you officially out of contract now,' he said, when she appeared in the kitchen, expecting a sandwich – or a 'shambly', as Ned called them. Presenting her with an envelope, he added, 'It's your wages. You'll find I've been more than generous.'

Without opening it, she slipped it into her pocket. 'Fair enough, but I insist on driving. I'm not going anywhere in that death-trap of a Land Rover. At least two of the tyres are bald and I bet it hasn't been anywhere near a garage for years.'

He put up a show of resistance that got him nowhere, and after she had changed out of her filthy work clothes, they set off.

'Can I have chips, please, Mummy?' Ned called from his rear seat as they turned into the market square. 'And ketchup?'

'It's market day,' Gabriel said. 'You might have trouble parking.'

'Beans would be nice.'

'Of course, if you'd let me drive my death-trap, we'd be able to slip into any old space.'

'Mm . . . and lots of vinegar, please. I like vinegar. I like it when my lips go white because I've had too much.'

'Damn! You'll have to go round again.'

'Can we have a pudding as well?'

'There! There's a space. Quick!'

'For goodness' sake, Mr Liberty, calm down! You'll give yourself a heart-attack at this rate.'

'No chance. I'm saving that pleasure for when I've over-feasted on a coronary lunch-time special.'

They were met by Shirley and a raised eyebrow when she saw who they had with them. 'We missed you last Friday, Mr Liberty,' she said, handing them each a copy of the menu. 'Thought perhaps you'd taken your business elsewhere?'

'You mean you hoped I had.'

She smiled at Clara. 'Shall I get you some drinks while you choose?'

Gabriel took off his cap and thwacked the table with it. 'You make it sound as if you're offering us something decent, like a glass of single malt whisky.'

'Just give my sour friend a pint of your finest malt vinegar and ignore him,' said Clara.

'Don't worry, I always do. So what'll it be? How about a nice strawberry milkshake? We've just had a new machine installed and I'm itching to give it a whirl.' This last remark was directed at Ned, who nodded enthusiastically.

It was Ned who brought up the subject of their leaving. Expertly dipping the end of a chip into the pool of ketchup on his plate, he said, 'Will you miss us when we've gone, Mr Liberty? Will you be sad when you're all alone again?'

Clara willed the old devil to say something nice. But not too nice.

'That depends, doesn't it?' he said evasively, his gaze flickering over Clara.

'Why?' asked Ned.

'If I thought I was never going to hear from you again, that *might* make me sad.'

They both looked at Clara. Expectation was etched over their faces. 'You could send Mr Liberty the occasional postcard, Ned,' she said, thinking fast, while hiding her surprise that Gabriel had said something so refreshingly agreeable and tactful. 'That way he'll know what we're up to.'

Another chip went into the tomato sauce while Ned thought about this. 'But how will we know what Mr Liberty is doing?'

'You won't, lad. No one ever knows what I'm up to. And that's the way I intend to keep it.'

Ned's frown showed that this wasn't the answer he wanted. 'Couldn't we stay longer, Mummy? You could clean a bit more of Mr Liberty's house for him.'

Clara smiled. 'Mr Liberty's house is like the Forth Bridge. I could go on cleaning it for ever and ever.'

Ned's face brightened at the possibility. He turned to Gabriel, a chip dangling from his fork. 'Would you like Mummy to clean your house for ever and ever?'

'I'd like nothing better, but I suspect your mother wouldn't. Now, are you going to eat the rest of those chips or watch them grow?'

Over pudding – the obligatory Bakewell tart and custard – Gabriel said, 'Do you really have to rush off, Miss Costello? We came to an arrangement a week ago, couldn't we do something similar again?'

'And what about the holiday Ned and I are supposed to be enjoying? I told you, I'm making this trip to spend more time with my son, not spend my every waking hour cleaning for you. Or anyone else for that matter.'

'But wouldn't you agree that your son has benefited from his time at Mermaid House?'

She looked at him sternly, kept her voice low. 'Don't play dirty, Mr Liberty, it doesn't become you.'

'In my experience, there's no other way to play.'

Her patience was waning. 'Look, Ned and I have been here for over a week and we still haven't had so much as a glimpse of what we came to see. We want to see the sights. We want to be tourists. We want to laze around eating overpriced locally made fudge, and turn up our noses at tacky souvenirs and buy them all the same. We want to be day-trippers trudging round in the rain. We want to—'

'Then stay on at Mermaid House for a few more days as my guests, and you can do all the day-tripping you want to do in this area.'

She hesitated, and in that instant knew that she had lost the upper hand in the argument. Gabriel leaned in towards her. 'Miss Costello, hear me out. I would very much like you to stay so that I can repay a little of your kindness.'

'But you've done that already. You've paid me.'

'It's not always about money.'

She smiled. 'Is this the same man who once said everything had a price, that everything was for sale?'

He shifted in his seat. 'Well, maybe I've . . .' His words petered out.

'Maybe you've what?'

He drew his eyebrows together, screwed up his paper napkin, tossed it into his empty pudding bowl. 'Changed,' he mumbled.

It was difficult for her not to laugh at his discomfort. The poor man had come a long way in just one week. 'Well,' she said, 'just so that we're clear on a few points. If, and I say *if*, we were to stay, there would be no more scrubbing and polishing?'

'Agreed.'

'No more—'

'I said *as my guests*. Don't you ever listen?'

'Only if I like the sound of what's being suggested.'

'And do you?'

'In parts. But before I commit myself, I have to mull it over with the boss.' She turned to her son. 'Ned, what do you think we should do?'

His eager face was answer enough.

Chapter Thirty-Five

At bedtime that night, Clara knew it was important to put the brakes on Ned's excitement by stressing that they would only be extending their stay by a few days. 'We'll be moving on first thing on Monday morning, Ned,' she told him. 'There's so much more to see and do. Who knows what's round the corner for us?' He nudged the book she was supposed to be reading to him. He hasn't been listening, she thought, when she eventually turned out his light and gave him one last kiss. He thinks two more days will turn into three, then four, then goodness knows how many.

She sat at the narrow table with a glass of wine, a plate of crackers and a gooey wedge of Camembert, enjoying the peace and quiet of her own company, and wondered why she was so reluctant to hang around Mermaid House for much longer. It would still be a holiday for them, so what was the problem?

Because it hadn't been part of her original plan.

She cut into the soft cheese, picked the sticky lump off the knife, slipped it into her mouth, and let its creamy smoothness melt on her tongue. Helping herself to another piece, she thought of her original plan, designed to make her and Ned feel like intrepid explorers. She had wanted to show Ned what an exciting world he lived in, so that he would grow up knowing that there were endless possibilities out there for him. Getting caught up in the lives of a handful of folk – however interesting – had never been a part of it.

Once again, she heard Ron and Eileen extolling the virtues of their easy-come, easy-go lifestyle. 'Oh, yes, we always start out with a plan,' Ron had said, 'we like to tease ourselves with a map of intent, but half the fun in life is changing your mind and abandoning the rule book. Spontaneity is the name of the game.'

That's all very well, thought Clara, getting up and reaching for her writing things from the overhead locker, but sometimes spontaneity had a habit of getting above itself. If it wasn't too much of a paradox, spontaneity needed careful managing.

Putting these thoughts aside, she settled down to write a letter to her parents in Australia, with a separate page enclosed for her brother, Michael, and then she turned to the postcard she had bought in Deaconsbridge that afternoon. It showed a colourful selection of mermaid shop signs.

Dear Louise
On the verge of leaving Deaconsbridge, having
completed our missionary work – the natives are
almost civilised now! We're finally getting to see the
local sights this weekend (the mermaids are a clue!)
and then we'll be moving on to who knows where.
Further north probably. I'll give you a ring some time
next week just to check all is well.
    Lots of love,
        Clara and Ned

Now that she had put down their departure date in writing, it made their leaving on Monday seem more real, which pleased Clara. And, as Louise would be the first to say, seldom did Clara Costello change her mind or go back on her word. U-turns, according to the Clara Costello School of Management, were for back-pedalling wimps.

She tidied away the remains of the cheese and crackers, put her writing things away in their allocated place, and made up her bed. As she pulled her duvet out of the cupboard beneath the seat, and caught sight of her filthy jeans hanging on the hook of the shower door, she remembered that Gabriel had offered her the use of his washing-machine before they left. She also remembered the envelope he had given her, and which she had stuffed into her back pocket. Better remove it now before she forgot about it and threw it into the washing-machine tomorrow morning. Ripping open the envelope she extracted a slip of paper on which was written, 'Don't even think about turning this down!' Paper-clipped to it was a cheque. When she saw the amount – he had doubled the agreed sum – she shook her head, partly with disbelief, but also with affection. 'Silly old fool,' she murmured. A rush of fondness for him brought tears to her eyes. She was deeply touched. 'Silly, silly, *silly* man. I was right all along, more money than sense.'

The next morning Ned woke first. He got dressed without disturbing Clara, and she only realised he was up and about when he slipped under her duvet for a hug.

'Shall we ask Mr Liberty to come with us today?' he asked, when he surfaced from her embrace.

'Do you think he'd want to? He's probably seen the Mermaid Cavern hundreds of times.'

'But not with us.'

'True.'

He smiled and slid out of the bed. 'Shall I go and ask him?'

'How about some breakfast first?' But he was already standing by the door, a hand working at the lock. 'Oh, go on, then.' She gave in. 'But don't be surprised if he shouts at you for disturbing him.'

Yawning, she dragged herself reluctantly out of bed, wiped the condensation from the window above the table and watched Ned scamper across the courtyard. The back door opened before he reached it and she saw Gabriel staring down at his early-morning caller. She strongly approved of Ned's suggestion and she hoped Gabriel would accept the invitation with good grace: it would be her way of thanking him for his more than generous cheque.

Armed with a map and several guide books, Gabriel in the front with Clara, and Ned in the back with Mermy, they embarked on a day's worth of sightseeing.

But first they had to make a stop in town.

'Just let me pop into the bank,' Clara said, switching off the engine and grabbing her bag. 'I need some cash.' She also wanted to offload Gabriel's cheque. Inside the bank, and because it was only open for the morning on a Saturday, she joined a long queue that snaked its way round the small building. Minutes later someone else joined the queue behind her. It was Archie.

'Hello,' she said. 'Didn't think you bothered with banks. I thought you were strictly a cash-only man.'

'Ah well, my mattress gets uncomfortable if I put too much underneath it. It plays havoc with my back. Has the Commandant let you out for an hour or two?'

'I've finished work now. Ned and I are officially on holiday again. We're taking Mr Liberty to see the Mermaid Cavern.'

'Does that mean you'll be leaving us soon?'

'Monday morning.'

He looked disappointed. 'That's a shame. The place won't be the same without you.'

'I expect you'll manage pretty well.'

Someone at the front of the queue moved away and they inched forward.

'By the way,' he said, 'I wanted to thank you for passing all that work in my direction. I really appreciate it. Oh, and you might like to know, I took your advice. I've got myself organised with a solicitor. The ball is definitely rolling, as they say.'

Another person at the head of the queue moved off, and they shuffled forward again.

'I hope it works out for you, Archie. I'm sure it will. Eventually.'

He shrugged. 'You're probably right. Anyway, cheer me up by promising you'll come and say goodbye before you and Ned disappear. Leave town without doing that, and the sheriff and I will have to send a posse after you.'

'It's a promise.'

The Mermaid Cavern was only a few miles from the centre of Deaconsbridge. The road climbed out of the town, and in no time the landscape became markedly different: it was softer, greener, more curvaceous. This was limestone country, where the White Peak reigned and the harsher, darker terrain of the High Peak receded into the northern distance.

According to the guidebooks, the Mermaid Cavern was often overlooked in favour of the bigger and more commercialised show caves in nearby Castleton. None the less, they agreed that it was of geological and historical interest and worth a visit.

But the million-dollar question was: did the mermaid rock formation really look like a mermaid?

Parking Winnie between another camper-van, which had a Dutch numberplate, and a people-carrier containing two panting, slobbering Labradors, Clara asked Gabriel if he knew the answer.

'It's so long since I saw it, I can't remember,' he said.

'How long ago? Time for her to have grown taller?'

'It was 1963, if you must know.'

'Oh, well before I was born, then.' She leaned through to Ned. 'Okay, Buster, you can unbuckle yourself now. We're all set.'

'I came here with Anastasia. We went for a picnic afterwards, but it rained. It came down so hard, so suddenly, we had to shelter under a tree. She joked we would get struck by lightning and that we would both die and go to heaven. I told her I was already in heaven.'

Moved by the unexpected tenderness in his voice, and the vivid picture his words had just painted, Clara turned slowly to look at him. 'And you've never been back?'

He gave her an odd look. 'What? To heaven?'

'No.' She smiled. 'Here.'

'Wouldn't have been the same.'

Signposts directed them to a path that ran alongside a row of pretty cottages where yellow daffodils, purple crocuses, and tiny blue scillas brightened small neat gardens. Twists of smoke plumed from chimneys and the crisp morning air was filled with the old-fashioned smell of burning coal.

The entrance to the cave was reached by a series of steps carved into the rock. In places they were slippery from the rain that had fallen overnight. Clara held Ned's hand and was tempted to take Gabriel's, too, but thought better of it: he would have his pride, after all. And pride seemed to have influenced his appearance that day. If she wasn't mistaken, he had spruced himself up, even wearing a tie beneath his V-necked pullover, which didn't have any holes in it.

They paid for their entrance tickets at the wooden booth and were shepherded through to a dimly lit tunnel where they joined a group about to embark on the tour of what had once been an old lead mine.

Fifteen minutes later Clara was glad she had bundled Ned up in his warmest clothes. It was bone-numbingly cold with no escape from the icy damp that had already seeped through the thick soles of her shoes to gnaw at her toes. The tips of her ears and nose were tingling too, and the occasional splash of water from the low roof on her exposed skin made her shiver. As she listened to the guide and watched the direction of his torch, which he used to indicate points of interest – the flowstones, the stalactites and stalagmites – she thought of the harsh conditions in which those early miners had worked.

The guide led them further into the series of caves, warning them to be careful and to hold on to the rail as they took the steep descent down towards the pool.

'Are we going to see the mermaid now?' whispered Ned, squeezing her hand.

'Any minute.'

When they reached the bottom, a boat was waiting for them. They were helped into it and when all was secure, they moved smoothly through the water. It didn't seem very impressive at first: the ceiling of the cave was still quite low, and though a few lights were fixed into the rock-face there wasn't much to see.

But then they turned a corner and there was an *aah!* from everyone in the boat. Even Gabriel, that stalwart of indifference, looked impressed. The vaulted roof of the cave soared above their heads, and shimmering lights gave it a serene, cathedral-like quality. People reached for their cameras, including Clara. After they had taken their pictures, the guide took them on further.

They came to a large rock that jutted out into the pool, steered round it and there before them, raised out of the water and subtly illuminated with softly glowing lamps, was the mermaid. To Clara's surprise and delight, no leap of imagination or suspension of belief was needed to make out what she was. There was her tail, the forked end skimming the surface of the pool, and her curvy body reclined gracefully against another rock.

For the benefit of those who enjoyed a good yarn, the guide told them how she came to be here. The story went that she had been a real live mermaid who had got lost at sea and had somehow found her way to the cavern – that she was so far inland was glossed over. She had liked it so much that she had made it her home, and after wishing that she could stay here for ever, she had been turned to stone to make wishes come true for others. As tales went, it was far-fetched and fanciful, but it satisfied Ned, and as Clara drew him closer to her, she hoped he would never lose the sense of wonder she could see in his eyes. Everything was such a pleasure for him. New, exciting, full of mystery. Heaven forbid that life should ever become a chore for him.

Just as she was thinking this, the guide pointed the beam of light from his torch at the small raised pool behind the mermaid. 'If you want her to grant you a wish,' he said, 'you have to throw a coin into her pool.'

Judging from the number of coins already tossed into the crystal-clear water, there had been plenty of people here before them who had gone along with the lark. Clara reached for her bag. 'Go on, Ned,' she whispered, 'make a wish.'

He took the ten-pence piece from her. 'But what about you, Mummy? Don't you want a go? And, Mr Liberty, you have to make a wish too.'

Gabriel pulled a face. 'I've never heard anything so absurd in all my life. A lot of stuff and nonsense.' But then he smiled – reminding Clara of the big bad wolf in *Little Red Riding Hood* – and produced a pound coin from his pocket. 'Shall we make it a good one, Ned, eh? Come on, Miss Costello, get your money out. After your visit to the bank this morning I know you can afford it.'

They waited for the rest of the group to throw their pennies and make their wishes, and then, at last, it was their turn. 'Don't say it out loud,' Ned informed Clara, 'it won't come true if you do.' Four years old and how well versed he was in these matters. 'And you mustn't tell anyone what you wished for,' he said afterwards, as the guide steered the boat away and they waved goodbye to the mermaid. 'Telling people what you wished for brings you bad luck, and we don't want that, do we, Mummy?'

'No, Ned. We certainly don't.'

Clara's wish had been the same as it always was whenever irrational reliance on omens and charms was called for: she wanted Ned to be happy. But on this occasion she had tagged on an extra request: that the months ahead would be as enjoyable as the last two weeks had been.

She glanced at Gabriel's face in the subdued light. There was no knowing what he had wished for.

Chapter Thirty-Six

On Monday morning, as Clara unhooked Winnie from Mermaid House's electrical supply, Ned was anything but happy. He wanted to stay longer. The weekend had passed all too quickly, with most of it spent sightseeing. They had visited Peveril Castle, the plague village at Eyam, Buxton, and even another cave – the Blue John Cavern in Castleton. But now they were preparing to leave.

'There's still more to see,' Ned said, showing her the evidence to support his argument. He was pointing to a picture in one of their guide books that showed a place in Matlock Bath where they had cable-cars to get you up and down the wooded hillside. 'Couldn't we go there today? Oh, please.'

She stopped what she was doing, sat down, and pulled him on to her lap, knowing that if she wasn't careful, she'd have a tearful rebellion on her hands. She flicked through the pages of the book to the next section. 'And look,' she said, 'even more to see.'

He stared at the picture of a traditional steamer crossing Lake Windermere, then at the one showing the Beatrix Potter museum. Clara hoped that the sight of Peter Rabbit in his blue jacket nibbling a carrot would tempt Ned to get back on the road.

Originally the plan had been to use the Peak District as a stepping stone for Yorkshire, before carrying on towards Berwick-upon-Tweed and Scotland, where they would then work their way round the coast, to the top, then drop down the west coast and keep on going till they hit Devon and Cornwall for the summer. But in bed last night Clara had decided to change the route. The Lake District, which was full of all things cute and wonderful, would give her a better chance of luring Ned away from Deaconsbridge.

She wasn't ready for what Ned said next.

'Couldn't we take Mr Liberty with us to see Peter Rabbit? He'd like that, wouldn't he?'

She put an arm round him. 'I'm not sure he's a Beatrix Potter kind of man, Ned. Besides, he has his friends and family here to think of.'

Ned shrugged away her arm and gazed at her intently. 'He doesn't have any friends. He told me. He said most of them are dead.'

'I'm sure that was just another of his exaggerations. He's not that old.'

'He is! He's going to be *eighty* on his next birthday.'

'I'm sorry, Ned, but the answer's still no. Winnie is only big enough for the two of us. Imagine having a great big man like Mr Liberty sharing it with us.' It was such an awesome prospect Clara felt her face twitch with the threat of laughter. Keeping her expression under control, she added, 'And I bet he snores as loud as a giant.'

For the first time since getting out of bed that morning, Ned smiled. 'He'd be just like the giant in *Jack and the Beanstalk*. When he snored it was so loud all the buttons fell off Jack's coat.'

Clara giggled. That colourful little detail had been her father's. He was always contributing his own lines to the stories he read to Ned. 'Pepping it up,' was what he called it. She hugged Ned close. 'Well, we wouldn't want *our* buttons falling off whenever Mr Liberty had a nap. It would be too embarrassing for words.'

With the situation more or less under control, and Ned rounding up his cuddly toy collection, Clara carried on tidying the van. She was almost through with checking for potential rattles in the lockers and cupboards when there was a loud thump at the door. 'Time you were going, isn't it?'

It was Gabriel.

'Always a mistake to outstay your welcome,' he growled, filling the doorway and blocking out the light. 'Remember that, Ned. When it's time to go, you go. No hanging around.'

Clara felt a wave of gratitude towards him for being his usual blunt self, for not making things worse for Ned by giving him a show of treacly affection. 'And a good morning to you, Mr Liberty.'

He stepped inside, looked at his watch. 'It's afternoon, as near as damn it.'

'Mr Liberty, guess where we're going?' Ned chimed in. 'We're going to see Peter Rabbit and some big lakes and mountains. Do you want to see?' He held up the guide book that he and Clara had been reading earlier. 'Mummy says we'll go on a really old boat that has steam coming out of it. And there's a museum where we can see pencils being made. And when we've done—'

'Sounds much too exhausting to me,' Gabriel interrupted, scarcely glancing at what Ned was showing him.

'I think we're about done now,' Clara said, shutting the last cupboard with a clunk. She took the book from Ned and stowed it in the rack with the rest of the maps and guides. 'If you'd like to say goodbye to Mr Liberty you can climb into your seat and strap yourself in.'

But all at once Ned didn't seem able to move from where he was standing. He put his hands behind his back and screwed a shoe into the floor. His eyes lowered to the level of Gabriel's knees, but not before Clara saw them fill. Then a little voice mumbled, 'Goodbye,' and his lower lip wobbled and she knew they were in real trouble. She moved towards him, to put a comforting hand on his shoulder but, with a creak of bones, Gabriel got there before her. He bent down to Ned, gently picked him up with his big-knuckled old hands and carried him outside.

Staying where she was, Clara watched them go. This was their moment. For something to do she repacked one of the cupboards and tried to ignore the large lump in her throat and the tears that were threatening to do their worst. Damn the man, why and how had he got to them both?

Finally they were in their seats with the engine running, and it really was time to go. Coming round to the driver's side of the van, Gabriel poked his head through the open window. 'You take good care of yourself, won't you, Miss Costello?'

'Is that an order?'

'If needs be, yes.'

'And you'll take care as well, won't you? Don't lose any of those instructions I spent ages writing out for you. The dishwasher will need salt and Rinse-aid adding now and again, and you'll also have to—'

'Yes, yes, *yes*, Miss Costello. I have your infernal instructions Sellotaped to the inside of the cupboard, just as you insisted. I'll have them tattooed on my chest if it will make you feel any better.'

She revved the engine and knocked the gear-lever into first. 'Well, then, nothing more to be said. Apart from thanking you for having us to stay. Ned and I have had a great time. We won't forget you in a hurry, that's for sure.'

'Pah! You'll forget me so fast you won't even remember to send me a postcard.'

'We will remember,' cried Ned, fiercely. 'We'll send you one every week.'

'Goodbye, Mr Liberty. Despite everything, it's been a pleasure.' His grizzled head was still close to the window and, seizing her chance, she leaned towards him and kissed his bristly cheek.

'What was that for?'

'What do you think, you silly old fool?'

'I never thought I'd say it, Miss Costello, but if I were a younger man—'

She laughed. 'If you were a younger man, I wouldn't have dared to kiss you.'

'Oh, so old age makes me less of a sex object, does it?'

'It makes you more accessible, you whingeing old pain in the proverbial!'

He laughed too, then reached through the window, lifted her right hand off the steering-wheel, raised it to his lips, and very gently kissed it. 'I'm going to miss you, you delectable sharp-tongued girl. You've been a breath of fresh air for me. Goodbye now. Drive safely. And if you're ever passing . . .' but his voice trailed away.

Touched, she said, 'We wouldn't dream of not calling in on you if we were in the area. You can take that as a promise. Or maybe a threat!'

Steering Winnie out of the courtyard and tooting the horn, they gave one last wave to the solitary figure that stood in the shadow of the archway. He didn't linger.

Neither Clara nor Ned spoke until they had reached the midway point down the long drive. Ned looked out of his window and said, 'Shall I wave one more time in case Mr Liberty's watching us from the tower?'

She patted his knee. 'Good idea.'

He kept on waving until the house was almost out of sight. When they were nearly at the end of the drive, they saw a car approaching. It was Jonah.

Clara was glad to see him. She reckoned Gabriel could do with some company right now, even if it was only someone he could bully. She pulled over so that Jonah could come alongside the van. They wound down their windows at the same time.

Clara said, 'How was it on the Western Front with your school trip?'

'All quiet when we left it. Wet and cold too.'

'Too bad. So, not at school today shaping fertile young minds?'

'No, we've broken up for the Easter holidays. I've come to see if Dad wants some shopping fetching. Where are you off to?'

'The Lake District. You'll be pleased to know I've given

up trying to marry your father and swindle him out of his vast fortune.'

'You're leaving?'

'Yes, Ned and I are moving on to pastures new, where scheming gold-diggers are given the proper respect they deserve.'

He smiled, not hugely, but enough for her to realise how attractive he was. Yet what struck her most about him in that split second, as she took in the curve of his mouth and the way his hazel eyes caught the light as he looked up at her, was that everything about him was reminiscent of the young woman in the painting in his father's library. The likeness to his mother was unmistakable and she wondered if he was aware of it, and whether or not Gabriel found it a comfort or a painful reminder of what he had lost.

'Caspar will be relieved to hear that,' he said good-humouredly. 'Scaring off a potential step-mother would have been a time-consuming business for him.'

'I bet it would. But do me a favour, will you? Persevere with your father.'

The smile was gone and his face turned awkward and defensive. Annoyed that she seemed to have an uncanny knack for rubbing him up the wrong way, she said, 'I might have misjudged you when I first met you, but . . . well, a week with your father and I think I understand things better now.'

But the smile didn't reappear as she had hoped it might. 'I doubt that,' he said, with feeling. 'Anyway, thanks for everything you've done for Dad. I'll do my best to carry on where you've left off. That's if he'll let me.'

'I find the shotgun approach usually works. You ram it up his nose and lay out your demands. Nothing to it. Goodbye.'

Chapter Thirty-Seven

9 April

Dear Archie,
Apologies for sneaking out of town without saying
goodbye. Ned was so upset about leaving Mermaid
House I thought it better to keep the farewells to a
minimum. As you can see, we're in the Lake District
now – weather damp, scenery stunning, people almost
as friendly as those in Deaconsbridge.
   Thanks for all your help at Mermaid House.
      Regards, Clara and Ned

P.S. What happened to the posse?

10 April

Dear Louise and associated rabble,
The hardship continues! Currently languishing beside
beautiful Lake Windermere with Mrs Tiggywinkle and
chums and getting fat on cream teas. Tomorrow we're
going in search of lonely clouds and hosts of golden
daffodils. Sorry I still haven't got round to phoning –
will try to mend my ways. Do hope you're all
behaving yourselves and missing us terribly.
      Love from Clara and Ned

P.S. Happy Easter!

11 April

Dear Mr Liberty,
Just to prove we keep our promises, Easter greetings
from Dove Cottage, the home of William Wordsworth.
Maybe you should pen a few lines of poetry and open
Mermaid House to the public, I'm sure you'd love
thousands of tourists tramping through your home.
Think how rude you could be to them!

Ned says thank you very much for the money you
gave him – that was v. naughty of you (slapped
wrists!), but v. kind. He's used some of it to buy
himself a pocket-sized Peter Rabbit.

Take care,
Ned and Miss Costello

P.S. Have you advertised for a cleaner yet?

Bateson, Hardy, Willets and Co.,
Chartered Accountants,
Dean Street,
Manchester
M10 9PQ

16 April 2001

Dear Caspar,

Re: Tax Return – C. Liberty

Please find enclosed copy of latest letter received from
the Inland Revenue.

In view of the claims made, I suggest we meet and
discuss the matter so that we can devise some sort of
strategy that will satisfy our friends at the IR.

Kind regards,
Harvey Wilson

2 Canal View,
Manchester

21 April

Dear Damson,
What the hell's going on? Why won't you speak to
me?

Five times I've tried to get you on the phone and on
each occasion some *Guardian*-reading, bean-eating
beardy type has told me it's not convenient. Since
when is it not convenient to speak to your brother? Or
is this all part of the brain-washing process that's
going on up there?

Damson, surely you can see what's happening.
Divide and conquer, it's how these cults operate. They
isolate you from those who care about you, telling you
it's for your own good.

If I don't hear from you soon, I will personally come
up there and beat the **** out of that patronising
wimp of a man who won't let me speak to you.

Caspar

P.S. How much money have they stung you for?

Rosewood Manor Healing Centre,
Blydale Village,
Northumberland

Saturday, 26 April

Darling Caspar,
If you really care about me, don't be silly and drive all
the way up here just to take out your frustration on
poor Roland – who is neither vegetarian nor the
wearer of a beard, and he certainly doesn't read the

Guardian! Instead, why don't you write and tell me what's wrong. And please don't deny that there is anything bothering you – as twins, you know I always feel it when something is wrong with you.

    Love and warmest wishes,
      Damson

27 April

Dear Louise and everyone,
Here we are north of the border! Glasgow is terrific! Moira, you'd love it – more designer shops than you can shake a stick at. Wall-to-wall Rennie Mackintosh stuff as well, tho' not sure Ned shared my enthusiasm for it! Tomorrow we're setting sail for the bonnie banks of Loch Lomond – Rob Roy country.

    Och aye the noo!
      Clara and Ned

P.S. It was great to speak to you on the phone last week, Louise – it almost made me miss you!

28 April

Dear Mr Liberty,
Saw this wonderful card of a fierce-looking Scotsman playing the bagpipes and thought of you! Ever thought of dyeing your hair red?

    Hope you're taking care of yourself and haven't slipped back into your bad old ways.

    Best wishes,
      Ned and Miss Costello

Bateson, Hardy, Willets and Co.,
Chartered Accountants,
Dean Street,
Manchester
M10 9PQ

1 May 2001

Dear Caspar,

Re: Tax Return – C. Liberty

Once again I enclose a copy of the latest
communication from the Inland Revenue. As you can
see from the detailed documentation, they leave us with
little choice or room for manoeuvre.
   Kind regards,
    Harvey Wilson

2 Canal View,
Manchester

5 May

Dear Damson,
I would much rather discuss this over the phone, or
even face to face. Please let me speak to you.
   Caspar

P.S. I might have guessed his name was bloody
Roland!

Rosewood Manor Healing Centre,
Blydale Village,
Northumberland

Monday, 5 May

Dearest Caspar,
So much anger!
Please, just tell me what's wrong.
   Thinking of you, all my love,
      Damson

17 Cross Street,
Deaconsbridge

7 May

Dear Stella,
Before the solicitors get too carried away with their
expensive games, why don't we meet and discuss
matters in private, just the two of us? It's the least we
owe each other.
   Yours hopefully,
      Archie

P.S. We don't have to meet in Deaconsbridge if you
don't want to. You choose.

2a Carlisle Terrace,
Macclesfield,
Cheshire

12 May

Dear Archie,
I could meet you a week next Tuesday after work in
Buxton, but only for a short while. I'll see you 6.00
by the bandstand.
    Stella

Date: 14/05/01 14.44 GMT Daylight Time
From: ClaraCost@hotmail.com
To: GuyXXX@Phoenix.co.uk

Hope I'm in luck and that you're sitting in the office
twiddling your thumbs as you always used to!
    It had to happen sooner or later; I've found myself
in a cyber café in the middle of Edinburgh e-mailing
you silly boys. How goes it? Who and what is the
latest gossip? Don't hold back on the dirt!

Date: 14/05/01 14.49GMT Daylight Time
From: GuyXXX@aol.co.uk
To: ClaraCost@hotmail.com

Hey, Clarabelle, is that really you? This is like old
times. Makes me realise how much I miss your sharply
worded e-mails! I'm working from home today, so we
can gossip quite freely – no chance of the surfing police
earwigging! We have it on good authority (David) that
the big chiefs in Wilmington are dispatching a couple
of their smart-alecky types to suss out the takeover –
Les Francais Garcons are definitely putting their francs
on the table so it's all systems go. Not that anyone is

supposed to know this, of course, but I don't need to tell you that it's been common knowledge here for some time that the plant doesn't fit in with the strategic direction of the CEO's thinking. And guess who's coming to see us? None other than the big honcho lawyer himself, Fenton Bexley, and the stellar-rated finance director, Todd Mason Angel. Aren't we the lucky ones?

    Fondest etceteras,
      Guy

P.S. Didn't you get to know TMA during your stint in Wilmington? What's he like? Is he likely to drive the women on the packing line mad with desire? You know what they were like with the last blue-eyed wonder boy who crossed the water to see us! Sexual harassment didn't come close!

Chapter Thirty-Eight

It was five weeks since Gabriel had received the first of the postcards from Ned and Miss Costello and he had kept each one they had sent. He had them carefully lined up along the kitchen window-sill and every day, around twelve o'clock, when the postman finally got round to making a delivery at Mermaid House, he hung on to the hope that there would be a new addition for his collection.

It was a mild, sunny morning in May and he bent down to gather the scattering of envelopes that were spread so far and wide that he wondered if the postman made a game of firing the mail through the letterbox to see how far it would go.

Once again, there was no card and he tasted what was now the familiar bitterness of disappointment. Silly old fool, he berated himself. Get a grip, man. But then, hiding beneath a buff-coloured envelope addressed to 'The Occupier', he glimpsed a flash of blue sky. The pendulum of his emotions swung from disappointment to delight. Without looking at the card – not wanting to spoil his enjoyment of it – he took it through to the kitchen where he dropped the buff-coloured envelope into the bin. Next he scanned his monthly bank statement for any anomalies, threw away a book-club offer and the chance to take out a fifteen-thousand-pound loan, then got down to the card, drawing out the process slowly, wanting to make it last.

The glossy picture showed a busy harbour: there were fishing boats, large and small, steep rows of terraced houses with red pan-tiled roofs and the ruins of an abbey on a distant clifftop. He recognised it instantly. It was Whitby. How well he knew it.

For three years running his father had taken him there when he was a boy. Just the two of them. They had stayed in the same modest boarding-house each time and always in the first week of August. The routine never varied: fishing in the morning, lunch overlooking the quay, and the afternoon spent going for long invigorating walks. Seventy years on he could still hear his father's voice booming above the crashing waves on the rocks below them as they marched along the cliff: 'Come on, Gabriel. Keep up, no lagging behind.' The last time they had made the trip he had fallen over and cut his knee on a rusty tin, but he hadn't cried, hadn't wanted to make a fuss. His father wouldn't have tolerated that. It wasn't until they were at home two days later and he woke in the night with a thrashing fever that had induced nightmares of goblins chasing him over a cliff that he allowed his mother to look at his leg. Straight away she called the doctor: the gash to his knee was infected and his temperature was soaring dangerously.

Gabriel turned over the postcard and smiled. Miss Costello had written it but Ned had added his own name and his topsy-turvy, oversized writing was thrown across the bottom of the card like tumbling building bricks.

Gabriel read it through once more then placed it on the window-sill. But, unlike the rest of the postcards, he positioned it so that the writing faced him. And while he made himself an early lunch, hacking at the remains of a loaf and adding a slab of Wensleydale to the thick hunks of granary bread, he continued to stare at Ned's handiwork, picturing the lad in the camper-van, kneeling up to the narrow table, his fingers gripping the pen, his hair falling into his eyes and his tongue poking out of the corner of his mouth as he concentrated. The thought of Ned's determination and the attachment he seemed to have made to an old man he scarcely knew, caused Gabriel to stop chewing his sandwich.

His *shambly*.

A few moments passed before he could swallow what was in his mouth.

If someone had told him two months ago that he could be so moved, he would have laughed in their face.

But every time he thought of Ned, he experienced a tightening in his chest. And if he pictured that moment in April when the boy had tried to say goodbye to him, he felt overwhelmed by sadness so heavy his breath caught. It happened to him now, made him feel as if his heart had just been torpedoed.

On impulse, that day, he had carried Ned round to the front of the house and together they had sat on the curved stone bench beneath the library window. 'I don't want to go,' the poor blighter had sniffled, rubbing his sleeve across his face, his legs swinging. 'I like it here. Nowhere else will be as nice.' The plaintive note in his voice had cut right through Gabriel.

'Now that's where you're wrong, Mr Smarty Pants,' he had said, putting an arm around him and tucking him into his side – he was so small. 'Do you think your mother would take you anywhere she thought you wouldn't like? No. Of course not. She's much too good a mother to do that to you.'

Ned had wrinkled his nose. 'I wish you could come with us. I asked Mummy if you could but she thinks you'd snore and keep us awake at night.'

Laughing, he had said, 'Your mother's a very wise woman, but Ned, and you must promise to keep this under your hat, it's not something I want everyone to know – I'm too old for travelling.'

'I know you're very old,' he had said, so solemnly it had made Gabriel want to smile, 'but you wouldn't have to drive. Mummy would do all that.'

'And she has enough on her hands without having me along for the ride and getting in her way. Now then, dry your eyes and promise me one more thing, that you'll look after her. When you're older, you'll discover that the people who least appear to need help are those who need it most. Do I get a hug goodbye?'

Ned had squashed himself against Gabriel, burrowed his head into his neck and held on to him tightly.

Even now, all these weeks on, Gabriel could smell the sweet warmth of the boy and the bubbling sense of energy within his little body. It was a happy memory, but at the same time it made him feel low and weary. And so very alone.

The emptiness of the house – the deathly quiet of it – had never seemed so oppressive as it did now, and that was with Jonah constantly making a nuisance of himself. Solitude had never bothered Gabriel in the past, but now he wanted none of it. He craved the sound of a small child's excited voice calling to him, the hurried, purposeful footsteps of a young woman, the crisp humorous taunt, the robust mocking smile. But he knew he could crave those things all he wanted and he would never know them again.

Through the window, beyond the courtyard, he watched a kestrel hovering on the wind, its wings beating the air. Seconds passed, and then it was gone, attracted by something a long way off.

Oh, how he missed that little firecracker and her son.

It was against school policy for a member of staff to visit a pupil at home on his or her own, especially if the pupil was a girl, so Jonah had wisely enlisted the help of Barbara Lander – an experienced, seen-it-all-before geography teacher – to help him get to the bottom of why Sharna Powell was missing from school yet again. He had a pretty good idea of what was going on, and had decided it was time for him to put in a personal appearance. He was taking this slightly unorthodox approach, rather than bringing in the Education Welfare Service, because, rightly or wrongly, he believed he could resolve the problem. In his opinion it was all too easy to pass on the difficult children to a higher authority and wash one's hands of them, but he didn't think that was the way to improve the pastoral system at a school like Dick High.

The Powell family lived on the same estate as Jase O'Dowd, along with the majority of the kids at Dick High, but unlike most of the others, who occasionally stayed away from school for the hell of it, he was certain that Sharna's frequent absences were due to a more worrying influence than mere peer-group pressure to bunk off classes.

Parking outside number twenty-three Capstone Close – predictably, the letter R had been inserted with a black pen into the road sign – Jonah said, 'Thanks, Barbara, for doing this. I appreciate your help.'

'No problem. Just don't be too hopeful that we'll get anywhere. If it is the mother who's deliberately keeping Sharna home, our presence is likely to be inflammatory.'

'I know, but it's worth a try, isn't it?'

Barbara slipped her bag over her shoulder. 'As I said earlier, I'm going to leave you to do all the talking. This is your show and if *you* can't charm this particular birdie down from the tree, I don't know who can.'

He shoved open his door and got out. 'And what's that supposed to mean?'

She looked at him over the top of the car. 'Don't sound so shocked. It's common knowledge in the staff room that your crusading techniques leave the rest of us standing. Must be something to do with that fine-boned face of yours and the disarming boyish smile. It takes the little sods by surprise, makes them want to help you out. The old dragons like me only get results by beating them into submission. I'm just pleased you picked me for this assignment because I'll get to observe you in action, and at close range.'

'I had no idea I was such a focus of attention,' he said drily.

'Come off it, Jonah, surely you know that everyone in the staff room calls you Walker behind your back.'

'Walker?'

'Yes, Walker as in crisps, as in potato chips, as in—'

'Mr Chips,' he finished for her. 'Great! Just what I need, a sobriquet from the Dark Ages.'

She laughed. 'Do you want to know what's also being said about you behind your back?'

'In or out of the staff room?'

She laughed again. 'What the hormonally charged girls say about you is unrepeatable, but it's hotly rumoured in the staff room that you're going to be put in charge of the sixth form in the autumn.'

'You're kidding?'

'Nope. At the rate you're going, you'll be Dick High's very own Moses, parting the water with a flick of your angelic curls. Don't frown like that, Jonah, it spoils the whole effect. You can't be a shiny-eyed enthusiast with stress and worry lines like the rest of us.'

The Powells' semi-detached house was as run-down as the neighbouring properties – the fascia boards needed replacing, the windows were filthy, the net curtains were torn, and the overgrown front garden was a dismal sight: home to a tangle of two dismantled motorbikes, several burst bags of cement and a supermarket trolley minus its wheels.

They picked their way through the debris and knocked at the door. It was ajar and Jonah could hear the sound of a television from somewhere within. He knocked again, louder this time. The volume on the television was turned down and a woman's voice shouted, 'Get that, will you, Shar?'

'Hello, Sharna,' Jonah said, when the door opened fully to reveal an overweight girl with a pasty complexion that flushed ten shades of red and clashed with the skimpy purple halter-neck top she was wearing. The lower part of her was covered, just, by a crotch-hugging skirt, and as if to lessen the effect of so much exposed thigh, she tried to hide one leg behind the other.

'Sir! What're you doing here?'

'I might ask the same of you. Okay if we come in?'

Reluctantly she took them through to the back of the small house, to the kitchen. Next to a steaming kettle there were two full mugs of coffee, an opened jar of Nescafé and a carton of long-life milk. As well as the aroma of instant coffee, there was a less appetising smell that came from a gas cooker where a charred grill-pan contained a blanket of solidified cooking fat. It looked as if it had been used many times: blackened scabs of burnt food poked through its hard, rancid surface.

With some of her fourteen-year-old spirit returning, Sharna said, 'Not expecting lunch, are you, Sir?'

'No, but I am expecting a good reason for why you're not in school. *Again*.'

'It's me asthma. Same as before.' She gave her substantial shoulders a heave and produced a corroborative cough.

'Then perhaps you ought to cut back.' His gaze fell on an overflowing ashtray on the draining-board where two packets of frozen sausages were defrosting.

'I've given up. It's only Mum and me brothers who smoke now.'

'Good for you. Is your mother in?' He saw her hesitate and knew he had put her on the spot.

'Um . . . she's not well, Sir. She's having a lie-down.'

'She's probably thirsty too. Shall we take her coffee through? It seems a shame to keep her waiting.' And before she could stop him, he picked up one of the mugs, went back to the hall, then opened the door of what he assumed was the front room. The air was blue with the fug of cigarette smoke. An enormous television, with a china dray horse on top of it, squatted in the furthest corner of the room – John Leslie was putting a contestant through the rigorous hoops of *Wheel of Fortune*.

'And about time too. How long does it take to boil the kettle and make us a drink? Who was that at the door? Go on, mate! Spin the bloody thing!' The voice was thick and husky and emanated from a woman sitting on the

308

edge of a PVC sofa that crackled with her agitated movements. Sharna's mother was a larger version of her daughter – the pasty complexion and the broad shoulders were the same, as was the shaggy permed hair.

'Mrs Powell?'

She swivelled her head and looked at Jonah with breathtaking hostility. 'Who the hell are you?'

'I'm Mr Liberty, your daughter's form teacher, and this is Mrs Lander, a colleague from school.' He handed her the coffee and, uninvited, sat down beside her. 'If it's not inconvenient,' he said, 'we'd like to discuss why Sharna is absent from school so often. We're very concerned for her. You see, every day she misses puts her at a disadvantage with her GCSEs, and that strikes me as a great shame, given her ability.'

Mrs Powell shifted forward and reached for her cigarettes. She flipped open the packet, took out a Marlboro, hunted for a lighter among the mess on the table in front of her. 'It's her asthma. How many times do I have to tell you lot?' She found the lighter and lit the cigarette. Inhaling deeply, she stared him in the eye, her expression sullen and challenging. 'What's more, I put it in that note last week when she was off.'

'It has nothing to do with this, then?' He picked up a two-inch-square polythene bag of tin-tacks from the coffee table, then poked at a pile waiting to be bagged up. 'Piece-work can take for ever, can't it? An extra pair of hands makes all the difference – really lightens the load.'

She threw down the lighter, scattering tin-tacks on the carpet. 'What're you on about? It's me who does this. *On my own.*' She placed the cigarette between her lips, drew on it hard, then blew a cloud of smoke into his face. 'Coming round here with your bloody fancy posh voice accusing me of friggin' knows what! And why, I'd like to know, aren't you in school doing what you're paid to do?' Her tired, lined face blazed with insolence.

While her manner didn't bother Jonah, it upset Sharna, who hadn't said a word. Now she stepped forward.

'Mum! Don't shout at him like that, you'll get me into even more trouble.'

'Shut up and leave this to me.'

'But Mum—'

'If you can't be quiet, get out.'

'He's only trying to help. It's his job.'

Keeping his voice low and smooth, in contrast to Mrs Powell's bullying screech, Jonah rose to his feet and said, 'I think we've said all we need to, Mrs Powell. You're a busy woman and we have no right to take up any more of your valuable time. Sharna, perhaps you'd show us out.'

Standing at the front door, the volume of the television in the sitting room turned up again, Sharna said, 'Sorry about that, Sir. She loses it now and again.'

He looked at her kindly. 'It's okay. But, Sharna, you do have a choice in this. If you see yourself in years to come earning your living from packing tin-tacks, like your mother,' he paused meaningfully, 'then so be it. But if there's the slightest chance that you might want more out of life, I'd be delighted to see you in school first thing tomorrow morning. Think it over. It's your decision. Nobody else's. The law says you must attend school in one form or another, but nobody has the right to bully you into making the wrong decision. Not me, not your mother, not even Mrs Lander here.'

The girl put a finger to her lower lip, pushed it against her teeth, chewed at it anxiously. 'I'll . . . I'll see y' then, Sir.'

'Soon, I hope.'

The door closed slowly behind them, and when they were driving away, Barbara Lander said, 'Creeping bloody ivy! So it *is* true what they say about you. You were as slick as an oiled eel.'

'Do you think so?'

'Oh you know so! The moment that horrible woman started attacking you, the daughter leaped to your defence, just as you knew she would. Me, I'd have blown it by throwing the letter of the law at the mother and getting both their backs up. But not you, you cunningly got the girl on your side. And if there isn't a tick by her name in the register tomorrow morning, I'll cover your lunch duty for the rest of term.'

'And it's two whole weeks until half-term – how very generous of you. However, the hard part will be ensuring we keep her at school. She'll need a lot of support to stand up to that mother of hers. And we don't want to cause so many waves that the heavy brigade get brought in. That would be totally counter-productive.'

He slowed down to let a car pull out in front of him. It had come from the road where Jase lived, and Jonah was almost tempted to take a detour and see how he was getting on – year eleven was officially on home study leave for their GCSEs. The first of the history papers was set for next Tuesday and Jonah was giving an eleventh-hour revision lesson on Monday after school. Jase had said he would be there, but would he?

Shuffling through his collection of dusty cassettes, and not looking too impressed with his choice of music – Barbara was a country-and-western devotee – she said, 'I'm intrigued, Jonah. Where did you learn to deal so effectively with bullies?'

He smiled wryly. 'It comes from being a coward. I don't like confrontation. I prefer to disarm rather than mobilise the tanks of aggression.'

Of course it had nothing to do with growing up at Mermaid House.

That evening he stayed on at school to do some marking, but instead of going home straight away when he had finished, he drove to Mermaid House. He was concerned about his father. Since the miraculous Miss Costello had moved on, Gabriel had been morose. Only a fool would think that her influence had been restricted to overhauling an uncared-for house: Jonah knew that it had gone much further than that. She had touched Gabriel Liberty in a way that few people ever had. Amazingly, she had made him happy.

But what worried Jonah most, was that his father's trademark fighting spirit had dwindled to nothing. He had mentioned this to Caspar on the phone, but all his brother had said was, 'Well, it was bound to happen at some time or other. He can't go to his grave snapping and snarling – we'd never get the lid down on him.'

'For pity's sake, Caspar, how can you talk like that? He's our father.'

'He's also a miserable old man who won't listen to a word of common sense, and who, I might add, took malicious pleasure in making me look a fool over that Costello woman.'

Jonah had put his brother out of his misery about their father supposedly marrying for the third time. Predictably Caspar's anger had been cataclysmic. 'I thought you might have been relieved,' Jonah had reasoned.

'Relieved he despises me so much that he had to humiliate me in front of a complete stranger? Are you mad? And why do you always have to miss the bloody point?'

Changing tack, and hoping to move on to safer ground, Jonah had said, 'So how's business?'

But the ground had opened up beneath him. 'And what the hell do you care about my business?' Caspar had sniped. 'Since when have you ever cared about anything I do?'

'Hey, I'm only asking.'

'Well, don't! Take your snivelling civility and stick it—'

Jonah had ended the conversation by putting the phone down quietly. There was nothing to be gained from talking with his brother when he was in that kind of mood. He didn't hear from Caspar in the following weeks, which meant that he was no longer under any pressure to do his bidding. There had been no further mention of selling Mermaid House – their father had made it clear that there would be no question of it – but privately Jonah still thought it was the right thing to do.

It was still light when he arrived at Mermaid House, and he found his father in the gun room, locking the glass-fronted cabinet. 'Bloody crows,' he said, pocketing the key. 'They've been at the lambs again. Vermin. Should be wiped off the face of the earth. What brings you here? And what's that smell?'

'It's this.' He held up a paper carrier-bag. 'Indian take-away. Thought you might fancy a change from your usual bean-feast.'

Gabriel eyed the bag suspiciously. 'You did, did you?'

'It'll need heating up in the oven for a short while. Shall I see to it?'

'Feel free.'

A week had passed since Jonah had last called in and he was relieved to see, as he slid the foil packages inside the oven, that his father was still keeping the place relatively clean and tidy. There were no feminine touches of flowers or tablecloths, but the kitchen was still hygienically sound. 'Any luck with finding a cleaner?' he asked, bending down to a cupboard for two plates, then opening the cutlery drawer. He knew that Gabriel had placed an advert in the local paper.

'No. Word's probably gone round the whole of Derby-shire that I'm a no-go area. Drink?'

'Thanks. But only a small one. I'll add some water.' Despite his father's look of disapproval, he took the tumbler of whisky over to the sink. He ran the cold tap for a while then added an inch to the glass. He noticed the postcards lined up along the window-sill and looked at the latest addition. He picked it up and turned it over to see where it had come from. 'I see the Costellos are in Whitby,' he said, his back still to Gabriel. 'Didn't you go there with your father when you were a boy?'

'How much longer is this meal going to take?'

Acknowledging that prising any information out of his father about the past was as productive as trying to squeeze blood out of a stone, he replaced the card on the sill. 'Another five minutes should do it.' He raised his glass. 'Cheers.'

While they ate, Jonah kept up the conversation as well as he could, but it was hard going. His father was even more uncommunicative and morose than usual. For something to say, he told him about Sharna and her mother.

'Sounds like you're wasting your time there,' Gabriel said, picking at his food uninterestedly. 'If people don't want help, you can't force it on them.'

Jonah looked up from his chicken korma. 'So you think they should be left to dig themselves a deeper hole from which there's no hope of them ever climbing out?'

Gabriel lowered his gaze. 'I didn't say that.'

'So what did you mean?'

'You have to wait until people are ready to accept your help. Or ask for it. Go blundering in as a self-appointed champion of the underdog with scant regard for anyone's feelings and you'll find yourself up against a brick wall.'

'But not everyone knows how to ask for help.'

'True. But maybe in the end they do.' His father pushed away his plate.

Jonah hadn't expected the conversation to take this turn and he steeled himself to ask, 'Dad, who are we really talking about here? Disadvantaged teenagers or . . . or you?'

As soon as the words were out, he regretted them. Gabriel glowered at him, his thick eyebrows drawn together, his mouth set so firmly that his lips had all but disappeared. Oh, God, he recognised that look. He had seen it a million times and felt the consequences. Why couldn't he have kept quiet?

But when his father spoke his voice was anything but firm – anything but recognisable. It shook almost as much as the knobbly hand that reached clumsily for the glass of whisky. 'I . . . I would have thought that was patently obvious, Jonah.'

It was madness to go any further, but with the thought of Miss Costello's parting words echoing in his head – about the shotgun approach and laying out one's demands – he felt compelled to force his father, just once, to be honest with him. 'Are you saying what I think you're saying? That you want my help but don't know how to ask for it?'

The heavily loaded question trapped them in a long, silent pause, and they stared at each other across the table. It was as if they were frozen with fear. Then, to Jonah's horror, his father's eyes were swimming with tears.

'Dad?' Jonah rose from his chair uncertainly. He could cope with irate, booze-sodden parents threatening him and thuggish students disparaging him. That was a breeze. But this? His father crying? Dear God, what had he done? He moved slowly round the table, every step filling him with alarm and confusion. His father's tears were flowing freely now, his body had slumped forward, his head was in his hands, and his breathing was coming in sharp, noisy gulps.

Jonah bent down to him cautiously, and for the first time in his life, he placed a tentative hand on his father's shoulder, expecting it to be pushed away roughly, to be told, 'Don't touch me!'

But there was no rejection. Gabriel turned into him, rested his head against his shoulder, and continued to weep. Words streamed out of him, but Jonah could make no sense of them. It didn't matter, though. Understanding would come later. For now, comforting his father was all that was needed.

Chapter Thirty-Nine

Gabriel woke with a start. There was someone – *something* – in his room! He sat bolt upright. A shadowy figure was coming towards him.

'Dad, are you all right?'

'Jonah?'

'I've brought you a cup of tea. How are you feeling? Did you sleep okay?'

The painful rush of adrenaline that had coursed through his veins now abandoned him and a heaviness, not unlike a hangover, pushed Gabriel back against the pillows. Through dry, gritty eyes he watched Jonah draw the curtains, letting sunlight spill into the room. He blinked at the brightness. 'Why are you here?' he croaked. His throat felt as if it had been sandblasted and his voice sounded distant, not like it normally did. Nothing made sense, and forcing his brain to battle its way through the lethargy that was consuming him, he wondered if he had been drugged. But who would have done that to him?

Jonah came and sat on the bed. There was an expression on his face that made him look different somehow. Something in the eyes, the mouth too. It was something oddly familiar ... something that made Gabriel's heart miss a beat and made him, inexplicably, want to cry. Overwhelmed, confusion closed in and he felt as weak as a baby. He swallowed hard but his mouth was so parched he couldn't.

Panic-stricken, he was terrified suddenly that something awful had happened to him while he had slept. He sat forward so that he was eye to eye with Jonah. He gripped his son's hands, and drew a deep, shuddering breath.

'Jonah, has something happened to me? Tell me the truth. Have I had a stroke? I feel different. Strange. Not myself. Am I making sense to you?'

'Dad, calm down, you're fine.'

But the frown on Jonah's face only made him think he was being lied to. 'The truth,' he demanded. 'Tell me why I feel so strange and why you're here.'

'Don't you remember last night?'

'What about last night?'

'You were . . . you were very upset.'

'Was I? What about?'

The frown deepened. 'We were having supper together, we were talking and . . . Dad, do you really not remember?'

But suddenly Gabriel did have a glimmer of recall. 'You brought an Indian meal . . . we were talking about somebody called Charlene—'

'Sharna. She's one of my pupils.'

He waved aside the interruption. His befuddled brain had started to piece together the bits of the jigsaw and he didn't want it to be put off by unnecessary details. Not when he could feel a new, disturbing emotion growing inside him. Finally, like a wreck being raised out of the water, it surfaced and he recognised it as shame. He groaned, remembering vaguely that something had caused him to lose control in the kitchen. Appalled, he closed his eyes. How had that happened? He concentrated hard, and saw himself bent over the table, heard himself howling. Then he recalled his younger son holding him, and later helping him upstairs to bed. And all the while he was blethering like a lunatic. But even as he felt the debilitating shame of what he had done, and could recall the reasons why, he sensed a closeness to Jonah that he couldn't explain. He knew though that he could never talk to him about it. He would never be able to find the right words. And there was always the danger that if he tried he might lose control again.

He jerked his eyes open, and said, in his firmest voice, 'I

think it would be better all round if neither of us referred to last night again.' He saw hesitation in Jonah's face. What was left of his dignity lay in his son's hands and Gabriel willed him to do as he had asked. Do this small thing for me, Jonah, he urged.

'Is that really what you want, Dad?' Jonah asked.

'Yes, it is.'

'But . . .'

'But what?'

'You don't think we ought to talk about what happened?'

'No, I don't!'

'Okay,' he said soothingly. 'If that's what you want, that's fine by me.'

Relieved, Gabriel sank back into the softness of the pillows. He was home and dry. The relief was as potent as the earlier rush of adrenaline had been. Jonah passed him his tea and as their eyes met, his son smiled and suddenly Gabriel wasn't so sure that he *was* home and dry. He knew that smile so well, had loved it. A hot wave of panic flooded him, his heart thudded painfully in his chest and his hands shook so much that he had to put the mug on the bedside table. He wanted to speak, but couldn't. Consumed with the absurd need to weep on his son's shoulder again, he summoned all his strength, heaved himself out of bed and blundered blindly from the room.

His head spinning, frightened he was going to be sick, he locked himself into the bathroom and sat on the edge of the bath. He pressed his clenched fists to his eyes and wept as silently as he could. God in heaven, why had it taken him almost thirty-five years to see just how like his mother Jonah was?

Chapter Forty

The May sunshine had warmed the wooden bench Archie was sitting on, which helped to relax him a little. He wasn't a jumpy man, but today his nerves were shot to pieces. Which was crazy: he was only meeting Stella, for heaven's sake – a woman he'd known for most of his adult life.

But perhaps he hadn't ever *really* known her. If he had, surely he wouldn't be sitting here in Buxton, in the Pavilion Gardens, waiting to meet her so they could discuss their divorce in a civilised and amicable manner.

It had seemed the right thing to do when he had written to Stella earlier in the month, and it had still seemed right when she had penned a hurried note last week to say she couldn't make it that day after all, but would the following Tuesday be okay? He had sent a note back saying it would be fine.

But now it felt anything but fine. What would they say to each other? Would they argue and cause an unpleasant scene that would play right into the solicitors' hands?

The sun and nervous energy were making him sweat – he unbuttoned his cuffs and rolled his sleeves up. He was ten minutes early, and he watched the people around him enjoying themselves. Picnic blankets were laid out on the grass where cool-bags, discarded socks and shoes had been scattered, and groups of tiny children, their lips and clothes stained with ice-lolly juice, squealed and laughed while their mothers chatted. Through the leafy trees, and down by the lake, where ducks were being fed chunks of processed bread, the miniature train rattled along its narrow-gauge track, whistling. In the shade of an oak tree, a girl and a boy were oblivious to the world around them as they kissed.

He sighed. Oh, what a world it was, at one minute so beautiful and full of golden opportunities, and at the next hopelessly confusing and fraught with difficulties.

'Archie?'

He started. 'Stella!' He got to his feet. Was it really her? Surprise must have been stamped all over his face.

Self-consciously she patted her short, flicked-back hair. 'I'm still getting used to it,' she said.

But the dramatic change in hairstyle and colour – from mousy grey to harsh teak – wasn't the only thing that was different. She had lost weight, more than a stone. And since when had she had such long nails? They must be false – she had never been able to get hers to grow. She had always complained they were too brittle. The jewellery was new too, and there was too much of it, he thought. Gifts from the new man in her life, perhaps. The silky overshirt covered a camisole top that was low at the front, and between her breasts an amber pendant he didn't recognise caught the sunlight. She had changed the colour of her lipstick too. It was darker. Too red. It gave her teeth a yellowed appearance. 'You're looking great,' he said.

'You too.'

They sat down and Archie cringed at how easily she could lie. He knew he looked far from well. Only that morning when he had been shaving he had noticed the unhealthy pallor of his skin and the extra lines and shadows around his eyes.

'How's the shop going?'

Pride made him want to say that business was booming, that since she had gone the money had poured in, that he spent every evening counting his new-found booty and devising ways to spend it – a yacht here, a second home there. And that was when he wasn't fighting off the women! Oh, yes, all the gorgeous young women he'd had in his life since he had become a single man – banging on his door they were. 'Oh, same as ever,' was all he said, thinking that this was the answer his circumspect solicitor would expect of him – '*Make the shop sound too profitable, Mr Merryman, and she'll want a cut of that too!*' 'Business is up and down,' he added, further obliging the lawyer in his mind.

'And your mother?'

'A little better.' No thanks to you, he wanted to say, with an uncharacteristic spurt of malice. Oh, this was no good! They wouldn't get anywhere if he carried on like this. What was done was done. Bitterness wouldn't help either of them. 'Do you fancy an ice-cream?' he asked, catching sight of a tot leaning forward in his pushchair, trying to grasp the cornet his mother was keeping at a safe distance.

'I shouldn't, really,' she said, smoothing out a crease in her skirt, then crossing her legs and revealing a shapely calf. 'I'm on a diet.' She made it sound like it was the 'in' thing to be doing, that over in cosmopolitan Macclesfield that's what everyone was up to.

'Oh. Sure I can't tempt you? Not even a small one?'

She shook her head. Not one hair moved, he noticed. 'But don't let me stop you.'

Childishly, he took her words as a challenge and strode off to the nearest ice-cream seller. With a strawberry Cornetto in his hand, he took the return journey more leisurely. Come on, he told himself, drop the pathetic dumped-husband routine and relax or this meeting will be a waste of time.

'So what was it you wanted to discuss?' she asked, when he joined her on the bench again. He saw her sliding two gold bracelets apart on her wrist so that she could look at her watch. Couldn't she have done that while he'd been gone? And how come she was so cool? He was sweating and squirming like a pig.

He moistened his lips and launched into what he wanted to say. 'This isn't easy for me, Stella, but I just wanted you to know that . . . that I'm sorry.'

She looked at him blankly. 'Sorry?'

'Yes. For not being the husband you needed. I let you down and this . . . this awful awkwardness between us seems . . . Oh, Stella, this coldness between us seems a heck of a price to pay, especially when you think how happy we once were.'

She continued to stare at him, and in such a way that he wondered if what he'd said hadn't made sense. He opened his mouth to try to make himself clearer.

'I don't understand,' she said, her tone icy. 'Is this some sly trick of yours to make me feel guilty?'

'Huh?'

'I know what you're doing, Archie, you're clinging to the past. You're trying to—'

'I'm not!' he blurted out. 'I was trying to say that I want you to know I understand. Or, rather, I think I understand. Over the years we both changed without either of us realising it, and—' A high-pitched squeal of laughter distracted him. He turned to see a small child lying on his back waving his legs in the air as his mother tickled his tummy. 'Perhaps if we'd had kiddies, things might have been different,' he said flatly.

'This isn't about us not being able to have children,' she said pointedly. 'It's not even about you forcing your mother on me.'

That really hurt. He tried to respond, but his voice failed him.

'I'm not coming back, Archie. I thought I'd made that perfectly clear. I have a new life now. One that makes me happy. Happier than I've been in a long while. I only came here to make sure you understood that.'

He was stung by her hardness and felt himself shrivel inside. Melting ice-cream trickled down his thumb. 'Stella, I asked you to meet me so that we could try to make things easier between us. To make our divorce less painful. I thought it would give us the chance to go our different ways with a more positive attitude.'

'I don't believe you. You wanted to drag me here to

flaunt your forgiveness at me, to make me feel bad about what I did. You always did want to be the good guy – self-righteous Archie Merryman. Well, now you've got what you always wanted. I'm the villain for walking out on you and you're the hard-done-by man everyone feels sorry for.' Her voice was tight with recrimination, her words spilling out as though she had been storing them up specially. Suddenly she leaped to her feet. 'There's nothing to be gained from this. I knew it would be a mistake. And look!' She pointed to his left hand accusingly. 'You're still wearing your wedding ring. You haven't accepted any-thing at all.' Without another word, she wheeled round and marched away.

He was dumbfounded. He watched her stride out in the direction of the opera house, her unfamiliar hair bobbing through the strolling holiday-makers. Her arms swinging, she veered off-course only once to avoid bumping into a man with a pushchair. Then at last she disappeared.

Archie thought, if your new life makes you so happy, Stella, why do you look and sound so miserable?

He drove home to Deaconsbridge more confused than when he had set out. What had she meant by him always wanting to be the good guy? Sure, he liked to be liked. Who didn't? It was human nature to want to get on with other people. The belief that there was good in everyone was at his core. Take that Mr Liberty, for instance. He certainly wasn't everyone's cup of tea, but Clara Costello proved his point perfectly: she had seen something worth digging for beneath the layers of prickly rudeness or why else had she put herself out for him?

To his surprise, by the time he reached home and was locking the car, he no longer felt so sorry for himself. It was Stella his heart went out to. Her bitterness seemed so much greater than his own.

He let himself in at the back door and saw that his mother had managed to peel some potatoes for their supper – a hopeful sign. He went through to the sitting room where he could hear *Emmerdale*'s theme playing on the television.

'Hi, Mum,' he said, forcing himself to sound carefree and jolly. He had told her where he was going, that he was trying to smooth things out between him and Stella, and he wanted her to think that the meeting had gone well, that he had it all under control now. He reached for the evening paper, which had slipped on to the floor beside her armchair and passed it to her. It was then, when she made no move to take it from him, that he realised she had had another stroke.

The doctor said there was no need for him to stay. 'You might just as well go home and get a decent night's sleep in your own bed,' she advised.

But Archie said no. 'I wouldn't sleep anyway.'

The doctor, a woman in her early forties with a kindly, understanding smile, nodded. 'I thought you'd say that. But do your best to grab the odd nap. We don't want you conking out on us. You look too useful a chap to lose.'

With the curtain drawn around the bed, screening them off from the rest of the ward, Archie sat alone with his mother while she slept. Except it wasn't a true sleep. She was now in a world where he couldn't reach her.

Dr Singh had warned him that a second stroke was on the cards, that it would probably strike within a year of the first, but when it had happened, he had been taken unawares. 'No use looking for warning signs and symptoms,' Dr Singh had said, 'it'll just make you more anxious, which will make Bessie more anxious.'

He laid a hand on his mother's and hoped she could feel his touch. He wanted to believe that she knew he was there and that she wasn't facing this alone. With her head turned away from him, she looked just as she always did when she slept. But the other side of her face told a different story. The corner of her mouth was open and looked as if it was waiting to have a pipe or a cigar popped into it. Her eyelid looked as if someone had tied a thread to it, then pulled it down towards her cheek. It was a heartbreaking sight.

Still with his hand on hers, he sank back into the chair, tilted his head, closed his eyes and listened to the noises beyond the curtain. Someone was coughing – a dry, tickly cough – another patient was muttering in her sleep, and beyond the ward, voices rose and fell. A phone was ringing and hurried footsteps squeaked on the polished floor.

This last sound dredged up a pleasant memory for Archie, of his first visit to Mermaid House and Clara Costello's confident step as she led him the length of the impressive hallway towards the drawing room.

As sleep claimed him, he wondered where she was now. What wouldn't he give to pack up his troubles and take to the road?

Chapter Forty-One

That night Clara dreamed she was running. Her legs carried her effortlessly through fields of long, dry, swaying grass. Her feet were bare and a warm breeze blew through her hair – not short as it was now but streaming out behind her – and in her arms she carried Ned. There was no weight to him and together they were almost flying. In the distance, there was a hill, and Ned asked her to take him to the top. Their laughter rang out like birdsong as she ran sure-footed up the steep incline. The higher she climbed, the lighter and freer she felt. From the top, where the sun was brighter, the wind keener, they looked down on to a small town. It was Deaconsbridge. There was the church, the bustling market square, Archie's shop and the Mermaid café. Away from the town, and perched on a hill which he had all to himself was a man. He was waving to them. Standing beside her, Ned clapped his hands. 'Mummy, there's a man waving to us. Is it Mr Liberty? Has he come to see us?' But as she shielded her eyes from the glare of the sun, she caught Ned by the hand and started running again, down the hill, her feet scarcely touching the ground beneath them. 'That's not Mr Liberty,' she cried, the wind tossing her words over her shoulder, 'that's your father.'

She woke violently from the dream, her heart racing. That was twice now she had dreamed of Todd.

Didn't you get to know TMA during your stint in Wilmington?

How innocently Guy had typed those words, never once thinking they would have such an effect on her. How hard it had been to e-mail him back and say casually, *Oh,*

*I met him once or twice. And yes, you'd better keep him
safe from the women on the packing line!*

It was stupid of her, really, but she should have guessed
that Todd would be assigned to visit the plant and oversee
the buy-out. It was part of his job. She wondered if he was
anxious about bumping into her.

Probably not.

She was measuring the depth of his response by her
own, which couldn't be the same. He didn't know that
their brief love-affair had created Ned.

Since she had returned from Wilmington, she had
observed his progress within the organisation from company reports and morale-boosting in-house magazines.
She had also tuned in discreetly to any snippets of
transatlantic gossip that buzzed around the plant. But last
year she had been brought up short when she had
unexpectedly come across him in the pages of the
Financial Times. It had been an article about Phoenix's
latest rise in profits after the US drug regulator had given
the green light to its new anti-depressant drug, but all she
had been interested in was the photograph that showed
the company finance director. It was clearly an up-to-date
picture because he was wearing glasses, which he hadn't
needed when she had known him. Two thoughts had
occurred to her as she looked at the photograph: (a) the
frameless glasses suited Todd, and (b) she would need to
check Ned's vision as he grew older.

She straightened the duvet and turned on to her side,
knowing that sleep would elude her for a while yet. She
wished there was someone in whom she could confide.
For more than four years she had kept her own counsel,
and convinced herself that she would never have to deal
with Todd again. She supposed it said a lot about her
controlling nature that she had believed she could wrap
things up so tidily.

But now, because she knew Todd would soon be
arriving in England, a voice was asking if she had done
the right thing in keeping the truth about Ned from him.

Her intentions had been good, though: she hadn't wanted to jeopardise the relationship he needed to rebuild with his wife and daughters. But would it have been fairer to give him the facts and let him decide what to do? And would he be angry, if he were to find out about Ned, that he had been denied the right to know his son?

That was what worried her most.

Even so, part of her was convinced that it would be better to go on keeping Todd in the dark – what the eye didn't see, the heart couldn't miss. But what if he discovered that Clara Costello had jacked in her job to spend more time with her son? She could imagine the conversation all too well. 'She has a son? When did she marry?' An awkward pause. 'Oh, not married. How old is the child?'

When he had done the sums, would he track down those to whom she had been closest at work, and through them seek her out?

And that was where the need to talk to somebody came in. Should she confess to her friends so that Guy and David could be on their guard for any unfortunate slip of the tongue, and prime them to lie about Ned's age?

She knew that to expose them to such a secret wasn't fair.

No. Her only hope was to carry on as before and pray that Todd wouldn't ask after her. He hadn't up till now, had he?

But the next morning Clara was tempted to phone Louise. She thought she would go mad if she didn't confide in someone. The need to be told that she had done the right thing, that no blame could be apportioned to her, was so great she could think of nothing else.

Ironically, it was Ned who provided her with the means to stand firm. With him around, there was no opportunity for her to make such a telephone call. After breakfast, and following a lengthy, fun-filled washing-up session, they left the campsite in Pateley Bridge – which had been home for the last three days while they had toured Ripon, Harrogate and Skipton – and set off for Haworth. This was primarily Clara's choice – she had always wanted to see where the Brontë sisters had lived – but there were plenty of things to interest Ned too. A trip on a steam train run by the Keighley and Worth Valley Railway, and a visit to Eureka!, the Museum for Children in Halifax. They might even drive over to Leeds to see the Armoury. Education as well as entertainment was the order of their trip.

She had been worried that Ned would tire of being a perpetual tourist, but they had yet to encounter boredom. The trick, it seemed, was to provide a wide-ranging variety of places to visit, as well as allow themselves occasional days of doing nothing so they could relax and catch their breath. They did this when they were fortunate enough to find themselves on campsites with plenty of facilities – a swimming-pool (preferably indoor), a play area, a woodland trail, a crazy-golf course. One place they had stopped at in Northumberland, not far from Bamburgh Castle and Holy Island, had had its own ten-pin bowling alley and they had spent a hilarious afternoon trying not to drop cannon balls, as Ned called them, on their toes.

They arrived at the Haworth campsite shortly after twelve. They checked in and hooked up to the electricity supply. As they had already stocked up on groceries, fresh milk, a loaf of wholemeal bread, some Edam for Ned, Stilton for her, and a bag of treats – chocolate fingers, crisps and a bar of Fruit and Nut – they decided to have lunch. It was warm enough to sit outside, and while they ate Ned kept his eye on a family a few pitches away. Two small girls were laughing at their father as he danced around like a gorilla with a rubber mallet in his hands; their mother looked on, amused, as she brushed grass off a large plastic groundsheet.

Clara watched Ned closely. What was going through

his mind as he took in this ubiquitous family unit? Did he ever feel he was missing out in some way?

Inevitably Ned had enquired early on in his young life where his father was: the children he mixed with at nursery school seemed to have one, if not two, in their lives – there were plenty of step-fathers on the scene. Clara had been dreading this question, but had believed she would wing it when it surfaced. Ever since Ned had started to talk, Clara's mother had been on at her to devise a reasonable explanation, saying that it wouldn't be fair to Ned to be anything but honest. She had also been concerned that Ned might ask *her* the crucial question, and had needed to know what she should say.

It had crossed Clara's mind, and for no more than a nanosecond, to say that his father was dead, but the consequences of such a lie were too awful to contemplate. As were those of saying she didn't know who his father was. In the end she had told him the truth, or as near to it as she could. She had explained that sometimes adults had to make difficult decisions, and the hardest one she had had to make was to bring him up on her own because his father lived a long way away and wasn't able to be a real father to him. She had waited for him to probe deeper, but the questions didn't come. He seemed satisfied with what he had, and once more, she put his happiness down to the fact that he was blessed with wonderful grandparents and other people who truly cared for him. She didn't fool herself that she could get away so lightly for much longer, though. The older he became, the more enquiring he would grow, and in turn she would have to be more honest with him. As his mother, that was her responsibility.

As her son, it was his right.

Haworth was beautiful. Surrounded by deserted, unspoilt moors, it was easy to conjure up the brooding sense of melancholy conveyed in Emily Brontë's classic novel. Windswept moors, abandoned hope, neglect and decay, it was all here. It was a place of pilgrimage for anyone whose heart had ever been broken. The long walk up to Top Withens, reputedly the ruins of the house that had inspired Emily's *Wuthering Heights*, almost defeated Ned, and Clara had to carry him for a short while, but afterwards they rewarded themselves with tea in a pretty café in the steep main street of Haworth. Fortified by strong tea, with lots of milk in it for Ned, and floury scones, home-made raspberry jam and cream as thick as butter, they joined a guided tour of the parsonage where the Brontë family had lived. Then they dawdled through the leafy graveyard, where they played an impromptu game of hide-and-seek. Ned was easy to find: he always had a foot or an elbow sticking out from the lichen-coated headstone he was giggling behind. They had a leisurely snoop through the gift shops – it was still early in the season and the vast crowds of sightseers were yet to invade – and found some beautiful handcrafted wooden toys. Ned picked out a funny little acrobat who swung his brightly painted body when the sides of the toy were squeezed, and they added to their collection of postcards, as they did in every place they visited. Clara also bought herself a copy of *Wuthering Heights*. It was years since she had read the book, and apart from being a perfect memento of the day, it would be a nostalgic treat.

Ned went to bed early that night, worn out, and while he slept, Clara read. When she had finished the first chapter, she laid it aside and fished out the tapestry kit she had bought in Glasgow. She had never tried tapestry before, condemning it as a time-wasting occupation for those with not enough to do, but she found the repetitive motion of pushing the needle in and out of the canvas oddly relaxing. It was also addictive: the steady process of producing neat rows of orderly stitches had its own appeal for her. She studied what she had done so far, trying to make up her mind which piece of the intricate pattern to do next, and settled for the bottom right-hand corner, where a dusty-skinned Victoria plum had rolled away from the bowl of fruit that made up the majority of the design. She selected a length of wool, threaded it, and thought, as she made the first stitch, how like the plum she was: she, too, had rolled away from what had been the mainstay of her life – her career.

The decision had not been taken lightly, but it made her smile to think how dramatically different her life had become. Here she was, in a second-hand camper-van, surrounded by stunningly picturesque scenery, spending her evening sewing while her son slept. She had never felt so full of energy: the closeness she now had with Ned was truly uplifting. But who was this rejuvenated Clara Costello, who had been so happy to let go of her old life? And where did she see herself in the months ahead when it was time for Ned to embark upon his sixteen-year sentence of scholastic hard labour? Did she really want to slip back into the rat-race she had left behind and become again the frazzled woman she had allowed herself to turn into? Was there something she would rather do?

She rethreaded her needle. What *did* she want to do?

She felt confident that she could resume her career more or less where she had left it, maybe not with Phoenix, but there were plenty of other pharmaceutical companies. The all-important question, though, was: did she want to pick up where she had left off? Perhaps it was time to change direction and do something new.

Not so long ago she would have been annoyed and frustrated that she couldn't find an answer to this but now she was content to take each day as it came; it was enough to be happy with what she had right now. And because she had never been a spendthrift she had sufficient funds to tide them over for some time yet. Come the New Year she would have to get a job and start bringing in a decent salary again, but that was months away. It wasn't even June, and they had the whole of the summer stretching gloriously ahead of them. Three wonderful months of come-what-may. How lucky she was.

It was when she was lying in bed, having just turned out

the light, that her thoughts slipped back to where they had been first thing that morning.

Todd.

All at once her anxiety about him returned. It was a warm night and, with several windows open, she tossed and turned for nearly an hour listening to noises from their fellow campers – a dog barking, a car door slamming, a kettle whistling. Before long, the surge of worry turned into a thumping headache and, knowing she would never get a decent night's sleep if she didn't take something, she slipped out of bed and opened the locker above the cooker. It was too high for Ned to reach and she kept in it the first-aid kit and the bottle of paracetamol. It wasn't easy to find in the semi-darkness, not with all the important documents she had stored in there: the vehicle insurance details, her cheque book and building-society pass book and a file of other essential records. She continued to rummage for the paracetamol. She pushed aside a bulging A4 envelope and her mobile phone, then found something large and bulky that she didn't recognise. Then, with a flash of guilt, she realised what it was: the tied-up bundle of Val Liberty's diaries.

She let out a smothered moan of self-reproach – how many times had she made a mental note not to forget to put them back? – and lifted the notebooks down from the locker. Despite herself, she couldn't resist the pull of Val's story-telling. She found the paracetamol, slipped back into bed, switched on the overhead light and flicked through Val's last diary. Scanning the pages for something of interest, her eyes were drawn to the final entry.

The writing was a lot less sure than it had been on previous pages. She must have known she was dying when she wrote this.

To whoever is reading this (and it will probably be Jonah, he is the only one who would be interested), all I ask is that you give my diaries to Gabriel when I am dead and ask him to read them. I know he won't sort through my things (just as he didn't with Anastasia), but I do so badly want him to know that in my own way I did love him. There was so much unsaid in our marriage – so much that needed saying – that this is perhaps the only way I will be able to communicate my feelings to a man who has been too hard on his family, but mostly too hard on himself. He wasn't able to offer his children the love and affection they needed, for the simple fact one can't give what one hasn't got. A broken heart is exactly that – a broken vessel with the love drained out of it.

I've tried to give a fair picture of life at Mermaid House, and though Gabriel might not like what I've said, I want him to know that he has to forgive everyone he thinks has let him down. He needs to forgive himself and be reconciled with the truth that all any of us can ever do is our very inadequate best.

There were tears in Clara's eyes as she closed the book. It wasn't so much the poignancy of the words that touched her but all the blank pages that followed.

She turned out the light and knew that she had no choice but to return the diaries to their owner. And, just as surely, she knew that the task had to be performed in person. There could be no cheating, no sending them anonymously in the post.

She had no idea how she was going to explain to Gabriel why she had 'borrowed' them.

Chapter Forty-Two

It was just as Caspar feared: the bank had pulled the rug out from beneath him. They had turned down his request for another thirty days' grace. And with no one else to turn to, it was financial melt-down time.

He threw the letter on to the pile of bills on his desk with contempt and directed his anger at those who could have helped.

His accountant for not moving fast enough to save him from bankruptcy.

His vindictive father for being such a tight old buzzard and too stubborn to sell Mermaid House.

The bloodsucking man at the Inland Revenue for hounding him so relentlessly.

The European Commission for insisting that the special relationship between car manufacturers and dealers had to be shaken up, and that forecourt prices had to be cut.

He also blamed the hordes of cheapskate cowboys who were ruining decent businesses like his by bringing luxury cars into the country by the back door. He supposed it said a lot about the calibre of his customers who were now taking their money to these fly-by-night Johnnies with their low overheads, fast turn-around, cheaper imports and undercut prices. Never mind the after-sales problems they experienced. Never mind the fake documents with which these cars often came. Never mind that men like Caspar Liberty were forced to rob Paul to pay Peter and go to the wall in the process.

Through the glass panel of his office, which looked out on to the showroom, he watched a young man of no more than twenty-five approach a Jaguar XKR. It was late afternoon and sunlight was shining in through the plate-glass window, showing off to perfection the car's smooth, sleek lines and glossy red finish. The man slipped into the driver's seat, one hand cupping the head of the gear-lever, the other stroking the steering-wheel. With his well-cut suit, open-necked shirt, gold watch, ostentatious bracelet, deep tan and collar-length hair, he bore all the hallmarks of a vulgar young blood: in other words, a genuine punter. He was probably a professional footballer, or big in the world of popular music. God knows, there were enough of them in Manchester. What he couldn't be mistaken for was a member of the anorak crowd; pathetic time-wasters who came in to drool over something they could never afford.

Caspar waited for one of his salesmen to materialise. Minutes passed, and no one appeared. He was about to go and deal with the man himself when the telephone on his desk rang. He hesitated, caught between the two. Then he thought, What the hell? The business was sunk.

He sat at his desk with his head lowered, and let the phone ring until the caller gave up.

In the staff room at Dick High, Jonah put down the phone. He had never rung his brother at work before, but then, he had never been so worried about their father.

It was four days now since he had witnessed the unimaginable: Gabriel Liberty crying. Since then he had called at Mermaid House every day, intending to carry on where Miss Costello had left off, but his father had had other ideas. 'I'd rather you didn't meddle with my things,' he had said, taking from Jonah the roll of plastic sacks for the bin he had just emptied. 'And what, I'd like to know, has got into you all of a sudden? Why have you taken it upon yourself to keep pestering me?'

He had wanted to say, 'Because I'm worried about you,' but his courage had failed him: showing concern was tantamount to showing weakness, and that was something no Liberty was ever allowed to do.

His father's stolid manner and desire to pretend that there had been no breakdown at the kitchen table proved that he was determined the matter should never be referred to again. But Jonah knew he would never forget the night when he had helped his father upstairs and put him to bed. Gabriel had fallen asleep almost immediately his head had touched the pillow, and not wanting to leave him alone, Jonah had found himself a blanket and passed an uncomfortable night in an armchair beside the bed, imagining that the morning would bring a degree of openness between the two of them. His hope had been misplaced. The next day his father had indicated that once more the shutters were down. But his words had been at odds with his actions, for seconds later he had fled the room, locked himself in the bathroom and stayed there for nearly an hour.

Jonah was convinced that his father was depressed, that in his current state he would isolate himself further and his health would suffer. On more than one occasion he had found him standing in the library staring blankly at Anastasia's portrait. He had tried several times to get him out of the house, suggesting they go for a walk while the weather was warm and dry. But anything he put forward was thrown back at him with the same taciturn reply: 'Why can't you just leave me alone?'

Jonah had to face facts. As ever, his presence was adding to his father's discomfort. Or, more accurately, his presence was the cause of his pain. He had considered getting in touch with Dr Singh, but, again, his courage had failed him.

Yet the concern that was uppermost in Jonah's mind, and the reason why he had taken the unprecedented step of phoning Caspar at work, was that he felt their father's mental state might deteriorate to the extent that one day he would go out for a walk with one of his guns and never come back.

Though why he thought Caspar would be of any use, Jonah didn't know. He would probably offer to load the gun. But perhaps turning to his brother reflected the depth of his concern. In desperation, he even wondered if it would be worth his while to get in touch with Damson.

He sighed deeply. Why was it always he who had to sort things out? It had been the same when Val had died. Everyone had expected him to deal with the funeral arrangements. 'But you're so good at these humdrum things,' Damson had said airily, when he'd hinted that maybe she and Caspar might like to give him a hand. 'And anyway,' she'd added, 'you wouldn't want me organising a funeral. I'd feel duty-bound to turn it into a theatrical event.' Jonah hadn't doubted it. His sister's idea of a funeral would probably include a pair of black horses pulling a Victorian glass hearse, with a cortège of professional keeners trailing behind.

In the staff room, standing at the window looking down on to the playground, he saw a familiar figure striding across the tarmac: a lad wearing a Marilyn Manson T-shirt and hugely baggy jeans hanging off his hips. Talking into a mobile phone, Jase O'Dowd was pushing against the tide of shambolic gangs of jostling home-leavers, one of whom was Sharna Powell. It was early days yet, but since Jonah's visit to twenty-three Capstone Close, Sharna's attendance at school had been a hundred per cent.

Checking his watch, Jonah saw that it was four o'clock and time for his eleventh-hour revision lesson for his GCSE history set. Gathering up his briefcase, pleased that Jase had shown up, he set off for his classroom, thinking how easy it was to motivate his pupils but how impossible it was to do the same with his family.

That evening, to the sound of church bells – it was bell-ringing practice night – Jonah cooked himself supper. After he had eaten, and while it was still light, he went outside to work in the garden. He was in just the right frame of mind to deal with the ancient honeysuckle.

He hacked away at the woody growth, thinking how

sad it was that the only person who could lift their father's spirits was not a member of the family but the redoubtable Miss Costello.

He stood back from what was left of the mutilated bush and decided to have a bonfire. It was almost dark now, very quiet – the bell-ringers had gone home – and there was little wind, so he bundled up the honeysuckle, took it down to the bottom of the garden, and dropped it on to the blackened remains of a previous fire. He fetched some sheets of newspaper and a box of matches from the shed. Twigs were soon snapping and crackling and tiny flames flickering, and before long, small billowing clouds puffed into the still night air. As Jonah stared into the darkness, at the outlines of the distant hills, spotted here and there with glowing lights, he found himself wishing he could track down his father's fairy godmother. He would drag her back to Deaconsbridge and make her wave her magic wand over Mermaid House once more.

As he absorbed himself in this scenario, he was forced to admit that his altruism was transparently thin. He didn't want Miss Costello back just for his father's benefit: since her departure from Mermaid House, he had thought of her frequently. He wanted to figure out what had attracted him to her. Had it been her challenging manner? Or the sharpness of her mind and the way she always seemed to be one step ahead of him? He smiled wryly. Or perhaps it had been nothing more than the pose she had struck that day in the courtyard? Was he merely the same as the next man, aroused simply by the thought of a woman's body and the potential pleasure and gratification held within?

Disconsolately, he poked the charred end of a long stick into the glowing embers of the fire. What did it matter anyway? She was never coming back.

Chapter Forty-Three

Yorkshire was behind them now. They had left Haworth early that morning in a blaze of sunshine, taken the A629 to Halifax, then on to Huddersfield and Holmfirth – *Last of the Summer Wine* country – before crossing the boundary into Derbyshire. If they kept up their current speed, Clara reckoned they were less than an hour from Deaconsbridge. She had thought of ringing Mermaid House to announce their arrival, but Ned had begged her not to: he was desperate to surprise Mr Liberty.

Just as she had anticipated, Ned had been overjoyed when she had told him that they would be making a return trip to Mermaid House – though, of course, she hadn't told him the reason behind their visit. His eyes wide with excitement, he had burst out that this was what he had wished for when he'd tossed his coin into the mermaid's pool in the cavern. 'You see, Mummy,' he'd said, hopping from one small foot to the other, 'wishes do come true!' He had wanted to pack up there and then, but she had insisted that they finish visiting what they had come to see in Haworth and the surrounding area. But now, and much to Ned's delight, they would shortly be seeing Gabriel Liberty. His excitement gave him an extra bounce and she wished she had half his vitality. As she concentrated on the winding road, she was aware that a nagging headache was developing and that she felt drained.

The cause was anxiety – and guilt: she was nervous about coming clean with Gabriel over Val's diaries. She just hoped he could forgive her for what she had done.

340

She didn't know why, but his forgiveness was important to her.

Gabriel pushed his stockinged feet into his walking boots, and after a brief stab at tying the laces with his useless fingers – they were particularly painful that day – he slipped a shotgun over the crook of his arm and shut the door after him. He crossed the courtyard and skirted round the front of the house, across the sloping lawn where the daffodils had long since gone over, and carried on towards the copse. The rhododendrons were in full flower, splashes of vermilion brilliant against the dark green of glossy leaves. He trudged on, his boots sinking into the soft grass. Sheep scattered at his approach, bleating mournfully, and above him, the sun shone on the back of his neck, making him regret putting on the waxed jacket.

His thoughts, never far from his younger son these days, turned to Jonah and how badly he had treated him – and was continuing to treat him. But it was too late to make amends for the damage he had wreaked. What good would it do to tell Jonah that he was sorry? It wouldn't change anything, not the words, the gestures, the neglect, or the downright cruel way he had excluded and blamed the boy.

If only he had been a better man – a better father – he would have realised that his younger son had never deserved such rough punishment. It hadn't been Jonah who had killed Anastasia: fate had done that. But for all these years, ever since Gabriel had come home in the middle of the night and had been told that his wife was dead, he had needed to lay the blame on someone. And he had done it that night when the young nurse had handed Jonah to him. He had turned his back on her and his baby son, and walked out of the room, out of the house. In the darkness, he had stumbled down to the copse and stayed there until dawn had bruised the sky, tearing it apart with harsh streaks of sunlight. Eventually he went back to the house, but didn't look at that newborn baby, not until after the funeral, and only then for a few seconds. How could he, when he saw him as the cause of his beloved wife's death? It was years before he was able to lay eyes on the child without wishing he had died instead of Anastasia.

For years, tolerance was the best he could manage. A thin veneer of tolerance that was often stripped back to reveal his bitterness, and to let his child know what it was to suffer. Oh, how callous he had been.

And what had woken him to the truth?

It was the shock of recognising Anastasia's face so clearly in Jonah's. Seeing the two of them so inextricably bound together had brought him up short, had made him, for the first time ever, see Jonah for what he really was: his mother's son. He was not, as Gabriel had made him out to be, a malevolent stranger who had walked into his life and wrecked it.

He was the son of the woman Gabriel had never stopped loving.

Now, whenever he looked at his son, he saw Anastasia staring back at him. She was in Jonah's eyes, the turn of his head, the shape of his mouth. The pain of his guilt went so deep inside him that sometimes Gabriel had to sit down and wait for it to pass. But the one thing he couldn't do was face Jonah and confide in him. He was too ashamed. Ashamed to admit that for all this time he had harboured such a monumental and misplaced grudge. That was why he continued to rebuff Jonah. Having him around only added to his grief. Because that was what it felt like. Since that appalling night when he had broken down, it was as if he was being forced to grieve for his darling Anastasia all over again.

Plunged further into misery, he pressed on down to the copse where, in the dense shade of the trees that were in full leaf now, a blanket of bluebells shimmered, their colour brightening the darkness. Though not the darkness by which he felt so consumed. That would never lift. That was *his* punishment. It was no more than he deserved. But he'd had enough of the burden, the strain of knowing that in this life he would never be released from the shame and the guilt. It was too much for him. He wanted to be with Anastasia. He needed her forgiveness for what he had done.

The weight of the gun pressed heavily on his arm. He shifted it to a more comfortable position and entered the wood, feeling at once the welcome cool shade offered by the trees. He paused, making up his mind where he wanted to be. As to the rest, he had thought it all out, had prepared himself so that he could at least get this right.

The triumphant entrance Ned had hoped to make was spoiled by Gabriel not answering the door.

'Shall we go inside and find him?' Ned asked, assuming that the door would be unlocked. He pressed his forehead to the door, peered in through the letterbox.

Clara tried the handle and stepped inside, Ned at her heels. 'But we'll only go as far as the kitchen,' she said. 'We ought not to intrude any further.'

She was surprised to see that her hard work had not been in vain. While the kitchen had gathered a few extraneous piles of paperwork – mostly bills and bank statements – the place was still reasonably clean and orderly. She wondered if Gabriel had found himself a cleaner. Leaving Ned to call him, she noticed the post-cards lined up along the window-sill. Touched that he had kept them, she went over to look at them, recalling exactly when and where each had been written.

Still not getting any response to his eager cries, Ned joined her at the sink. 'Do you think he's gone for a walk?' he asked, his elation fizzling into disappointment.

'I think that's precisely what he's done. Shall we see if we can find him?' She had seen the battered old Land Rover in the courtyard, so it was a safe bet that he hadn't gone far. Unless, of course, Jonah had given him a lift somewhere.

They shut the back door and set off towards the copse, which, according to Ned, was where Gabriel liked to go. 'He makes sure the badgers are all right,' he informed Clara.

It was a truly glorious day. The sun shone brightly in a perfect canopy of blue, and the air smelt sweet from the grass beneath their feet. In the distance, the hills were golden with flowering gorse bushes. Nearing the copse, Clara was overcome by the most beautiful sight: bluebells, hundreds of them. She had never seen so many in one spot before. It was breathtaking: a magical infusion of colour. She stood for a moment to take it in. It was so tranquil here. So perfect.

High up in one of the trees, a wood pigeon broke the calm, clattering its wings as it flew out of the copse. It came towards them, and ahead of her, Ned came to a stop. He tilted his head so far back to watch the bird, she thought he might fall over. She caught up with him, and together they passed from the sunny brightness into the dappled, shadowy gloom. The fresh meadow-sweet fragrance of crushed grass was replaced by the earthy smell of moss, rotting bark and mouldy damp leaves.

'He usually goes this way,' Ned said knowledgeably, pointing towards a leafy path that twisted through the thicket of trees.

They had only taken a few steps into the cool woodland when Clara stood still. She craned her neck. Ned looked up at her. 'What?'

'I thought I heard something.' She smiled. 'It was probably one of Mr Liberty's badgers.'

But within seconds, they had stopped again, and this time she knew she wasn't imagining it. Someone else was in the copse. Remembering that day down by the river when they had first arrived in Deaconsbridge, she held Ned's hand firmly. The sound grew louder and she wasn't sure what it was she could hear. It was a groaning of such guttural rawness it was animal-like. Bravely she carried on, until at last they came to a small clearing and she saw the source of the noise.

It was Gabriel Liberty. He was on his knees, crumpled over the trunk of a fallen beech tree, and beneath his waxed jacket, he was shaking violently.

'Stay here, Ned,' she commanded. Confusion written all over his anxious face, he did as she said, and she moved in closer to Gabriel, who seemed to have no idea that they were there. She reached down to him, placed a hand lightly on his shoulder. He didn't react and the racking groans and rasping breath continued. 'Mr Liberty,' she said, 'it's me, Clara – Miss Costello. Are you hurt?'

He stiffened and turned towards her, his face contorted with abject misery. Disbelieving eyes, brimming with tears, focused on her. It was then that she saw the shotgun cradled in his arms. Her instinct was to step back, to get as much distance as possible between herself and the gun, but instead she prised it out of his shaking hands, and placed it on the other side of the tree-trunk. Then she got down on her knees on the soft cushion of leaves and took him in her arms. She held him tightly, hushed him with soothing words, as if he were Ned, until finally, he gave one last, shuddering sob, slumped against her and gradually became still.

It took all of her strength to pull him on to his feet and sit him on the damp, moss-covered tree trunk. When she had settled him and found a grubby old handkerchief in one of his jacket pockets, she beckoned Ned over.

'Mr Liberty isn't very well, Ned,' she said matter-of-factly. 'Come and sit down and help me make him feel better.'

With one of them sitting on either side of him, the poor man's first coherent words were 'I – I can't bear you to see me like this.'

She took the handkerchief from him and dabbed at his eyes. 'And I can't bear to think of you suffering like this all alone. What's been going on?'

He dropped his chin to his chest. 'It's – it's Jonah . . .'

'Jonah? What's happened to him?' Alarmed, Clara thought of the last time she had seen Jonah. How his expression had transformed when he had dropped his guard. She thought too of all she now knew about him from reading Val's diaries. 'Has . . . has there been an accident?'

Gabriel looked at her, confused. 'No,' he murmured, 'it's me. It's what I've done to him. Terrible things. I'm – I'm so dreadfully ashamed. And there's no going back. I know that.' His voice cracked and she felt a tremor run through him. She took his hands in hers and squeezed them firmly.

'There might not be a pedal for going backwards,' she said, 'but there's always one for going forwards. Do you think with my help you could make it up to the house?'

He raised his red-rimmed eyes to hers. 'Miss Costello, I honestly believe that with your help, I could do almost anything.'

She kissed his stubbly cheek, then helped him to his feet. 'Well, before we take on the world, let's start with the short walk home, shall we?'

Chapter Forty-Four

In Clara's opinion, the best place for Gabriel was bed, but he refused point-blank to do as she said. Just as he had vehemently rejected her suggestion that she ought to ring Jonah or Dr Singh. So she removed his cumbersome jacket, sat him in the chair next to the Aga and sent Ned upstairs to fetch a blanket – the poor man was in shock and shivering despite the warmth of the day.

While Ned was out of the room, Clara knelt in front of him. She rubbed his hands. 'We can't talk now,' she said, 'not really talk, but later tonight, when Ned's asleep, I want you to tell me what's been going on here. But for now, all I can do is dose you with hot, sweet tea and some chocolate cake we brought for you from Haworth.'

He turned his bloodshot eyes on her. 'Dear girl, why are you so good to me? I don't deserve such kindness.'

'Ulterior motive, I'm still hoping to seduce you and get that ring on my finger.'

He laid a hand over hers. 'What made you come back so soon? Did you forget something?'

'In a manner of speaking,' she hedged, 'but we'll talk about that later too.'

Puffing from his exertion, Ned burst into the kitchen. 'Will this do?'

Clara took the heavy, feather-leaking eiderdown from him with a smile. 'Perfect, Ned. Here, help me to wrap up Mr Liberty. We want him as snug as a bug in a rug.'

They sat with their mugs of tea and plates of cake. Clara let Ned do all the talking: sitting on Gabriel's lap, with cake crumbs falling from his fingers as he waved his arms in the air, he told him all about their travels: of the castles they had seen, the mountains, the lakes, and the people they had met. 'We even stayed on a farm,' he said proudly, 'where I learned to milk a goat. And I fed the chickens. And I rode a pony too. I had to wear a hat that kept slipping over my eyes.' Drawing breath, he paused before saying, 'But nowhere was as nice as this. We didn't meet anyone as nice as you, Mr Liberty.'

'I'm delighted to hear it.'

Clara topped up Gabriel's mug with more tea, relieved to hear a glimmer of his old spirit returning.

When the time came for Ned to go to bed, Gabriel said he wanted them to be proper guests and stay the night inside Mermaid House. Apart from his bedroom, Val's old room was the only one Clara had cleaned and sorted, and though she had irrational reservations about using it, she made up the double bed to share with Ned.

When she bent to kiss Ned goodnight, he hooked his hands round her neck and pulled her closer. 'I'm glad we came back,' he said.

'I'm glad too.'

Then, more seriously, he said, 'Is Mr Liberty better now?'

She kissed him and unhooked his hands. 'He'll be fine. He just needs a little tender loving care. He's like a flower that someone has forgotten to water. We need to water him and make him nice and strong again.'

He considered this. 'How long will that take?'

'I don't know. We'll have to see.'

'Two days? Three days?'

She kissed him again, amused that he was subtly negotiating with her. 'Like I say, we'll have to wait and see.' He seemed happy enough with her reply and didn't push her any further. Instead, he yawned; he suddenly looked sleepy. 'Come on,' she said, 'it's late and you need to get some rest or you'll be the one in need of watering. Enjoy your night's sleep in a proper bed. And no kicking me when I join you later.'

He yawned again, turned on to his side, and reached under the pillow for Mermy. 'I promise,' he said drowsily.

Turning out the light, Clara felt the day catching up with her. More tired than she had felt in a long while, she took the stairs slowly, knowing it would be several hours before she would lay her aching head on a pillow. It was now time to get to the bottom of Gabriel's problems. Having read Val's diaries, she had a fair idea that raging guilt would be mostly to blame. Chances were it had finally caught up with him. The question was, why?

She thought of that moment when, just before entering the copse, she had paused to admire the bluebells. She remembered thinking then that she was in the right place at the right time. She wasn't one of those cranky types who believed in synchronistic events shaping collective destinies – making sense of coincidence with the benefit of hindsight was child's play – but there was no avoiding the extraordinary timing of her arrival here today.

Call it luck, call it predetermination, call it what you will, but it was a good thing that someone had been there for Gabriel Liberty when he most needed a friend. Thank goodness for Val's diaries! Thinking of the diaries, Clara decided that it would be better to hang on to them until Gabriel was feeling a lot stronger. In his present state they might upset him too much.

He was waiting for her in the kitchen. He had moved from his chair by the Aga and was clumsily stacking their supper things in the dishwasher. Despite his protests, she shooed him back to the chair. 'Leave that to me.'

'I'm not an invalid,' he argued, a little more of his old spirit shining through the clouds of his melancholy. But he relented anyway.

She tidied up, then poured two glasses of whisky, wondering who needed it more. She felt unaccountably lethargic and headachey, and wondered if she had a cold coming. When they were settled at either side of the Aga, she said, 'So what drove you to think about killing yourself?'

349

Gabriel flinched. He had known that this straight-talking woman would not couch her questions in polite euphemisms, had known, too, that her candid approach was what he needed and that it would bring him equal measures of pain and relief. But even so, hearing her put into such plain words what he had tried to do filled him with self-loathing. How desperate he had been. And how typically self-centred. Once again, he had put himself first, prepared to leave his family to clear up the mess he had made of his life . . . and his death. He was nothing but a coward.

He took a gulp of his drink. 'Failure,' he said, at last. 'I've been a lousy father and it's only just dawned on me the harm I've done.'

She looked at him over the rim of her glass. 'Who do you think you've failed the most?'

'The lot of them. But especially Jonah. I've . . . I've also failed Anastasia.'

'Not Val?'

He kept his eyes lowered. 'Her too. I never gave her the credit she deserved. She was a good wife and, against all the odds, a good mother.'

A silence settled on the room. Not rushing to fill the pause, Gabriel took a long sip of his drink.

'Tell me about Anastasia,' Clara said softly. 'She was the true love of your life, wasn't she?'

He took another swig of his whisky. 'That phrase doesn't even come close.'

'How did you meet?'

'At a wedding. And let me tell you, she outshone the bride by a long stretch. She was the most beautiful girl present – the most beautiful I had ever seen.' He cleared his throat, shifted in his seat. 'I was no spring chicken, no innocent, but she dazzled me from the moment she spoke. She was so compassionate, so genuinely warm-hearted. So full of joy. She had this wonderful ability to make me feel special. Corny I know, but the truth. She had that same effect on me even when we were married. We could be at a party, separated by a roomful of tedious people whom I had no desire to talk to, and our eyes would meet, and it would be as if we were alone.'

'You're lucky to have experienced that depth of love. Few people do.'

'It didn't feel lucky to have so much one minute, then have it snatched away the next.' His tone was bitter. 'Sorry, back to wallowing in self-pity again.'

She waved aside his apology. 'Did you ever allow yourself to grieve for Anastasia when she died? And I don't just mean going through the motions of accepting well-meant platitudes and attending a funeral. I mean, did you let yourself howl? Did you give in to the pain and let it render you helpless? Did you put yourself beyond caring what anyone thought of you?'

Fiddling with his glass, he said, 'You know the answer to that, or you wouldn't be asking.'

'But today you did put yourself beyond caring, didn't you? Today you did openly grieve for her, and for everything that has happened since.'

He nodded. 'And I know what you're going to ask me next. You want to know what precipitated all this ghastly baring of the soul and the realisation that I've let Anastasia down, quite apart from what I've done to Jonah—'

She raised a hand to interrupt him. 'Forgive me for splitting hairs, but you've known that all along. It's why you've suddenly acknowledged it that needs explaining.'

Swirling the last of his drink round, then downing it in one, he said, 'I see, as ever, that you have your gloves off and are sparing me nothing.'

'Business as usual. So what was the catalyst?'

'You, my dear.'

'*Me?* But how? Why?'

Until that moment Gabriel hadn't known the answer to that question, which he had asked himself earlier that day. But now he knew with certainty just how important a role this young woman and her son had played in opening his

351

eyes. 'You and Ned made me feel better about life,' he said simply. 'You made me realise what I'd been . . . what I'd been missing out on.' He swallowed, suddenly frightened that his emotions were in danger of sliding out of control again. He was being so honest it hurt. As if understanding, she reached for the bottle of Glenmorangie on the table and refilled his glass. When she had sat down again, he said, 'In a nutshell, you cared.'

Oh, there was so much more he could say, so many truths he now understood. How she had never judged him, never looked at him with eyes that feared or despised him. How she had never hated him because he had neglected his family. How she had amused him with her spirited put-downs. How she had charmed him by not treating him as a decrepit old man. He could have said all this, if only he trusted himself to get the words out without looking and sounding foolishly sentimental.

As ever, she said just the right thing. 'I might have known you'd try and lay the blame on me.'

He managed a small smile. 'How do you think it makes me feel, knowing that in our politically correct society, which as you know I abhor, our roles have been reversed and I've been cast as Sleeping Beauty while you've taken on the role as the Prince who's awakened me with a kiss.'

She laughed. 'Perhaps Beauty and the Beast would be a more comfortable analogy for you. And, in case you're wondering, you're the Beast. So how did you get from seeing life as a more worthwhile proposition to viewing Jonah differently?'

'After you and Ned had left I realised how lonely I was.'

'And you shared this with Jonah?'

'No. Oh, I wanted to, but have you any idea how hard it is to admit that you're lonely?'

'You've just done it with me.'

'That's because you're . . . you're different. You're a girl of unique charm and sensibility.'

She raised her glass to him. 'Still up to speed with the

schmaltz, I see. But back to Jonah. What changed between the two of you?'

'I . . . I stopped blaming him for his mother's death.' Keeping his voice as steady as he could, he explained about the night he had broken down in front of Jonah, how a connection had been made between them, but which he had found impossible to acknowledge or discuss. 'And it was all because I suddenly saw the likeness between Jonah and his mother.'

'And you'd never seen it before?'

'It sounds absurd, doesn't it? But no. Not consciously. What the hell's been going on inside my brain all these years is anybody's guess.' With a deep sigh of regret, he added, 'What does any of it matter? Jonah will never forgive me for what I've done.' He stared at her miserably.

She met his gaze with a shake of her head. 'Be warned, I'm about to split hairs again. You know jolly well, just as I do, that Jonah is one of the most compassionate people alive, and that he'll forgive you at the drop of a hat. What you're scared of is how that will make you feel. That all this time his love and forgiveness were there for the asking, but you were such a heel you chose to ignore it.'

'You don't think it's too late for reparation, then?'

She looked at him sternly. 'No, I don't. And, what's more, the sooner you do it, the better. Because then you'll realise that Jonah was one of the many gifts Anastasia left you. Perhaps the best gift of all.'

'But how will he react when I tell him that all these years I blamed him for her death?'

'You don't think he's always known that? Come on, it's time to be brave. Jonah's a big boy, he can take whatever revelations you throw at him.'

He took a moment to absorb this idea. To let faint hope take root. Finally he said, 'And what about Damson and Caspar? What do I say to them?'

She rubbed her eyes and yawned. 'If you don't mind, I'd

rather leave those two until tomorrow. For now I need to go to bed. I'm shattered.'

'Yes, of course. You must be tired after your long drive.'

They both rose to their feet. After they had locked up and turned out the lights, Clara slipped her arm through his. They climbed the stairs together. She said, 'Would you ever consider seeking professional help? I mean, someone qualified to discuss what you've . . . Well, it was a close call today, and if I hadn't—'

He squeezed her arm. 'You're professional enough for me, my dear. And don't worry, I've learned my lesson.'

'Which is?'

'That while one is caught in the throes of a low and unhappy mood, it's not the ideal time to distinguish a right course of action.'

When they reached the top of the stairs, Clara said, 'I might not be as old as you, or have gone through as much, but my guess is there's no magic cure or easy way to cope with grief or guilt. You have to plough headlong through it, take whatever it chucks at you, good or bad.'

'You sound as if you're talking from experience.'

'This might come as a shock to you, but you don't have a monopoly on self-reproach. Most of us scourge ourselves from time to time with a little bit of soul-searching.'

'Even you?'

'Oh, yes. Even me.'

He walked her to Val's old room, and as she pushed open the door, causing a shaft of soft light to spill from the landing across the carpet to the bed where the cause of her own soul-searching slept, she suddenly felt emotional and overwrought. She was tired, she told herself firmly. Nothing that a good night's sleep wouldn't cure.

But she slept fitfully, tossing and turning in the large creaking bed, one minute hot, the next freezing cold, all the while crashing from one bizarre dream sequence to another. Next to her, Ned slept on, blissfully unaware of

354

her discomfort. By the time daylight filtered through the gap in the curtains, she had managed to chase away the nightmares and fallen into a deep, more restful sleep.

She woke to find the other side of the bed empty and her head thumping. She was drenched in sweat but icy cold. Her eyes were sore, her throat felt dry, raw and lumpy, and her chest was as tight as a drum. She had only experienced full-blown flu once, but she suspected she was in for a second taste of it. Determined to prove herself wrong, that it was only a cold, she launched herself out of bed. A hot shower was all she needed. That, a cup of tea and a couple of paracetamol. She was half-way across the room when the door opened and Ned came in. He was dressed in the clothes he'd worn yesterday, and a few paces behind him was Gabriel with a breakfast tray. He took one look at her and said, 'Good Lord, what've you been up to? You look dreadful.'

'I feel dreadful,' she croaked.

She was immediately chivvied back into bed. Pillows were shaken and plumped, and the duvet straightened while Ned opened the curtains to brighten the room. Gabriel fetched some paracetamol from the bathroom and she washed them down with the mug of hot strong tea. She couldn't face the toast and marmalade he had so kindly made for her, and within minutes her head and eyelids were drooping and she was faintly aware of a door shutting quietly. Sleep sucked her into a nightmarish maze of hunting for Ned, but never finding him; of driving Winnie up and down a network of narrow lanes and hills that always brought her to where she had started. She dreamed she was back at work, that she and the boys were conversing in German, even though they were working for French-speaking gnomes who sat cross-legged on their desks with little fishing-rods and on the stroke of each hour burst into Rod Stewart's old song, 'Do You Think I'm Sexy?'

When she surfaced again she needed to go to the loo.

Shivering, and squinting against the brightness, she focused on her watch. Heavens! It was four o'clock!

Rallying her aching body, she made her way to the bathroom. When she had traversed the landing – which felt as unsteady as the deck of a ship on the high seas – and had locked the door after her, she had the second shock of her day. Damn! Her period had started. She groaned, recalling that she didn't have any of those wonder items tucked away in Winnie that would enable her to swim, roller-skate and skydive to her heart's desire – she had used them all up during last month's extravaganza of sporting events. She groaned again. There was nothing else for it: she would have to rouse herself and drive into Deaconsbridge. She would need to buy super-strength painkillers too. Something lethal enough to stun a charging rhinoceros. Otherwise she'd be in for several days of rolling around on the floor in agony with a hot-water bottle strapped to her stomach. With chattering teeth, and her head feeling like pulsating cotton wool, she unlocked the door, pulled it open, then jumped back, startled. Looking for all the world like a welcoming committee, Ned and Gabriel were waiting for her.

'We heard a noise and came to check on you,' Gabriel said, making a show of looking anywhere but at the rumpled state of her *déshabille*. 'No need to ask how you're feeling. You look ready to drop. Back to bed with you.'

She wrapped her arms around her shivering body. 'Er . . . actually I need to go into Deaconsbridge.'

'Yes, my dear, and I need to marry Lucrezia Borgia. But before I send out the wedding invitations, you must go back to bed.'

'No, really. You don't understand, I *have* to go shopping.' But even as she was speaking, she was being taken by the arm and steered towards the bedroom. Too weak to disentangle herself from the firm hands that were guiding her, she was in bed before she knew it. Sitting next to her, his legs stretched out alongside hers, Ned said, 'Mummy, are you very sick?'

She forced her dry lips into a smile. 'Just a little. But I'll be fine. Honestly.'

He dipped his head towards her shoulder so that she could put an arm around him. 'I told Mr Liberty about us having to water him to make him big and strong again, and he said it was his turn to water you now.'

Right on cue, Gabriel passed her the mug of tea he had brought up. She took it gratefully, then remembered about her need to go shopping. She knew, though, that in her current state, driving would be a monumental challenge, as well as putting others on the road at risk. Yet the thought of asking Gabriel to buy her such personal items seemed far more daunting.

Down in the kitchen, while Ned organised the draughts board for another game, Gabriel cringed at what he had been asked to do. Though he had been married twice and had raised a daughter, 'intimate womanly matters' had been an accepted no-go area of secrecy and mystery. Nothing had ever been divulged to him, and he had certainly never felt the urge to probe. Now, though, he was expected to walk bold as brass into the chemist in town and hunt through the shelves for . . . for . . .

He ran his hand through his hair and shuddered. He couldn't bring himself to say the words, not even inside his head. Worse still, he had no idea what the wretched things looked like.

And yet he had to do it. Miss Costello – Clara who had shown him such kindness – was upstairs in bed, relying on him. This was no time to be squeamish and embarrassed. He tried to remember the last time he had been into the chemist. It was when he'd burnt his arm and had needed antibiotics. He saw himself in the shop, waiting for the prescription to be made up. Closing his eyes, he tried to recall where everything was kept. Tissues. Toilet rolls. Shampoo. Nappies. Combs. Brushes. Makeup. Camera films. Plastic rainhoods. Nail-clippers. Pumice stones. Sponges. Sponge bags. Toothpaste. Throat lozenges. Vitamin tablets. Witch hazel. Laxatives.

Oh, it was hopeless! He could practically do a roll-call of everything in the damned shop and still not locate the crucial items Clara required.

Hearing his name called, he opened his eyes and turned round. 'What's that you're saying, Ned?'

'The telephone's ringing, Mr Liberty, can't you hear it?'

He looked about him, confused – his brain was still in the chemist's searching the shelves for the elusive items. 'Oh, so it is.' He crossed the kitchen, went out into the hall to where the phone was ringing. He picked up the receiver, glad of the diversion.

'Hello, Dad, it's me, Jonah. I'm just nipping to the supermarket and I wondered if you needed anything. I noticed you were getting low on cereal the last time I was there. Anything in particular you fancy?'

Thank God for Jonah, thought Gabriel, five minutes later, when he had explained that the Costellos were staying with him again and he had offloaded – after a few false starts – the task that had been thrust upon him.

Chapter Forty-Five

Jonah was still smiling to himself as he worked his way methodically round the supermarket, which was busy with early evening shoppers.

Weaving a path through the stop-start traffic of trolleys, he didn't know what amused him more: his father's excruciating embarrassment as he mumbled into the phone, trying to avoid the unmentionable T and ST words, or the fact that Miss Costello was back, albeit under the weather with flu and 'female malaise'.

Arriving at Mermaid House, and parking alongside the Costello camper-van, he thought of how, only the other night, he had wished for its owner to return to Deacons-bridge so that she could wave her magic wand over his father. Well, amazingly, the first part of that wish had come true. Now it was a matter of getting her back on her feet so that she could fulfil the rest. As to any pleasurable hopes he might have secretly harboured for himself, time would tell on that score.

He opened the boot of his car and lifted out two carrier bags. One contained everyday bits and bobs for his father, and the other everything necessary to get the patient on the road to recovery.

His father met him at the door. He looked anxious. 'Did you get everything?'

'Everything,' Jonah reassured him, and stepped into the kitchen. 'Hi, Ned. Nice to see you again. How're you doing? Hope you're not going to come down with flu. You ought to be careful too, Dad.'

Ned got down from the chair by the Aga where he had

been reading a book and came over. 'Have you brought some medicine to make Mummy better?'

'That's right, lots of medicine. We'll soon have her well enough to chase you round the garden.' He passed one of the bags to Gabriel. 'Do you want to take it up?'

His father's face coloured. 'Er . . . no, I was just about to start cooking some supper. You do it.'

'Okay, but why don't you hang fire on the cooking and let me do that for you?'

He realised when he was climbing the stairs that he hadn't asked his father which bedroom had been turned into a sick room. But the sound of coughing directed him towards Val's old room. He knocked on the partially open door. A croaky voice answered, 'It's okay, I'm as decent as I'll ever be, you can come in. Oh, it's you.'

'You sound disappointed.'

She blew her nose. 'I haven't the strength to be disappointed. You can come closer, if you want. I promise not to breathe over you. What have you got there?'

He handed her the plastic bag, hovered awkwardly at her side, then sat in the chair next to the bed. At once he felt history repeating itself: how many times had he sat here in this chair chatting to Val when she was ill? 'I was going shopping anyway and Dad enlisted my help.'

Despite her discomfort, she smiled knowingly. He could see now just how ill she was. Her complexion was flushed, and beneath her eyes, puffy dark arcs bruised the skin. Her breathing was shallow and echoed with a trace of a wheeze that made him want to clear his throat. 'Your poor father,' she said hoarsely, 'I've never seen anyone dissolve into such a heap of toe-curling embarrassment.'

Jonah smiled too. 'Not his scene, I'm afraid. Womanly matters were always taboo in this household. He would much rather you were suffering from something less indelicate, something dignified with backbone. Bubonic plague, for instance.' Lowering his eyes to the plastic bag, he said, 'I've tried to cover every eventuality, but if I've forgotten something or got the wrong thing, just say, and

I'll make another trip. The supermarket stays open until eight tonight.'

She rummaged through the bag. He could see the relief in her face. 'Good heavens,' she said hoarsely, 'I'm looking at a small chemist's shop. You're a real life-saver, Master Liberty. You've thought of everything. Super-strength painkillers and a selection of feminine hygiene to suit every occasion. I can even go swimming now.' She coughed, then reached for a tissue and blew her nose. 'That's if the mood takes me, of course. Mind if I make a timely exit?'

He rose quickly to his feet. 'Shall I bring up a drink so you can take the painkillers?'

'Tea would be great. Though don't make it as strong as your father does. With the amount I'm getting through, I don't want to risk sprouting chest hairs.'

She was back in bed when he knocked on the door again. He noticed she had brushed her hair and sprayed on something pleasant. She took the mug from him and said, 'Maybe this is the moment to say that you can call me Clara, seeing as we've been so intimately thrown together.'

'I'll call you Clara if you stop calling me Master Liberty.'

'Agreed. So – and given your stunted upbringing at the hands of a father like yours – where did you pick up such a wonderful understanding of female needs? How come you're not so bashful?'

'No big deal. My last girlfriend suffered badly every month. She found yoga helped. Shall I pop out the pills for you?'

She nodded, then settled back into the pillows and sipped her tea. Suddenly she looked doubly tired, as though just talking to him was taking it out of her. 'You're too much, Jonah, you really are.' She sighed. 'Emily was a fool to let a saint in human form slip through her fingers.'

He put the tablets into her outstretched hand. 'How did you know her name was Emily?'

Her eyes wavered away from his, looked out of the window at the distant crest of Kinder Scout bathed in the soft early evening sunshine. 'Your father must have told me,' she said. 'How else would I have known?'

It seemed unlikely that his father would have discussed something as personal as his younger son's love-life, but Jonah let it go. She started to cough again, her shoulders jerking violently. He took the mug from her and put it on the bedside table next to the box of tissues. From the carrier bag that was now at the end of the bed he pulled out a bottle of cough mixture. He read the instructions on the box. 'You're not pregnant or asthmatic, are you?'

'Not asthmatic, and certainly not pregnant. Not unless this is a contagious bout of immaculate conception I'm suffering from.'

He unscrewed the metal top of the bottle, measured the specified dose into the plastic cap provided, and gave it to her. 'Every four hours, it says.' He checked his watch. 'So the next dose will be at eleven.'

She gave him a limp salute. 'Yes, Doctor.'

'I'm on cooking duty next. Any special requests?'

She shook her head weakly. 'No, I'm not hungry.'

'Not even a boiled egg? Everyone likes a boiled egg when they're not well.' Smiling, he added, 'Perhaps I could rustle up a soldier or two.'

'Sorry, but uniforms have never done it for me.'

He emptied some of the contents of the bag on to the dressing-table behind him, lining up the packets of Lemsip, throat lozenges, vitamin supplements, and the extra soft tissues. He caught her eye in the mirror as she watched what he was doing. Thinking that she had probably had enough of his company, he folded the bag, and said, 'Well, I'll leave you to it then. Shout if you change your mind about something to eat. And don't worry about Ned. Dad and I will take good care of him.'

362

He was across the room and standing by the door when she said, 'Thank you for the tea, Jonah, and . . .'

'And?'

'And for everything else. Give yourself a gold star and go straight to the top of the class.'

'I guess it's the least I can do, given the amount you did here for Dad.'

A burst of coughing rattled her chest and when she had recovered, she said, in a voice laden with sleep, 'You need to talk to him, Jonah. There's something he wants to say to you, something he *needs* to say. Help him to seize the moment. He's not brave enough to do it on his own.'

Puzzled, Jonah went downstairs. He could hear the animated sound of his father's voice in the kitchen. He stood in the doorway, taking in the scene. By the Aga, sitting on Gabriel's lap, Ned was enthralled with the story that was being read to him with relish and enthusiasm.

How perfect they looked together. It seemed a shame to disturb them.

The vote was carried by a unanimous show of hands that Jonah should cook cheese-and-ham omelettes and Ned's favourite vegetable, sweetcorn. He was a happy and remarkably trusting little boy, who appeared to take everything in his stride – a trait he had probably inherited from his mother, thought Jonah. Though moderately concerned that she should soon be well, he wasn't put out by her absence. It was only when he started to yawn and Gabriel announced that it was his bedtime and that he ought not to share a bed with his mother that night that he became anxious. 'But where will I sleep? In Winnie on my own? What if I have a bad dream?'

Jonah stepped in quickly. 'You could have my old room if you like. It's next door to your mother's. Let's go and have a look at it, shall we?'

It was a dreary sight in the dim light cast by the low-wattage bulb hanging from the ceiling rose. There were several boxes on the double bed, but when these had been removed and the bed made up with a clean sheet and Ned's own pillow and stripy blue and white duvet, he seemed happy enough with the arrangements. Especially when he found a collection of Jonah's long-forgotten books in a chest at the foot of the bed. There were ancient *Rupert Bear* books that Val had given him at Christmas, as well as an old *Blue Peter* annual. Despite their age, they were in pristine condition, but Jonah had always been careful with his things.

'Will you check my teeth for me?' Ned said to Jonah, when he had changed into his pyjamas and stood poised with his toothbrush in the bathroom, his chin level with the basin. 'Mummy always does that. I have to do them first, then she brushes them again to make sure I've done them properly.'

This duty carried out, Ned then asked if he could see if his mother was awake to give him a goodnight kiss.

'Okay, but be sure to be very quiet, just in case she's asleep.' Jonah waited for him outside the door, not wanting to intrude. Seconds later, Ned reappeared, disappointed.

'She is asleep. But I climbed up on to the bed anyway and gave her a kiss.'

As he walked Ned to his bedroom, Jonah was surprised when the youngster slipped a small hand into his and said, 'Will you tell me a bedtime story, please? A made-up one? I like those. They're fun.' A winning toothy smile appeared on his face.

He was hard to resist, so after Ned had settled himself beneath the duvet, Jonah sat on the edge of the bed and started his tale. He soon realised that he was cheating and was giving Ned a jumbled-up version of *The Selfish Giant*. Deciding that there were too many deaths in it for a four-year-old, he improvised and gave the tale a different spin so that everyone lived happily ever after.

His eyes glazed with sleep, Ned said, 'Why didn't the giant like the children who came to play in his garden?'

'Because he thought they were noisy and might spoil his garden.'

'But they didn't, did they? They made it nice for him. The flowers grew and the sun shone.'

'And he was jolly lucky to realise that before it was too late,' said a gruff voice at the door. Ned lifted his head from the pillow and Jonah turned round. How long had his father been standing there? He came into the room. 'Do I get a goodnight kiss from my favourite house guest, then?'

Jonah patted Ned's shoulder affectionately. 'I'll leave you to it. Goodnight.'

'Will you be here tomorrow?'

'I'm at school during the day, but maybe I'll pop in and see you in the evening. Sleep well.'

While he waited for his father to join him in the kitchen, Jonah decided to take Clara at her word. *Help him to seize the moment.* Well, perhaps that moment had come.

But what if the consequences were as devastating as the last time he had tried to talk to his father?

Driving home later that night, Jonah brought his car to a sudden stop. For a long moment he sat and stared at his hands as they gripped the steering wheel in front of him. Then, in a swift, decisive movement, he switched off the engine and got out of the car. Breathing hard, he went and leaned against the drystone wall alongside which he had parked. He gazed across the darkened landscape, back towards Mermaid House. He saw that his hands were shaking. It was shock.

What had just passed between him and his father had gone well beyond anything he had thought might come of a heart-to-heart chat. To hear his father asking him for his forgiveness had been unbearably painful. It had been the culmination of a lifetime of confused guilt and regret. A lifetime of wondering how things might have been for his father, and for his brother and sister, if he had never been born . . . if their mother had lived.

Forgive me, Jonah. Please.

He had never thought to hear those words. Never imagined such a moment when his father would lay a hand on his shoulder and say that he was sorry. Almost too choked to speak, he had mumbled something about it being okay, that there was nothing to forgive. That it was all in the past.

'It'll never be in the past,' his father had said, 'not until I know you forgive me.'

They were standing in the library, symbolically beneath the portrait that Jonah had made countless wishes upon as a child: *Make my father happy . . . Make him notice me . . . Make Caspar and Damson like me.* Caspar had once caught him staring up at the painting and had taunted him cruelly. 'You killed her, you know that, don't you? If it hadn't been for you, she'd still be alive.'

'Please, Jonah,' his father had said, 'I know I've done everything wrong, but I want to change all that now. It's not too late, is it?'

A shake of the head was as much as he could manage, and with an unsteady hand, he had taken the glass of whisky his father had just poured for him. He'd downed it in one, willing its warmth to relax his throat so that he could speak. It worked. 'It's okay, Dad. Really. I've never held anything against you. I knew it was all down to circumstances.'

It was then that his father had told him about going down into the copse with one of his shotguns – just as Jonah had feared he might. 'No, Jonah,' he'd said, raising his hand to stop him from interrupting, 'and don't look at me like that. I don't deserve your sympathy. Not one ounce of it. I've been a damned silly fool. I can't promise to change overnight, but I want you to know that I do care about you. I care very much. Another drink? You look like you could do with it.'

'I'd better not, I'm driving.'

'Of course.'

An awkward silence then followed when neither of them spoke. Not until Jonah said, 'It's getting late. I ought to go.'

They parted at the back door, not with a great show of new-found emotion, not with an uncharacteristic hearty embrace, but with a warm handshake, as though they were two people who had just met for the first time and had decided they quite liked each other.

Turning from the drystone wall, Jonah got back into his car and drove home.

Chapter Forty-Six

That same night, in Cross Street, Archie was eating his supper in front of the television. The news was on, but he wasn't listening to it. He was too tired. It was as much as he could do to cut into the chicken and mushroom pie he'd picked up on the way home.

It had been a long, long day, with a house clearance in Whaley Bridge that had taken more effort and time than he'd anticipated. Valuable hours had been wasted because the relatives of the deceased owner of the house couldn't decide who should have what. It should all have been settled before he and Samson had arrived but it hadn't, and they were soon caught up in a classic family dispute with the dead woman's daughters-in-law arguing over who had been promised a pretty little carriage clock from the front room. When things had got ugly, he and Samson had retreated to the kitchen to start on the cupboards, leaving the rapidly dividing family to resolve matters alone. It wasn't as though there was much worth fighting over: the house was small and the possessions meagre. Maybe that was the problem: the fewer the bones to pick over, the more frantic and bitter the feeding frenzy.

Perhaps it was some folk's way of handling grief, letting off steam by bickering among themselves; it distracted them from what was really going on. But this lot had been mean and grasping. They hadn't been interested in sentimental keepsakes: they only wanted the stuff they thought had a bit of value.

It had been left to him and Samson to clear out the rest, which the family plainly regarded as rubbish. Archie always felt he owed it to the person who had spent a lifetime gathering these mementoes to do his best by them. It was the bedside tables that invariably got to him. It was in those little drawers that, often, the most personal and poignant objects had been kept, and which gave the deepest insight into that person's habits and thoughts. Today's bedside table had revealed the usual old tubes of ointment, packets of indigestion tablets, buttons, rusting safety-pins, bent hairpins, and a string of cheap, gaudy beads. There was a tiny-faced watch that didn't work, a money-off voucher for washing powder (dated October 1988), a pair of tweezers, a throat lozenge that had oozed a sticky trail across an envelope of black and white holiday snaps, a crumbling bath cube that had lost its scent, and a small trinket box containing a collection of Christmas cracker jokes, unused party hats, two plastic whistles and a key-ring. There was also a small Bible, its pages thickened with use.

He had got away from the house just in time to nip home, clean himself up, then drive to the hospital. He went every day, hoping for some sign of improvement in his mother. He always came home disappointed. Her condition had remained the same since she had been admitted: unmoving, lost in a world where he couldn't reach her. He talked to her all the time, though, needing to believe that while she couldn't make any movement, not even a flicker of her eyelids, she could still hear him. He couldn't bear the thought that she might be lonely, that she might feel he had abandoned her. So he kept her abreast of everything that was going on around her. He told her about the attractive nurse who had just got engaged and was planning to marry on a far-away Caribbean island, and with his voice deliberately low, he gossiped about her fellow patients – the uppity woman opposite who was always complaining about the food, the woman who was addicted to crossword puzzles, and the woman in a risqué nightdress whose husband was smuggling in a regular supply of illicit hooch for her. He didn't tell her about the woman in the nearest bed, who had died and whose place had been taken by someone new. She had appeared on the ward yesterday, an elderly woman with badly fitting dentures who wouldn't stop interrupting Archie as he talked to Bessie. Maybe she was lonely and didn't have anyone to visit her, but she had tested his patience. 'What did you say your name was?' she had asked him, for the hundredth time.

'Archie,' he replied, for the hundredth time.

'I knew an Archie once. He was a terrible man. Kissed me outside the butcher's for all the world to see.' She laughed loudly, her loose teeth sliding around in her mouth. 'What did you say your name was?'

'Archie.'

'I knew an Archie once. He was a terrible man. He—'

Feeling trapped, and hating himself for his rudeness, he had drawn the curtain around his mother's bed. Looking down at her still body, it was as if her features had been stolen from her face. All the warmth and light had gone from it. The true essence of Bessie Merryman was no longer there.

He ached for her to open her eyes and say something. Anything would do. 'Archie, be a love and fetch me a cup of tea, will you?' Or: 'Archie, where am I? What am I doing here with all these poor old dears?'

Oh, to have one last conversation with her, to say all the things that needed saying. What he'd give to hear just one of her nonsensical words from her creative lexicon.

Forking up the remains of his chicken and mushroom pie, he realised that he'd never hear another word from Bessie, that he was days away, maybe hours, from the end.

When the telephone rang again, Caspar could have knocked whoever it was to the ground. He was sick of the phone ringing constantly. Word had soon gone round that he was on his uppers and the vultures had gathered. Friends, they called themselves, well-wishing friends who were concerned about the rumours they had heard.

To hell with that! They just wanted to gloat.

He poured himself another glass of wine from the second bottle he'd opened that evening, staggered to his feet, and grabbed the cordless phone. 'Whoever you are, why don't you take a one-way trip to hell.'

'Mr Liberty?'

'Sorry, did I make that too complicated for you to understand?'

'Mr Liberty, this is Roland Hall. You might recall that we have spoken before.'

'Too right I remember. You're the patronising wimp who wouldn't let me speak to my sister. What do you want? Are you hoping I might be as stupid as Damson and want to join you?'

'No. I'm calling to say that I think you should come and visit her.'

Though Caspar was very drunk, enough of his brain was functioning for him to hear something in the man's voice to make the hairs on the back of his neck stand on end. 'Why? What's going on? And why isn't Damson saying this to me?'

A pause.

'Damson doesn't know I'm making this call.'

'Is that how you operate, then, sneaking behind your punters' backs, tittle-tattling to friends and relatives?'

'Mr Liberty, our alternative way of life here at Rose-wood Manor may not—'

'Look, buddy, I'm all out of rapture and patience, so cut the drivelling waffle about your Arcadian existence and get to the point.'

There was another pause. 'Your sister is ill and I think you should come to see her.'

After drinking copious amounts of head-clearing espresso coffee, Caspar lay in bed cursing the day Damson had ever been introduced to Rosewood Manor Healing Centre. Oh, he knew what had happened up there, all right. They'd fed her some wishy-washy diet of ginseng and cabbage, had made her ill and were now frightened at what they'd done to her.

He punched his fist into the pillow, regretting the amount of wine he had drunk. If he hadn't knocked so much of it back he would have been able to drive straight up there and fetch Damson home. As it was, he had to wait until he was free of the risk of getting done for drink-driving. He already had six points on his licence, and on top of everything else, a year-long ban would be the final straw.

As soon as it was light, Caspar was ready for the journey north. He'd managed a couple of hours' sleep, and with yet another fix of strong black coffee inside him, he gripped the steering-wheel with steely determination. He had it all worked out. He would arrive at Rosewood Manor, give that Roland Hall a piece of his mind, put Damson in the car and get the hell out of it.

Then he would drive south, stopping somewhere for the night. Harrogate perhaps, somewhere half decent. He had enough cash on him to stump up for a twin-bedded room for him and Damson, but he would have to be careful: credit cards were a no-go area now. He had a bit stashed away that not even his accountant knew about, but that was real rainy-day stuff. And, of course, there was always Damson. Once she knew of the bother he was in, she would tide him over until he got himself sorted and was on his feet again.

Unless, of course, those manipulative, brainwashing weirdos had bled her dry.

This thought had him pressing down on the accelerator and, flashing his lights at the car in front of him, he sped on towards Northumberland.

Clara opened her eyes, wanting to believe that she would feel better today.

But she wasn't. She was worse. Her skin was so flushed and sensitive it felt raw all over, as if someone had taken a cheese-grater to her in the night. Her joints seemed to have tightened while she slept and ached horribly. Her throat was so sore she would have sworn on a stack of Bibles that she had gargled with broken glass. Her chest ached from prolonged bouts of coughing and her head throbbed. Added to this, her stomach was cramping painfully.

She eased herself into a sitting position and reached for the box of tissues, then took a sip from the glass of water someone had thoughtfully left for her and forced down a couple of painkillers.

From downstairs, she could hear voices: one high, one low. She glanced at her watch on the bedside table and saw that it was half past nine. This was no good, she had to get herself moving – she had to get back into the land of the living. She pushed away the duvet and swung her legs out of bed, her mind set on having an invigorating shower – on the other hand, given that the plumbing at Mermaid House was not for the faint-hearted, a bath might be a better option.

But when she reached the bathroom, it was as much as she could do to brush her teeth and use the loo. Then she shuffled back to bed and pulled the duvet over her. A knock at the door interrupted a coughing fit. 'Come in, if you dare,' she rasped.

'How's the patient?' asked Gabriel.

'Are you feeling better, Mummy?'

The look of hope on their faces was enough to make her cry. 'Sorry,' she said, 'but I think I'm worse.'

'I'll send for Dr Singh,' said Gabriel, so resolutely that she knew it would be useless to try to overrule him. 'It's about time Sonny Jim did something worthwhile round here.'

The doctor called later that afternoon. But it wasn't the much maligned Dr Singh, it was a locum, a diminutive young man with the beginnings of a moustache on his top lip and a pair of nervous blue eyes. He checked her over, diagnosed flu, wrote out a prescription, and advised her to drink plenty of fluids.

'As if we hadn't thought of that,' Gabriel growled, when he'd shown the doctor out and Clara told him what he had said.

'Sorry to be such a nuisance,' she said. 'Sorry, too, that I'm not making a speedy recovery.'

He sat on the end of the bed with Ned. 'Can't be helped. Just glad that you're here with me and not stuck on a campsite in the middle of nowhere. Do you feel like eating anything yet? All you've had since yesterday is a bowl of tomato soup.'

She shook her head, then wished she hadn't. She closed her eyes, waited for her brain to stop spinning inside her skull, and at once felt herself drifting on a tide of sleep. In the distance she heard Gabriel say, 'Make haste, young Ned, we need to get your mother's prescription made up before the shops close for the day.'

Rallying herself, she said, or thought she said, 'Make sure you strap yourself in, Ned.'

The room went quiet and sleep claimed her fully. She sank into a dream that held her in an endless loop of knocking nails into the hull of a boat to stop the sea flooding in. Again and again she frantically banged the hammer against the nails.

Bang. Bang. Bang.

Tap. Tap. Tap.

She roused herself out of the dream, only to slip straight into another. She was dreaming of Jonah. He was dressed in a pair of jeans with a loose-fitting pale blue shirt, his sleeves were rolled up to the elbows, and he was carrying a large vase of flowers. 'Put them in the cupboard with the rest,' she told him, 'but don't try eating them. They'll make you shrink.' He raised an eyebrow, tilted his head to one side, and gazed at her quizzically. She giggled, thinking how gorgeously fresh-faced and kissable he looked. 'Well, Master Liberty, I'll wager you've broken a few hearts in your time, you being such a romantic cutie.'

That was the nice thing about dreams, you could think and say what you liked with delicious impunity. He came closer, still tilting his head, and still, it had to be said, looking adorable.

A slow smile appeared on his face. 'You're not mixing your medication, are you?' he asked.

She grinned back at him, but then began to feel that something was wrong with the dream. It was too real. Too three-dimensional. She focused on the vase of flowers and realised she could smell them – could even identify the particular scent of carnations. Was that possible? Did things really smell in dreams? She decided not, and raising herself into a sitting position, she dragged her sluggish brain into a more alert state and registered that he was assessing her a little too intently for her liking, as if trying to decide if she was a candidate for Care in the Community. 'Did I just say something silly?' she asked.

'Very silly. But it's my fault, I shouldn't have disturbed you.'

She cringed. 'Sorry about that. I keep having these awful dreams that don't make any sense. I thought I was still dreaming when you came in.'

'Ah, well, that would explain the *romantic cutie* bit,' he said playfully. 'These are for you, by the way. Where would you like them? And no worries about me eating them, I'm not hungry.'

She groaned. 'Oh, go right ahead, why don't you? Make fun of a girl when she's too weak to defend herself. If you put them on the window-ledge, the breeze will waft the scent in my direction. And before you think I've lost my manners completely, thank you, they're beautiful.' She watched him put the vase on the ledge, noting that he did everything with carefully considered movements, just as he had yesterday when he had set out the items from the chemist on the dressing-table: there was nothing slap-dash about him. With his back to her as he looked out of the window, she said, 'School finished for the day?'

He turned, the sunlight shining from behind him and

375

making his hair glow with a coppery warmth. 'Yes. And for the next week. It's half-term now.'

'Goodness, you're always on holiday when we meet.'

'Not quite.' He came back towards the bed. 'Are you up for a chat?'

'Sure.'

He settled in the chair next to her, stretched out his legs in front of him, and smoothed the wrinkles in his jeans with long, straight fingers. 'Where are Dad and Ned?' he asked.

'The last I heard they were going into Deaconsbridge to get my prescription made up.' She checked her watch. 'That was more than two hours ago.'

'You've seen a doctor?'

'Yes. Your father insisted on calling one out. A boy not much older than Ned diagnosed I had flu.'

He smiled. 'He's very fond of you, isn't he?'

'Who? The pubescent doctor or my son?'

'My father.'

'This may surprise you, but I'm quite fond of the old devil myself.' She coughed, then coughed again, and once she'd started, she couldn't stop. She held a tissue to her mouth while her chest crackled and her ribs ached, and as she struggled to catch her breath, he stood up and rubbed her back. Within seconds the spluttering convulsion passed and she flopped exhausted against the pillows. 'Sorry about that,' she wheezed.

'Can I get you anything?'

'A new body would be nice, I'm tired of this one, but I'll make do with some cough mixture and a cup of tea, if it's not too much trouble.'

'Your wish is my command. You see to the cough mixture and I'll organise the tea.'

He soon returned with a tray on which he'd placed two mugs of tea, a segmented orange, and a plate of chocolate biscuits. 'Vitamin C and something to give you energy. If the crumbs are too painful to swallow, you can make do with licking off the chocolate.'

He made himself comfortable in the chair again, and after he had persuaded her to take a biscuit, he said, 'I thought you might like to know that I took your advice last night.'

She dunked the biscuit in her tea. 'I'm having trouble remembering my name, never mind what I said last night. What did you do?'

'I got Dad to talk to me.'

She looked at him blankly. 'Did *I* tell you to do that?'

'Yes. You told me to seize the moment.'

She thought about this. There was a vaguely familiar ring to the words, but she couldn't be sure they had been hers. 'I think I may have been delirious when I said that. Was it good advice?'

He nodded. 'Excellent advice. I have a lot to thank you for.'

It seemed an age since she and Ned had found Gabriel on his knees in the copse, and Clara wondered just how honest he had been with Jonah. 'He's had a lot to come to terms with recently, hasn't he?' she said, prompting Jonah into expanding on what he had just said.

He ran a hand through his thick wavy hair – an elegant movement that momentarily caught and held her attention. 'That's putting it mildly. I just wish he could have opened up years ago.' He raised his eyes to hers. 'Dad told me about you finding him in the copse.' For a long moment his words, and what they implied, hung between them. 'I feel I've let him down,' he continued, 'that he reached such an awful point and—'

'Don't, Jonah. There's been enough self-recrimination going on in this family already. You tried your best with someone who wasn't ready to be helped. Just be glad that the two of you are reconciled. And remember, it wasn't your fault that he kept his feelings under house arrest all that time.'

He smiled that soft hesitant smile of his and passed her another biscuit. 'Yes, ma'am.'

She waved the plate away.

'Feeling tired again?'

'Yes.'

'Anything I can get you before you slip away on another of your hallucinogenic trips?'

She thought about this. 'Actually, yes, there is. I need some clean things to wear. Take Ned with you to the van when he gets back with your father, and he'll show you where everything's kept. The keys are in my handbag.'

'Is that all?'

'Mm . . . something to read would be good. Though not the copy of *Wuthering Heights* in the rack above the table. My brain will crash completely if I attempt that. Pick me something else. Something light and comforting.'

'Something romantic?'

She closed her eyes, all her energy now spent. 'No. A nice gory murder would suit me better.'

Chapter Forty-Seven

Caspar's day wasn't going as smoothly as he had wanted it to. A snarl-up on the motorway had added an extra hour and a half to his journey, and now it was taking him for ever to find Rosewood Manor. He'd gone round in circles, doubling back on himself again and again along roads that cleaved through windswept moors and all looked the same. It was a wild inhospitable place of craggy bleakness with few houses, and in places it reminded him of Hollow Edge Moor. He had left Manchester in the sun earlier that morning, but up here, in this godforsaken land where the rain was pouring and the wind gusting, it wasn't difficult to picture the tribes of marauding savages from the north that the Romans had been so keen to keep out by building Hadrian's Wall.

Whatever had possessed Damson to settle here?

Eventually he stopped to risk lunch at a pub, where the copper-topped tables were sticky with beer and scarred with cigarette burns; the padded stools were so filthy he thought twice about sitting down. His order was taken by a charmless old hag who was more interested in watching the wide-screen television hanging from the wall at the far end of the overheated room than serving anyone. There were few other punters: a wizened man with his nose dipping into his pint, and a group of youths lolling around a pool table.

He planned to stay just long enough to satisfy his growling stomach and to ask the whereabouts of Rosewood Manor Healing Centre.

Nobody had heard of it, but he was informed that Blydale Village wasn't a village as such. 'Nothing more than a sprawling place that's got above itself,' the hag said, with a disapproving sniff, when he handed over a ten-pound note for a plate of artificially pink microwaved gammon steak and a glass of unspeakably rough brandy.

Just because the Romans had departed aeons ago, it didn't mean the natives had gone soft on tribalism, Caspar observed, as he slipped back into the refined comfort of his Maserati. He knew the sensible thing to do was phone Rosewood Manor and ask for directions, but he'd be damned before he was reduced to doing that. Getting that nerdy wimp Roland Hall on the phone and asking him for help was out of the question.

He drove on determinedly, back towards Blydale. Ten minutes later, luck shone on him when he saw the remains of a wooden sign he hadn't noticed before, although he had driven up and down this stretch of road several times. He stopped the car, got out and, with the rain pelting down on him, poked around in the long, sodden grass with his foot. Flipping the rotten piece of wood over, he saw the words 'Rosewood Manor Healing Centre' carved in a pretentiously curlicued script. Hallelujah! Now, at long last, he was getting somewhere.

Back in the car, he took the next left, as the sign had originally indicated. The road dipped and narrowed, twisted and climbed and all but disappeared up its own access before it brought him to the brow of a hill and a T-junction. There were no helpful signs, but in the distance, submerged in the misty gloom of a verdant coniferous plantation, he saw a large house.

He drove on hopefully. At the approach to the house, a metal gate barred his way. Attached to it was a sign that read, 'Private Property' and 'Keep Out' in red. A brick-built postbox stood to the left of the gate, but there was nothing, other than a strong feeling in his guts, to suggest that this was where he would find Damson. He made a lightning dash to the gate, swung it open, then dived back into the car. Driving on, he left the gate swinging in the wind.

The house was as he had visualised it: Victorian and unrelentingly grim. It had probably been used as a school, or even a remand home, at some time: it had that institutionalised look about it. Ugly and over-extended, it was a solid mass of brickwork with staring windows. With a shudder of revulsion, Caspar thought of the elegant flat in Bath Damson had given up in favour of this remote, heartless monstrosity. What had she been thinking of when she came here this time last year?

He parked the car as near to the front door as he could, bolted across the gravel towards the shelter offered by the porch, and yanked on the metal bell pull. Getting no response, he thumped on the door loudly and waited. Was it his imagination, or could he detect the whiff of institutional cabbage?

Predictably it was some time before someone eventually deigned to open the door. A scrawny barefooted individual with a shiny bald head stood before Caspar, placed his palms together, and bowed from the middle. 'Welcome to Rosewood Manor Healing Centre. My name is Jed, how may I help you?' His gormless face was insufferably beatific and made Caspar want to ram a fist into it.

'Oh, save it for someone who cares. I've had the devil of a day so don't waste any more of my time. I'm Damson's brother, so take me to your leader and then do me the kindness of scarpering.'

Not a flicker passed across the man's face. He bowed again, stepped aside to let Caspar in, then shut the door silently. Suddenly Caspar felt uneasy, as though he had entered a strange, eerie world and the only escape route had been closed off.

He was shown into a large room that had probably been built as an impressive drawing room for some Victorian industrialist. A hundred years on, it was cold and reminded Caspar of Mermaid House, except it was shabbier and a lot less inviting. A circle of assorted chairs dominated the oblong space; the floor was bare, and the walls had been painted an insipid shade of mint-green with the intricately carved cornice and ceiling rose picked out in a darker green. And where, presumably, pictures and mirrors had once adorned the walls, there were now rows of pin-boards. While he waited, he read some of the notices. The first was full of silly mantras:

Make the renewal of your soul your priority.
A hardened heart is an impoverished heart.
Know thyself and be at peace.
Self-esteem comes from confronting your insecurities.

It was nothing but the crazy psychobabble that every New Age hippie traded in these days, he thought. The next board revealed a series of rotas. There seemed to be one for almost every mundane domestic activity: cooking, cleaning, laundry, shopping, even scrubbing out the toilets. He noted that Damson's name was absent from any of the lists. A separate piece of paper showed another range of activities, from cheese-making and bee-keeping to the construction of wooden toys and hammocks.

'Mr Liberty?'

He turned. 'Yes.'

Caspar recognised good-quality clothes when he saw them, and striding across the room, his hand outstretched, was a man of about his own age and height who clearly took pride in his appearance. He was wearing cream chinos and a Ralph Lauren striped shirt with a navy-blue cashmere sweater draped around his shoulders; a gold watch hung loosely from one of his wrists. With mounting satisfaction, Caspar knew that he was face to face with the devious brain behind this whole scam. 'And you are?'

'Roland Hall. It's good to meet you at last.'

Hiding his surprise, Caspar ignored the outstretched hand and gritted his teeth. It was time to get down to business. 'Damson. Where is she?'

'Yes, of course, I quite understand your eagerness to see her. But perhaps a drink first? How was your journey? The weather must have slowed you considerably.'

The fraudulent act of smooth charm and slickly offered hospitality incensed Caspar. 'My sister's welfare is the only reason I'm here, so let's dispense with the small-talk.'

The man's expression remained impassive. 'As you wish. But I feel it only right that I should warn you that your sister—'

Caspar held up a hand, jabbed a finger at the man's face. 'I'm not interested in what you have to say about Damson. Whatever comes out of your mouth is guaranteed to be one hundred per cent garbage. The half-baked drop-outs you're used to dealing with might be taken in by your cool, calm and collected manner, but I'm not. I know a man on the make when I see one.'

He was almost disappointed that Hall's response was restricted to a noncommittal nod. 'I'll take you upstairs,' was all he said. There was something annoyingly self-possessed about the man. He led the way out to the entrance hall where, at the foot of the stairs, a small group had gathered. There looked to be equal numbers of men and women, and they all turned and smiled when they saw Hall advancing towards them. Caspar detected the look of naked lust in some of the women's faces as they watched their leader climb the stairs. So it wasn't just greed for money that had brought him here: it was the pumping up of his gigantic ego too.

They came to a room at the furthest end of a long, thin corridor and a door that had had many layers of paint added to it over the years; it was chipped in places, particularly around the handle. Hall knocked softly. 'Damson, it's me, Roland. I've brought someone to see you.'

So the weasel hadn't even bothered to tell her he was coming!

As they entered the room, it was impossible to know who was more shocked: Damson at the sight of Caspar, or Caspar because he couldn't believe the devastating change in his sister.

Shock rendered him immobile. He stood staring at the

woman sitting in the bay window. For a moment, he almost convinced himself that this was some cheap trick on Hall's part. Where's my sister? he wanted to shout. What have you done with her? Who is this bone-thin woman with hollow cheeks and gruesomely short hair?

But the words that came out were, 'My God, Damson, what have these charlatans done to you?' Then he was across the room, kneeling on the floor in front of her, clasping her cold hands in his.

Caspar wasn't aware of Hall leaving them, but when he raised his eyes to Damson's pale face, he saw that the door was shut and they were alone.

'Oh, darling Caspar, why have you come? I didn't want you to see me like this.' She brushed the hair back from his forehead, and kissed him tenderly.

Still holding her hands, which had no strength in them, he moved to sit in the chair beside her. 'I don't understand what's going on, Damson. I got a call saying you were ill, that I ought to come and see you. Not for one second did I think it was anything serious. That smug crook, Hall, should have said something. Why didn't you ring me yourself?'

She sighed. 'It's complicated.'

'Please don't fob me off. Give me the truth. Do that much for me, tell me what's wrong. I mean, for God's sake, you're . . . you're in a wheelchair. Have you been in an accident?'

She shook her head. 'No accident, Caspar. Truth is, I'm dying.'

The shock of her words winded him and he gasped. She reached out and placed a hand on his forearm. 'Too much honesty hurts, doesn't it, darling?'

'But – but you can't be! Not you. Anyone but *you*!' His head spun and a rushing sound filled his ears.

'Oh, Caspar, didn't you know? It happens to the best of us. And who knows, this might be something I get right.'

He simply couldn't accept what he was hearing. She

was being much too cavalier and flippant. He stood up, towered over her frail body, spread his arms in an accusing gesture. 'It's this place. They've done something to you. If I get you away, you'll be well again. You're probably not eating properly. You could be anorexic.'

'Please sit down, and please calm down, Caspar. This is just why I didn't want you to see me. Don't you think I would know if I was anorexic? No, my darling, I have ovarian cancer and I'm in the final stages. We're talking a tumour as big as a fist. Conservatively, I have weeks to live rather than months. Though, personally, I think it might be less.'

He collapsed on to the chair. 'No! This can't be happening. Damson, you have to listen to me, you have to fight this. I don't care what you've been brainwashed into believing.'

'No, it's you who has to listen. I've been ill for some time. In fact, that's why I came here. I met Roland in Bath at a party, a month after I was diagnosed with cancer. He told me about Rosewood Manor, which he had just started up, and the more he told me about it, the more I thought it would be the ideal place for me to live out my remaining days. I needed somewhere to rest. Somewhere I could resolve things. And before you say anything else about Roland, he didn't know I was ill when we met. I kept it from him . . . from everyone.' She paused to take a small shallow breath. 'You see, Caspar, I knew I wouldn't have the courage to cope with all that chemotherapy – the nausea, the tiredness. Nor did I want to be constantly in and out of hospital, treated like an experiment. So I decided to be a coward and let nature take its course. It's for the best.'

Clutching at straws, and with his voice cracking, Caspar said, 'So if you haven't tried conventional medicine, how – how do you know it won't work for you now?'

She smiled at him wanly. 'Roland made me see a doctor earlier this year when he realised that something was wrong, that I was in pain and had been hiding it from him. After agreeing to see the local man, I saw several specialists who all said the same, that the cancer was so advanced nothing could be done. In a way, I was glad. It meant that I was finally in control of something. You know how flighty and out of control I've always been.' She gave a little laugh, with a brittle, hollow ring.

To his horror, tears filled Caspar's eyes and he knew real despair. 'But Damson, you're not in control, the cancer is. It's – it's killing you and I can't bear it.'

Once again he was on his knees, and with his head in her lap, he began to cry.

Oh, God in heaven, he was losing the only person who had ever meant anything to him.

Damson was the only person he had truly loved.

Chapter Forty-Eight

Seldom did Gabriel consciously keep track of the days, but since Clara had been struck down with flu, he was unusually aware of them. It was now Saturday and this was her third day of being confined to quarters. Each morning when he looked in on her he willed her to feel better, but she seemed to be withering before his eyes. Seeing her so incapacitated made him realise that she wasn't invincible after all, and that having her here at Mermaid House, where he could look after her, he was repaying a little of her kindness.

He was glad, though, that he had Jonah to share the load, and in more ways than one. Since Thursday night, when he and Jonah had talked – really talked – he had come to know the truth of Clara's words: Jonah was indeed a gift from Anastasia, and his forgiveness had been instant.

To thank Clara for what she had instigated, Gabriel would go to any lengths. He had told her as much this morning when he and Ned had taken up her breakfast on a tray the lad had decorated with one of his drawings and some flowers picked from the garden. At Jonah's insistence both Gabriel and Ned were under orders to stay at the foot of her bed, as if her germs were too stupid to travel that far, and from there, Gabriel had thanked her for everything she had done and told her that if there was anything she needed, she had only to ask.

The sound of laughter broke into his thoughts and he turned to look out of the library window. Ned and Jonah were in the garden playing football; the little boy was chasing Jonah, who was heading for a pair of makeshift goalposts – two upturned flower-pots.

Suddenly they caught sight of him and waved. Gabriel waved back, then pointed at his watch, indicating that it was time for lunch.

And time was something he had wasted too much of since his retirement and Val's death – he had wantonly frittered it away. Well, not now. What he had left, he would make good use of. What had Clara said when she had agreed to sort out Mermaid House? Oh, yes: 'I'll give you one week of my precious time, Mr Liberty.' She was right, time was precious, and he had squandered so much on living in the past. He had allowed himself to feed off his grief and turn it into a destructive force that had nearly cost him everything.

But to make things completely right there was something else he had to do. He was reconciled with Jonah, and now he had to do the same with Caspar and Damson.

'When were you going to tell me, Damson?' The question had been on Caspar's lips since yesterday afternoon when his sister had told him she was dying, but until now, he hadn't had the nerve to ask it.

They were lying together on her bed, her head turned towards him, and the afternoon sunshine streaming through the windows. It was years since they had lain like this, although as children they had done it all the time, cutting themselves off from the rest of the world.

'I hadn't thought that far,' she said. 'Cowardice, I'm afraid.'

'You were never a coward.'

'We both were, Caspar.'

He raised himself so that he was leaning on his elbow and looking down into her face.

'Don't look at me like that, darling, not when you know I'm speaking the truth. Help me to sit up, and let me tell you what I've learned while I've been here.'

Caspar slid off the bed and went round to his sister's

side. He lifted her frail body gently so that her shoulders were against the pillows. He had to force himself not to wince when he touched her because there was nothing to her. The cancer had hollowed out her body until she was just the shell of the beautiful woman she had once been.

Last night, he had listened in horror to her acceptance that her life would soon be over. She had told him that she had everything arranged. When the time came, and she felt it was no longer fair to inflict herself on Rosewood Manor, she planned to go into a hospice: she wanted the minimum of fuss. 'Just this once, Caspar, I shall behave myself. I intend to go gently into the night.' He had wanted to go on talking, but she hadn't had the strength and had fallen asleep. He had tucked a blanket around her, then sat in the growing shadows as night fell, just staring at the face that had captivated so many men in her wildly extravagant life. Always unpredictable, always exhilarating, she had lived each day as it came, as though – as though it would be her last.

When darkness had fallen, he had gone in search of Roland Hall. It was supper time and the rest of the inmates had their noses in the trough in the dining room, their voices bright as they chatted. He had experienced a surge of rage as they stuffed their faces while his sister endured untold pain.

'How is she?' Hall had asked, when Caspar finally tracked him down.

The man's mild tone had infuriated him and he'd turned on him savagely. 'Oh, she's fine! Bloody marvellous for a woman who's dying! Why the hell didn't you tell me?'

'You must believe me when I say it wasn't what I wanted, but she made me promise not to. I had to respect her wishes.'

'So why disrespect her wishes last night and phone me to say I should come?'

'I thought it was time.'

He'd grabbed Hall by the shoulders. 'And who do you think you are making all these decisions? God Almighty?'

Still Hall didn't react. His calmness made Caspar let go of him. He stepped back. 'I'll sue you. I'll sue the shite out of you. You've wilfully let my sister go beyond help. You've as good as murdered her.'

'I can assure you, I've done no such thing. I only ever wanted the best for Damson. Perhaps when you're calmer, we'll talk more. For now, you must be hungry. I'll send something up on a tray for you both.'

Caspar had gone back upstairs to Damson. She was still sleeping. He switched on lamps and drew the curtains, wanting to block out the rest of the world. There was a knock at the door and a red-haired girl with a large tray stepped in. She placed it on the low table in front of Damson's wheelchair then left without a word. Caspar lifted the stainless-steel domes from the plates and saw that the food had been labelled: for Damson there was a bowl of vegetable soup, and for him, poached salmon with a baked potato and a green salad. Pulling out the stops to impress him, no doubt. He woke Damson, and after she had shaken off her drowsiness, and swallowed a handful of tablets, they ate their supper. He tried not to notice how little of the soup she spooned into her mouth. No wonder she was so thin.

'You must stay the night,' she said, when she pushed her tray away. 'I'll get Roland to organise a bed for you. There's a room next door that's free.'

'Can't I sleep in here with you? I could manage in a chair.'

'No, I'd disturb you. I sleep lightly at night and often read to pass the time.'

'I could read to you – like old times.' He nearly choked on his words.

She shook her head. 'Not tonight. You need to rest.'

He was too dazed to argue with her. Under no other circumstances could he have imagined spending a night at Rosewood Manor, but the world had found a new axis on which to spin and everything was sliding out of his grasp. Nothing felt real any more.

Now, sitting on the bed with Damson nearly twenty-four hours later, the situation didn't feel any more real to Caspar. But knowing he had no choice, he was beginning to resign himself to it. He had to accept that, before long, his sister would be dead. He listened now to what she had to say.

'I know you think Rosewood Manor is a ghastly place full of the lost and insecure,' she began, 'and you'd be right. People come here suffering from all sorts of problems: executive burn-out, failed marriages, abuse – oh, yes, I've heard heartbreaking life-stories that would bring even you to your knees, Caspar. What Roland has created here is an oasis of—' She held up a hand. 'No, please, don't interrupt, I don't have the energy. I wish you could see Roland for what he is. He's the most honourable and decent man I've ever met. He's helped me so much. There's nothing bogus about him, Caspar. Truly, there isn't. But I've wandered from what I wanted to talk to you about.' Her voice trailed away and she seemed caught up in her own thoughts, a long way from him. Slowly she drifted back. She said, 'We need to discuss your future, Caspar.'

'It's hardly important to me now, Damson.'

She seemed not to hear him. 'Did you know that when there's not much future left, the past magnifies itself and becomes much clearer?' She didn't wait for an answer, but continued. 'We need to talk about Mermaid House, about Dad and Jonah. I want you to promise me something. It won't be easy, but take it as a woman's dying wish.'

He swallowed hard. Didn't she realise how distressing it was for him to hear her speak like this? But then, as if sensing his pain, she touched his cheek. 'No hiding or running, Caspar. We're beyond that now. Remember when we used to say, "It's the two of us against the world"?'

He nodded jerkily, remembering the first time she had

ever uttered those words. It had been the night their mother died. He had crept into Damson's room and stood at the side of her bed. 'I can't sleep,' he had whispered. Without a word she had pulled back the bedclothes and let him in. She had cradled him in her arms, already assuming the role of protector to him. 'It's just you and me now, Caspar,' she had said, 'you and me against the world.' They had fallen asleep, and the following morning, with their lives changed irrevocably, and unable to penetrate the wall that had sprung up around their father, they knew they could rely on no one but themselves.

'Caspar, are you listening to me?'

'I'm sorry, what did you say?'

'I was saying we got it wrong. We should never have isolated ourselves as we did, or been so cruel to Jonah and Val. We treated her despicably.'

Caspar felt his body tauten. He didn't want to think about Jonah or Val, the woman who had dared to try to replace their mother.

A knock made them look up. The door opened and Hall poked his head round it. 'Damson, the nurse is here to see you. Okay if I show her up?'

'Of course, Roland. Caspar, would you mind leaving me now, please? These nurses can be very thorough and I don't want you to see more of me than is necessary. Why don't you go for a walk? It's such a lovely day.'

But Caspar didn't go for a walk. He shut himself in the room he had been given last night and wondered how Damson could be aware of what the weather was like. Since his arrival he had been oblivious to what was going on outside Rosewood Manor. Every thought revolved around the appalling knowledge that he would soon be without his beloved Damson.

Now he regretted every bad word he had ever spoken about the way she had recently chosen to live her life. He should have tried harder to understand what she was doing instead of condemning it. He had considered her weak and deluded, and he had never stopped to ask why she was doing this.

It hurt that she hadn't turned to him when she knew she was ill. But it hurt more to know that, although they were together now, it was too late. With painful clarity he realised that most of the derisive comments he had made about Rosewood Manor had been based on jealousy. It had been impossible to accept that his precious Damson had chosen to be with a bunch of misfits rather than with him.

He lay on the bed and stared up at the ceiling rose, tracing the circular pattern of leaves with his eyes. He remembered doing the same as a young child in the summer months when his bedroom was still light and he couldn't sleep. He could recall one particular occasion, before their mother died: Anastasia had come in to kiss him goodnight before going out to a party. Dressed in an elegant evening dress that showed her shoulders – the fabric was silky soft and whispered as she moved – she had kissed his cheek and let him twist her lovely long hair around his fingers. Then Dad had come in and kissed him too. How happy he had felt, lying between them, so loved, so safe.

And as Caspar drifted off to sleep now, he was back in his old bed in Mermaid House. He was covered with a blanket of love . . . It reminded him that Damson hadn't been the only person he had truly loved.

Before everything had gone wrong, he had loved his parents.

Jonah took Clara's supper in to her. She was sitting up in bed reading, which he took to be a positive sign.

'On a scale of one to ten, how are you feeling?' he asked. From where he was standing, she looked a little better, less flushed and feverish.

She lowered the book. 'Around four,' she said, 'bordering on five.'

'That's good. I hope you're well enough to eat this.' He

placed the tray on her lap. 'Scrambled eggs with smoked salmon and a glass of freshly squeezed orange juice. I trust everything's to Madam's liking.' He shook out a white linen napkin with a flourish and offered it to her.

She smiled. 'I could get used to this.'

He passed her a knife and fork. 'Eat it while it's hot.'

'Yes, Teacher.'

'That's "Sir" to you. Are you in the mood for some company, or would you rather eat alone?'

'Company would be fine. The house is quiet, where is everyone?'

He positioned a chair in front of the open window and sat down. 'Dad's taken Ned to the stream. They've gone fishing, with the most high-tech equipment they could find: a plastic sieve and a jam-jar. How's the book going? Decided who the murderer is yet?'

She finished what was in her mouth. 'Two chapters to go and I think I have it in the bag.'

He smiled. 'When you've proved yourself right, do you want me to fetch another book for you?'

'Please, if it's not too much trouble. Also, if you could bring me my mobile, I'd be grateful. Though to be honest, I think it's high time I pulled myself together. I feel guilty about you and your father having to amuse Ned.'

'Well, don't. Dad and I are quite happy to look after him. He's a great kid. I'm used to hulking great teenagers, so a four-year-old is a novelty.'

'I'm not sure I like my son being described as a novelty, but I'll let you off if you tell me about the school where you work. Your father says it's full of hooligans.'

He started warily, but when he saw she was genuinely interested, he talked at length about the pupils at Dick High, his frustration with some of the other teachers, and his hopes for the school. He even told her about Jase. 'I just hope the wind was blowing in the right direction for him when he sat the first history paper this week. He's never been given any encouragement before, and I want to prove a point to him, and everyone else.'

394

She smiled. 'You're a real heart-on-your-sleeve crusader, aren't you?'

Thinking of the conversation he'd had recently with Barbara Lander from school, he recrossed his legs and frowned. 'I don't see it like that. And please don't make me out to be a naïve idealist. I'm not. I'm a determined, hard-working optimist.'

She drank her orange juice and looked at him thoughtfully. 'And would I be right in thinking this isn't the type of school you, Caspar and Damson went to?'

'More or less, but there are comparisons between Dick High and the first boarding-school I attended. The number of demoralised teachers and the degree of bullying were certainly the same. I hated the place and spent most of my time planning my escape.'

'But your brother loved it?'

Surprised at her insight, he laughed. 'It made Caspar the man he is today. So what about you, then? Tell me about the job you gave up to become a happy wanderer.'

It was the first conversation they had shared without his father as the focus, and because Jonah was curious to know more about Clara, he listened attentively to her husky voice, trying to read between the lines of what she was saying. When she had finished, he said, with a touch of irony, 'And you don't miss all that? The money, the power, and the kudos of being a corporate high-flyer?'

'I'd hardly describe myself as a high-flyer, but there are bits I miss, mostly the camaraderie with some of the people I was close to. David and Guy were great colleagues, friends too.'

'It must have been hard to juggle a demanding career with bringing a child up on your own,'

Clara laid her knife and fork together neatly on the plate. She wondered why Jonah was suddenly giving her the third degree. But then she realised she was overreacting: always on her guard to protect the identity of Ned's father, she was too sensitive to any question she thought might lead her to giving the game away. 'I've been extremely fortunate,' she said carefully. 'My parents have been wonderful and helped out selflessly with Ned.'

'And Ned's father, where – where does he fit in?'

She looked up sharply. 'Nowhere.'

'I'm sorry,' he said hurriedly. 'I had no right to ask that.' He got to his feet and took the tray from her. 'Ready for pudding now?'

'No, thank you,' she said stiffly. Then, 'I'm full. That was more than enough. It was delicious too. Thank you.'

'Sure I can't tempt you with a strawberry meringue bought fresh from the baker this morning?'

She hesitated. 'Well . . .'

'One meringue it is. Tea?'

'Need you ask?'

While he was downstairs in the kitchen, Clara relaxed and stared through the window at Kinder Scout. Suddenly she wanted to be out there in the hills, to feel the wind on her skin, to breathe in the peaty smell of the moors. She was tired of being in bed with nothing to do but read or sleep. Which was why Jonah had become such a comfort, she supposed. She was sorry that she had just been so curt with him when she liked him so much. She thought of his enthusiasm for his job and envied him. When had she last felt like that about her work?

He had reminded her of Todd's imminent visit to England, and it occurred to her that Jonah, who was a good listener, might be just the person with whom she could discuss the problem. He was so detached from her life back home that he would be a safe pair of ears. There was the added bonus that he could give her not just an objective opinion but a considered male view.

She waited for him to reappear. When he did, she said, 'Jonah, would you mind me using you as a sounding-board?'

'I've been used for far worse things, believe me.'

She sank her teeth into the meringue he'd just given her.

'Mm . . . heavenly,' she murmured. After another mouthful, she said, 'Now, what I'm about to tell you, you must promise never to discuss with anyone else.'

Leaning against the window-ledge, he raised an eyebrow. 'Sounds intriguing.'

'Do you promise?'

'Hand on heart.'

'You asked me earlier about Ned's father. I'm sorry I was a bit short with you, but back home, people know better than to press me on who he is. I've got rather used to shooting people down in flames if they get too close.'

'Does that make me incredibly brave, or very foolish?'

She smiled. 'Neither.' Then she plunged in, and told him about her relationship with Todd and its consequences, ending with, 'So, what I want to know is, how would you feel if you were in Todd's shoes, if a secret like that had been kept from you?'

Jonah rubbed a hand over his jaw. He had wanted to know more about Clara, but this was way beyond anything he had expected her to share with him. Putting his surprise to one side, he tried to imagine how he would feel if Emily, whom he had loved and wanted to marry, turned up now with a child and announced that it was his. Shock would come first. Then anger. Yes, he would definitely be angry that he had been kept in ignorance of something so important. But next would come acceptance, and delight that he was a father.

Looking steadily at Clara, he said, 'If I were in Todd's shoes I would want to know the truth. No matter how complicated it might make my life.' He pushed his hands into his trouser pockets. 'Does that help?'

She nodded. 'I think it's the conclusion I'd reached too, but I needed someone else to confirm it for me. Thanks.'

Later, when his father and Ned had arrived back from their fishing expedition, Jonah remembered Clara had asked him to fetch her mobile phone. He had the key already in his pocket, so he went out to the camper-van, thinking, as he turned the key in the lock, that when Clara was feeling better, he would invite her to have dinner with him. He had already suggested that he could take her and Ned on a walk to show them some of his favourite haunts, and she had accepted quite readily, but would the idea of dinner – just the two of them – go down so well?

He let himself into the van, and was just acknowledging how much he would enjoy an evening alone with Clara when he realised she hadn't given him any clue where her phone would be. He began hunting through the racks and overhead lockers. He found lots of maps and colouring books that belonged to Ned, and a copy of *Wuthering Heights*, but no phone. There was one last cupboard, the one above the cooker. He opened it and peered inside. Moving aside a first-aid kit and a lot of buff-coloured envelopes, he found the mobile and was about to let the door click shut when something caught his eye. He did a double-take, thinking he must be imagining things.

But he wasn't. He'd know those notebooks anywhere. He had seen Val with them hundreds of times, but had never let on to her that he knew she was keeping a journal. But since her death, and until this moment, he hadn't given the notebooks a thought. But what on earth were they doing here in Clara's camper-van?

He sank down on the bench seat behind him, untied the ribbon, and opened one of the books. He read the first page, the second, the third, and kept going, turning the pages and absorbing every painful word his step-mother had written. But with every instalment he took in, he was conscious that Clara had been there before him.

So that was how she knew about Emily!

Furious, he slapped the diaries together, tied them up, and wondered at her nerve.

Chapter Forty-Nine

By the time Clara was feeling better, May had slipped into June and summer had arrived. The weather was glorious, sunny and warm. The yellow gorse bushes scattered over the surrounding hills were ablaze with golden flowers and the sky held wisps of fresh white clouds. Everything seemed sharper, more intense. Although Clara's temperature was normal now, and the racking cough little more than an occasional annoyance, she was still under orders from Gabriel to take it easy.

To her amusement, Gabriel continued to fuss over her, insisting at every opportunity that she rest and build up her strength. He had also stressed there would be no talk of her and Ned moving on until he was convinced she was fully recovered. 'And be warned,' he'd barked at her, 'I'll confiscate your keys if I detect any insubordination in the ranks, young lady. So behave and do as you're told.'

Now she was in the library doing some of her tapestry. Sitting in the bay window, where the sun shone warmly through the glass, she could hear the trill of birdsong with the occasional bass note in the echoing call of a dove. Other than this, there was no other sound to be heard. Gabriel had taken Ned into Deaconsbridge to post some letters and to buy some cheese, and ham and a loaf of bread for lunch. She knew, though, because she'd caught Gabriel whispering to Ned, that they would be gone for a while – they were planning to slip in a don't-tell-your-mother visit to the Mermaid café for a clandestine sticky bun or two. Thick as thieves, the pair of them.

Whatever adventures she had envisaged for Ned during

this time away from home, acquiring a second grand-father had not featured. But that was exactly what had happened: Gabriel had won Ned's devotion. Ned had played his part too: he had befriended an old man nobody else had wanted. But that was children for you: they saw things the way they wanted to see them. And now that Gabriel, like her, was feeling so much better, she felt the time had come for her to give him Val's diaries: they contained the final truth he needed to confront and accept.

She knew that when the time came for them to leave, she and Ned would always stay in touch with him, for a connection had been made between them.

Once again, she recalled what had led her to Mermaid House, and it all came down to Mermy. Who would have thought that when her parents gave her that little bit of nonsense, it would lead her and Ned to Gabriel?

It made her wonder if there really might be such a thing as fate.

And if there was, what did it have in store for Ned in the foreseeable future? Was Todd about to make his appearance in his son's life? It seemed likely. From the moment she had received that e-mail from Guy in Edinburgh she had known that events were conspiring against her. Her conversation with Jonah had also flagged up what she had known already: that Todd had a right to know about Ned.

But this didn't take away the fear: she was terrified of losing control of a situation at which she had worked so hard to stay on top. Despite what people thought of her, she did have moments of self-doubt – not often, and not over trivia, but with something as important as this, she needed to know she was doing the right thing, and for the right reasons. Which was why she had confided in Jonah.

To her disappointment, there had been no sign of Jonah for some days now. The last time she had seen him was when she had told him about Ned's father. She missed his company, his thoughtfulness and quiet sense of humour.

It had been nice having somebody of her own age to talk to.

She put down her tapestry and looked out of the window. Who did she think she was kidding? Her enjoyment of Jonah's company went deeper than that. She had liked having an attractive man around – she hadn't experienced that in quite a while.

And Jonah was, to use a Louise-ism, borderline gorgeous. He was patient and attentive with a sensitivity that one rarely came across in a man. Beneath it, though, she sensed a strong will and spirit. How else could he have survived his childhood and hung on to his sanity? She thought of the entries she had read in Val's diaries, the fight he had got into at school, and she didn't doubt that, if sufficiently provoked, the mild-mannered Jonah Liberty would come out fighting.

So why had he disappeared? It was so unfair, just as she was feeling better and looking less like a bag-lady, he was nowhere to be seen.

She tidied away her tapestry and reached for *Wuthering Heights*. Perhaps it was reading of such passion and unrequited love that was making her long for Jonah's quiet, responsive company. With this in mind, she decided to test herself. It was a game she and Louise had played late at night, when they were more than a little mellow. You had to close your eyes, picture a man you knew and imagine kissing him. If the image made you cringe and squeal, you could safely assume that he had as much charm and sexual magnetism as a landfill site. But if . . .

Well, the 'if' was obvious.

She sat back in the armchair, closed her eyes, and conjured up the necessary scenario: a backdrop of rugged moorland against which she and Jonah were indulging in a slow, tentative kiss. However, before long it had developed into a wallopingly good, lip-smacking, heart-thumping, knee-buckling snog of monumental proportions.

She snapped her eyes open, faintly embarrassed by such an enjoyably erotic image.

Archie let the door of the estate agent's office close slowly behind him. He had agreed to sell his home, or more correctly, his and Stella's home. It was practically a done deal, with no reason why contracts couldn't be exchanged within two months.

It was all happening so fast.

The For Sale board had only gone up on Friday afternoon, but by Sunday three couples had viewed the house and the first – who were planning to get married in the autumn – had offered him the full asking price. They weren't in a chain and, as the estate agent had just said, they were a safe bet, as eager to buy as he was to sell. Except he wasn't eager to sell. It was his *home* and he was parting with it reluctantly.

He crossed the busy market square to go and view what might well become his new home, albeit a temporary one. It was a small, unfurnished flat above Joe Shelmerdine's antiquarian bookshop, which he let on a strictly short-term basis. 'Nothing worse than to be stuck with a bad tenant,' he had told Archie yesterday afternoon. Archie hadn't been able to view the flat then, because the carpets were being cleaned, but Joe had told him to come back today. 'It's not very big,' he warned Archie now, as he handed him the key, 'and the carpets haven't come up as clean as I'd hoped they would. It needs a lick of paint too.'

The entrance to the flat was via a gloomy alley at the side of the shop, and in the half-light, Archie stepped cautiously round a wheelie bin and an upturned rusting metal stool. He put the key in the lock and climbed the narrow stairs, determined to like what he found at the top.

A lick of paint was an optimistic understatement. The walls of the sitting room were covered in dirty marks, and there were holes where picture hooks had once been. Chunks of plaster had come away from one wall where there was clearly a damp problem, and the window that overlooked the square had two cracked panes.

However, he told himself, as he stood in the middle of the room, it wasn't a bad size, and there was a working fireplace, which would make it nice and cosy in the winter. But the thought of winter depressed him. He saw himself celebrating Christmas alone here.

The floorboards creaked as he moved through to the tiny kitchenette. It looked big enough to accommodate the cooker and fridge freezer he would bring with him. But there was no room for a table, or for all the crockery and glassware Stella had collected over the years and which they had hardly used. But that wasn't a problem: she would probably take it. If she didn't, he'd sell it.

The bedroom, like the kitchenette, overlooked what had been the backyard: Joe had turned it into an attractive courtyard. There were vines covering the white-painted brick walls, some raised beds with flowers growing in them, and a wooden bench and table. He imagined Joe sitting there during a lull in the day, enjoying a glass of wine.

There was an ominous smell in the bathroom, but the modern suite and shower over the bath appeared new and clean. He located the smell to the stained cork tiles around the toilet and wondered if Joe would object to him replacing them.

It would do, he decided, returning to the sitting room and visualising it with his own furniture, until he had made some real decisions about what he was going to do permanently. Really, when all was said and done, compared to others, he was a lucky man. What's more, Shirley had offered to lend a hand with curtains and the like, stuff he was useless with. She had even offered the decorating services of her son, Robbie. 'Not that I'm saying you can't manage yourself,' she'd said, 'but it's time, isn't it? There's never enough of it.' And when he had a bit more time on his hands, he ought to do something about thanking her for all her kindness.

He stood at the window and stared down at the crowded market square; a car horn tooted, a door slammed. Over the weekend, the council had put up hanging baskets, as they did at this time every year, and the bright splashes of colour gave an added gaiety to the shop fronts. Everywhere he looked the place was buzzing with people, cars and tourist buses. Now that it was June, and visitors were pouring in, the place had a jolly, prosperous air, but by next month it would feel the strain of so many visitors: the roads would be clogged and tempers would fray as people fought over too few parking spaces. He watched a dusty old Land Rover reverse into a space that looked perilously small, but the driver seemed to know what he was doing. Having accomplished the impossible, he got out and walked stiffly to the nearest pay-and-display machine. Archie recognised the tall, slightly stooping figure: it was the Commandant from Mermaid House. He continued to watch the man as he returned to his vehicle. He put the sticker on the dashboard, then went round to the passenger door to let someone out. It was young Ned, Clara Costello's boy.

After taking one last look around the flat, he locked the door and returned the key. 'I'll have it, Joe,' he said. 'Okay if I come back later to tie up the loose ends?'

'Any time you want. By the way, I forgot to mention the floor tiles in the bathroom. I'll see to those for you.'

Out on the street, Archie saw the Commandant with Ned again. They were crossing the road in the direction of the post office. Archie needed some stamps, so he decided to wander over and see if Ned remembered him. He caught up with them as the Commandant was lifting Ned so that he could slip some letters inside the postbox. When Ned saw him, he said, 'Look, Mr Liberty, it's Archie.'

'Archie who?'

Archie smiled to himself. Trust the Commandant not to remember him. 'Hello there, Ned, what are you doing back here?' With a tilt of his head, he added, 'Archie

Merryman, Mr Liberty, Miss Costello's disreputable rag-and-bone man.'

'Ah, yes, I remember you now. You came to the house a couple of times, didn't you?'

'That's right.'

'Mummy thinks we're only here to post some letters and buy some bread,' Ned said importantly, 'but we're going to have a cake and a milkshake in the café as well.' He leaned in close to say this last bit, as though it was a big secret.

'Well, aren't you the scallywag? And how is your mother?'

'She's been very ill with flu and Mr Liberty has been looking after her. Do you want to come and have a cake with us?'

Archie laughed. 'I'd love to, but I've got to get back to the shop. Will you give your mother my best wishes when you get home? Tell her I hope she's soon feeling better.'

Ned nodded, then said, 'Have you got any more jigsaws in your shop? Mummy gave me a pound to buy myself something. A jigsaw would be nice. I liked the last one you gave me.'

'As a matter of fact I have got some more. Why don't you come and have a look?'

'Can we, Mr Liberty?' He looked up eagerly at the Commandant, who had been silent throughout this exchange.

He said, 'I should think that could be arranged.'

Ned swivelled his head back to Archie. 'Do you have anything that Mummy might like? I wanted to buy her a present too.'

'I'll have to think about that. You go and see Shirley in the café, and I'll have a fossick and see what I can find for you. How does that sound?'

Archie walked back to Second Best wondering what Clara might like. She had far too much taste and class to want anything from his tatty old shop. But then he remembered the teapot Samson had nearly smashed yesterday morning when he was emptying a box from a house clearance. It was a novelty teapot, with a pair of stumpy legs, an arm for a handle and another for the spout. He could easily get more than a pound for it, but Ned's pennies were good enough for him. Quickening his pace, he hoped no one had bought it while he'd been out.

As he let himself into the shop and saw Samson with his feet up, reading the paper, his mood was lighter than it had been when he'd gone out. He had been miserable at having to go to the estate agent and accept the young couple's offer on his house. Now things didn't seem so bad: he'd found himself a decent flat that was cheap and conveniently handy. Okay, it wasn't anything special, but it would tide him over until he'd sorted himself out. If there was one thing he'd learned recently, it was that you never knew what was around the corner.

Half an hour later the irony of those words was brought home to him. The hospital phoned to say that his mother had just died.

Chapter Fifty

With the house still empty, and confident that she would be alone for some time yet, Clara decided to be brave.

Well, brave-ish.

Although she'd had her mobile phone with her since Saturday, and had intended to ring her friends while she was housebound, she had not got around to doing so, for the simple reason that she had lacked the courage to set in motion the sequence of events she knew would unfold once she spoke to Louise.

But now she was determined to grasp the nettle.

To seize the bull by the horns.

To seize—

Oh, get on with it! she reprimanded herself.

She tapped in Louise's work number, muttering that there was to be no more yellow-bellied prevaricating. It was time to see what Louise knew about the latest goings-on at Phoenix – specifically if the corporate wonder-boys were over from the States yet. It made more sense to speak to one of the boys, but she was in the mood for a good old girlie gossip with Louise. But Louise's voice-mail informed her that she was out of the office for the next two days. Clara mentally tossed a coin: Guy or David. Guy won. She tapped in his number and waited for him to pick up.

'Clarabelle!' he said, when he heard her voice. 'How's it going?'

She pictured him leaning back in his chair with his feet up on his desk. 'I'm fine. Well, not that fine, I'm recovering from a nuclear attack of flu.'

'Poor you – but that explains why your voice is husky

and sounds so dead sexy. So where are you now? Outer Mongolia?'

'We're back in the Peak District. It's a long story, but do you remember we stayed with an eccentric man in a place called Mermaid House?'

'Yes.'

'Well, we're with him again. He's been fantastic and taken care of Ned while I've been flat on my back with—'

'Clarabelle, please, you're shocking me. I've told you before, your private life is your own.'

'Guy Morrell, the only thing that would shock your delicate ears is if Moira told you she was pregnant.'

'Ooh, as sharp as ever. So how's Ned? Still as cute as a button? Missing us all, I hope.'

'Of course he is. He's grown. He's already gone through two pairs of shoes and is due for another haircut. My mother would claim it's all the fresh air he's getting.'

'She might be right. Hey, and before I forget, you were right about that Todd Mason Angel dude, the women on the packing line have been drooling over him ever since he arrived.'

Clara tightened her grip on the small mobile phone, pressed it harder to her ear. 'You always did say I was a good judge of character,' she said lightly.

'What's even more galling is that he's a nice bloke into the bargain.'

'You've met him?'

'Don't sound so surprised, of course we have. David and I took him out for a drink. We discovered he was a keen squash player and the next thing we knew we were being thrashed within an inch of our lives. But to get our own back, David invited him home for a typically English barbecue. The rain never stopped, and the poor bloke thought we were mad when we put the brollies up and carried on as though nothing was wrong.'

Clara couldn't believe what she was hearing. Her

friends were socialising with Ned's father! The meddling hand of fate was up to its tricks again.

'Oh, and I mustn't forget,' Guy carried on blithely, 'when he realised you were a close friend of ours, he sent his best wishes. I have to say, it strikes me that you were holding back on us, Clarabelle. We're all getting the impression that you knew him a lot better than you've been letting on.'

He laughed and Clara wondered if he was fishing. But then a more worrying thought occurred to her. 'Guy, is your door shut or are you broadcasting this conversation to the whole of Phoenix?'

'The door's shut, but the phone's on monitor and I'm in the middle of a meeting.' He must have heard her sharp intake of breath. 'Hey, I'm only joking. Clara, what is it? What's wrong?'

She kept her voice level. 'Nothing's wrong, silly. So what else have you been up to with your new-found chum?'

'Not a lot. In a way, we all feel sorry for him. He's obviously homesick. You know what these Yanks are like, no place like the old homestead. He got some photographs out of his wallet during the barbecue, showed us pictures of his wife and daughters, even phoned home while he was with us. A true blue-blooded family man, I guess. A rare breed.'

Clara couldn't take another word. 'Guy, are you sure your door's shut?'

'Yes. I told you it was. Why, what's up?'

She took a deep breath and threw herself into the abyss. 'The thing is, Todd is Ned's father.'

There was a stunned silence. Then, 'Gee whiz, girl, does he know? I mean, does Todd know about Ned?'

'No. I never let on that I was pregnant.'

Another silence. Until: 'But Clara, he's seen pictures of you and Ned!'

It was her turn to fall silent.

Filling the gap in the conversation, Guy said, 'It was

late and we'd all had a bit to drink. Well, *we* had, he hadn't, he's practically teetotal, but, oh, Clara, don't be cross, we were in the kitchen and he was looking at the collection of photos David and Louise have on the wall, you know that montage Louise made.'

Clara knew it well. Quite apart from a range of silly pictures of her and the gang, there was a large picture of her with Ned slap-bang in the middle of it – she had an arm around him while he puffed his cheeks with air ready to blow out the four candles on his birthday cake. 'Go on, Guy, tell me the worst. He asked who the boy was, didn't he? And then he counted up the candles, I'll bet?'

'He did.' Guy's voice was miserable.

'Oh, well, that would do it. Did he say anything?'

'I can't remember. It was one of those crazy moments when we were all doing something. Moira was making the coffee, and David and I were sorting out the dishwasher and making our usual hash of it. We weren't taking much notice of him to be honest.'

'So it was Louise who was talking to him?'

'Yes.'

'Then I have to speak to her.'

'I think she's away on a course in London. But she's at home in the evenings.'

'I know. I tried her office before ringing you.'

'Well, I wish she'd been there, then she would have been the one to get the grilling.'

Clara felt awful. 'Guy, I'm sorry. It's not your fault. It's mine.'

'I don't understand why you didn't tell us.'

'I . . . I couldn't. I thought the fewer people who knew, the less danger there was of Todd ever finding out.'

'You don't think he had a right to know?'

'Come on, Guy, you said it yourself, he's a family man. I couldn't rock the boat for him.'

'He's not that committed if he had a fling with you.'

'It wasn't a fling.' She explained that when she had met Todd he had thought his marriage was over.

'So what will you do?'

She sighed heavily. 'I think I have to tell him, but I'm frightened of the consequences. I don't want to do anything that might jeopardise his marriage.'

'And what about you?'

'What about me?'

'Do you still have feelings for him?'

'How sweetly put, Guy. But if you're asking am I still in love with him, the answer is no.'

'Are you sure? Or is this why there's been no one since? From the little I know of the man, I'm under the impression he might be a hard act to follow.'

'Don't give up the day job, Guy, you'd make a hopeless agony aunt. You're wrong on all counts. Look, I'm going to have to go, I can hear a car – it must be Ned coming back with Mr Liberty.'

'Okay, but before you go, do I have your permission to tell the others so that we can be on our guard? And what do we do if Todd starts interrogating us? If he's guessed, and let's face it, he must have, he's probably going to want to know where you are and how he can see you.'

'For now, tell him the truth, that I'm in the Peak District, but you don't know where. But don't let on to him that we've had this conversation. Play it as dumb as you can.'

'You mean, play it like a man, don't you?' The wry laughter in his voice lifted Clara and she said a hurried goodbye, then waited for Ned to come rushing in with Gabriel following behind.

But Ned didn't come bursting into the room as she had anticipated. He ambled in, his face downcast. He came over to where she was sitting, climbed up on to her lap and said, 'I wanted to buy you a present but I couldn't because when we went to Archie's shop it was closed. His mummy had died and he wasn't there.'

Hugging Ned to her, she got up from the sofa and went to find Gabriel so that he could elaborate on what Ned had told her.

He was in the kitchen, and while they put some lunch together, he explained how they had met Archie outside the post office and after they had been into the Mermaid café they had popped along to Second Best to find Ned a jigsaw. 'The door was locked,' Gabriel said, as he hacked at a wholemeal loaf and laid out the uneven slabs of bread on a plate, 'but because we knew he was expecting us, we knocked on it to get his attention. Anyway, someone else, a brute of a man with few words at his disposal, came to the door and told us they were shut as a mark of respect. Apparently Archie's mother had just died and he'd left for the hospital.'

Although Clara had met Bessie Merryman only once – and Gabriel not at all – lunch was a sombre affair. They both admitted that the faintest association with death tended to make one re-evaluate what was important.

It made Clara realise that the sooner she talked to Todd about Ned, the happier she would feel. She also sensed that now wasn't the right time to hand over Val's diaries, not when Mr Liberty was so quiet and downcast.

Across the table Gabriel was thinking of what he had done in Deaconsbridge that morning with Ned, when he had posted a letter to Caspar and another to Damson.

He had written late last night, asking his elder children to come and see him: he had something important to discuss with them.

That night, when Ned was fast asleep and Gabriel had also gone to bed, Clara phoned Louise at home. 'Have you heard the news?' she asked, without preamble. 'Has Guy been beating those tom-toms?'

'He has. But I'd guessed already, Clara.'

'You had?'

'Yes. Whenever your name came up, I noticed that Todd showed a little too much control over his reaction. Then when I saw his face while he was looking at the photos of you and Ned, the penny dropped and I knew for sure. He went so pale I thought he was going to faint. He excused himself and spent ages in the loo. He might even have been sick. He looked very green about the gills when he came back into the kitchen.'

Clara groaned. 'And the boys didn't reach the same conclusion?'

'Oh, come on, you know the boys never reach any kind of a conclusion on their own.'

'So why didn't you put them in the picture?'

'Because, Clara my sweet, I'm not the ditsy blabber-mouth you clearly have me down as. You could have confided in me, you know. I feel quite hurt that you didn't trust me.'

'I'm sorry, it's just that once a secret is shared, it has a ripple effect that's impossible to contain. Forgive me, please?'

'Done already. So what happens next? Guy says you're going to come clean with Todd about Ned. Are you really?'

'Yes, I am. I have to.'

'Not that you've asked for my opinion, but I think you're right. The day was always going to come when you would have to be straight with Ned. You might just as well bite the bullet now. And from what I hear, this sell-off that Todd's over here for will soon be wrapped up, so you'd better get your act together. I'm assuming you want to do it face to face and not over the phone.'

'You assume correctly.'

'So, tell me about you and the lovely Todd Mason Angel. I must say, I'm pretty envious – he's very attractive. No wonder Ned turned out to be such a great-looking boy. It also explains why you haven't looked at another man since.'

'Not you too! I had enough of that from Guy this afternoon. And for your information I *have* looked at another man with lustful thoughts – quite recently too.' Immediately Clara regretted saying that. 'Strike that from the record,' she said. 'I never said it.'

'Not on your life. If there's a man up there and you

have the hots for him, I need to know all about him. Give.'

Clara squirmed. 'There's absolutely nothing to tell.'

'Thank you, but in view of how close to the chest you play it, I'll be the judge of that. Who is he and what's his name?'

'Louise, this goes no further than you. Not a word to another living soul. Do you hear me?'

'Loud and clear. Come on, I'm all agog. What's he like?'

'Um . . . tall, dark and handsome.'

'Oh, please, spare me the cliché!'

'But it's true. He is tall, he is dark and he is handsome. His name's Jonah and he's a history teacher and he's the same age as me.' She told Louise how sweet he'd been while she'd been ill in bed.

'Hot diggity, the man's a gem!'

'I think could be right.'

'And talking of *bed*, is he a *lurve* machine between the sheets?'

'Louise, keep it focused!'

'That's exactly what I'm doing. I want you to promise you'll be careful. You got pregnant during your last away match and I don't want a repeat performance.'

'Believe me, there's no danger of that happening again. And if he is a *lurve* machine, I wouldn't know.'

'What, no nooky? None at all?' Louise sounded incredulous.

Clara laughed. 'Certainly not. He doesn't even know I like him.'

'Is he soft in the head? Oh, I get it, he's another married man, isn't he? For crying out loud, Clara, what is it with you?'

'What a blast you are, Louise. Now, stop leaping to conclusions and pay attention. He's not married, he's pleasant to have around and as every good celeb says, Jonah and I are just good friends.'

'Mm . . . but let's not forget those lustful thoughts you have for him, eh?'

Having made the fatal error of getting herself drawn into the conversation, Clara knew it was going to take real effort on her part to end it: Louise would be reluctant to let go of this one. She realised too, having heard herself openly discuss Jonah, that he was the first man, since Todd, who made her feel that he might be worth taking a risk for.

On the landing, just the other side of Clara's door, and having been downstairs to make himself a drink, Gabriel considered what he'd overheard.

Now, who'd have thought it? The lovely Clara carrying a torch for Jonah.

Taking care where he placed his slippered feet on the wooden floorboards, he crept back to his bedroom. By jingo, he hoped that Jonah had the sense to see what was right under his nose.

Sitting at the kitchen table, the last of Val's diaries now read, Jonah stared at his step-mother's final entry and wished that her life had been happier. She had deserved better than she had received from the Liberty family. She had tried so hard to pull them together, to make everything better for them. And what had they given her?

Nothing but trouble, heartache and bitterness.

Caspar had always been particularly brutal. 'Don't think for one minute you can seduce us with a slice of home-made apple pie,' he'd said to her one afternoon, when they were sitting down for tea. 'You'll never replace our mother, so don't bother to try.'

How Val had coped and never lost her temper was a mystery to Jonah. She must have been angry at times, had to have been, but she had never shown it. Not once.

He poured the last of the wine into his glass, then went and stood at the back door that opened on to the garden. Staring into the darkness, he considered the reasons behind his own anger, which had increased with each page he had read of Val's diaries. It was bad enough that Clara had read them, but it was worse that she had kept them from him. From his father too. He did not doubt that his father had no idea what she'd been up to behind his back.

Draining his glass, and feeling he had been taken for a fool – that Clara had derived some kind of perverse pleasure from stringing him along – he decided he would go to Mermaid House tomorrow morning and confront her.

It would be interesting to see how she would justify her actions.

Chapter Fifty-One

While she was hanging out a basket of washing in the warm sunshine, Clara congratulated herself on feeling better than ever that morning. She felt so good she was even humming a little tune, slightly off key. She stopped, though, when she heard a car approaching. She continued to peg a row of Gabriel's shirts on the line, until the car turned into the courtyard and she saw it was Jonah. In view of what she had admitted to Louise on the phone last night, she felt awkward suddenly at the prospect of talking to him.

She watched him shut his car door and walk towards her. He was dressed, as he so often was, in jeans with a loose-fitting cotton shirt, the sleeves rolled up. But there was something unusually purposeful about his step, which was curiously at odds with his appearance: it made Clara think he had come here with a specific task to complete. Or perhaps he was just in a hurry.

'Hi,' she said, 'long time no see. We've missed you.'

'I've been busy. How are you feeling?'

She pegged the last of the washing on the line – Murphy's law dictated it was a pair of her knickers – and said, 'Much better, thanks to you and your father cosseting me and—'

'Good,' he cut in. 'Are you up to a walk?'

Something jarred with her in his unfamiliar clipped tone, and it occurred to her that maybe he was nervous. Was it possible that he had reached the same conclusion about her as she had of him? 'I should think so. I'll go and get Ned.'

'I thought we could go on our own.'

She bent down to pick up the empty washing basket and allowed herself a small smile that had a hint of *Yesss!* tucked into it. It was to be a romantic stroll, just the two of them. 'Okay, then, I'm game if you are. Shall we go inside and see if your father will agree to look after Ned?'

Gabriel greeted the suggestion with such enthusiasm that Clara was prepared to put money on it that he was in on the whole thing. Perhaps, and in view of their new-found relationship, Jonah had confided in his father.

'Quite all right by me,' Gabriel said, putting an arm around Ned and ruffling his hair. 'You go off and enjoy yourselves. Ned and I will be fine, won't we, lad?' And then to Jonah, 'But be careful – mind you don't go too far and tire her out.'

After she had swapped her slip-on shoes for a pair of trainers, they set off in an easterly direction across the fields. They climbed over a wooden stile that had been built into the drystone wall and soon Mermaid House was far behind them. They were alone, surrounded by a patchwork of lush green slopes. Filled with a lightness of heart she hadn't felt in a long while, Clara felt sorry for anyone who didn't have the opportunity to experience such a golden summer's day. It was what her mother would call a Grateful Day – a day to be glad one was alive. In the distance sheep bleated and overhead she heard the call of a bird she didn't recognise.

'What's that, Jonah?' she asked.

'It's a skylark,' he responded, without interest. Puzzled at his terseness, she decided that he was one of those people who preferred to take his nature walks in peace and quiet.

They walked on, the path rising steeply, the sun warm on their backs. She tried not to steal too many sideways glances at him, but found her gaze drawn irresistibly to his face: it was set as if he was deep in thought. There was no sign of a smile, or that he was enjoying himself. They crossed a tumbling stream, and in front of them, Clara saw a gathering of large rocks. She opened her mouth to suggest that they rest awhile, but before she could speak Jonah said, 'I expect you're tired. Let's sit here.'

Glad of the opportunity to catch her breath, and grateful for his intuitive consideration, she chose a comfortable-looking stone on which to sit, one that was large enough to accommodate the two of them. But he remained standing, his back to her, his hands thrust into his trouser pockets as he stared at the view. A soft breeze blew at his hair, rippled his shirt, and Clara had to fight back the urge to reach out and touch him. Irrationally, she wanted him to turn and kiss her. 'I used to come up here on my own when I was a child,' he said, turning slowly to face her. 'In fact, it's one of my favourite places, where I like to come and think.'

His expression was serious and made her want to touch him even more. Kiss me, she willed him. One kiss to make me feel young and wild again. One divinely long-drawn-out kiss and I'll never trouble you again. How about it?

'But you know that, don't you?'

She stared at his sexy mouth, not listening to his words, but taking in the soft curve of his lips and how they might feel pressed against hers.

'Like you know that this is where my brother clinched matters with Emily. Just as you know all about my family.'

Suddenly she saw that the beguiling softness was gone from his mouth, and a feeling of sick dread swept through her.

'Jonah, what is it?' But she knew what was wrong. Knew it with painful and shameful clarity.

He stared down at her, his eyes dark and hard. 'I'm talking about Val's diaries. I found them among your things in your camper-van when I was looking for your mobile.'

There was no point in denying it. 'I – I was going to put them back,' she confessed, accepting that while she had to give him the truth, it would not lessen the seriousness of her crime. She lowered her gaze. She had nearly made a fool of herself. Jonah hadn't brought her up here for a passionate smooch, as she had hoped, but to take her to task. Oh, how stupid and misguided she had been!

'So you admit you took them?' He was towering over her, blocking out the sun and everything around her – everything but his simmering contempt.

She nodded. 'I'm sorry. It was awful of me, I know. But it was when I was sorting through Val's things. I started reading them and was fascinated by what she—'

'You took them and read them,' he said sharply, as though she hadn't spoken. 'Despite their intensely private nature, you felt you had a right to read them. What Val wrote was private. She never intended a stranger to read them. A lying stranger at that. They were meant for my father. No one else.' His voice was cold and stinging, utterly condemning. He was every inch the tough adversary she had imagined him to be if sufficiently provoked. But he hadn't finished. 'What gave you the right to do that?' he persisted.

'It was wrong of me,' she murmured, 'and I'm sorry. But it was why I came back to Mermaid House. I forgot I still had them, and when I'd got to the end, when I read Val's last entry, I knew I had to give them to your father . . . I've been waiting for the right moment.'

He turned away from her. 'Perhaps it would have been better if you hadn't come back.'

She let this last comment sink in, then realised she couldn't let it go, and with her humiliation and meekness subsiding, she said, 'If I hadn't come back when I did, your father might have gone through with what he'd intended to do down in the copse.'

He swung round. 'If you're going to take that line of argument, I could say that if you had never come here in the first place my father would never have got so depressed.'

Clara was getting angry. She didn't like illogical arguments, and this one was heading that way. 'Oh, please, enough of the self-righteous fest, Jonah! If it

420

wasn't for me, you and your father would still be carrying on like a couple of bickering children.' She saw she'd hit home. And, oh boy, he looked as mad as hell now.

'Don't you dare denigrate what my father and I have been through in so offhand a manner!' he thundered.

She leaped to her feet, stood just inches from him. 'Time to bring the truth trolley round! What bothers you most about me reading those diaries? Could it be something to do with the fact that I know more about you than any other living person? That I know your weaknesses as well as your strengths. That you ran away from school all those times because you were so desperately unhappy. That you've never stood up to your brother because, deep down, you're scared of him. Oh, I think it's all of that and more, but what probably irks you most is what we both know, that if you had kicked Caspar into touch years ago, you would have married the woman you loved and be standing with her here. Instead you're stuck with me, a "lying stranger". Which begs the question, who do you despise more? Me or yourself?'

For a moment she thought she had gone too far. His face turned white and his eyes took on a wild, shining darkness that made her step back from him. His body was taut with barely concealed rage. 'I'm sorry,' she said. 'I shouldn't have—' But she got no further. He stepped in close, pulled her to him and kissed her. She resisted at first, unnerved by the rough suddenness of what he was doing, but then the desire she'd felt for him earlier came flooding back and she relaxed into him and let herself be kissed. And before long, the dreamy, knee-buckling kiss she had fantasised about was a thrilling reality. His arms held her tightly and she pressed her hands into his shoulders, wanting to feel the warmth and strength of his body through the soft fabric of his shirt, wanting to absorb every bit of him.

But, annoyingly, the need to cough got the better of her desire. 'I'm sorry,' she said, releasing herself from his embrace. 'I hope I'm no longer infectious.'

He waited for her to finish coughing, then circling her waist with his hands, drew her gently back to him. 'What you said a moment ago about Emily, you're wrong. I'd much rather be standing here with you.' He smiled hesitantly, his handsome face now devoid of all animosity. 'May I kiss you again but this time without the threat of world war breaking out? And when I've done that, it might be a good idea for us to talk.'

Chapter Fifty-Two

The mail at Rosewood Manor was delivered by van, usually at around ten o'clock, and after someone had carried it up the long drive from the postbox by the gate, it was sorted and placed in the appropriate pigeonholes in the purpose-built shelving unit in the dining room. Damson's was brought up to her by one of Roland Hall's acolytes, a frumpy earth-mother type in sandals. That morning Caspar decided he would check Damson's pigeonhole himself.

It was Monday and he had been at Rosewood Manor for over a week, and while the place and its creepy inhabitants continued to get on his nerves – had him wanting to nuke all of the brain-dead idiots – its isolated location and day-to-day routine made him focus on what was important. Being with Damson was all that mattered now. The rest of the world could go hang, as far as he was concerned. He didn't know how much longer he would stay, that depended on his sister, but he didn't care. It was a relief to have escaped his problems at home.

When he had arrived, he'd been worried sick about the loss of his business – the money he owed, and the humiliation. Previous business ventures that had gone belly-up on him had involved other partners and backers so the fallout had been shared. This time the buck had stopped with him and there had been no one to bail him out. But stuck here in the middle of nowhere, he was experiencing a strange, unexpected sense of freedom. It was as if he was in exile, buffered from the raging storm the Inland Revenue and his creditors had whipped up, and he felt absurdly safe.

It was weird and he had told Damson about it, just as he had told her everything since his arrival. She had smiled – especially when he confessed to having thrown away his mobile phone so he could be doubly sure that no one would track him down. He had driven into the nearest town for some items of clothing to tide him over – some new shirts, underwear and socks, paid for by Damson – and on the way back he had stopped the car and hurled the phone into the air. Hearing it crack open against a drystone wall and smash to a thousand pieces had been surprisingly satisfying.

Damson had made no comment on what he had just told her, but had asked if he would do something for her. They were sitting in a secluded spot in the garden, the afternoon sun was shining down from a clear sky, but despite its warmth, Damson needed a rug over her legs. On the other side of a wall, they could hear the irritating chatter of a group of inmates who were working on the vegetable plot: they were discussing the most humane way to deal with the army of slugs that, overnight, had invaded their organically grown crops. 'What is it?' he had asked, his heart bursting with the need to make her well again, to have her as she'd once been.

'I want you to accept that what we did as children, and continued to do as adults, was wrong.' Her voice was faint and he had to strain to catch her words. 'We held Jonah responsible for destroying our family, for taking our mother away, and for making Dad so unhappy. But we both know the truth, have known it since the day we first blamed him.' She paused, as if stocking up on air and energy. 'We both held on to that anger in the misguided hope that it would protect us from the pain. But Caspar, it caused us so much more. It still is, for you, isn't it?' Covering his hand with hers, she had held his gaze steadily. 'We turned ourselves into victims, when really we're survivors. Remember that, Caspar. And here's a little Rosewood Manor truism for you, one that will make you shudder with cynicism, but I want you to think about it. For every sixty seconds of anger you experience, you deny yourself a minute of happiness.' From nowhere a smile had appeared on her face, and suddenly the real Damson was there beside him, the beautiful, bright-eyed twin sister who had comforted and empowered him, and meant everything to him.

There was just one letter in Damson's pigeonhole and Caspar instantly recognised the handwriting on the envelope. Climbing the stairs, and ignoring the moronic greetings of passers-by, he gripped it and felt that his haven was under attack. The outside world was never far away, no matter how much he kidded himself.

Damson was sitting in her wheelchair by the window when he tapped on her door and stepped inside. She was combing her cropped hair. When he had asked her why she had had it cut, she had said, 'It seemed frivolous in the circumstances. You don't like it, do you?'

'Not much,' he'd said. He found women with long hair attractive; he had never looked twice at a woman with short hair.

As he looked at Damson now, he saw that she appeared weaker today. He held out the letter to her. She hesitated, then said, 'You open it for me, darling.' It was almost as if she had been expecting it.

'You don't seem surprised. Does he write to you often?'

She put the comb down on the table beside her. 'No, but I was expecting this one. The pieces are all coming together, just as they should. Just at the right time.'

He slit open the envelope. There was just one sheet of paper. The writing was uneven, the lines badly spaced, and there were crossings-out in several places.

Damson sank back into her chair. 'Read it to me. Please.'

'Are you sure?'

She sighed heavily. 'Yes. And read it nicely.'

He caught a hint of a smile as she said this. 'Nicely does it, then,' he said.

Dear Damson,

Just lately I have been forced into thinking a lot about the past and I'm ashamed to say it's been a painful process and made all the worse by knowing that I put you and Caspar through a hell of a time.

I know you will probably regard this letter with cynicism, and I can hardly blame you for that, but please, I would very much like to see you again. Caspar too. I have written to him in the hope that the pair of you might be prepared to forgive a stupid, selfish old man who should have known better. It would mean everything to me if you would get in touch.

Regards,
Your father

Caspar lowered the letter and looked at his sister. Her eyes were shut, her head tilted back against the chair. He was used to seeing her fall asleep without warning, but he had never seen her so still. He cleared his throat. 'Damson?'

She didn't answer.

He bent down to her. 'Damson?' He was frightened. He reached out to her. At his touch, her eyelids opened and relief, like none he had ever known, washed over him. He swallowed his fear.

She took the letter from him and stared at it, tears filling her eyes. 'I said the pieces were coming together, didn't I?'

'I'd rather they didn't if it meant you could be well again.'

'It's the way forward, Caspar. If the future is going to mean anything for you, you must do as he asks.'

'What about you?'

She held the letter to her chest. 'This is enough for my future. He'll understand.'

Understanding only one horrible truth in all of this, that a future without Damson would be worse than any hell

his father could imagine, Caspar left her sleeping peacefully. He went downstairs, and sat in the garden where
yesterday he and Damson had chatted. It was another
warm, sunny day, and as if he were locked in a time loop,
he could hear the same people arguing the toss about the
best way to deal with the slugs – jars of home-made beer
was held up as the ideal solution. 'Take a bloody great
spade to them!' he yelled at the brick wall. 'Smash their
stupid brainless bodies in!'

The voices went quiet.

'For once I'm in agreement with you.'

Caspar turned his head sharply and saw that Roland
Hall had crept up on him.

'Oh, it's you. What do you want?' Though Damson had
told him repeatedly that Hall was a good, sincere man,
that he had never tried to turn their friendship into
anything more, or to inveigle money out of her, Caspar
still didn't trust him. But then, other than Damson,
whom had he ever trusted?

Hall sat down. 'I want to talk to you about Damson,'
he said. 'It's been your sister's intention to move into the
local hospice when she felt she couldn't cope with the pain
any more. I think that time is drawing near.'

Caspar wanted to take a spade to Hall and smash him
to smithereens. To see the man's infuriating face pulped.
'You want to be rid of her now, do you?' he muttered
savagely. 'She's become a nuisance, is that it? Frightened
that the smell of death will scare the punters off?'

Hall's expression was impassive. 'It's what she wanted,
Caspar.'

Exasperated, he dragged a hand over his face. 'Tell me,
Hall, what the hell did you do before you took up
scamming deluded fools who are more concerned about
the finer feelings of slugs than themselves? You're so
bloody inscrutable. What were you – an MI5 interroga-
tor?'

'Actually, I was a monk.'

Caspar laughed nastily. 'A monk? Oh, that's a good

one. But, don't tell me, the celibate life proved too much of a challenge for you?'

'I had no problem with the vow of chastity. It was the other monks I found difficult to live with. There was no escaping them and their inbuilt prejudice of right and wrong.'

'So what's different about this place?'

Hall sat back, steepled his hands together in front of him, the tips of his fingers just meeting. 'I'm not saying it's perfect here – community life can never be that. Put a group of people together and it's human nature for them to disagree over something or other. Here at Rosewood Manor, in our search to build a caring and sustainable lifestyle, we value autonomy and independent thinking. We try to support one another and support ourselves in any way we can, for instance, by growing and selling organic food.' He canted his head towards the brick wall. 'But even that provides a breeding ground for dispute. It means we have to try harder, to be more self-aware. And while we're striving to achieve all that, no one at Rosewood Manor is forced to be what they're not. So long as one isn't harming another person, one can be oneself here, without fear of being judged. It's why your sister has enjoyed being with us.'

Caspar took this as a criticism of his sister, which he couldn't countenance. 'Damson has never been frightened of anyone, or anything.'

Hall looked at him hard. 'That really isn't true, Caspar, and it's time you realised it. Damson was terrified of herself and what she was capable of inflicting on her mind and body. She came to us crippled by fear and regret. She'd had two abortions by the age of twenty-two and she never forgave herself. It's haunted her for most of her life.'

Caspar's jaw dropped. 'No! That can't be true. I don't believe you. She would have told me.'

'She never wanted you to know. She told me you idolised her and saw her as perfect. She hated knowing that she wasn't, hated knowing that she had let you down.'

'But she didn't!' cried Caspar. 'She hasn't let me down. She could never do that. Not ever.'

Hall's voice was steady. 'Are you sure about that? What about her coming here? Didn't that annoy you? Didn't you berate her for hitching up with a bunch of sad losers whose only interest in her was to relieve her of her worldly goods?'

Caspar had the grace to turn away. He tried to take in what Hall had told him. He was mortified that he had added to Damson's problems. And, worse, that he was perhaps the source of some of them.

'When you're thinking more clearly,' Hall said, 'you'll understand that Damson has spent most of her life searching for something to make her happy, something to take away the guilt. She's told me about the series of unsuitable men who used and abused her, and who, in her own words, she used as a means to inflict yet more punishment on herself.'

'Stop! I don't want to hear any more. Just be quiet, will you?' Caspar pushed the heels of his hands against his eyes. It was too much to take in. Unable to speak, he got to his feet and left Hall sitting on the bench alone. He went back inside the house. He needed to be with Damson. Needed to apologise to her.

She was sitting in the window where he had left her no more than half an hour ago. The sun was shining through the glass and its rays lightened her hair – the same colour as his own. He remembered how she used to dye it during the school holidays, much to Val's and their father's horror. One summer, having already dyed it jet black, she had another go at it and it turned a vivid orange. She didn't care: she just laughed and tied it up on top of her head with a green silk scarf and said, 'How's that for a carrot head?' Nothing bothered her. 'It's just another experience to add to the rest,' she said.

But some things had bothered her and she had not shared them with him.

Why hadn't she? The truth bit into him. Because she had been selfless in her love and support for him and, like a spoiled child, he had greedily accepted her unconditional love. By putting her on a pedestal, he had imposed restrictions on what she could do with her own life. He was allowed to change and make untold mistakes, but she wasn't. She was his sister, but he had treated her as a mother. And everyone knows a mother must be constant in a world of chaos and upheaval.

He crossed the room silently. There was so much he had to say to her. More than anything, he wanted Damson to know that she would always be perfect in his eyes, no matter what.

But when he knelt beside her, took their father's letter that was still on her lap and laid it on the table, he saw that he was too late.

Damson was dead.

He held her in his arms and wept. Wept as he had never wept before. 'Oh, Damson,' he groaned, 'I'm so sorry for what I did to you. I didn't realise.'

Jonah had spent the afternoon on tenterhooks. His GCSE history class was sitting its last paper. Once the exam was under way he had slipped in at the back of the sports hall and had scanned through the questions, reassuring himself that there weren't any horrible surprises in store for his pupils. Or him. But it had been fine. He had covered all the ground in his lessons. He went back to his classroom to share the joys of the 1832 Reform Act with 7B, confident that so long as his students kept their cool they would do well.

When it was all over and the papers had been gathered in, he was waiting outside the sports hall to see how they had survived. He was greeted with a mixture of relief, anxiety and cautious optimism. And an element of cockiness from an unexpected quarter. 'Did you get the eight main points to the Treaty of Versailles?' he asked the group.

Jase grinned at him. 'No sweat, man. It was a breeze.'

Jonah smiled. 'Atta boy. You off home now?'

'Nah. Thought I'd stick around and polish up the candelabras. 'Course I'm off home. Were you offering a lift?'

'I wouldn't inflict that on you again, Jase. I wouldn't want to be held responsible for damaging your image.'

'A word of advice, Sir, you wanna get yourself fitted with a flash set of new wheels or you'll never pull a decent woman.'

'I was wondering where I was going wrong.'

Driving home, Jonah wondered how Clara might have responded to Jase's worldly wisdom. From what he had learned of her lifestyle before she'd upped sticks in favour of taking to the road in a camper-van, she had owned a smart car herself. And, like shoes, he had always believed that a car gave away a lot about its owner. He could easily imagine Clara dressed in a power suit sitting behind the wheel of a sports car, mobile phone ringing, head-lamps flashing.

In contrast, his rusting Ford Escort, which would pass its next MOT by the skin of its teeth, shouted from the rooftops that his attitude to life had a more casual slant. Sure, he could splash out on a better car if he wanted, he certainly had the money, but so long as his existing one provided him with a safe, reliable drive, he didn't much care what it looked like.

And, anyway, he *had* managed to pull himself a decent woman. He was seeing Clara that evening.

His father would baby-sit Ned, and instead of taking Clara to a restaurant, Jonah had offered to make dinner at his cottage. 'Having already sampled your cooking and enjoyed it, I'll take the risk,' she had said. What surprised him most about the evening ahead was not that Clara had agreed to see him, but that his father was so keen for them to enjoy themselves. Jonah had anticipated a somewhat less than enthusiastic response to his poaching Clara away from Mermaid House for the evening, but it seemed that the opposite was true. 'No, no, don't you worry about me, Jonah, you go ahead and have a little fun. It's high time you did. Ned and I will have a grand old time of it.'

Jonah was always suspicious when things came to him too easily. Everything he had really wanted in life he had had to fight for.

It was only yesterday that he had behaved like a pompous idiot with Clara over Val's diaries – oh, he'd gone the full nine yards – but it felt like days ago. She had apologised over and over again for what she had done, and each time she said she was sorry he felt a bigger heel. He had tried hard to make her understand why he had been so angry.

'It was reading them and having everything brought back so vividly,' he had said, still with his arms around her. 'It was a shock reliving it, I guess.'

She had looked deep into his eyes and said, 'I'm sorry, Jonah. Truly I am. It wasn't a gratuitous act on my part, I was genuinely interested in you all. I wanted to understand why your father behaved as he did and why you had such a bad relationship with him. I admit it was wrong of me to do it so sneakily, but it just sort of happened. I wish I could apologise more. I feel awful. I should never have said that bit about you and Emily.'

'It's okay, forget it. Though I ought to 'fess up the reason I became so angry and Joe Regular turned into Stormin' Norman. I didn't want you to think I was a spineless wimp.'

'I'd already decided that anyone who enjoyed teaching at a school like Dick High was anything but a wimp.' She'd kissed him, then added, 'I've been lucky, Jonah. I've had what must seem to you a very boring middle-of-the-road but happy upbringing, and it's made me the way I am. Just as your upbringing has made you wary and guarded, not to say perceptive, it's also, I suspect, made you determined to fight for what you want. So don't go selling yourself short.'

'In that case, dare I ask you to have dinner with me?'

'Just the two of us?'

'Is that a problem?'

'Only if your father doesn't want to baby-sit.'

They had walked back to Mermaid House, hand in hand, and as though to underscore what he had already told her, he said, 'I'm not devaluing what Val wrote, but I can think of any number of kids at Dick High who have suffered far worse than any member of my family has. Some of those kids survive levels of violence, abuse, degradation and neglect that make my childhood look like something out of *The Waltons*. I don't want your sympathy.'

She had come to a stop and given him one of her stern but sassy looks. 'Don't worry, it's the last thing you'll get from me.'

Clara's first impression of Church Cottage was that she liked it. She could see why Jonah had bought it: it was him down to the ground, from the cosy proportions of the rooms to the eclectic taste in décor and furniture. She had plenty of time to poke and pry, as the moment he had opened the door to her the telephone had rung. 'Don't worry about me,' she had told him. 'I'll make myself at home while you see to that.'

Standing in the sitting room, which looked out on to the street where she had parked Winnie, she studied the small, simply framed pictures that had been squeezed in where there was space between overfilled bookcases. In front of the window, there was a mahogany desk and two piles of exercise books along with a collection of wooden puzzles – she pictured Jonah patiently piecing them together. Either side of the fireplace, where there was a wood-burning stove, there were two sagging armchairs and, set out neatly on the mantelpiece, a collection of old clockwork toys: a performing seal with a ball attached to its nose, a marching soldier beating a drum, a laughing policeman and a strutting sausage dog with a bone in its mouth. She wandered over to the largest bookcase and ran her eyes over his taste in reading matter. It was mostly historical, with biographies coming a close second, and the complete works of P. G. Wodehouse, Oscar Wilde and Evelyn Waugh bringing up the rear. An interesting mix, she decided. Scholarly with a dash of whimsy.

And no slacker when it came to matters of the heart, she thought, remembering their embrace on the moors. Their second kiss had been just as intense as the first, but in a completely different way. Slow and gentle, but sublimely erotic, it had held her firmly in a dizzy state of longing. Him too, if she wasn't mistaken.

Through the open door she could hear him winding down the call. Seconds later he was back with her. 'Sorry about that,' he said. 'A neighbour wanting me to keep an eye on their house while they're away.'

'Does everyone rely on you?'

He raised an eyebrow. 'Meaning?'

'Hey, no criticism. I just get the feeling people see you as rock steady, someone they can turn to in their hour of need.'

'A bit like you, then?'

She smiled. '*Touché*. First point of the evening to you.'

He smiled too. 'Well, that's the pleasantries dispensed with. I thought we could eat outside, if it's warm enough for you. Come through to the kitchen and I'll pour you a drink.'

The kitchen smelt heavenly, and she said so.

'Thai fish cakes. Wine?' He held up a bottle of white for her approval.

'That's fine. Anything I can do?'

He passed her a glass. 'No, it's all done. I'm quite organised for a mere man, don't you think?'

'Young Master Liberty, you wouldn't be casting your net in search of a compliment, would you?'

'Credit me with more sense than to do that.' He chinked his glass against hers. 'Cheers.'

They ate on the small terraced area just off the kitchen. It was still light, and just above a pretty lilac tree, a cloud of gnats danced in the warm evening air. The view from where they were sitting was stunning. 'This is lovely,' she said. 'You've created yourself a proper home here, haven't you?'

He leaned back in his chair. 'It's going to take something very special to make me want to leave. Caspar thinks it's a hovel, but it suits me perfectly.'

'And what kind of house does Caspar live in?'

'A clinical wasteland. An airy loft apartment in Manchester. Very grand, and very expensive. What about you? What's *chez* Costello like?'

'Oh, executively smart – four beds, two baths, double garage. Not very imaginative, I'm afraid.'

He smiled. 'But eminently practical, like its owner?'

'Eminently practical. With the demands of my job I had to buy something that would fend for itself and leave me free to enjoy my weekends with Ned. Patching up leaking gutters was the last thing I needed. Though I suppose you're the opposite. I bet after a tough week at school you like nothing more than to get stuck into some house-restoration therapy.'

'Something like that. Between you and me, my next-door neighbours keep dropping hints that they might be putting their house on the market. If so, I'm hoping I might get first refusal. Knocking the two together would make a great conversion. I'd love to get my teeth into a project like that.'

'Here's to knocking through, then.' She raised her glass. 'You're a man of many talents, Jonah.'

'If you say so.'

They continued eating in contemplative silence, until the church bells struck the half-hour and Jonah said, 'Clara, it's none of my business, but have you decided what you're going to do about Ned's father?'

435

She put down her knife and fork. She had been wondering at what stage in the evening to bring up the subject that had occupied her mind for most of that day. And the decision she had reached after speaking to Louise on the phone again. 'Yes. I'm going home to see him before he returns to America.'

'When will you leave?'

'In a couple of days.'

'Have you told Dad?'

She shook her head. 'Not yet. I only decided this afternoon.'

'He's going to miss you when you've gone.'

'It works both ways. I'll miss him.' She wanted to add, 'and I'll miss you,' but her nerve failed her: her come-hither skills were too rusty to dish out romantic one-liners. Instead, she said, 'And goodness knows how Ned will take it. He loves being here. Mermaid House has become a second home for him.'

Another silence grew between them. Finally, Jonah said, 'Is there any chance you'll come back? You've still got a few months before Ned starts school in the autumn. You know you'll always be welcome.'

She knew what he was really asking and she knew she had to be straight with him. 'Each day as it comes, Jonah. I need to keep the plans to a minimum. That's what I've learned from this trip. Nothing works out quite the way one thinks or hopes it will.'

'Would it be pushing things to ask you to keep in touch? Just as friends, perhaps?'

She stretched out her hand across the table and made contact with his. 'I think I'd like it to be more than that. But first I need to settle things with Todd.'

'I understand,' he said. Turning her hand over so that her palm faced upwards, Jonah laid his on top. Dispirited, he had the feeling that maybe this was the end between them, and not the beginning as he had hoped. He could tell from the way she spoke about this Todd character that he'd meant a lot to her. He was the father of her son, after all. And now, after more than four years of not seeing him, who knew what the outcome might be of their meeting up again?

The shrill ringing of the telephone made them both jump. 'That's probably Dad checking up on me, making sure I'm behaving myself and not besmirching your good name.'

She laughed. 'Tell him we're being very respectable, and that although we're making mad passionate love in full view of the neighbours, I've still got one foot on the floor.'

He answered the phone in the kitchen, but the smile was wiped off his face when he heard Caspar's distraught voice and what he had to say.

Chapter Fifty-Three

'How can this be? It's against nature for a parent to outlive his children.'

Gabriel's voice was thick with tiredness and bewildered grief. 'Three women. All gone! Tell me why. Just tell me why.' He thumped his fist on the table, sent an empty coffee mug flying and hung his head. While Clara picked up the shattered pieces from the floor, Jonah went to his father.

It had been a long night with only a few hours of sleep for any of them. After he had received the call from his brother, he and Clara had driven straight over to Mermaid House to break the news. Gabriel had been sitting alone in the library, enjoying a glass of whisky and reading. 'What's this, Miss Costello?' he'd joked, closing the book and putting it aside. 'I didn't expect to see you back so early. Jonah's cooking frightened you off?' But he must have seen from their faces that something was wrong.

Once the words were out, he had looked at Jonah as if he hadn't understood. Within seconds, though, his eyes had filled and his hands had started to shake. He had tried to stand up, but his body had failed him, and he had remained slumped in his chair. Clara had made them all tea, and while she was in the kitchen, Jonah had pulled up a footstool beside his father, taken his trembling hands and held them firmly. Gabriel had suddenly looked old and confused.

Now, at six o'clock in the morning, as Ned slept peacefully upstairs, Jonah and his father were setting out on the journey to Northumberland. Neither knew quite what to expect when they arrived. Caspar had sounded a broken man on the phone, but if his grief had turned to rage, it was anyone's guess what kind of reception awaited them.

Before going to bed last night – Jonah had spent the night at Mermaid House – he had made two telephone calls. One was to a colleague from school to say he wouldn't be in for the next couple of days, and the second was to get more information from Rosewood Manor about his sister's death. He spoke to a helpful man called Roland Hall, who had stressed that he would do all he could to take care of Caspar. He had explained about Damson's illness and how Caspar had been with their sister in the last week of her life. He had also given Jonah directions on how to find Rosewood Manor.

Armed with these and an AA road atlas, he was now helping his father into the front seat of his car. For the first time ever, he regretted the state of his old Escort and just hoped that it would get them up to Northumberland in one piece.

Gabriel was too dazed to say goodbye to Clara, but Jonah stood with her for a moment. Nothing had been said between them, but Jonah knew that she and Ned wouldn't be at Mermaid House when he returned. 'I'm not sure when we'll be back,' he said, 'but when are you going?'

'Tomorrow morning. It feels the right thing to do. If you're bringing Caspar back here, my presence won't help him. We didn't exactly hit it off.'

'I know the feeling. But I have a hunch that Caspar is going to need what's left of his family.'

'You'll take care, won't you?' she said, opening her arms and hugging him.

He squeezed her hard, then pulled away. 'You take care as well. If you want to ring, or drop me a line, you know where I am.'

'I will. And please, explain everything to your father for me. I feel bad that I won't be here to help, but—'

He silenced her with a feather-light kiss, held her gently, pressed his cheek against hers, then walked away.

Clara took Ned to the Mermaid café for breakfast. Shirley greeted them as if they were old friends and gave them a table in the window.

There was a lot Clara had to tell Ned: why Gabriel had gone away with Jonah so unexpectedly, but more importantly why they were leaving. She hated lying to Ned, but she could hardly tell him the truth: that they were going home so she could arrange to meet his father.

Instead, she told Ned that she was feeling homesick and wanted to see her friends.

He listened to what she told him while he munched on a piece of fried bread, holding a corner of it delicately between his thumb and forefinger – he was such a tidy eater. 'Does this mean we're going home for ever?' he said finally. 'No more Winnie?'

She sipped her tea. 'Not at all. We still have two and a half months left before we have to part with Winnie.'

He dipped the fried bread into the yolk of his egg. Stirred it round a little. 'Then I start school?'

'That's right.'

'Will I like it this time?'

'You'll love it. Think of all the tales you'll have to tell the other children. They'll be so envious of what you've been up to.'

He frowned and wrinkled his nose, and Clara knew that if she looked under the table his legs would be swinging. 'I didn't really like St Chad's,' he confided.

'Maybe we'll find a different school. But don't forget, you're older now and it will feel better. Also, you were missing Nanna and Granda.'

His face cheered up at the mention of Nanna and Granda. 'Will they be home from Australia now?'

'No. They're not back until after Christmas.'

Another frown.

'But don't worry. When I've seen Louise and the gang, we'll be off on another adventure.'

'Back here?' The change of expression on his face was so rapid, so telling, that Clara didn't know what to say. There was a danger that if they came back to Deaconsbridge, they might never leave. There was so much about the place she had grown to love, from the beautiful countryside, to the busy market square, so pretty in its summer finery to the friendly people who lived here. Unwittingly, she and Ned had become a part of it, and *it* had become a part of them. It had also caused her to consider abandoning her old life and creating a new one here, where the pace was slower, the people more genuine.

Deaconsbridge aside, there was also the small matter of their involvement with the Liberty family. She would never forget the protective love Gabriel had showered on her and Ned.

And there was Jonah.

With his benign social conscience, his understated charm and thoughtful kindness, he had achieved the impossible: he had tempted her to wonder what it might be like to be in a relationship with him. But where could it lead them? When she and Ned were back in their old routine, what use would a long-distance relationship be? How soon before it fizzled out?

She felt sure, however, that even if it did run out of steam, they would remain friends. And friends, as she had come to know, were what counted.

'You look lost in thought. Where were you? Lying on a tropical beach having coconut oil rubbed in somewhere pleasant?'

Clara smiled and passed her empty plate to Shirley, who had arrived to clear their table. 'Not even close.'

'Oh, well, how about a teacake?'

'Ned? Can you manage anything else?'

Kneeling up on his chair and wobbling from side to side with his bottom balanced on his heels, Ned puffed out his cheeks. 'No, thank you. I'm very full.' He patted his tummy.

Passing him a lollipop from her apron pocket, Shirley said, 'You're the politest little boy I know.' Then, in a more serious tone, she said to Clara, 'Have you heard about Archie's mother?'

'Yes, I have. How's he getting on? They were very close, weren't they?'

'Cut up something rotten but, like he always does, he's putting a brave face on it. It was the same when that stuck-up grabby wife of his left him. It was ages before he let on that she'd gone. If you want my opinion, he's better off without her. It was what everyone told me when my old man left me. Thing is, you don't believe it at the time. But I'll tell you this for nothing, she was a snooty whatsit, always looked down her nose at the rest of us.' She paused to let a customer squeeze past, then continued, 'The funeral's the day after tomorrow. I thought I'd get an hour off and go along. Moral support and all that. Did you know he's sold his house? He's moving into the square, above Joe's bookshop. I thought I'd get him a house-warming present. Something small. Just a token. No point in being flash when discreet will do.'

Goodness, thought Clara, when Shirley left them to serve a middle-aged couple dressed in shorts and walking boots, what a lot Shirley has to say about Archie. And how highly she regards him. She wondered if Archie realised what a devoted friend he had in Shirley.

Clara paid for their meal and they left the café. Standing on the step outside, waiting for a young mother with a pushchair to trundle by, Clara felt a pang of sadness: Ned and she had probably eaten at the Mermaid café for the last time. It was going to be even more of a wrench leaving than she had anticipated. 'Shall we go and see Archie?' she said, forcing brightness into her voice.

The bell tinkled as she pushed the door of Second Best. It was a cheerful sound that had to be at odds with how the owner of the shop was feeling. There was no one about, so she called Archie's name. She heard the scrape of a drawer being pushed in and Archie's head appeared from behind a pine veneer wardrobe. 'Hello there,' he said, 'and what a sight for sore eyes you two are.'

'How's things, Archie? I heard about Bessie.'

He pushed his hands into his pockets, jangled the loose change in them, rocked on his feet. 'Oh. Not brilliant. Funeral's the day after tomorrow.'

She nodded sympathetically. 'I know, Shirley's just told me. I'm so sorry, Archie.' He seemed lost for words, so she said, 'Shirley also said you were moving into the square. It's all change for you, isn't it?'

'It's probably for the best. Nothing like a shake-up. Fancy a brew? I was just about to make one.'

Clara was awash with tea from Shirley's generous ministrations, but she said, 'That would be nice. Thank you.'

Turning to Ned, Archie said, 'Have a good old forage in that box over there. If you're lucky, you might find a couple of jigsaws.'

Clara went through to the back of the shop with Archie, to a tiny kitchen area where there was only just room for the two of them. He filled the kettle at the sink where a bowl of used mugs lay waiting to be washed. 'Sorry about the mess,' he said, catching her glance. 'It's always the same, the moment I leave Samson in charge . . .' His voice trailed off. 'Hang on a minute, that sounds like the door.'

By the time he had joined her again, she had made their tea and given the kitchen a blitz.

'Here, there was no need for that.'

She smiled and flicked the tea-towel at him. 'Drink your tea and be quiet, Archie Merryman.'

Leaning against the sink, he relaxed visibly. 'That's what I like about you, you always cheer me up. So what's new at Mermaid House? Apart from you having had flu. You look as if you've recovered well. Fresh as a daisy, I'd say.'

'And you can save the flattery for the punters.'

'Just speaking as I find. One look at you and I feel made up. Now, did Mr Liberty take good care of you? I bet he terrorised you into getting well, didn't he?'

'I've told you before, he's a poppet.' She went on to explain about his daughter. 'I think her death coming out of the blue has hit him very hard.'

'Oh, God, the poor man. To have lost two wives and now a daughter.' He lowered his eyes and delved into his pocket for a handkerchief. 'Life, eh? If we had any idea how tough it would be we'd give it up as a bad job.'

Clara's heart went out to him. What he needed was a great big hug.

She was still hugging him when a crisp voice said, 'If I'm interrupting, I'll come back later. Or maybe it would be better if I didn't bother.'

Neither of them had heard the shop bell, or the sound of footsteps, and they sprang apart, which made an innocent embrace seem altogether more furtive.

'Stella, what – what are you doing here?' Archie's voice shook with alarm. He fumbled with his handkerchief, pushed it back into his pocket.

'I heard about your mother and came to offer my condolences.' The brittle formality of her words was as flinty as the look she gave Clara, which left no one in any doubt of what she thought had been going on.

Clara decided to make a tactful exit. She didn't like the look of Stella. Too much makeup. Too much jewellery. And way too high and mighty. Shirley had been right. Picking up her bag to go, she said, 'I'll leave you to it, Archie. Excuse me, please,' she added, when Stella made no attempt to let her pass.

'And you are— ?'

'Clara is a friend of mine, Stella,' Archie said gamely, 'but I think you gave up the right to know who I mix with the day you left me. Thanks for the condolences. Was there anything else?'

Good for you, Clara applauded him silently. And, even

better, the horrible woman took the hint and departed as quickly as she had arrived, slamming the door behind her and making the bell jangle long after she'd gone.

They watched her through the window as she crossed the road to the square until she became lost in the crowd of shoppers and tourists. Archie looked anxious. 'Do you think I was too hard on her?'

Clara smiled. 'Given the circumstances, you played it just right.'

He laughed. 'And just think, she now imagines that her boring soon-to-be-ex-husband is capable of pulling a woman as young as you.' He laughed so hard the tears rolled down his cheeks. 'What a joke! What a huge joke!'

His mirth didn't ring out with pure happiness though. There was a strained false note to it that Clara knew echoed the emptiness of his new life. Watching him wipe his eyes with the back of his hands, she said, 'Archie, how's your social life these days?'

He shrugged. 'About as good as an agoraphobic hermit's. Why?'

'In that case, I think it's time you did something about it.'

He smiled. 'You asking me out on a date?'

'Oh, dang! You've rumbled me.' She smiled. 'Actually, I had Shirley in mind. Why don't you ask her out? I've a feeling she's quite fond of you. And just think of the great perks on offer. More fry-up breakfasts and Bakewell tart than you can shake a stick at.'

He rubbed his jaw, unconvinced. 'You think she'd say yes? I mean . . . well, we've been friends for a long time, but this . . . this would be different.'

'Oh, come on, Archie, try listening to me. The woman's mad about you.' Clara wasn't sure that this was strictly true but, hey, what the heck? If she was going to start flinging Cupid's arrow about, she might just as well make a proper job of it and aim for a bull's-eye. Besides, Shirley wouldn't have gone on and on about Archie in the way she had, if she wasn't just a little bit sweet on him.

They stayed with Archie until Ned had chosen three boxes of jigsaw puzzles – having tried them all out – and Clara had explained that they would be leaving the next day.

'Is this the last I'll see of you both?'

'Who knows?' she said evasively. 'When the wind changes Ned and I might just roll into town again.'

He gave her a final hug goodbye. 'You're a regular Mary Poppins, you are. Not got a carpet bag and an umbrella with a parrot's head on it, have you?'

She was almost out of the door when she was struck by what she thought was her second great idea of the day. She turned back. 'I know this is a lot to ask of you, Archie, but I don't suppose you'd do me a favour, would you?'

'For you, sweetheart, anything. Just name it.' But when Archie had waved them goodbye and shut the door, he wasn't so sure he would be able to carry out her request.

Unlike Clara Costello, he wasn't a miracle worker.

Before leaving the next day, and with Ned's help, Clara prepared Mermaid House for the days ahead. Intuition told her that Jonah would suggest that Caspar stay with their father while their sister's funeral was organised. Caspar had been adamant on the phone with Jonah the other night that Damson was to be buried in the churchyard in Deaconsbridge, where their mother was buried. Clara had never thought of it before, but Jonah lived next door not just to his mother's grave but his stepmother's. It was a weird thought.

She changed the sheets on the beds and, working on the assumption that Caspar would be staying, made up the bed in his old room. She cleaned the bathroom, and even did her best with the guest bathroom, which hadn't been used in years – the massive iron bath had more than a dozen rust spots scarring its interior and a dripping tap had left an ugly stain. She put some flowers from the garden on the table in the kitchen, and left a note for

Gabriel saying that she had been to the supermarket and had stocked up on easy-cook meals for them. She also promised him that she would be in touch soon. Lastly, she added a postscript:

This is obviously a time for you and your family to be alone. But I want you to know that I'll be thinking of you often.

All my love,
Clara

She wrote a separate note for Jonah, put it into an envelope, and stuck it down. That was definitely not for Gabriel's eyes.

She locked the door, slipped the key through the letterbox, and turned her back on Mermaid House, wondering whether she would ever see it again. She wanted to say that she would. That she would make it happen. But she knew as well as the next person that life was full of unexpected twists and turns.

Chapter Fifty-Four

The silence in the car lay over the three of them like a shroud. On the back seat, his father slept, and in the front, next to Jonah, Caspar was sitting with his head resting against the window. His eyes were closed but Jonah knew he wasn't asleep.

Never before had Jonah seen such a change in a person. Normally fastidious about his appearance – to the point of obsession – Caspar was unshaven, his hair unkempt, his clothes rumpled, and his face sallow and ravaged through lack of sleep. He was almost unrecognisable. His grief was so tangible it shocked Jonah almost more than the death of their sister.

When they had arrived at Rosewood Manor, yesterday lunchtime, Roland Hall had been waiting for them. Jonah had approved of him instantly, grateful for his quiet, reflective manner, though his father had been less impressed. He had demanded to know what kind of a healing centre had allowed his daughter to become so ill that she had died without proper medical care. Roland had explained that Damson had chosen the care she wanted and that she had been seen regularly by an excellent doctor.

Next, he had taken them to Caspar. He was in Damson's room, sorting through the few belongings she had brought with her to Rosewood Manor. Quietly shutting the door behind him, Roland had left them alone. For what seemed for ever, they had stood in awkward silence, not knowing what to do. Nothing had prepared them for this moment.

Seeing a framed photograph by the side of the bed,

Jonah went over to it. It was of Damson and Caspar when they were teenagers. Dressed in matching velvet flared trousers and cheesecloth shirts, they looked wildly attractive and were undeniably brother and sister: they had the same long straight nose, the challenging flashing eyes and high cheekbones that gave them an air of lofty grandeur.

'Please don't touch it,' Caspar murmured from the other side of the bed, where he stood hunched like an old man sheltering from the rain. In his hands he held a silk scarf, which he was twisting around his fingers. 'Don't touch anything.'

Jonah and Gabriel exchanged glances. 'So what can we do to help?' their father asked gruffly.

Caspar stared at him blankly. 'Nothing. Absolutely nothing. I don't know why you've come. I didn't ask you to.' There was no cruelty to his voice, just painful detachment.

'We're here because we care.'

The blank stare swivelled round to Jonah. 'Well, as you can see, your care has come too late.' There was a trace of blame in his tone.

Gabriel moved slowly across the room, and with his big, rough old hands, he gently removed the scarf from Caspar's whitening fingers. 'I know how you feel, son. Believe me, I do. I lost someone who meant the world to me. But don't make the same mistake that I did. Let people help you.'

Jonah had never admired or loved his father more than he did then. What courage had it taken for him to lay down the past and reach out to Caspar in the way that he had?

Raising his head, Caspar looked his father in the eye, but there was no clue in his face as to how he was going to react. From his back pocket, he slowly pulled out a piece of paper. 'The letter you wrote to her . . . I . . . I . . .' He swallowed. 'I read it to her yesterday morning . . . She said it came just at the right time.'

Gabriel closed his eyes. 'Too late,' he groaned. 'Too

bloody late. I should have done it years ago.' His body sagged. Worried, Jonah shot across the room and, with Caspar's help, manoeuvred him into the nearest chair. Gabriel sobbed openly. 'My poor girl,' he wailed. 'What have I done?'

'What have we all done?' murmured Caspar, the colour gone from his face.

There had been a lot to organise, and with Caspar and Gabriel in no fit state to do it, Jonah had dealt with everything. Damson's body had already been taken to a chapel of rest by a local firm of undertakers, who were delivering it to Deaconsbridge for the funeral later that week. There was endless paperwork and phone calls to get through, but with Roland Hall's help, Jonah got it all done. Roland wanted to attend the funeral, so he offered to drive Caspar's car down to Deaconsbridge and catch the train home afterwards.

'It might be better if we did a swap,' Jonah said, thinking of his brother's reaction to anyone else driving his expensive car. 'Caspar might prefer to have his own car when he gets home. Which means, I'm afraid, you'll have my old wreck to cope with.'

'Whatever you think best.'

Jonah and Roland had stayed up late, talking long into the night. Jonah was glad of the opportunity to talk to someone who seemed to have understood his sister better than anyone. 'Does everyone here get such special treatment?' he had asked, conscious that his question sounded disagreeably loaded.

But Roland took it in his stride. 'Damson was special to me.'

'You loved her?'

'Not in the physical sense, if that's what you mean. I didn't exploit her like so many had before. She needed someone to love her for what she was. Battle scars and all. We were friends. Close spiritual friends.' He looked away, stared into the distance, lost in his own thoughts. Jonah realised that this man, who had taken Damson under his wing and given her unconditional love, which she had had from no one else, was grieving privately for her.

They arrived home to find Mermaid House empty, just as Jonah had known it would be. But there were still some comforting signs of Clara's presence, from the freshly made-up beds to the flowers on the kitchen table and the two letters she had left for them.

Jonah had told his father in the car on the way up to Northumberland that Clara and Ned would be gone when they returned. He had explained the reasons why, and Gabriel had said, 'She once told me that we all scourge ourselves from time to time with a bit of soul-searching. Obviously, she knew what she was talking about. I hope the boy's father behaves decently.'

It was strange being home. Strange because, though it felt familiar and welcoming, it no longer felt like home. Which was an absurd reaction, Clara decided, they hadn't been away for that long.

But it was great to see Louise and the gang again. When she had phoned Louise to ask if she and Ned could stay with her and David, she had been met with, 'Oh, so you're bored with being cooped up in a camper-van, are you? No danger of me being proved right, is there?'

'Rule number one for us travelling folk, we grab the chance of free facilities whenever and however we can.'

'You're nothing but a freeloading parasite,' Louise had laughed.

They had arrived at David and Louise's last night, after a long, tedious journey. Guy and Moira were there too, and they'd stayed up late with several bottles of wine and a Chinese takeaway. Ned had fallen asleep on the sofa and David had carried him upstairs and put him to bed. 'Just like old times,' he said, coming down shortly afterwards, 'except that he's grown and he's heavier. I'll have to get down to the gym and build up my muscles if he's going to keep growing at the same rate.'

451

It was now Thursday morning and Louise had managed to get the day off work, so that she could indulge in a marathon gossiping session with Clara. She had devised a simple but guaranteed way to keep Ned amused. He had been denied access to a television since March, so he was putty in her hands when she switched on David's latest toy, an enormous wide-screen telly. Sitting cross-legged on the floor with a tube of Pringles and a pile of videos, he was hypnotised.

'I don't approve of you brainwashing my son,' said Clara, when they retreated to the kitchen and Louise put a large cafetière of coffee on the table, with two mugs and a jug of milk.

'Now don't come over the perfect Goody-Two-Shoes mother with me,' said Louise. 'Let me have you all to myself, just this once. And I said it last night, and I'll say it again, you look fantastic. Better than I've seen you in years. You're glowing with so much good health I almost hate you. I love the hair too. Makes you look years younger.'

'You should have seen me two weeks ago when I had flu – I looked like death on legs.'

Louise smiled. 'So bring on the lovely Jonah who took such great care of you. Give me a proper run-down on him.'

'I told you everything last night.'

'No, you didn't. That's what you were prepared to tell us as a group. Now that it's just the two of us, I want the important bits you've held back.'

Clara reached for the cafetière, pushed the plunger down, then poured their coffee. 'Honestly, there really isn't much more to tell.'

'But you think you could go the distance with him?'

'I think I could, but I'm not sure that it's worth the trouble of trying. My life is here, and his is there. Why invest valuable time and effort, not to say emotion, in something that has no future?'

Louise added milk to her coffee and stirred it. 'You

don't know that, not for sure. You wouldn't be hedging your bets, by any chance, would you?'

'Meaning?'

'Meaning Mr Todd Mason Angel. Don't forget I've met him. He's knock-out smart and extremely easy on the eye, just your kind of man, I'd say.'

Clara frowned. She straightened the mats on the table, squared them precisely. 'I admit he *was* my kind of man,' she said thoughtfully, 'which is why I fell in love with him in the first place. But I certainly haven't come back here to meet him under the delusion that we'll magically pick up where we left off. I'm not that stupid.'

'But how would you react if he suggested you did do exactly that?'

She was saved from answering the question by the telephone. It was David calling to say that the first part of Clara's plan had been put into place.

Todd had accepted an invitation to meet for a drink after work. Except it wouldn't be a drink with Guy and David as he thought.

Ned didn't bat an eyelid when Clara said she had to go out for a while that evening. He was much too busy to worry about where she was going or what she was doing. He was showing Louise his scrapbook and he was telling her all about Mr Liberty and the amazing house he lived in; about the tower, the secret passageway in the library, and the badgers down in the copse. Clara kissed the top of his head, gave her friend a grateful smile, and slipped away.

Louise had kindly loaned her the use of her BMW, and with the soft top down she drove to the Kingfisher Arms where Todd was expecting to meet Guy and David.

It was a lovely summer's evening, and the car park at the front of the pub was almost full. Though it was mid-week, it seemed that everyone had decided to come out and enjoy the warm weather. David had told her that Todd was driving a hired bronze-coloured Lexus. She saw it straight away and her heart began to pound.

Inside the pub, she scanned the bar, but drew a blank. She ordered a glass of fizzy water and took it out to the garden where she flipped down her sunglasses and surveyed the tables of drinkers. She eliminated them one by one. Then she saw him. He was sideways on to her, dressed in his work clothes – a lightweight suit and pale blue shirt. He had loosened his tie, undone the button on his collar, and there was no denying that he stood out from the crowd. He had that indefinable quality that made it obvious he was from across the Atlantic. Part of it was the confidence in his bearing, the head held high, the neatly cut hair, the firm jaw. He looked well, and just as handsome. Just as she had remembered him. The only thing different about him was the glasses, but they enhanced rather than detracted from his features.

She began the long walk across the garden, shaking so much that she was spilling her drink. She tried to steady her hand, as well as her nerve. She was almost upon him when he turned. For a moment he looked as if he had seen a ghost: his mouth dropped open and he simply stared. Then disbelief propelled him to his feet. 'Clara?'

She raised her sunglasses, as though it might convince him it really was her, that she was no ghost. 'Hello, Todd. Mind if I join you?'

There was so much they had to say but neither knew where to start, other than with a polite exchange.

'I like your hair. It suits you.'

'Thank you. The same goes for you and the glasses.'

'I hear you've been away, travelling.'

'Yes. Life on the open road. How are you getting on with the French?'

'Fine. We should be done by next week. The shares will really hit . . . Oh, hell, Clara, this is no good. Talk to me properly. Tell me how you really are. Tell me about Ned . . . about our son.'

Her mouth clamped itself shut. She repeated his words inside her head.

Our son.

Our son.

Suddenly she felt as if all the strength had been ripped out of her. If she hadn't been sitting down, she would have fallen to the ground. All this time Ned had been *her* son. Now, just like that, he was to be shared.

To her horror, she began to cry, but didn't know why. She felt Todd's arms around her and she leaned into him, remembering how good he had always felt. How good it had been between them.

Through blinding tears, she felt him pulling her up, then leading her away. He took her down towards the river, to the shade and privacy of the willow trees that arched their graceful branches over the water.

'I'm sorry.' She gulped and sniffed. 'I had no idea I was going to react like that. It's just—'

He held her tightly. 'How do you think I feel? When I found out about Ned I nearly went crazy. I've been out of my mind, not knowing what I should do. I so badly wanted to turn to your friends, but it was clear they didn't know about us. Oh, Clara, why didn't you tell me?'

She straightened up, pulled away from him. 'You know the answer to that. I didn't want to ruin everything for you. I knew how much your wife and children meant to you, and the day I discovered I was pregnant, you came into my office and told me you and Gayle were getting back together.'

'Oh, my God, you knew then.' He took his glasses off and passed his hand over his eyes. 'If only I'd known.'

'It wouldn't have worked, Todd. Ned and I would have got in the way of what you really wanted. What you already had . . . Gayle and your girls.'

She could tell from the look in his eyes and his silence that she had been right. She had been right all along. Vindicated, at last. She turned away from him, let her gaze fall on a pair of mallard ducks that were kicking up a row further along the river. Composed now, she said,

'Let's go back. I don't know about you, but I'm in need of a real burn-the-back-off-your-throat drink.'

Their table was still free, and after Todd had fetched two glasses of Jack Daniel's, she said, 'It's important that you understand I expect nothing from you. I made the decision to have Ned and he's my responsibility. I'm not about to make any demands of you.'

'Now hold on a minute, Clara. I hear what you're saying, but the situation has changed. I can no more turn my back on Ned than I could disown my children back home. Don't I have a say in anything to do with him?'

Clara felt a knot of panic tighten in her stomach. If Todd wanted to feature in his son's life, she would have to part with him. Todd would want to have him over in the States for prolonged stays. And the more that happened, the more likely it was that Ned would grow away from her. Tears threatened again, but she fought them back and took a gulp of her drink. She was being irrational, she told herself. She looked at Todd warily. 'What are you proposing to do?' she asked. 'Tell your wife?'

He lowered his gaze and played with his glass, turning it round slowly. She knew she'd hit him below the belt, that she had deliberately tried to score a point off him. She felt cheap and unworthy. 'I'm sorry,' she said, 'that was uncalled-for.'

He let out his breath. 'It's a perfectly valid question, though, and one for which I don't have a ready answer. It's what I've thought of ever since I guessed who the boy with the neat smile was in the photographs your friends showed me.'

On firmer ground now, she relaxed a little and said, 'It's your smile.'

He shook his head. 'That's great. Just wonderful. My daughters look like Gayle, but the child I've never seen takes after me.'

'My mother describes his smile as a gift from the angels.'

'Oh, my. And who says we Yanks don't get irony?'

456

They sipped their drinks. 'You haven't married, then?'

'No, Todd. Probably something to do with not having the time or energy to bag myself a good 'un.'

'But you've managed okay on your own? I mean, financially.'

She bristled. 'Financially I've been fine. Making money hand over fist.'

'I'm sorry. That was rude and patronising of me. But it can't have been too easy bringing up a child on your own.'

'Everyone says that to me, but it's been okay. Mum and Dad have been great. My friends too.'

As if sensing he was treading on thin ice, and thinking a change of subject would be a good idea, he said, 'So what made you trade in Phoenix for a camper? I would never have had you down as doing something as off the chart as that.'

People change, she wanted to say, feeling another frisson of antagonism. 'It was Ned,' she said. 'I wanted to spend more time with him before he starts school in September. It was now or never.'

'So what kind of school have you got in mind for him?'

Again, she felt herself tense with possessive defensiveness. 'A dreadful school, of course.'

He looked at her, puzzled. 'What is it, Clara? I'm getting the feeling I'm saying all the wrong things.'

She drained her glass. 'Forget it. It's me. I can't handle this. I thought I could. But the truth is, I'm not sure I want to share Ned with you. I've done everything for him, made all the decisions, wiped away all the tears, read all the books, sat up all the nights—'

He laid a firm hand on her arm and stopped her. 'You did all that, and much more, because you chose to do it, Clara. Don't sit there throwing hurtful accusations at me. While you were doing all those things, I never even knew Ned existed. So don't try to make me feel guilty.'

She pushed his hand away. 'And if you had known of his existence, what would you have done?' She watched him collect his thoughts before making his measured reply.

'You're angry with me, I can see that. And I can't blame you. But please, don't think I don't care about Ned now. I do. I have no idea how to resolve things, but I promise you, I'll do my best by him. Which doesn't mean I'm about to wade in like an FBI agent and take him from you. You're his mother, and as we all know, it's mothers who make the important decisions when it comes to children. Dads are just hangers-on who need to know their place.' He gave a small smile and said, 'You can put down your weapons now.'

She relented and smiled too. 'So, when do you want to meet your son?'

Chapter Fifty-Five

The back door slammed so violently that the windows rattled. Caspar was leaving the house to go for another of his long walks. Since they had arrived back from Northumberland, he had done a lot of walking, always alone and always for hours at a time. It was as if he was trying to walk his grief out of his system. Gabriel knew from bitter experience that it wouldn't work.

They had buried Damson yesterday. It had been an exhausting, emotionally draining day. An unlikely mixture of people had turned up for the funeral.

Jonah and Roland had gone through Damson's address book and had contacted as many people as they could, working on the theory that because Damson was so pragmatic, if she had entered a name in the book, it was because she liked that person: ex-husbands' and boyfriends' names were conspicuously absent.

Not knowing how Caspar was going to survive the day, Gabriel had concentrated on keeping people away from his son: their looks and words of sympathy, no matter how well meant, were not what he needed. Once the service was over, they had walked next door to Jonah's house where he had laid on a modest buffet of sandwiches and drinks. While Jonah and Roland had poured drinks and chatted politely with the guests, Gabriel had grabbed a plate of sandwiches and taken Caspar back to the churchyard. 'Your brother has it all in hand,' he'd said. 'Let's have some time on our own.' They had sat on a wooden bench in the warm sun, just yards away from Damson's grave. The gravediggers had finished their work and the hole was now filled in, decorated with flowers. To the right of this was her mother's grave, and further along, her step-mother's. Gabriel had deliberately avoided coming here since Val's funeral and it surprised him to see how well tended the plots were. There was only one person who could have been caring for them so diligently. And how typical of Jonah that was. There was never any song and dance about him. He never went out of his way to look for thanks and glory. It was a trait that was wholly reminiscent of his mother.

'Is this supposed to help?' asked Caspar, his gaze on his sister's grave.

Putting the plate of sandwiches on the bench between them, Gabriel produced a dented silver hip flask from his suit-jacket pocket. He passed it to Caspar. 'Can it make it any worse?'

Loosening his tie, Caspar took a swig of the brandy, then another. He wiped the back of his hand across his mouth. 'No. You're right. Wherever I am, I'll always feel the awful loss of her.'

'Better to accept the truth of that than spend the rest of your life running from it.'

'Is that what you did with Mum?'

'I never stopped running. It's why I buggered up things with you three children so spectacularly. I turned away from you, left you to cope with something you weren't able to deal with. It's only now that I've come to realise the harm I caused through my selfishness. Heartbreak rots our integrity, Caspar, remember that. And I'm telling you this because I'm being selfish once again. I need you to know why I behaved as I did.' He cleared his throat. 'My biggest regret is that I didn't have a chance to apologise to Damson. Are you going to drink that flask dry?'

Caspar passed it back to him. 'I think Damson was ahead of you, had worked it out for herself.'

'She had?'

'She was always the smarter one of the two of us. More astute than anyone gave her credit for. One of the last things she said to me was that we're survivors, not victims.'

Gabriel pondered on this. 'From what Jonah's told me, Roland Hall played a crucial part in her life towards the end.'

'Are you saying I didn't?'

At once Gabriel felt Caspar's body turn rigid on the seat next to him. 'No, I'm not,' he said emphatically, keen to avoid upsetting his son. There had been enough explosive outbursts from Caspar lately, when he had ranted and raved and thrown things, then left the house to tramp across the moors, returning hours later exhausted, his rage spent. It was just what Gabriel had done when Anastasia had died. 'I'm saying you, me, Jonah, we weren't the people she needed at that time.'

Caspar's chin dropped. 'So what's brought on all this understanding, Dad? Bit of a change of tune, isn't it?'

Gabriel ignored the dismissive tone, and after a swig of brandy, he said, 'I came very close to killing myself last month.' He waited for the words to sink in, then saw the disbelief in his son's face.

'You? But why? How?'

'Yes, me – of all people. But you see, I suddenly understood how much I hated being alone and the reasons why I was alone. Having reached that conclusion, it seemed the perfect moment to take my cue to exit stage left. As to the how, well – picture the scene if you will – I went down to the copse with a shotgun, all ready to blast my stupid head off.'

Caspar looked suitably horror-stricken. 'What happened?'

'You mean, what went wrong? I didn't have it in me when push came to shove. Oh, I meant to do it, I really did. Maybe if I'd taken some Dutch courage with me I would have done it. But there I was, bawling my eyes out, the gun shoved up under my chin, and an angel of mercy appeared from nowhere.' He watched Caspar's expression change to one of time-to-humour-the-old-boy. 'She was an angel of sorts,' he went on, 'although she doesn't have wings.' He smiled. 'It was Miss Costello.'

Caspar looked confused. 'But I thought she'd left weeks ago.'

'She did, but she came back that day. Was it fate, or just good timing?' He shrugged. 'Who knows? Sandwich?'

'No.'

'You need to eat, Caspar.'

'I will. Just not today.'

The sound of knocking jolted Gabriel out of his reverie. He was expecting Jonah – it was the weekend – but Jonah never knocked twice. He knocked once then let himself in.

He opened the back door and was momentarily nonplussed. It was Clara Costello's junk-dealer friend, Archie Merryman.

They stared at one another warily.

'I was sorry to hear about your daughter—'

'I was sorry to hear about your mother—' they said simultaneously, and in a perfect mirror image of each other, they looked down at their feet, not knowing what to say next. Crippled with embarrassment, they were like a pair of schoolboys who had been forced to apologise for fighting in the playground.

Clutching a carrier bag, Archie hoped that he could live up to Clara's expectations of him. She had asked him to visit the Commandant with a view to keeping an eye on the old boy. 'He's going to need someone to cheer him up in the weeks ahead,' she had said, 'and I can't think of anyone better suited to the task.' Personally, Archie thought he was the last person on earth fit for such a task. But still, she had thought him capable of it, so here he was.

'I've brought you this,' he said, dipping his hand into the bag and pulling out a bottle of whisky. 'Just by way of saying I reckon I know what you're going through.'

Gabriel stared at the bottle. He thought of the letter

Clara had written for him on his return from Northumberland, in which she had asked him, when he felt able to, to keep an eye on Archie Merryman in her absence. 'I know you like to think of yourself as an unsociable crosspatch,' she had written, 'but underneath it all, I know you're the sweetest man alive who won't think twice about doing this one small thing for me.'

Just for the sheer hell of it, he'd show her what he was made of.

He took the offered bottle and said, 'Mr Merryman, it's a little early, but how do you feel about a pre-lunch snifter?'

'Please, it's Archie, and thank you, a drink would slip down a treat. Especially after the week I've had. Though yours can't have been much better.'

'You're not wrong there. Not wrong at all.'

'For once it looks as if we'll get through an entire barbecue without a drop of rain.'

Clara passed Guy a glass of wine and agreed with him absently.

'Oh, come on, Clara,' he said, 'lose the long face. It'll be okay. Anyone would think Ned was being put through some kind of test.'

Louise came over from where she and Moira had been setting the table. 'You're not still worrying, are you?' she said to Clara.

'Of course I am! Wouldn't you be, if your child was meeting his father for the first time?' Though Ned was at the bottom of the garden playing football with David and well out of earshot, Clara kept her voice low.

'The important thing is that Ned doesn't have a clue what's going on,' Guy said, equally circumspect. 'As far as he's concerned, Todd is just another of his mother's many friends.'

Clara knew that what Guy was saying was right. But, oh, she just wished this day could be over. It had seemed so reasonable when Louise and David had offered to invite Todd to a lunchtime barbecue so that he could meet Ned in a relaxed setting. But now she was regretting the whole idea. What if Todd suddenly felt the need to blurt out to Ned who he was? Common sense told her that Todd would never do that: he was one of the most rational people she knew.

They had discussed this important day on the phone several times and had even met up again for a drink last night. He was as concerned as she was that Ned was not put through any emotional upset. It helped enormously that he was the same understanding Todd with whom she had fallen in love, and while it seemed a paradox, she frequently found herself thanking her lucky stars that she had had an affair with such a considerate man.

Determined to safeguard Ned, Clara had laid down the ground rules straight away. She had told Todd that until he had decided whether he was going to tell his wife about Ned and therefore offer a real, open commitment, he could not reveal who he was. It was harsh, but it was Ned's feelings that mattered, not hers, not Todd's.

Yet she wasn't without sympathy for Todd. She knew he was up against the worst dilemma he would probably ever have to face. But the cool, efficient and detached woman within her reasoned that it was *his* problem. She had cleared her conscience by telling him about Ned; what happened next was down to him. She could do nothing to help him.

She was a hard-headed realist, if nothing else.

She had said this to Jonah on the phone late last night – she had phoned him several times, always when Louise and David had gone to bed and she could be sure of talking to him without Louise listening in. 'Nothing wrong in being hard-headed or a realist,' he'd said.

'Did I say there was?'

'No, but something in your tone suggested you were defending yourself.'

'Goodness, you're being mighty forward all of a sudden.'

464

He'd laughed. 'Only because I know I'm out of slapping range.'

After he'd brought her up to date with how his brother and father were getting on, he'd said, 'It's a pity you're not here, it's a beautiful night.' He hadn't said he was missing her, but the implication was there.

'Are you in the garden?'

'On the terrace with a glass of wine and a bag of pistachio nuts.'

'Sounds good. Describe the view for me.'

'Mm . . . it's dark and starry.'

'Come on, you can do better than that.'

'Did I mention the moon?'

'No.'

'It's very white and looks like a clipped toenail.'

'Stop! You're spoiling it for me. Where's your romantic, chivalrous soul, Jonah Liberty?'

'It's cowering under the table too scared to show itself.'

'Then tell it to pull itself together.'

'I've tried but it's no good. It said, "What's the point? Who's here for me to sweet-talk?"'

It had been good talking to him, and not just because he took her mind off Todd.

Todd arrived exactly on time, just as Clara had known he would. One look at his face as he stepped out of his car and she knew he was as nervous as she was. It made her feel better, took away some of her edginess.

Which couldn't be said of her friends.

They tried too hard to show that they were relaxed with the situation. Louise and Moira laughed too loudly at Todd's joke about the weather, and Guy took the bottles of Californian wine he'd brought with such expansive gratitude that anyone would have thought he had been presented with the Holy Grail.

And while they tried to hide their awkwardness, a piercing squeal came up from the bottom of the garden. Seconds later, Ned came running towards them, his dark

465

hair shiny in the bright sunlight, bouncing with each step he took. His face was a huge grin of delight. 'Mummy, Mummy, I beat Uncle David. Ten goals to five!' Breathless, he threw himself at her legs and raised his arms for her to scoop him up as she usually did. But on this occasion, she didn't. 'Ned,' she said, 'this is an old friend of mine. He lives in America and his name is Todd. Have you got enough puff to say hello to him?'

Ned looked up at him and smiled confidently. 'Hello, Mr Todd. Do you like playing football?'

It was such an emotionally charged moment that everyone suddenly found something to do – the barbecue coals needed lighting, the salads had to be dressed, and a new bottle of wine opened. Clara watched Todd's face as he hunkered down to be on eye level with Ned. 'Hi,' he said, 'I'm more of a baseball fan, but I'll give football a shot if you'll teach me.'

Ned grinned. 'I'm very good. Jonah taught me when Mummy was ill in bed. He showed me how to tackle. Do you want to see?'

Todd glanced up at Clara and her heart twisted as she saw both sadness and joy in his face. 'Would you mind?' he asked.

She smiled. 'Not at all.'

They were three very important words, she thought later that evening when Todd had left for his hotel, and she was kissing Ned goodnight.

'Todd was nice,' Ned said, snuggling down beneath the duvet and holding Mermy up for her to kiss as well. 'I like the way he talks. Will he come and see us again?'

'I don't know. He's very busy at the moment and then he has to go home to America.'

She pushed the hair out of his eyes, and was about to get up from the bed when he said, 'Mummy?'

'Yes?'

He gave her one of his melting looks. 'What do you think Mr Liberty is doing right now?'

'Probably wondering what you're doing right now.'

He seemed pleased by this thought. 'Do you think so?'

'Absolutely. You're a hard boy to forget, Ned.'

'Can we go back to Mermaid House to see him?'

She had known it would only be a matter of time before he asked her this question.

'Don't you like being here?'

He hesitated, as though not wanting to cause offence. 'Mm . . . it is nice, but I miss Mr Liberty.'

'Well, that's not a bad thing. It means you care about people, and that's good.'

'It doesn't feel good. It feels . . . horrible.' His lower lip wobbled.

'Oh, Ned.' She lifted him out of bed and sat him on her lap. It wasn't often he cried, but when he did, Clara knew it was with good reason. She cuddled his warm body against hers, but the tears had taken hold of him and there seemed no way to comfort him. Hearing the noise, Louise popped her head round the door.

'What's wrong?' she asked, concerned.

'A surfeit of good times, I think.'

Eventually Clara settled him by promising that they would ring Mr Liberty tomorrow morning so that Ned could speak to him. When she joined her friends downstairs, she sensed they had something to say to her: they had formed themselves into what looked suspiciously like a deputation.

Guy patted the seat next to him on the sofa. 'Clarabelle, for once in your life you're going to take the advice of your friends.'

'And please don't take this the wrong way,' Louise said, 'but quite frankly you've outstayed your welcome.'

'Yes,' agreed David, handing round cups of coffee. 'So you can pack up your things and go. We've had enough.'

'More than enough,' said Guy. 'If I have to hear one more word about Ned's superhuman friend, Mr Gabriel Liberty, I think I'll go mad.'

'And as for the wonderful Jonah Liberty,' said Moira, 'well, please, is any man that perfect?'

'Oh yes,' groaned Louise. 'If I have to eavesdrop on another of your midnight phone calls, I'll die of envy.'

Clara stared at them confounded. 'What's going on? What are you up to?'

'Get real, sister,' laughed Guy. 'You and Ned have done nothing but go on about Deaconsbridge. If we've heard it once, what a fantastic time you had, we've heard it till we're ready to go up there and see for ourselves the Utopia you've discovered.'

'But—'

'No buts,' interrupted Louise, with a warning finger. 'If you hadn't come back here to see Todd, you'd still be up there in the Peak District, wouldn't you?'

Clara nodded. 'Possibly.'

'No possibly about it! Now, what's stopping you from taking off tomorrow and seeing how the land lies?'

'But why would I want to do that?'

Nobody answered her. They just stared at her hard. She knew she was being pushed into a corner, and that her friends wouldn't let the matter drop until they were satisfied. She decided to humour them.

'Look, the truth is, it has crossed my mind to do just as you're suggesting, but—'

'We told you, no buts!'

'But, Louise, I'm worried if Ned and I do go back we might not want to leave.'

'I'm sorry, call me a dumb old bloke,' said David, 'but what's the danger in that? You've found somewhere you like, where you've made friends, and where there's even the chance of you getting off with a real live man. Explain the problem.'

'The problem is you lot! What would I do without you all?'

'Oh, so we're just here to be used, are we?'

'Guy, don't you dare try twisting my words. I meant, how would I survive without your friendship permanently on hand?'

Moira shook her head. 'Poor excuse. We're not having that one, are we?'

'Certainly not,' agreed Louise. 'You left us behind in March without so much as a second thought. What's different now?'

'Are you trying to get rid of me?'

'*Yes!*' they all shouted together.

'But this *is* different,' she said, trying not to get carried away with their enthusiasm. 'If Ned and I go back, and we find that we want to stay, what then?'

David sighed as if she was being particularly dense. 'You'll get a job, get Ned into school and find yourself somewhere to live.'

'And if it doesn't work?'

'You come back here,' Guy said. 'But what would be worse, doing that, or knowing you were too much of a coward to try it?'

'You sneaky dog, Guy Morrell. Nobody gets away with accusing me of cowardice.' Smiling, she thumped him with a cushion. 'I'm beginning to think that I *would* be better off living miles away from you lot.'

Louise grinned. 'I think we're getting somewhere. We're wearing her down.'

'Oh, you did that a long time ago. But be serious for a minute. Do you really think I should go back for the rest of the summer and see how it pans out?'

'All you have to do is ask yourself, what have you got to lose?'

Louise's question stayed with Clara as she fell asleep that night. The only answer she could come up with was that she had a resounding nothing to lose – but maybe everything to gain.

With her fondness for having everything organised, and every conceivable contingency catered for, Clara spent the following week planning. At no time did she let on to Ned what she was doing.

There was one important phone call she had to make,

to her parents. 'I just wanted to know how you would feel if Ned and I weren't here when you came back from Australia,' she said to her mother.

Her mother went very quiet and said, 'Whatever decision you make, you know we'll go along with it. We always have and there's no reason why we would change now.'

'You're the best, Mum.'

'I know.'

'Wonderfully modest too.'

'You would know, dear – like mother like daughter. Now, explain what you're up to, but quickly, this call must be costing you a small fortune.'

After Clara had outlined her plans, her mother wished her luck and asked if Ned was around for her to speak to.

'I'll go and get him, but don't mention anything I've just told you. I want it to be a surprise for him.'

The night before she planned to drive north with Ned, she met up with Todd one last time. His work was almost finished at Phoenix and he was due to fly home in two days.

They sat in the garden of the Kingfisher Arms once more, but Clara didn't press him for details about the future. She had no right to do that.

'I want to thank you for being so understanding,' he said, 'and for letting me see Ned. A lot of women wouldn't have acted as generously as you have. I'm more grateful than I can say.'

'But I have so much more to be grateful for,' she said. 'I have Ned. He means the world to me.'

'I know he does. I can also see how much you mean to him. He's a wonderful boy, you've done a fine job of raising him. I'm just envious and shamefaced I haven't been there for you both when I should have been.'

There was an awkward moment when he brought up the question of financial support. 'I'd feel a whole lot better if you'd take this, Clara.' He handed her a cheque.

Without looking at it, but knowing instinctively that he would have been generous, she passed it back to him.

'And I'd feel a whole lot worse taking it. When you know exactly what you want to do about Ned, then we'll discuss money. Not before.'

'Fair enough,' he said. Then, looking faintly embarrassed, he added, 'By the way, what . . . what did you put on the birth certificate?'

She smiled and covered his hand with hers. 'What do you think? Your name, of course.'

He swallowed. 'You always did play it dead straight, Clara. Thank you for doing that.'

They exchanged addresses and telephone numbers, and after they'd drunk a toast to Ned's future, Todd took her by surprise.

'So who's this Jonah I kept hearing about from Ned when he was trying to teach me to kick a ball?'

Annoyingly, she felt the colour rise to her face. 'A friend.'

'A special friend?'

'Maybe.'

'Ned seems quite taken with him. What's he like?'

Driving back to Louise and David's, Clara felt sorry for Todd. How complicated his life had suddenly become. He had arrived in England a happily married man with, presumably, few cares in the world, and he was returning home with the knowledge that he had a son. Not only that, he had an unexpected emotion to deal with. One that Clara certainly hadn't anticipated.

Jealousy.

In his brief cross-examination of her about Jonah, he had clearly been troubled by the idea of another man forming a relationship with Ned.

Funny that Guy and David hadn't undergone the same scrutiny.

Chapter Fifty-Six

For the last day or so, the weather had alternated between blustery showers and intermittent sunshine, but now it had settled again and the sky was blue save for clouds of fluffy whiteness that bubbled up then drifted away on the light wind that blew in from the west.

Standing in front of the mirror, Gabriel straightened his tie and admired his new blazer. He pushed his shoulders back, turned to the right, then to the left, and decided it wasn't a bad fit. He was glad now that he had asked Caspar to take him shopping for some new clothes, and even more so that he had taken his son's advice and chosen the single-breasted rather than the double. Next he turned his attention to his hair. Again, Caspar had intervened and pushed him to have it cut dramatically shorter than he wanted. Grudgingly Gabriel admitted that it was a great improvement. It made him look younger, distinguished – with a dash of jauntiness, he liked to think. He tilted his chin up, raised an eyebrow like Roger Moore did in all those old Bond movies and mentally declared himself a handsome devil.

Chuckling, he turned his back on the mirror and left his room. Enough of the preening. Time was of the essence. He still had lots to do. Ned and Clara would soon be here. He paused on the landing outside Val's old room, then went in. With Archie's help, he had had it spruced up for Clara. When he had mentioned to Archie that he wanted to have it redecorated, he'd said, 'I know just the chaps you need.' Turned out that Shirley from the Mermaid café had a son who, with a friend, had started up his own painting and decorating business and was looking for work. 'You'd better be cheap,' he'd said to them when they arrived on their motorbikes to give him an estimate. 'Just because I live in a large house, don't imagine my wallet is a bottomless pit.'

The following day they'd shown up in a wreck of a van with a ladder strapped to the roof. Dressed in overalls, they plugged in a large radio that belted out something that could never be described as music and got down to work, stripping off the old flowery wallpaper that had been there for more than twenty years and replacing it with a cheerful yellow paper that brightened the room. Shirley's son, Robbie, had explained to him that there was a range of bed linen to match the paper and border they'd used, so he'd instructed them to get that too. 'Might as well go the whole hog,' he'd said, handing over more money. They had transformed Jonah's old room too, giving it a fresh new look that they swore blind would appeal to a small boy. They had worked quickly and tidily, and Gabriel was so pleased with the results that he thought he might get them to have a go at some of the other rooms. His own, perhaps.

Shirley had been a great help too. Funny, that – he'd only ever talked to her in the café when he was ordering his lunch, but she had been ready to lend a hand when he had mentioned the party he wanted to give. 'You'll be needing food, then,' she'd said. 'Want any help with that?'

'I don't want anything fancy.'

'You mean you don't want anything expensive, you old skinflint.'

She and Archie were somewhere downstairs. It was only a small party he was throwing, but he didn't know how he would have organised everything if they hadn't offered to help. He supposed Archie still needed to be busy. He'd had a tough old time of it recently, what with his wife leaving him and his mother dying, and Gabriel was looking forward to telling Clara that he'd more than risen to her challenge of keeping an eye on him. Under the guise of clearing out yet more junk from the house, he'd seen quite a lot of Archie, had found him an agreeable man, and he was pleased, if not a little amused, that he and Shirley were getting on so well. He knew, from first-hand experience, that it wasn't good to be on one's own too much. Having people around made things bearable.

And that was what he had wished for, that day at the Mermaid Cavern. He had tossed his coin into the pool and wished that he would have the pleasure of seeing Ned and his mother again. Because when they were around, life was infinitely better.

Downstairs, he found the kitchen empty. An appetising smell was coming from the oven, but apart from that, there was no sign of any activity. Like Clara, Shirley was a tidy worker and she put everything away after she had finished with it. She had been coming to Mermaid House for just over a week now to keep the place in order, and the arrangement was working well. She still had her part-time job at the café in town, but as she had said to him after Archie had come up with the idea, 'We'll give each other a trial run for a month. And this is what I'll do for you. For six pounds an hour, I'll keep your home sweet if you promise to keep your temper sweet. How does that sound?'

'It sounds to me as if we ought to spit and shake on it before either of us changes our mind.'

So far she had been as good as her word. The rooms that mattered were as neat as a pin. He had no complaints at all.

The only gripe he had was that Dr Singh wasn't around to see how smoothly he now had his life ticking over. He'd heard through Shirley that he had moved up to Blackburn. Or was it Bury? Anyway, wherever he had beggared off to, doubtless he was poking his nose into some other poor devil's affairs. Though, of course, despite his annoying interference, Gabriel was aware that if Dr Singh hadn't been such a nuisance, he might never have formed the friendship he now had with Ned and Clara. Or be reconciled with Jonah and Caspar. He still had a way to go with Caspar: his elder son had yet to recover from the shock of Damson's death. He was currently dividing his time between Manchester and Mermaid House, and though it was hard work having Caspar around, Gabriel didn't want him to be on his own. The more time they spent together, the more alike Gabriel realised they were. Neither suffered fools gladly, both were as stubborn as hell and they each possessed a temper that could scorch asbestos. And while Caspar's dandified arrogance and assumption that the world revolved around him would always infuriate him, Gabriel could, none the less, appreciate and admire his sharpness of mind. If only he would apply it to something more constructive than he had until now.

In the meantime, Gabriel took it as an encouraging sign that Caspar had agreed to join the party today. He had expected his son to turn down the invitation, denouncing it as in poor taste. Instead, he had said he would try to put in a brief appearance.

Jonah was the only person who didn't know what was going on. He didn't even know that Clara would be here this afternoon – he had been deliberately misled into believing that she was arriving tomorrow. Revelling in all the skulduggery, Gabriel had phoned Jonah and told him to get here when school was finished because there was something important they needed to discuss. Which was partly true, there *were* things he needed to say this afternoon. Things he should have said and done a long time ago.

It was reading Val's diaries that had clinched it for him. Jonah had given the notebooks to him last week, saying Clara had found them when she had been sorting out Val's room. Seeing the anxiety in Jonah's face, Gabriel had guessed that he wouldn't be the first person to see the journals. They had made for difficult reading, and it saddened him to know that Val had felt such an outsider at Mermaid House. What moved him most, though, was her determination to try to understand a family that had, in her words, 'had its heart ripped out of it'. More graphically, she had written, 'I've been brought in as a plaster for this family, but what they really need is a tourniquet to staunch the flow of their misery. I doubt they'll ever know peace of mind. Because, perversely, they don't seem to want it.'

After he had finished arranging the flowers on Damson's grave, Caspar straightened up. He flicked at a hover-fly that had landed on his sleeve and then stood still, his head bowed, his eyes closed. Anyone seeing him would have thought he was praying, but he wasn't. He was remembering Damson as a young girl. Vital and beautiful. Sharp and funny. Wilful and passionate. And dangerous to be with at times. 'I'm just like my namesake,' she would say to anyone meeting her for the first time, and commenting on the uniqueness of her Christian name. 'I have a dark and bitter-sweet soul.'

That darkness of the soul of which she had spoken frequently as a teenager had frightened him. She talked endlessly about death, and what it might feel like when you knew the end was near. Around the time of their twentieth birthday, she had taken to disappearing for weeks at a time. He hadn't liked her doing that, had hated not knowing where she was, who she was with, or what she was up to. Selfishly, he had felt excluded. But when she surfaced again, she was the same old Damson, ready to party and stir up some fun. In view of what Hall had told him at Rosewood Manor, it was possible that these absences had been connected with the abortions.

He opened his eyes and sighed. How was it possible to be so close to someone, and yet so far from them?

Checking his watch, he saw that he would have to leave soon. He wasn't in the mood to be sociable, but he had made his sister a promise, and he would do his damnedest to keep it. He had let her down when she was alive, he would not do the same now she was dead. So a party it was.

476

He knew exactly why his father had chosen today to throw a party, and he supposed it was about time, but it was a woefully sentimental and symbolic gesture. And what a lot of fuss he was making about it. New clothes. A hair-cut. Not to mention the bedrooms that had been tarted up for the benefit of the shrewish Clara Costello – the angel in the copse – and her son, who were coming to stay for the rest of the summer. Bizarrely, it seemed that his brother had fallen for the woman's sharp-tongued charms, and stranger still, their father was keen to play the part of Cupid and encourage the blossoming romance.

'Oh, Damson,' he murmured softly, 'I wish you were here with me to witness this madness.'

He turned and walked away, back down the gravel path and out on to the road where his car was parked in front of Jonah's house.

He was now the not-so-proud owner of a second-hand Rover. The Maserati had been sold, and his beautiful loft apartment was on the market. The bank, the creditors, the taxman, they were all feasting greedily on his remains, but he didn't give a monkey's. It was gone. Another chapter in his life dealt with.

Bruised and battered he might be, deserted by his so-called friends and treated as a social leper, but he was far from being down and out. Oh, not by a long chalk. It would take more rope than that to hang Caspar Liberty.

Ironically his father, after stubbornly refusing to help him, had changed his mind the other day and offered to bail him out when he discovered the mess he was in, but Caspar had rejected the offer. Pride had made him sensitive to pity. Besides, Damson had left him her pretty little house in Bath with a sizeable amount of money, which she had made from shrewd investments from her two divorce settlements. He planned to move down there and start afresh. A new beginning was what he needed. And, thanks to his sister, he had been given the opportunity to do just that.

Damson's will had been clear on two points in

particular, that (a) she had been of sound mind when she had written it, and (b) Caspar was to be the main beneficiary of her estate and that he was to agree to her instructions that Rosewood Manor was to receive a modest annuity from a trust fund she had set up.

He had no problem with this. He might not like Hall and all he stood for, but he would always respect Damson's wishes.

Darling Damson. How dull his world was going to be without her.

Ned was so excited, he was in danger of bouncing out of his seat. If he hadn't been strapped in, he very nearly would have when Clara swerved to avoid a large pothole. They juddered on, and suddenly Mermaid House appeared over the brow of the hill. It was the most welcoming sight, made her heart beat just a little faster. For the coming months it was to be their new home.

Before they had set off first thing that morning, Louise had threatened to come up in the next week so that she could see Mermaid House for herself.

'You're all talk, Louise,' Clara had said, giving her a huge hug goodbye. 'You've never been further north than the Cotswolds.'

'Yes, but I'm prepared to make an exception in this case.'

Guy had moved in for a final hug and produced an envelope from his jacket pocket. 'For you, Clarabelle.'

'What is it?'

He'd smiled. 'A bet's a bet. Open it and see.'

She'd laughed when she'd seen the cheque for two hundred pounds. She'd forgotten all about the bet he'd made with her that she would be crawling home within a month and applying for her old job.

Saying goodbye to her friends this time round had been tough, because in her heart she knew she wanted to give Deaconsbridge her best shot: she wanted to stay there and really make it work. Other than the brief sojourn in the

States and her time at college, she had never lived away from where she had grown up, she hadn't felt the need to break away.

But now she did. And tied into this was the realisation that she wanted to give herself the chance to discover what else she was capable of doing. The Clara Costello she knew was – and to paraphrase her friends – smart, unflappable, hard-working and supremely resourceful. Less flattering, and to paraphrase her brother, she was a regular bossy boots. 'Give it time and you'll turn into a formidable old battle-axe,' he'd said to her not so long ago.

Maybe she would, maybe she wouldn't. But unless she allowed herself this chance to find out what other talents she had, she would always regret it. She had never liked the expression 'down-shifter', but in essence that was probably what she was opting for. A simple life that would enable her to spend more time with Ned had to be more enriching than the hectic one she had tried before.

And if it didn't work out? Who was to judge and condemn the path she had taken? And was there really such a thing as a wrong path? Critics were ten a penny. They were people too scared to try it for themselves. Too scared to break with convention and enjoy life to the full.

But she wasn't without a back-up plan. Gabriel Liberty's part in all of this was crucial. In letting her and Ned stay at Mermaid House for the rest of the summer, he was giving her the luxury of time and space to reflect on her next move. For now, she had only vague glimpses of the future. She saw herself living here, having traded in her overpriced executive house for something old with character, and odds on, in need of some work. If she let her imagination break free, she pictured herself running a bed-and-breakfast. Okay, she might be deluding herself that she could scrape a living from it, but it was an idea that refused to budge, despite common sense waving a threatening stick at it. It would take a lot of thought before she committed herself to it, and she might even come up with something else, but the big plus was that she saw herself being happy. Ned, too.

And she would be the biggest liar that had ever walked the planet if she didn't admit to wanting Jonah to be a part of that happiness. Just to see if he fitted into her life. And if she and Ned could fit into his.

She pulled into the courtyard, and before she had yanked on the handbrake, Ned was out of his seat. She watched him hurtle across the cobbles and pound on the door with his small fists.

When Clara caught up with him, it was all noise and laughter in the kitchen. Archie was there, and so was Shirley. Wearing a PVC apron over a tight-fitting black dress, she was sliding a tray of sausage rolls out of the oven, her face flushed from the blast of heat. With Ned held aloft, Gabriel came towards her. He stooped to kiss her cheek. 'Welcome back. You're late.'

'Well, well, well. And who might this handsomely rakish stranger be with the smart hair-cut and snazzy blazer? Where's the scruffy Mr Liberty I know and love?'

'But Mummy, it is Mr Liberty! Look, it's him!'

She smiled. 'I know, Ned. I'm only teasing.'

'Ah, I see the first of the honoured guests have arrived.'

They all turned. It was Caspar. Brandishing a bottle of champagne, he said, 'A contribution towards the merriment.' He put it on the table and held out his hand towards Clara. 'We didn't ever really introduce ourselves properly, did we? Caspar Liberty, the family ne'er-do-well.' He clicked his heels together and bowed elegantly.

Clara shook hands with him, seeing him as other women might: handsome, charming, but above all else, dangerous. For a lot of women that might be his appeal. But he held no attraction for her.

'We need to hide your van,' Gabriel said, some minutes later, when the kerfuffle of their arrival had died down.

'I'll help you bring your stuff in if you like,' offered Archie.

They went outside together, and after Clara had put Winnie out of sight, and was passing Archie Ned's bag, she said, 'How have you been since I last saw you? You look much better, if you don't mind me saying.'

'Thanks, love, I'm feeling great, on top of things again. And you were right about Shirley.'

'No kidding?'

He smiled shyly. 'And I've moved into what she calls my bachelor flat. It's quite comfortable, really. Less to fret over, if you know what I mean. It's been quite liberating throwing off a lifetime of clutter. You'd think I would have sussed that long ago, given the work I do. Funny thing is, I needn't have moved. Bessie left me her house over in Derby and the money it's going to fetch, much more than I'd ever thought, could have been used to pay off Stella.'

She touched his arm. 'For what it's worth, I think you did the right thing in moving. Leave the memories behind.'

'Oh, aye, I don't regret selling up. It was the best thing I could have done. Now I've got a bit of spare cash to enjoy myself. I'm thinking of taking a holiday. Do a bit of travelling.'

'Good for you. Hey, I don't suppose I could interest you in a camper-van, could I? Generous rates for friends.'

He laughed. 'Oh, that sounds dangerous. I might do a Clara Costello – find somewhere I like and never come back.'

She wagged a finger at him. 'Not dangerous, Archie. Adventurous. Living life to the full. That's what you must do from now on. Just think of the fun you and Shirley could have in a camper-van.'

Jonah wondered what his father wanted to see him about. He had sounded serious on the phone and he hoped it wasn't bad news. There'd been enough of that recently.

He drove into the courtyard and parked alongside his

father's Land Rover. He knocked on the back door, then entered. 'Dad,' he called, 'it's me, Jonah.'

There was no reply.

Passing the gun room, he caught the smell of cooking. Bit early for his father to be getting his supper ready, wasn't it? He pushed open the kitchen door, but stopped dead in his tracks. 'Clara! What are you doing here? I thought you were arriving tomorrow.'

She put down the tea-towel she'd been using to dry some plates. 'I could go away and come back in the morning if you'd prefer.'

'Don't even think about it!' He moved forward, was all set to put his arms around her and kiss her, when he held back. 'Are we alone?' he asked. He glanced over her shoulder towards the hall. 'Or are we likely to be interrupted by a curious son and a jealous father?'

She smiled. 'We're alone. And you have full permission to make the most of it.'

He did.

Afterwards, he said, 'It's so good to see you again. When did you change your mind about coming?'

'Oh, days ago.'

'But you never said anything. We spoke on the phone last night and—'

'The plot thickens, Master Liberty.' Grinning, she took his hands in hers. 'I think it's time you came with me. But you have to promise to close your eyes.'

Puzzled, he did as she said and allowed her to lead him outside. He knew they were crossing the courtyard, but all too soon he became disorientated and didn't know where they were heading. 'No peeping,' she said, just as he was tempted to open an eye.

He heard a door creak and she told him there were two steps in front of him. He lifted a foot exaggeratedly. Then the other.

'You can open your eyes now.'

He was in the banqueting hall. It had been thoroughly cleaned, was almost unrecognisable. There were candles

482

everywhere, and balloons and streamers. A long, thin table ran the length of the room; it was laden with food. There was a square cake in the middle of it all and it had . . . small blue candles on it.

And then it dawned on him. It was a party. A birthday party.

His father came towards him with a glass of champagne. 'Happy birthday, Jonah.'

'But . . . it's not until next week.'

His father shook his head. 'This is your proper birthday, son. This was the day you were born, and from now on, this is when we celebrate that fact.'

Still recovering from the surprise of seeing Clara, Jonah now had this second shock to deal with. Nothing could have stunned him more. To anyone else it might have seemed an act of madness to accept what his father had laid down all those years ago, but it had never bothered him. All families had their foibles, their unique way of handling difficult situations, and Jonah had simply gone along with Gabriel's wishes. But it touched him deeply to know that his father now cared enough to rewrite the rule book. He took the glass from Gabriel's outstretched hand. 'I don't know what to say,' he murmured. 'I'm overwhelmed.'

Gabriel turned to the rest of the room. 'In that case, how about we all have a crack at it for him?'

With his arm round Shirley's waist, Archie raised his glass. 'Here's to new beginnings and making the most of what time we have.'

'Hear, hear!' said Shirley, chinking her glass against his.

'Or, how about here's to Clara not discovering that Jonah's gay?'

'Caspar!'

'Only joking, Dad. Here's to it, brother, may you always look older and uglier than me. May the heavens always rain on you and the sun shine its rays on me.'

Smiling, Jonah turned to Clara who now had Ned

483

resting on her hip – he was dipping a finger into her glass. 'And do you have any words of wisdom?'

'I think I'm with Archie on this one. It's got to be, "To new beginnings".'

They sat in the gathering darkness on the stone bench beneath the library window. The air was warm and still, and way off in the distance, a dog was barking. Archie and Shirley had gone home, Ned was in bed, and Gabriel and Caspar were in the kitchen tidying up.

Clara leaned into Jonah and he rested an arm around her shoulder. 'A good birthday?' she asked.

'The best.'

'Even if Caspar did try to bring your sexuality into question?'

He tilted his head back and smiled. 'I took that as a reassuring sign that my brother is on the mend. I'd rather have him like that than the shattered mess he's been since we brought him back from Rosewood.'

'How generous of you. I'm not sure I'd be so forgiving.'

'Don't go making me out to be a saint, I haven't always thought so well of him.' He picked up her hand, raised it to his lips and kissed it tenderly. After a companionable silence had passed between them, he said, 'Clara, this might seem a strange question, but why do you and my father still call one another by your surnames?'

'Because it's all part of the act we put on for one another's benefit. It would spoil everything if we ever stopped doing it. It's a sign of affection between us. A code, I suppose. A game that only the two of us are in on. Sorry if that excludes you.'

'Don't apologise. I think it's nice. You realise, don't you, that it's going to be a strange old courtship, trying to win the heart of a woman who lives with my father? Heaven help me if I don't get you home on time.'

She laughed. 'Only you would call it a courtship.'

He laughed too. 'What would you prefer I called it?'

She thought about this. 'Mm . . . after giving it my

fullest consideration, I think courtship will do just fine. Despite outward appearances, I'm a straightforward old-fashioned girl, who needs to take things slowly.'

'Just my kind of girl, then.'

'I bet that's not what you thought when you first met me.'

'That's true. If I remember rightly, it was fear at first sight. I thought, Here's a woman who could more than punch her weight.'

'No better basis for a long and lasting relationship.'

Smiling, he turned his head towards her. 'Dare I ask permission for an extremely long and lingering birthday kiss?'

'Permission granted.'

Having said goodnight to Caspar, who had decided to head back to Manchester and not stay the night as he had thought he might, Gabriel stood in the darkness at the library window. With a glass of whisky in his hand, he gazed at the silhouetted figures on the bench outside.

He raised his glass to them both. 'Happy birthday, Jonah. By God, you've earned it. And to you, Miss Clara Costello. I may have lost my daughter, but I have the feeling I might be lucky and have the gift of another.'

He turned and looked up at Anastasia's portrait, conscious that she had waited a long time for this moment. 'We got there in the end, my darling girl. It took a while, but I think we got there.'

Raising his glass once more, he said, 'To you, my dearest Anastasia. To Val, and to Damson ... In my clumsy inadequate way, I loved you all.'